Vault
of Shadows

Vault of Shadows

THE NIGHTSIDERS

BOOK 2

JONATHAN MABERRY

Simon & Schuster Books for Young Readers
New York London Toronto Sydney New Delhi

SIMON & SCHUSTER BOOKS FOR YOUNG READERS
An imprint of Simon & Schuster Children's Publishing Division
1230 Avenue of the Americas, New York, New York 10020

This book is a work of fiction. Any references to historical events,
real people, or real places are used fictitiously. Other names, characters,
places, and events are products of the author's imagination, and any resemblance
to actual events or places or persons, living or dead, is entirely coincidental.

SIMON & SCHUSTER BOOKS FOR YOUNG READERS
is a trademark of Simon & Schuster, Inc.
For information about special discounts for bulk purchases,
please contact Simon & Schuster Special Sales at 1-866-506-1949
or business@simonandschuster.com.
The Simon & Schuster Speakers Bureau can bring authors to your live event.
For more information or to book an event, contact the Simon & Schuster Speakers
Bureau at 1-866-248-3049 or visit our website at www.simonspeakers.com.
Also available in a Simon & Schuster Books for Young Readers hardcover edition
Cover design by Krista Vossen
The text for this book was set in Minister Std.
Manufactured in the United States of America
0817 OFF
First Simon & Schuster Books for Young Readers
paperback edition September 2017
2 4 6 8 10 9 7 5 3 1
The Library of Congress has cataloged the hardcover edition as follows:
Names: Maberry, Jonathan.
Title: Vault of shadows / Jonathan Maberry.
Description: First edition. | New York : Simon & Schuster Books for Young
Readers, [2016] | Series: The Nightsiders ; book 2 | Summary: "Milo must choose
between risking his life to save both the human and magical universes—or to live
and save only his own"— Provided by publisher.
Identifiers: LCCN 2015027662 | ISBN 9781481415781 (hardback) |
ISBN 9781481415798 (pbk) | ISBN 9781481415804 (eBook)
Subjects: | CYAC: Science fiction. | Supernatural—Fiction. | Monsters—Fiction. |
Extraterrestrial beings—Fiction. | Heroes—Fiction. | Magic—Fiction. | BISAC:
JUVENILE FICTION / Action & Adventure / General. | JUVENILE
FICTION / Science Fiction. | JUVENILE FICTION / Monsters.
Classification: LCC PZ7.M11164 Vau 2016 | DDC [Fic]—dc23
LC record available at http://lccn.loc.gov/2015027662

To Sara Crowe and her two little faerie
princesses—Lilo and Phoebe!
And, as always, to Sara Jo.

Acknowledgments

Thanks to Brandon Strauss, for important (though creepy) information on insects. Thanks to David F. Kramer and Janice Gable Bashman, with whom I researched and wrote several books about the things that go bump in the night. I've been mining those books and our shared research for source material.

FROM MILO'S DREAM DIARY

Last night I dreamed that the world opened its mouth
    and swallowed me up.
I really hope that it was just a dream.
But way too many of my dreams have been coming
    true.
So . . . yeah, I'm really scared.

Part
One

Far, far away, there is a beautiful Country which
no human eye has ever seen in waking hours. Under
the Sunset it lies, where the distant horizon bounds the
day, and where the clouds, splendid with light and colour,
give a promise of the glory and beauty which encompass
it. Sometimes it is given to us to see it in dreams.
—BRAM STOKER

Chapter 1

Milo Silk was trying very hard not to die, but the day was not cooperating.

It was that kind of day, in a week of days like that, and lately Milo seemed to have only those kinds of days and nothing else.

This one was a classic.

He ran through the thick foliage along the muddy banks of Bayou Sauvage, trying not to fall into the churning water, trying not to get eaten by alligators, and trying especially hard not to get shot by alien shocktroopers.

He wouldn't have bet a fried circuit board or a fused diode on his chances.

All around him the Louisiana swamplands seemed to be filled with lurching shadows, bizarre shapes, and the *clickety-click* sound of insect legs. Blue pulses of phased energy burned through the air all around him. One blast was so close that it set his hair on fire and he had to slap his head to put it out. It wasn't a big fire, but it was on his head, so it was big enough.

The stink of burned hair chased him through the swamp.

The hardest part, for Milo, was remembering that this was supposed to be an ambush.

Supposed to be.

It reminded him of an old saying his dad had said once when a bunch of things went wrong during a garage clean-out at their house: "When you're up to your armpits in alligators, it's easy to forget that you came here to drain the swamp."

Yeah. Milo hated that saying.

Because there were alligators all over the place.

And they wanted to kill him too.

Chapter 2

This is the story of what happened when everything Milo tried to do went wrong.

Chapter 3

And what happened after that.

Chapter 4

"**C**'mon, c'mon, c'mon," muttered Milo as he ducked under the low arms of a dying pecan tree. He did it just in time, too, because less than a heartbeat later, another of the blue pulse blasts shot out of the dense shadows and blew the tree limb to splinters. Milo dove forward, rolled down a mossy slope, jammed his feet against the exposed roots of a bald cypress, came up running, and splashed through ankle-deep water until he reached a thick stand of slash pines. Then he squirmed into the tight cleft between two of the pines.

And froze.

Even though he was panting from the exertion, he forced his breath to go in and out of his mouth without noise. He tried very hard to become the bayou, to blend into it the way he'd been taught in survival classes.

To be one with the swamp. Or, as his backwoods Cajun pod leader, Barnaby Guidry, put it, "To be dere like you ain't dere, you."

To be there like you're not there.

Milo tried to not be there while he hid and watched the aliens come hunting.

When he saw them, his heart nearly turned to ice. Even though he'd seen them before, fought them, killed them, the fear was always there. He knew he'd been lucky—luckier than he had any right to expect, because fully trained adult soldiers couldn't beat the Dissosterin shocktroopers one-on-one. The alien invaders were seven feet tall and powerful, with armored insect bodies, heads like praying mantises', bulging red eyes, quivering antennae, and six limbs. Sometimes they stood on two legs so they could fire four pulse guns simultaneously; other times they scuttled on four legs faster than greyhounds and simply ran people down. They wore nearly impenetrable body armor and carried guns, grenades, knives, and shock rods.

As he watched, the wild sugarcane that choked the slope quivered and parted and a shocktrooper stepped cautiously out. A crystal had been implanted in the center of its chest and it pulsed a ghostly green. Every soldier, every hunter-killer, every creature belonging to the Swarm had an identical jewel, and these "lifelights" were tied to the actual life force of the Bugs and their mutant creations. Soldiers spent hours in camp working on their marksmanship, because if you blew out the lifelight, you killed a Bug.

The alien warrior made a soft chittering sound. Milo wasn't sure if it was talking to itself, communicating with other hunters via radio, or just making creepy noises. Whatever was going on, it skeeved him out.

The reeds crunched under its weight as it moved slowly

down the bank toward the edge of the muddy water. It bent low and peered at the clear print of a sneaker.

Milo's sneaker.

Then the shocktrooper turned in a half circle, scanning the bank to follow the natural path of whoever had made the print. Those multifaceted red eyes glared right at the copse of slash pines. The long, slender trunks of the trees offered little cover except down toward the ground, where they grew together in tight bunches. The canopy of needles interlaced with the ceiling of leaves from big live oaks and cast everything in near darkness. Only the shocktrooper, standing exposed on the bank, was visible to Milo, and he was certain he was invisible to it.

At least he hoped and prayed that he was.

The insect warrior gripped a gleaming pistol in one hand, and its segmented fingers held it rock-steady. The glowing blue focusing crystal on the end of the barrel was like an azure eye trying to penetrate the darkness.

Please, Milo thought, screaming the words inside his head. *Please, please, please.*

He was not begging the creature to go away.

He didn't want the shocktrooper to go away.

In fact, Milo needed him to be right where he was.

No, actually, he wanted him to be about five steps to the left. Closer to the water.

But the alien held his ground, clearly suspicious, searching for his elusive prey.

Finally Milo decided that the creature was not going

to move in the right direction and this plan was going to fail and end very badly for him. Like so many attempts before this.

So, to save his own life, Milo Silk stepped out from between the pines, raised his slingshot, and yelled at the alien.

"Yo! Roach-brain!"

He fired the slingshot in the same instant the shocktrooper spun to face him. The stone hit the creature on the side of the head, bounced high, and fell into the water without having made so much as a dent in the alien. Milo wished he had something to fire that could shatter the shielding around the lifelight. No stone would do that.

The shocktrooper instantly raised its pistol and rattled off a string of clicks and buzzes that Milo figured were probably very bad words in a language he was glad he didn't understand.

That's when three things happened in rapid succession.

The shocktrooper fired its pulse pistol, and the bolt seared past Milo's cheek and blew a six-inch burning hole through the trunk of one of the pine trees.

Milo dove for cover behind a fallen log.

And the thing in the water, disturbed by the noise, the movement, and the fall of Milo's stone, lunged up, jaws wide, and *attacked* the shocktrooper. It burst from the surface of the bayou like something tearing its way from a nightmare into the waking world. Massive, muscular, scaled, furious.

A bull alligator.

Old Chompy. Fierce and murderous and evil tempered.

Milo screamed and shimmied backward up the slope as nine hundred pounds of gator snapped his powerful jaws shut. Teeth like daggers crunched through the armor and shell as easily as Milo bit through a corn dog. And Old Chompy bit the Bug soldier clean in half.

It was a horrible sight, and even though this had been Milo's plan, it was gross and shocking and mind-numbing. The alien's chittering turned into a single piercing shriek of pain, and then dwindled to a gurgle as the fourteen-foot-long reptile dragged his unworldly meal down into the muddy depths.

Old Chompy was the undisputed terror of this part of the bayou. The ancient gator had dragged down wild pigs and even a ten-point buck unlucky enough to come to this section of the bank for a drink. Now he had claimed a fully armed and armored Dissosterin shocktrooper.

Milo stared in horror as green blood swirled around and around in the vortex of ripples. He saw the glow of the lifelight beneath the surface, but it quickly winked out and did not reappear. Milo knew it never would.

Old Chompy never gave back what he took.

A ball of tension that felt like a knot of hot barbed wire burst from his lungs and he sagged to the ground.

It was a terrible, stupid, insanely dangerous plan.

And it had worked.

FROM MILO'S DREAM DIARY

I miss my mom.

All the time.

It's only been four days since she took a bunch
of soldiers to check on a report of some dead
shocktroopers down around the Atchafalaya River.
She was only supposed to be gone for a couple of
days.

But the Bugs attacked our camp the next day.

The Huntsman and an entire hive ship just came out of
the sky and . . .

God, I can't even write down most of what they did.

Mom and the soldiers were long gone by then, and
after the attack, we had to abandon what was left
of the camp. It's way too dangerous to go back
there.

I don't know if Mom's okay.

I don't know where she is.

I don't know if she thinks I'm dead.

I don't know.
I don't know.
I don't know.
And I'm so scared.
Where are you, Mom?

Chapter 5

The waters of the bayou gradually stilled, except for a line of bubbles that rose and popped on the surface. He didn't know if Old Chompy could digest what he'd taken for his lunch, and Milo tried not to think about it. Here in the bayou, the big reptiles were nobody's friends and they'd eat just about anything they could catch.

When it was clear that no other shocktroopers were coming to investigate, Milo hurried over to the remains, wincing at the mess. The gator had taken everything from the waist up, leaving the rest behind. The lower half of the creature still twitched, the way some insects do even when their heads are gone. That was so nasty.

But Milo gritted his teeth, held his breath, grabbed the alien warrior's foot, and dragged the remains up the slope. Once he was on solid ground, he went to work. He had a big canvas satchel slung across his chest, and he began filling it with the weapons and equipment strapped to the hips and legs of the corpse. It was an incredible haul: two pulse pistols, a fighting knife with a twelve-inch serrated blade, six shock grenades, four incendiary grenades, signal flares, and several items

Milo couldn't immediately recognize. Any kind of tech was worth scavenging, and alien tech ten times so. The Earth Alliance scientists had recovered very little of that tech intact, because taking down a shocktrooper usually resulted in most of the body and its equipment being turned into melted slag and ash. The drop-ships and scout craft tended to blow up when shot down— something about how the coolant systems on the Dissosterin engines worked. Superb designs for flying, but awful for trying to scavenge anything useful.

Milo Silk was a scavenger. That's what he'd been trained to do, every day of his life. Well, ever since the aliens came in their vast hive ships and conquered the Earth. Milo had been six years old when the invasion began. Now he was eleven, and even kids in the EA had to earn their place. Everyone had to work together to help the human resistance survive, to preserve life and connection and cooperation so that there could be some hope of winning back the planet. Scavengers like Milo, like his friends Lizzie and Shark and Barnaby, scoured the forests and ruined towns for anything that could be useful. To people who were both desperate and resource- ful, nearly everything had value, from broken laptops to car batteries to circuit boards of crashed planes.

A nearly complete set of weapons and equipment from a shocktrooper was worth ten times Milo's weight in gold. He finished shoving the pieces of tech into his satchel, missing nothing. Then he slung the satchel over his shoulder and set off for camp. On the way, he passed a burned and twisted bit of wreckage that had been dropped into the forest yesterday morning. Milo and his friends had watched under cover of camouflage tarps as the debris fell. He knew what they were and why the aliens had sent them raining down into the woods.

He'd passed this piece on the outbound part of his trip this morning, but seeing it again gave him the same feeling of sickening fear. The object was the charred remains of a food cart. The other objects were cars, trucks, parts of a tank, and various chunks of military vehicles that had once made up the caravan in Milo's camp. This cart and those other machines had been where Milo, Shark, Lizabeth, Barnaby, and all the others, including Milo's mom, had lived, worked, fought. And died. When the hive ship had attacked the camp, these vehicles were blown up by pulse-rifle blasts or torn apart by hunter-killers. Until yesterday, Milo hadn't given a thought to the destroyed machines, caring only about the living, the dead, the wounded, and the missing people. However, the Bugs had gone back to the site of that attack and collected the junk. A message had then been painted on each piece, the same message, splashed in bright red on the soot-stained metal.

I WANT WHAT YOU STOLE

Milo didn't think the Bugs could understand human languages. Not that it mattered, because he was absolutely positive that he knew whose hand had written these five words over and over again.

The Huntsman.

Once a human being. A murderer hiding behind the uniform of a soldier. A merciless and malicious serial killer who believed that by taking lives he would become more powerful than any ordinary human, that he would become a god of darkness.

That was bad enough. More than bad enough. Then the Swarm took him. They had been looking for a human whose inner darkness was so powerful that it would give them the edge needed to break free of their own technological stagnation. They craved his evil, his dark imagination, and they had used their own twisted science to transform the killer into something half human and half Dissosterin. A hybrid that belonged to neither species. A monster that was far more powerful, far darker, than even the hive queens could predict. His evil and his madness had flowed into the hive mind and corrupted it, turned it from the cold hunger of a swarm of insects into a shared malevolence. They had built a slave but created a conqueror.

The Huntsman had led the attack on Milo's camp, destroying it and killing most of the people Milo knew. A few survivors had been taken as slaves and as organic raw material for the hive ship to make more shocktroopers. It had been the worst day of Milo's life. His mom and most of the best soldiers had been out on patrol and had escaped the slaughter, but Milo had been forced to flee the destroyed camp, and now he couldn't find her.

And the Huntsman was looking for Milo. Not merely to complete the task of exterminating an Earth Alliance group, but to recover two objects the monster held precious. One—a glittering black jewel called the Heart of Darkness—rightfully belonged to the Nightsiders and was now in the possession of the young werewolf girl, Evangelyne Winter. The other rightfully belonged to the alien Swarm from the far reaches of space. It was a small crystal egg, and in it was stored the DNA of the Swarm. The aliens traveled across the vast gulfs of interstellar space in colony ships that were millions of years old. During the thousands of years of travel from one planet to another, the aliens died off, only to be reborn from new eggs laid by the undying queens. The information stored in the crystal egg not only allowed the queens to produce countless new soldiers, workers, and drones, but it contained knowledge and skills, which meant that each new Bug hatched fully trained and ready to serve the Swarm.

With the Heart of Darkness, the Huntsman could gain the secrets of magic, which would make him invincible. But if he failed to recover the crystal egg, the Swarm would very likely turn on him. To become the conqueror he dreamed of being, he had to prove himself worthy to his current masters.

The egg was not a simple piece of alien tech. Milo believed that on some level, it was alive. *Alive.* And when he and his new friends took it from the hive ship, the egg had seemed, to Milo, to call out to the Swarm, begging—or perhaps commanding—the Bugs to rescue it and bring it home. He hoped that he had simply been paranoid and that the egg had not actually been sending a homing signal. So far no Bug legions had appeared, and the Huntsman seemed unable to find him. For now.

Milo knew that couldn't last. The Witch of the World had given him a dire warning about the lengths to which the Huntsman would go.

He will burn the fields of the earth and topple mountains to find you and get back what you stole.

Milo could feel the Huntsman's hatred. It was like the smell of acid in the air. It was like an ache in his bones. It was a ball of sick dread in his stomach. He lingered for a moment and stared at the words.

I WANT WHAT YOU STOLE

Milo walked up to the burned food cart and spat on the red letters.

Or at least, that had been his intention. Unfortunately, his mouth was so dry with terror that he had no spit at all. The best he could manage was a weak sound, a pretend spit that had no real force or power behind it.

Embarrassed, and feeling small and powerless, Milo turned away and looked into the woods toward where his new camp lay. It was well hidden, but he did not believe it was any safer than the one he'd lived in a few days ago. This was an invaded and mostly conquered world. There was no such thing as safety anymore.

Not until and unless the Swarm and the Huntsman could be defeated.

The crystal egg seemed to burn like a cinder in Milo's pocket.

He touched it through the cloth of his jeans. Felt it pulse. Or maybe twitch. Like something alive trying to flinch away from his touch.

Milo took a steadying breath and melted back into the woods.

Chapter 6

He had gotten less than a hundred yards when he found something very strange in a small clearing. It was a group of mushrooms growing in a near-perfect circle. Milo stopped and crouched down at the edge of it. Like everyone else in his pod, he knew a lot about what grew wild in the woods. What was safe and what wasn't. Most of the mushroom species here in Louisiana were safe to eat, though there were a few he knew to stay away from. These, however, were a species he'd never seen before. At a glance, they looked like either straw mushrooms or Caesar's mushrooms, but he was sure they weren't either of those edible kinds. The caps were pale yellow and about six inches across, and the stipes—or stems—were flecked with gray scales. There were at least sixty of the mushrooms, and when he bent close to examine them, he realized that the circle they made really was perfect. It was only the occasional tuft of grass that made the ring appear warped. This bothered Milo, because nature has its own ways of being perfect—the flight of a hummingbird, the color of bougainvillea, the warm sun of a spring afternoon—but exact geometrical shapes are rare.

Perfectly straight lines and perfect circles were unusual. And yet this didn't seem like the sort of thing the Bugs would ever do.

However, Milo had come this way not three hours ago and hadn't seen this grouping of fungi. Surely mushrooms this large couldn't have sprung up by themselves in just a few hours. That was impossible.

Which meant what? Milo wasn't sure. Was this something belonging to the Swarm? Was this something tied to the Nightsiders?

He didn't know, but as he wondered about it he suddenly felt very strange, and without meaning to, he dropped slowly to his knees just outside the ring. The air around him seemed to change, become less humid, and the heat leached away, replaced by a deep cold. When Milo exhaled, his breath plumed with steam. He jerked back. Then stopped. Bent forward . . . and breathed out again. It wasn't just that he could see his breath—he could see it only as the exhaled air crossed the arc of the toadstool circle.

Milo's heart began to flutter, and he knew for sure that this phenomenon was tied to the world of shadows and monsters. It was almost the same effect he'd felt when he had discovered a damaged pyramid of stones in the swamps not too many miles from this spot. There had been a perfect ring of icy air around the pyramid, and Milo had later learned it was a shrine that was sacred to the Nightsiders. And it was from that ruined monument that the evil and terrifying Huntsman had stolen the Heart of Darkness—the jewel that was crucial to the survival of Evangelyne and her friends. And maybe crucial to the survival of everyone on Earth.

There had been no ring of mushrooms there, though, and there was no pyramid here. All he could see inside the circle was grass and mud and . . .

As Milo watched, he could feel something changing. Inside and out. His eyes began to drift shut, as if he were sliding toward the edge of sleep. He wanted to fight it, knew he should fight it, but all at once he had no will to try to stay awake. And yet he did not topple forward into sleep. Instead he wavered there on his knees, swaying as if to the rhythm of a distant piece of strange music. The air inside the circle seemed to shimmer like a mirage. His eyelids fluttered, but he couldn't tell if they were open or closed.

And then . . . then . . .

Something moved inside the circle. Tiny figures no bigger than crickets, but human in shape. Almost human. They were dressed like soldiers from some ancient painting of war. Each warrior was dressed in clothes similar to those Milo had seen in books about the Middle Ages. Shining armor and long doublets with strange creatures embroidered on them: fire-breathing dragons, griffins, unicorns, basilisks, sea serpents, and mermaids. Each soldier had a miniature sword hanging from a leather belt, and a helmet of polished silver. There were female

25

soldiers as well as male, dressed in the same armor and carrying the same swords. The soldiers were not really people, though. Small as they were, Milo could see that their skin was a pale green, almost the color of grass on the first morning of spring. A few of them had tapered helmets that did not hide their ears, and Milo saw that these ears rose to sharp points.

As they danced, the little soldiers sang a song in voices that were so heavy with a foreign accent that it was hard for Milo to understand them. He bent close, his nose almost touching the shimmering air at the edge of the toadstool ring, and listened to the song raised by their tiny voices:

He wha tills the faeries' green
Nae luck again shall hae;
And he wha spills the faeries' ring
Betide him want and wae.
For weirdless days and weary nights
Are his till his deein' day.
But he wha gaes by the faerie ring,
Nae dule nor pine shall see,
And he wha cleans the faerie ring
An easy death shall dee.

Milo couldn't easily follow what the creatures were singing, but as he listened, he found himself drifting ever closer toward the edge of sleep.

And toward the shimmering circle.

The creatures laughed and beckoned to him as they

broke their own circle and whirled, some dancing together, others doing jigs by themselves. A few stood and clapped to keep time, and though Milo heard the music of strange pipes and drums, he could see no instruments.

Milo felt his lips move and he heard himself whisper two words that he was absolutely certain he did not know and had never heard before.

"Aes Sídhe."

They came out almost as a sigh, sounding to his ears like "ays sheeth-uh," though somehow Milo knew this wasn't how they were spelled. He was too dreamy and faint to wonder how he knew that.

The dancing figures laughed aloud at the sound of the words. Their dances became faster and faster, and Milo was getting dizzy trying to follow their movements.

"Come to the Sídhe, *Milo. . . . Come play with us. . . ."*

"I . . . I . . . ," he began, but he had no idea what he wanted to say. Or whether he could say anything at all. The world swam around him, and it seemed as if the only real and stable point in the universe was inside that ring. Milo felt seasick and woozy.

"Come with us," cried the tiny dancing figures. *"Come play with us. Come be safe with us."*

Milo began to lift his hand, to reach out, to reach *through.* As his fingertips brushed the outside of the shimmering wall, a shock went through him. It was like touching electricity. Milo snatched his hand back.

Except he didn't.

He wanted to. He willed his hand to pull back.

But instead it kept reaching forward. Touching the wall of shimmering air was like touching flowing water. It was more solid than empty air, but not something he could grab. The ground seemed to tilt under him, to make him lean forward so that his fingers pushed through the outer surface.

Inside the circle, the little figures danced and laughed, but Milo suddenly felt very afraid. There was no humor on their tiny smiling faces. The grins were like jack-o'-lantern grins—cruel imitations of smiles, with no human joy. And there was a kind of hungry delight in their eyes that burned like coals.

"Come play with us," they cried.

Milo's fingers kept reaching through the shimmer, and his body tilted forward inch by inch so that his face was right there, almost close enough to feel it on his skin.

"Be safe with us . . ."

As they chanted, the shimmering air above them inside the circle began to change. At first Milo thought it was a column of smoke rising from a fire he couldn't see, but it wasn't that. It moved like smoke, though, swirling and rippling, becoming darker as it filled the air and towered above the figures. The chants of the tiny soldiers increased as they begged Milo to enter the circle.

"He comes!" cried the little figures, and Milo thought they were referring to him. Not so. They pointed at the swirling column of smoke. *"The destroyer comes at our call."*

The dark smoke was taking shape now. Slowly, though, as if time itself had become uncertain, or as if the very air were reluctant to witness what was forming.

"No . . . ," murmured Milo, but he could not look away, could not pull back.

"The destroyer comes at our call," the creatures repeated, and now Milo could hear a wicked joy in their voices. *"He will open the door and set us free!"*

Inside the ring Milo could see the figure more clearly with each passing second. It was huge and almost—*almost*—human. Male, massive, with broad shoulders and a body packed with so much muscle that it looked bestial and deformed, its torso was wrapped in layer upon layer of chitinous plates, just like the Bugs. And like those aliens, it had a set of pincer arms sprouting from its sides, just below the muscular human arms. Insectoid pincers snapped at the air on either side of its cruel mouth. Antennae rose from the sides of its head, and the eyes were the multifaceted eyes of a blowfly. The human arms had been transformed into something monstrous and were covered with plates and ridges from which spikes jutted. Weapon belts crisscrossed the massive chest.

This creature was not a Nightsider or a Bug, or even human. It was something else entirely. Unique in its hideous nature, and unparalleled in its towering, destructive madness.

Even as it took shape in the air, Milo could hear an

echo of what the Witch of the World had said when he'd first seen this monster.

This is the destroyer. This is the Huntsman who will hang us all like trophies on his wall.

Milo screamed.

The dancing figures laughed and cried out in triumph as the Huntsman took shape within their magic circle.

"Here is the one you seek, O champion," they shouted. *"Take this boy and do with him as you will. Then lead us to victory over all!"*

Milo reeled. These creatures were conjuring the most dangerous monster who ever lived.

The Huntsman, as if able to read his thoughts, threw back his hideous head and laughed. But his laughter was silent, as if he was not yet enough in this world, not real enough, to be heard. He reached out toward Milo, toward the point where Milo's fingers were penetrating the shimmering wall.

Milo felt his will melting away, felt his fingers pushing forward. He felt he was losing himself as the creatures danced and the Huntsman reached.

And then a sound split the air.

Sharp.

Loud.

Not inside the ring. The Huntsman had not found his voice.

No, this was an animal sound. A very particular kind of animal sound.

And it came from behind Milo, off to his left, farther up the slope and beyond the edge of the field of wild sugarcane.

Milo turned, and the action pulled his fingers most of the way out of the shimmering wall. The tiny figures stopped dancing and glared up at him with naked hatred. And the Huntsman's image flickered for a moment.

The sound came again, and again.

Louder. Closer.

Urgent.

And familiar.

Milo licked his lips and blinked, trying to clear his eyes. He heard the sound again and forced himself to turn away from everything in the circle. Something was out there. Something was coming. He tilted his head to raise one ear, trying to catch the full sound. Was it a wild dog? Or, worse, was it a Stinger? Was it one of the Dissosterin mutant hunting animals, the nightmare blend of giant mastiff and deadly scorpion, come to greet its alien master?

Milo made himself turn more so that he couldn't even see the little people out of the corner of his eye.

Don't look at them, he told himself. *Don't look at* him*!*

The sounds came from a patch of wild cane, and as Milo watched, the stalks rippled as something headed toward him with increasing speed.

I'm dead, thought Milo.

Then the canes parted and a figure moved into a patch

of sunlight. Much, much smaller than Milo had expected. White, with brown patches, about the size of a meat loaf, standing on four bandy legs, eyes dark and bright, mouth open to reveal lots of tiny sharp teeth. The animal looked around, sniffed the air, then jolted to a stop as it caught sight of Milo. The little creature's eyes seemed to bug out of their sockets, and the slender tail began whipping back and forth so fast it turned into a blur.

Then it raced toward Milo at missile speed.

It was Killer.

Milo jerked his fingers completely free of the wall and reached out as the dog jumped into his arms, bore him backward, and tried to lick all the skin off his face. Killer slobbered all over Milo, biting his hair, whimpering, and dancing on the boy's chest and stomach.

Milo laughed out loud, and it was that sound as much as anything else that changed the day. The deep cold vanished, and when Milo dared to look, he saw the little figures disappear one by one. For a minute, though, one remained—a tiny woman dressed in armor the color of rotting leaves, with hair as red as flame and a thick band of carved gold around her throat. Above her towered the swirling image of the Huntsman. The monster spoke, but Milo could not hear a single word. However, the red-haired woman seemed to understand. She nodded and then turned toward Milo, and there was a look of such intense hatred on her face that it chilled Milo to the marrow. She pointed a slender finger at him.

"You will scream as you die," she said. *"But only after watching everything you love burn. And then my champion and I will conquer this and all worlds."*

Then she, too, faded. A moment later, so did the hideous, silent image of the Huntsman, and every one of the toadstools. It was as if they had never been there. As if this had all been some kind of waking dream. Or a nightmare that had tried to invade the daytime. The grass was unmarked, and the warmth of the bayou rolled over him and reclaimed the day.

Killer barked at him, demanding his attention. Milo pulled the dog to his chest and hugged him, kissing his head, rocking him back and forth. Grateful to have found him, grateful to have been saved by him.

Four days ago, when the hive ship had attacked Milo's camp, Killer had gone missing. Everyone assumed the little dog was dead, burned to black bones by the firestorm of the attack. Killer's owner, Shark, was Milo's best friend, and Shark been grieving as much for the dog as for the friends they'd lost in that terrible attack. So many people were still missing—including Shark's adoptive aunt and Milo's mom—but finding the dog seemed to prove that being missing did not have to mean gone forever.

Still holding the wriggling dog to his chest, Milo climbed to his feet. There were tears on his cheeks but he didn't care, and besides, the dog lapped up the salty wetness.

"I got you, Killer," murmured Milo. "I got you. You're safe now."

Though he meant that for himself, too. Safe now.

Safe.

The clearing was empty. Not a single mushroom was in sight. And even the memory of that strange song and those cruel smiles seemed to be fading, racing away from him like roaches scattering to hide from the light. Had he really seen them? Had he actually seen the Huntsman?

The more he thought about it, the less certain he was that it had happened at all.

"I must have been asleep on my feet," he told himself. Killer wagged his tail as if Milo had said something to him. "Just me being weird."

Milo finally set Killer down and examined him. The terrier was thin and covered with scratches and cuts, and his coat was filthy. The last four days had clearly been cruel to the dog. Despite that, the defiant fires that had always burned in his eyes were undiminished. He might only weigh fourteen pounds, but all of it was grit and determination. Killer had very little "give up" in him.

"I know someone who's going to lose his *mind* when he sees you, boy," said Milo. "Shark's going to go nuts."

At the mention of his person's name, Killer began wagging even harder and uttered a high, thin whine.

"C'mon, Killer, let's get out of here."

Milo retrieved his slingshot, cinched the flap of his

satchel, did a full turn to check the surrounding woods, and then clicked his tongue for Killer. They set off through the cane, moving as fast as caution allowed, making sure to leave no marks of their passage, relying on skills and smarts to stay safe and to ensure that death did not follow them back to where their friends waited.

FROM MILO'S DREAM DIARY

So much has happened that sometimes I have to stop
   and think about it to keep everything straight.
   That's important because when I dream, the story
   sometimes changes. In my dreams, my mom was
   with me when I met the Nightsiders.
In my dreams, the Nightsiders weren't strange
   monsters. They were my brothers and sisters. All of
   them.
Evangelyne Winter—the strange, moody werewolf girl.
Oakenayl—the grumpy tree spirit, who, I'm pretty sure,
   would be totally cool with it if I got eaten by the
   Bugs.
Mook—the rock boy.
Halflight—the fiery little sprite who flew around on the
   back of a hummingbird.
And Iskiel, the fire salamander who could explode and
   then re—form like a phoenix.
In the real world they were strangers. Weird and a little

scary and completely cool. Except for Oakenayl, who really was a jerk.

But in dreams they were my actual family.

And the stone, the little black jewel called the Heart of Darkness, wasn't something that belonged only to the Nightsiders. In my dream, it was something that had always belonged to my family. When we snuck aboard the hive ship to steal it back from the Huntsman, it wasn't just to help the Nightsiders. It was because my <u>family</u> needed it back.

My family.

<u>This</u> family.

How weird is that?

And . . . what would Mom think of all this? I mean . . . what <u>will</u> she think, when I find her?

Chapter 7

After almost an hour, Milo and Killer had nearly reached the camp. As the crow flies it was a twenty-minute hike, but stealth requires a longer path. He found no toadstool rings and heard no more strange songs from tiny people, and with every step he doubted more and more that it had even happened. How could a bunch of little creatures like that conjure the Huntsman? If they were Nightsiders, why *would* they? It was so crazy and made so little sense that it only reinforced his belief that he had somehow managed to have a dream while walking through the swamp.

Something suddenly rustled in the leaves above them and they both froze, Killer with bared fangs and hair standing in a ridge along his back, Milo with a sharp stone in his slingshot.

But then the thing that had made the noise crept out onto a bare section of a heavy limb. It was bigger than an iguana, with smooth gray-green skin marked with glowing lines of intense red that swirled and eddied with fire. It was no illusion, Milo knew; those fires really burned beneath the creature's skin. Killer snarled with a mixture of brave defiance and obvious terror, but Milo lowered his slingshot.

"It's okay, boy," he said to the little dog. "Iskiel's a friend."

The fire salamander flicked out his forked tongue and hissed softly at Milo.

"Good to see you, too," said Milo, though in truth he had no idea whether the hiss was a greeting or not. A moment later he found out, because Iskiel half turned and used his jaws to pick up something that was out of sight on the limb, and tossed it down. It landed with a metallic clank at Milo's feet.

Milo and Killer both jumped backward, and once more Milo brought up his slingshot.

It was a hunter-killer.

Specifically, a boomer. A Dissosterin murder machine. Shaped like a yard-long steel centipede, with hundreds of legs made from stiff red wire. Each segment of a boomer contained a separate explosive charge packed with shrapnel. A single boomer could destroy a Humvee and kill everyone inside. Boomers were only one of dozens of insect-shaped robots employed by the Bugs to do exactly what their group name suggested: to hunt and to kill.

Milo lowered his weapon, because it was clear that this particular hunter-killer was never going to cause anyone any harm. There were deep punctures and claw marks on each of the many sections, and the edges of the fang holes were smeared with a purplish goo. When Milo glanced up, he saw Iskiel open his mouth to display his teeth. Drops of the purple goo gleamed on the tips. Even though Milo hadn't seen this substance before on the fire salamander, he was sharp enough to understand what the creature was showing him. It was some kind of venom, and from the burned-wire stink rising from the boomer, there was no doubt that Iskiel's venom was pure acid.

"Niiiiice!" said Milo in real appreciation. "That is so cool!"

The fire salamander made a short, choppy hissing sound that might well have been laughter. If creatures like him could laugh.

Killer barked at Iskiel, but Milo shushed him. "Quiet, Killer."

The terrier stopped barking but kept a suspicious eye on the glowing amphibian. The row of bristling hairs on his back did not lie down, either.

"Iskiel," said Milo, "there was a shocktrooper down by the edge of the bayou, but a gator got him."

The salamander bobbed his head. A nod? Sure, why not? Milo knew the creature could understand human speech.

"Do you know if there are any others around?"

Iskiel lifted his head and looked about as if he could somehow survey the whole of the forest.

"Or any more of the hunter-killers?"

Then Iskiel cocked his head as if listening, but all Milo could hear was the rustle of leaves and the drone of ordinary earth insects. In the distance a bullfrog thrummed. The salamander gradually relaxed and flicked his tongue once more in Milo's direction.

"Nothing out there?" said Milo hopefully.

Amphibians can't shrug, so Iskiel merely hissed. Softly and without urgency. Milo got the point.

"Nothing out there *right now*," Milo interpreted.

Iskiel bobbed his head.

Milo glanced back the way he'd come, then looked sideways up at the salamander. "Hey . . . you wouldn't know anything about a bunch of little guys in armor dancing around inside a circle of mushrooms, would you?"

The amphibian gave him a flat, level, and totally unhelpful stare. Then with a swish of his tail, he turned and vanished into the cool green darkness under the leaves. Milo and Killer stood for a moment, watching the trees, but Iskiel did not return.

"Everybody I know is weird," said Milo. Killer looked at him as if in wonder that Milo was just now getting that through his thick head.

They moved off, leaving the boomer were it lay. Milo took note of its location, but he didn't want to risk carrying it back to camp, not even to try to scavenge parts. Just because it hadn't blown up during the fight with Iskiel did not mean that it couldn't. Later, when there was time, Milo would come back and dispose of it properly. Ideally with Shark, who was much better at fixing— or deconstructing—things than any of the other kids.

The camp was close, and as they approached, he noticed a figure in the shadows beneath a massive old elm. Even in that gloom Milo could see the deadly point of razor-sharp metal on the hunting arrow.

Milo stopped in his tracks.

"You can stop right dere," said a cold and deadly voice, but all Milo could see was a shaggy silhouette that seemed to be made of leaves and twigs, with narrow and knobby shoulders and long arms. It looked like Oakenayl, but the voice was clearly not his.

"Barnaby, it's me."

"I know," said the Cajun scout as he stepped into the light. He lowered his arrow and grinned. "Just wanted to see how many shades of white you'd turn. You look like sour milk, you." Barnaby let out a donkey-bray of a laugh.

Milo glared hot death at him. "You're hilarious."

"You should see your face, you." Barnaby wore full deep-forest camouflage: patterned clothes augmented by leaves, grass, flowers, and sticks attached by loops of strong thread.

Milo cut a nervous look toward the camp. "Did Oakenayl see you?"

Barnaby touched the foliage on his clothes. "Yeah, and he mad as a scalded cat, him."

"He doesn't like us to cut anything off the trees and—"

"I didn't do that. I picked all this stuff off the ground."

"So why's he mad?"

Barnaby shrugged. "Maybe someone forgot to tell him that."

"'Someone' meaning you? He's an actual monster, you know. Messing with him's not smart."

The Cajun shrugged again. "I didn't do no harm. He don't like it, that creepy tree boy can go whittle himself a new smile."

In the four days since Milo and the Orphan Army of supernatural creatures had stolen aboard the hive ship, recovered the Heart of Darkness, and rescued some of the camp survivors, the initial feelings of gratitude and mutual need had given way to old superstitions and prejudices. Most of the humans kept well away from the Nightsiders, and the monsters didn't go out of their way to make human friends. It was depressing, and the tensions were increasing every day.

Milo was about to say something to the Cajun about it when Barnaby finally realized who it was standing behind Milo's legs.

"Oh my, my, my, my—where at you find this *tataille-tayau*, this scary hound dog?" He knelt down and held a hand out to Killer, who approached cautiously, sniffed, then wagged his tail with moderate enthusiasm. Barnaby stroked Killer from head to tail, and for a moment the Cajun looked genuinely pleased. He cocked an eye at Milo. "Big man know his dog be back, him?"

"No. Where is Shark?"

Again Killer perked up at the name.

Barnaby ticked his head toward the dense oak grove behind him. "Back there. Probably eating something he don't need to eat, him. Like he always doing."

It wasn't an entirely unfair comment. Shark had no qualms about stopping for a meal. Any meal, anywhere.

"Is Evangelyne around?" asked Milo, and saw the scout stiffen.

"Mademoiselle Rougarou is off on her own, her, which is just fine with me."

"Don't call her that," said Milo. *Rougarou* was a local name for a particularly vicious breed of werewolf. Barnaby had always worn a pierced dime on a piece of twine as a charm against the evil of that kind of monster. It wasn't a word he would dare say to her face.

"Why not? She ain't here right now, her," said Barnaby.

Milo took a small step toward him. "No, but I am. Don't call her that."

The scout was taller, stronger, and older than Milo, and he was a much better fighter. He could have knocked Milo out with one fast punch, and they both knew it. But instead he simply studied the look in Milo's eyes and after a minute gave a small nod. "Sure, whatever you say, you."

Milo returned the nod and began to walk past him, then stopped and told him about the boomer Iskiel had destroyed.

"Wait, you saying that reptile done that to a boomer, him?"

"Iskiel's an amphibian," said Milo, "not a reptile."

"I don't care if he a dinosaur. How he kill that metal bug?"

Milo explained about the acid venom.

Barnaby looked uneasy. "Now, that's just weird."

"Yeah, well, welcome to my world," said Milo, and he went off to look for Shark.

Chapter 8

The reunion between Shark and Killer made Milo want to cry.

His friend had not, in fact, been eating but was instead sitting on a log with his tool kit beside him as he worked on a circuit board from the alien ship they'd stolen. Behind him, covered in shadows beneath the oak trees, was the massive red bulb of the Dissosterin command ship that had once belonged to the Huntsman. When they'd all escaped the hive ship, the red craft had brought them down to Earth in relative safety. However, the following day the survivors had bullied Milo into trying to fly them all across the lake to find an Earth Alliance camp.

Milo got the ship off the ground, but then one of the computer panels blew up and the ship crashed. Hard. It had been a terrible catastrophe. Several of the refugees were badly injured, and a lot of the ship's circuitry was damaged. Shark, the best tech wizard in Milo's pod, was now trying to get the craft running again. It was still an iffy proposition, though that morning he had told Milo that this particular circuit could probably get the ship to fly, just not fly very well. It was a start, and it was a lot better than nothing. They knew they were being hunted. Staying in any one place too long was insanely dangerous.

"Shark," called Milo from the edge of the small clearing, "look what followed me home. Can we keep him?"

Shark was a stocky kid with big hands, big feet, a belly that, though not as ponderous as it had been, was still considerable, and a head that looked like a bucket covered in cornrows. His skin was the color of dark chocolate, and his intelligent brown eyes were flecked with gold. William Sharkey. "Shark" to everyone.

"Geez," said Shark impatiently as he looked up, "don't tell me you want to adopt a Stinger . . ."

His voice trailed off and tears sprang into his eyes. A half second later Shark and Killer were crushed into a huddle, laughing and barking and kissing and petting and wagging. And it was hard for Milo to tell where one left off and the other began.

"Where . . . where . . . where . . . *how* . . . ?" began Shark, but he couldn't finish the sentence.

"He found me," Milo told him, and explained about the trap he'd set for the shocktrooper and the subsequent encounter with the fierce little dog. He wasn't sure that Shark heard one word of it. Feeling immensely happy for his friend, Milo sat down on the log and picked up the circuit board. He saw what Shark had been working on, followed the logic of the repair, and set to work, letting Shark have some privacy and not intruding on it, which is what friends should do.

Later, after Shark had recovered his composure, fed Killer more than the dog could eat, washed him, and dressed his many small wounds, he sat next to Milo with the Jack Russell sleeping contentedly on his lap.

"I really, really, really, really want to thank you, man," he said, punching Milo on the arm.

"Hey, like I said, Killer found me."

Then there was an embarrassing instant when they were both aware that Shark was crying and neither of them wanted to comment on it.

Milo said, "So . . . um . . . how's it going . . . ?"

Shark cleared his throat and took the circuit board from Milo. "This is the last one to fix before we try to restart the engine. Then I think we'd better get our butts out of here. We've been in this swamp way too long."

"I know. That shocktrooper I fed to Old Chompy was getting too close to camp."

Shark grinned. "'Old Chompy'?"

"I figured he needed a name."

Shark thought about it, nodded. "Old Chompy," he confirmed. "Better than some of the things Barnaby's been calling him."

"Barnaby's got issues," complained Milo, "and not just with gators. He's going to get in trouble with Evangelyne and the others."

"Yeah, he is. Oakenayl nearly took his head off earlier."

"Why? Because of the camouflage stuff?"

"That and because he wanted to cut up a tree for firewood. I mean, the tree was old and dead already, so it's not like he'd be killing one of Oakenayl's relatives. Wouldn't be like tossing his favorite uncle onto the fire."

"Maybe it would. Like a funeral pyre."

Shark sighed and shook his head. "Man, this is really, really weird."

"Yeah, it is."

Killer began snoring.

Milo told Shark about Iskiel destroying a boomer, and his friend was deeply impressed. "Okay, that might be the second coolest thing that's happened today. Coolest being the return of the world's smelliest dog." Shark grunted. "A fire salamander with acid for venom. Life keeps on getting weirder."

"Yeah," agreed Milo, and he almost shared the story of his encounter with the tiny soldiers in the mushroom circle, but ultimately he did not. Despite his knowing several supernatural creatures, this encounter now felt too much like a daydream. Besides, try as he might, he couldn't really remember many of the details. It was like trying to remember an elusive dream. The harder he grabbed for it, the more it pulled away.

Instead he looked around. The camp seemed deserted and quiet. "Where is everyone?"

"Well . . . ," began Shark slowly, "your new friends

all kind of bugged out this morning after you left. Don't ask where because none of 'em wasted a lot of breath telling us 'Children of the Sun' much of anything. Or is it 'Daylighters'? I keep hearing both."

"Don't sweat it, Shark, they're not cutting you up. They're the Nightsiders and we're the Daylighters. 'Children of the sun' is mostly what the Witch of the World calls us."

Shark didn't even try to comment on that. He was having enough of a hard time accepting Mook, Oakenayl, Evangelyne, and the other supernaturals, but believing that there was some kind of witch who only existed in dreams was still beyond his reach.

"Daylighters, sunbathers, whatever. Don't really care. What I'm saying is that one minute they're all here, next—*poof.* And by 'poof' I don't know if I mean they just up and left or if they actually vanished in a puff of smoke."

"I don't think they can do that."

"Why not? They can do a lot of other really, really weird stuff."

"I guess."

"I tried to talk to Vangie to, you know, try to get to know her. To try to wrap my head around what it must be like to be a . . ."

"A werewolf?"

"Well, yeah, that too, but I was going to say I wondered what it was like to actually be supernatural. You ever talk to her about that? About what it's like?"

"I tried," said Milo, "but she's not the easiest person to have a conversation with. I mean, that first day, when we had to team up to fight the Huntsman and all, we talked a lot. And I thought we were, like, I don't know, becoming *friends*."

Shark nodded. "So what happened?"

"It's weird, but since we got back from the hive ship, since she got that Heart of Darkness thing back, we haven't said ten words to each other. Not that I haven't tried. She hangs around the camp and all, but she hardly talks. Oakenayl never does. Iskiel can't, and Mook only says 'Mook.'"

"'Mook,'" said Shark, and they laughed.

"So, no, we haven't really talked about the whole supernatural thing. I guess it just *is*."

Shark looked at him. "I don't get you, man. You act like hanging around with werewolves and fire salamanders is no big."

"It's big, believe me."

"So how come you're not freaked? I know I'm freaked. Everyone in camp's freaked. Barnaby is *totally* freaked. And *why* are we all freaked? Because this is pretty darn freaky. Freakity-freak-freak with a capital *FREAK*."

"I didn't say I wasn't freaked, Shark. It's just that it is what it is."

"You're nuts, you do know that."

"Yeah," sighed Milo, "probably. But are Evangelyne

and the others really any freakier than an invasion fleet of outer space insects?"

"Absolutely."

"How?"

"Because outer space alien insects are science. I mean, *weirdo* science, sure, but they're just another species and advance tech. The Nightsiders are actually supernatural. Magical. I'll bet you can find them in a dictionary under 'things that are never going to be possible.'"

"Guess the dictionary's wrong, then."

"Right. That doesn't help me stop being freaked out."

"C'mon, Shark, you know what I mean. So, okay, four days ago we didn't believe in any of this stuff and now it's right here. This is all actually happening; it's real. It's now our version of what's real. It's the world. If you're asking if it scares me, then, sure. Werewolves and monsters and magic? Of course that's scary. All the things from all those books we've been reading are real. Vampires and ghosts and all that. It's all real."

"Except dragons," said Shark. "I asked Vangie about that and—"

"I don't think she likes to be called Vangie."

"—and she laughed at me for being weird 'cause I wanted to know if dragons were real."

"I know. She did the same thing to me. The Nightsiders don't believe in dragons."

"Ah, yes," said Shark, raising a finger and looking sage, "but do dragons believe in the Nightsiders?"

"That doesn't even make sense."

"Dude—we're sitting here next to an alien spaceship we stole, in a camp we're sharing with monsters, and you just tricked an alligator into killing a shocktrooper. You want to go over the whole 'what makes sense' thing with me again?"

"Oh . . . shut up."

They both burst out laughing because it really was kind of crazy, and sometimes the world needs to be laughed at. Killer barked happily and wagged his little tail.

After a minute, Milo said, "Hey, you never told me where everyone else is."

After the raid on the camp, the Dissosterin had captured thirty-eight survivors, mostly children and older camp followers. No soldiers. The older folks were still recovering from injuries sustained during the raid and from the crash of the red ship. A few were also in deep shock. The kids—some of whom were older than Milo and Shark—were in no better shape, though they seemed better able to process the fact that monsters were real.

"Mr. Campos and the other grown-ups are in the ship. Mrs. Rostov isn't doing great."

The oldest of the adults was Inga Rostov, who had taught sewing and tailoring in the old camp. During the crash she'd banged her head, and since then she'd been sleeping a lot. Way too much, but none of the other survivors were doctors. No one knew what to do for her other than to make her comfortable.

Milo looked at Shark. "She's not going to . . . you know . . . ?"

Shark wouldn't meet his eyes. "All I know is that I overheard Mr. Campos tell Barnaby to prepare for the worst. I can't think of any way that is good news."

"This is so wrong," growled Milo, balling his hands into fists. "If we had a medic or if . . ."

His voice trailed off. They both knew what he had been going to say.

Or if Mom was here.

All the camp's soldiers were trained in first aid, and many of them had really advanced skills when it came to battlefield injuries. It was crucial in this terrible new world for everyone to possess skills that went beyond personal survival. The real fight was keeping the human species alive.

The kids in the training pods all knew first aid. Milo, Shark, and their friends could set a broken bone, stitch a cut, immobilize someone with a spinal injury, and more. They knew which plants were medicinal, and they knew how to use spiderwebs and certain kinds of moss as natural antibiotics. But Mrs. Rostov's injuries were beyond that level of skill. There was something wrong inside her head, possibly a skull fracture or brain injury, and all the portable diagnostic equipment had been destroyed in the attack on the camp. It was heartbreaking and frustrating in equal parts.

"What's freaking me out," said Shark, "I mean, apart

from *everything* else, is that the grown-ups aren't helping much. They stay in the ship all the time and they don't even try to tell us what to do."

"I know." They both looked at the ship for a long time, as if they could see the adults inside.

Shark said, "I always hated it when Aunt Jenny or anyone told me what to do, but right now I'd be okay with someone telling me to wash behind my ears or tucking me in at night. And if you make a joke I will punch the snot out of you."

"No," said Milo, "I feel the same way. I guess not everyone who's grown up can handle stuff."

"Yeah. None of the old folks are trained fighters, either."

"We have to find my mom and your aunt Jenny," said Milo decisively.

"Yeah, we do," said Shark. "I'm open to suggestions."

"Well . . . ," said Milo slowly, "first we need to finish fixing the ship and—"

"Yeah, yeah, yeah. Fix the ship and go look for them. I don't want to be a party pooper, Milo, but have you really thought that through?"

"I don't want to hear it. Barnaby's wrong."

The truth was that from the beginning, Barnaby Guidry had outlined why using the Huntsman's ship to search for the soldiers was a bad idea. Shark said it anyway, ticking the items off on his thick fingers.

"The Bugs are looking for the ship," he began, "and

I'm pretty sure they're going to shoot it the heck down as soon as we take off."

"Yeah, but—"

"Aunt Jenny and your mom don't know we have it, so as soon as they see it they'll hide. And they're really, really, really good at hiding."

"Sure, but—"

"We don't know where the soldiers are."

"I know, but—"

"And since we've stolen the crystal egg, crippled one hive ship, and nearly killed the Huntsman, the entire Swarm is going to be on the alert. We're better off *not* using the ship. In fact, we should hide it, strip out as much tech as we can, and go find another EA camp. Barnaby thinks there's one near Mandeville, over near Lake Pontchartrain."

Milo sighed.

A slim figure stepped out of the shadows on the far side of the camp, glanced briefly at them, and then wandered back into the woods. Small, fragile, with masses of wild blond hair, and eyes that were filled with wonder. Milo nodded toward her.

"Lizabeth's the only one who believed that all this stuff was real," he said quietly. "And we always told her she was crazy."

Shark stroked Killer's stomach. "Hey, just because the Nightsiders are real doesn't mean Lizzie's not crazy. She still thinks the Loch Ness Monster lives in the bayou."

Lizabeth, who indeed had always been drawn to the world of spirits and shadows, claimed to have seen monsters many times. Until four days ago, none of her claims had ever been verified. Now Milo wondered if their friend simply had some kind of gift. A second sight, or whatever it was called. He'd meant to ask Evangelyne about it, but the wolf girl was never around.

"Right now," said Milo, "I wouldn't bet a whole bag of tech that the Loch Ness Monster *isn't* in the bayou. She might be right about all of it."

"Maybe," conceded Shark. "I'm just glad she's okay."

"Wait—what do you mean? Why *wouldn't* she be okay?"

"Because of . . . ," began Shark, then stopped and started over. "Oh, that's right, you were already gone this morning when I found her."

Milo gripped Shark's arm. "Found her? Lizzie? Found her where?"

Shark gently pulled his arm free and pointed to the woods Milo had just come from. "Over there. I was out to do a circle around the camp, you know, just to make sure everything was cool before I sat down to work on the circuit. And I found Lizzie sprawled on the ground. Scared the heck out of me. I thought maybe a hunter-killer got her or something."

"What happened?"

Shark shrugged. "Not much, really. She said she wasn't paying attention and must have walked into a tree. Knocked herself out."

"Is she hurt?"

"Not that I can see. She's been a little loopy, but Lizzie's always a little loopy, so it's hard to really tell."

Milo studied the section of woods into which Lizabeth had vanished. "I went that way this morning," he said. "I didn't see her. When did it happen?"

"I don't know. She must have gone out right after you did. Doesn't matter, though. She's okay." Shark nudged Milo's pack. "Hey, you told me about what happened to the shocktrooper, but did you get any of his gear?"

Milo suddenly grinned. "Yeah, it's pretty much Christmas for—"

And that's when the tree they were sitting under exploded.

FROM MILO'S DREAM DIARY

I sometimes dream about an old woman called the
   Witch of the World. I'm pretty sure she's not real.
   Not normal real. Not flesh and bone and like that.
But she's real in a different way.
Evangelyne and the Nightsiders all believe in her. The
   witch is something magical, but whatever she is,
   she's so old there's no name for it.
She hasn't said much since we escaped the hive ship,
   but the last couple of nights I thought I heard
   her whispering. It's driving me nuts, because I can
   almost understand what she's saying . . . but not
   quite. It's like she's in pain, like she's calling for
   help, but she can't tell me enough so I can do
   anything.

Chapter 9

Milo heard a deep *whoosh*, and he looked up just in time to see a long blue line of pulse power streak down from the clouds. He screamed, grabbed Shark's shoulder, and yanked his friend off the log and down just as the force beam struck the closest oak and turned it into a massive fireball. The leaves ignited and flew like embers into the air, raining down on the surrounding trees and instantly setting them ablaze. The force and intense heat split the trunk of the tree that had been hit, and it fell apart in two halves.

Killer leaped from Shark's arms, barking in alarm, as the two boys rolled out of the way to avoid flaming debris.

"Up there!" cried Shark, pointing.

But Milo didn't need help spotting their danger.

High in the air was a Dissosterin drop-ship. It was thirty feet across, shaped like a flying saucer seen in old books, with a spherical pilot's compartment in the center. Shocktroopers crouched on small detachable platforms called sky-boards, guns in their armored fists. Milo knew that the 'troopers could either disconnect their sky-boards and swoop down like predatory birds, or rappel to the ground on steel lines.

The air split with the sound of a deep, furious voice amplified to an unnatural bellow.

"I want what you stole!"

It was the voice of the Huntsman. The colossal sound smashed through the air. It was strange, too, as if the Huntsman were shouting through a dozen mouths at once. Then Milo realized that the Huntsman's voice, repeating and repeating those five words, was booming at them from speakers mounted on the sides of each sky-board.

"I want what you stole!"

The shocktroopers all clung to the drop-ship, each of them firing blue pulse blasts downward, setting the forest ablaze.

Milo and Shark shot to their feet and began running for cover, screaming warnings to the other survivors even though everyone would already know that danger had found them.

"Shark, get the li'l kids down to the bayou," bellowed Barnaby, who had appeared from the swirling smoke as if by magic. He pointed to where a knot of scared little ones cowered on the red ship's entry ramp. "Make for the bolt-hole, you."

"On it!" Shark yelled, then emitted an ear-splitting whistle. The kids turned toward him, spotted him through the smoke, and ran from the attacking Bugs. Shark pushed them into the brush, with Killer herding them like a frantic sheepdog. They vanished into the dense woods. The camp was within a mile's hard run of one of the EA's many reinforced bunkers. The bolt-holes were small, cramped, but well concealed and stocked with provisions. Ten people could hide in one for a week.

Barnaby pivoted, aimed his bow, and loosed an arrow. It struck the heavy armor of a shocktrooper and bounced off. The 'trooper fired a pulse blast at them, and Milo pulled the Cajun out of the way just in time. The blast exploded a young pine into sawdust.

"*I want what you stole!*"

"They seem pretty mad, them," said Barnaby, fitting another arrow.

"Didn't think they came because they like your cooking," snapped Milo.

He looked back wildly at the damaged red craft. More than twenty people were in there, most of them old and wounded. The shocktroopers hovered directly above the ship, and though they were not firing at it, it was clear that they'd somehow finally managed to track the stolen craft.

He grabbed Barnaby's sleeve. "We have to get everyone out."

The Cajun's face was filled with equal parts fear and anger. "I'll go. You get Lizabeth and the others out of here, you. I'll hold these *gros cafards* off, me."

The big cockroaches, as Barnaby called them, were firing at everything that moved.

"With a bow and arrows?" demanded Shark. "You're nuts."

Milo whipped his satchel open, pulled out the two pulse pistols, and shoved one into Barnaby's hands.

"How you get these—?"

"Christmas present. Go!"

Barnaby slung his bow, snatched the pistol, and immediately swung the barrel toward the drop-ship. "Eat this!"

He began firing the pistol, sending blue force blasts up through the burning leaves. His first five shots missed, but his sixth hit the arm of one of the 'troopers and blasted the creature from its perch. It fell like a cinder, burning and caterwauling until it vanished into the flames of the burning oak.

"I got this, me," yelled Barnaby. "Go!"

Barnaby fired and fired, hitting two more of the 'troopers. Then the others spotted him through the smoke and trained their weapons down at him. Milo saw what was about to happen and shoved Barnaby as hard and fast as he could. The two of them fell into the mud, and the spot where the Cajun had stood seemed to erupt into a whirlwind of smoking dirt and burning grass.

Milo rolled onto one knee. "Shark, get Lizabeth and anyone else you can and go to the bolt-hole."

"But—"

Milo threw the second pulse pistol to him. *"Go!"*

"I want what you stole!" roared the amplified voices.

Shark caught the gun, lost one second looking doubtful and confused, and then was gone, with Killer at his heels. Milo heard the gun fire and saw blue flashes in the woods.

Barnaby wheeled on him. "What you doing?"

Milo fished a pair of grenades from the bag. "I'm a lousy shot but I can throw."

The Cajun grinned, then spun around to offer covering fire as the drop-ship began swooping toward them. Milo had never used a Bug grenade before, but it was like all their tech—incredibly simple. There was one switch and it had to be the arming mechanism. Most of the Dissosterin were dumb as boxes of hair, relying on hive mind guidance to fight. Their tech was designed so that even the stupidest of them could use it. Milo was a lot smarter than a Bug and he understood tech. He flipped the switch, prayed that the grenade had a good timer, wound up, and threw it with his best fastball pitch.

The grenade cut through the smoke, heading directly toward the drop-ship. Milo knew that he had no hope of a direct hit, not at that distance, but anything would help.

"I want what you stole!"

The pitch was good.

The grenade exploded thirty feet from the drop-ship, just as the 'troopers detached their sky-boards for a close assault. The blast shook the whole forest, knocking Milo and Barnaby flat, blowing out half the fires, and punching the drop-ship like a massive invisible fist. Three of the troopers fell off their boards and plummeted to the unforgiving ground. A fourth was in the direct path of the blast and caught the shrapnel in the chest. He flew apart. The drop-ship canted sideways and, true to its name, dropped.

In all the wrong ways.

It fell sideways into the burning oak. Several of the 'troopers were still attached to the machine as it collided with the giant flaming tree.

Their screams were a dreadful thing to hear.

Barnaby got to his knees, but he was wobbly and when he tried to stand he keeled over, clutching his chest. Milo crawled to him and stared in abject horror at what he saw. A splinter—a piece of body armor from the 'trooper who'd been blown up—stood out from the Cajun's chest like a knife. Dark blood welled from the wound, and Barnaby's face went dead pale as the pain hit him.

"God, Barnaby!" cried Milo. "I'm sorry—"

Three shocktroopers were left and they dropped through the smoke on their sky-boards.

"I want what you stole!" Now the voices were faint, the speakers damaged by the blast. The resulting distortion somehow made the demand more unreal and more dangerous.

"Leave . . . me . . . ," gasped Barnaby. "I'm done. . . ."

"No!" Milo tore a strip from his shirt and pressed it quickly and gently around the wound. He dared not pull the spike out, because that would almost certainly make Barnaby bleed to death. The spike, painful as it was, formed a kind of plug for the hole it had torn in the pod leader's chest. "It's going to hurt but I have to get you out of here. Can you walk?"

He tried to help Barnaby up, but the Cajun's legs buckled. When he crashed down, the impact tore a shrill scream from him. Blue pulse blasts exploded around them, but the 'troopers' aim was spoiled by the smoke and fire. That faint protection wouldn't last, Milo knew. He had to get Barnaby out.

And there were still the old and the sick aboard the red ship. Milo saw movement over there, and through the haze he saw an old woman—Ms. Han, the camp's assistant cook—lean out the hatch with a machine gun in her wrinkled hands. She began firing at the shocktroopers, the gun juddering in her grip, bullets flying everywhere and hitting nothing. One of the 'troopers whirled and fired at her, and Milo screamed as the old woman vanished in a ball of blue flame.

We're all going to die, he thought. *Right here and right now.*

In his pocket he could feel the weight of the thing he knew the shocktroopers wanted most of all. The red ship was really only a secondary objective. They wanted the crystal egg. That egg, and the Heart of Darkness, which was now in the possession of the Nightsiders. The egg was crucial to the survival of the Dissosterin species, while the Heart of Darkness was the last known link between the Nightsiders here on Earth and all the infinite magical worlds into which most of their kind had fled. Evangelyne and her friends hoped to somehow relearn the secrets of the Heart of Darkness so they could open those shut doors—maybe to escape, maybe to call back others of their kind to help in this war and try to save the planet from the Swarm. However, for the Huntsman, the black jewel had a similar but much more destructive potential. He wanted to discover its secrets and open those doors— not to save the world, but to conquer all worlds and all dimensions, to use the Swarm to conquer all of time and space. The Huntsman was obsessed with unlocking the secrets of magic because the Swarm had reached a limit to their own technological growth. The monster they had created—the alien-human hybrid—was not content with destroying his homeworld. He wanted to be a new, dark god of the entire universe. Losing that stone to Milo and the Orphan Army had been devastating. Milo lived in terror of what the Huntsman would do to get it back.

He will burn the fields of the earth and topple mountains to find you and get back what you stole. That's what the witch had told him.

So Milo had to ask himself what he was willing to do to stop these monsters.

Barnaby groaned in pain and tried to raise his pulse pistol, but he lacked even the strength to do that. There was no choice but to try to use another grenade. Milo fished one out and showed it to Barnaby.

"I have to . . . ," he said apologetically.

The Cajun's face, though now gray with agony, twisted into a wicked grin. "You throw that thing and let's all go down together. Booyah!"

"You're crazy," said Milo, but he flicked the arming

switch and hurled the grenade as far as he could. Then he pushed Barnaby flat and arched his own body over him, ready to shield his friend with his own vulnerable flesh.

The grenade vanished into the smoke.

"I want what you stole!"

Milo scrunched his eyes shut, waiting for the explosion, maybe waiting to die.

And absolutely nothing happened.

Nothing.

Until it did.

Chapter 10

What happened wasn't an explosion, though.

The grenade did not go off. Maybe he hadn't pushed the switch all the way, or maybe it was faulty. Milo never found out.

The shocktroopers kept advancing, their guns raised, their antennae clicking with the anticipation of an easy kill. Milo cracked one eye open and looked over his shoulder. Seeing the aliens, seeing their hideous faces, seeing the lenses of their glowing blue pulse pistols as each of them raised their weapons. . . .

And then something rose up from the ground between Milo and the 'troopers. The scorched grass lifted and the dirt tore apart as something pushed up from beneath. Chunks of limestone and granite, slabs of fossilized trees, and splinters of shale thrust upward as if pushed by some giant hand. Pebbles and stones and rocks slapped together, grinding and twisting to form powerful legs, a thick torso, and huge arms, and a boulder as big as a barrel rolled up against the pull of gravity and planted itself between the ponderous shoulders to form a head. Blunt stone split apart to form fingers, and then those fingers clenched into fists like mallets.

The shocktroopers skidded to a halt, stunned and confused as the figure of rock towered over them. They chittered in fear as they swung their guns up toward the impossible creature.

The head of the rock figure split apart to create the jaws of a great mouth, and from that mouth issued a single word that was a challenge, a name, a threat, and a promise.

"MOOK!"

And then the rock elemental swung his fists at the shocktroopers. Mook struck one and tore it to pieces as surely as if the grenade had actually exploded.

"I want what—"

The tinny voice was cut off, replaced by the less mechanical but no less alien shriek of a dying shock-trooper.

The other soldiers tried to flee, but suddenly they were blocked by a tree behind them that had not been there before. It was made of living wood and scorched chunks of the dying oak. Nestled beneath a wreath of flowers, leaves, and twigs was a face that was twisted into a mask of terrible rage and hatred.

"What have you *done*?" bellowed Oakenayl as he thrust forward with hands from which long tendrils of vine shot like silk from a spider. The vines wrapped themselves around one of the troopers and then tightened like a fist, crushing the alien into green pulp. "Filthy parasites!"

The last of the 'troopers snapped off a few wild shots as he backpedaled away. Then he turned and ran for his sky-sled, the Dissosterin speakers still repeating the same demand. Something dropped from the limb of a smoking tree and coiled itself around the 'trooper's throat. Milo saw green scales marked with glowing red lines, saw claws and a flickering serpentine tongue, and then the 'trooper's head burst into a fireball. As the dead Bug fell, Iskiel the fire salamander dropped to the ground and scuttled off through the brush, seeking other prey.

Smoke swirled through the battlefield, but the tinny growl of the Huntsman was silent now.

"Milo!" called a voice. High, female, and urgent. He turned to see a girl standing near the ramp of the red ship. She had long pale hair that looked almost silver, and eyes the color of a winter moon. She pointed toward the eastern sky. "There's another drop-ship coming. It'll be here in minutes!"

"Evangelyne," he yelled, "we have to get everyone out. . . ."

The girl nodded and vanished into the ship. Mook lumbered after her, while Oakenayl stood staring at the burning trees.

"I knew those trees," he murmured in a voice filled with great sadness.

"I'm . . . I'm sorry . . . ," began Milo, but the tree spirit ignored him, snatched up a barrel of drinking water, and hurried over to fight the flames. Milo heard a snatch of the vile things he muttered as he went. Oakenayl said "Daylighters" exactly the same way he said "parasites." As if he saw no real difference between the alien invaders and the human race.

A heartbeat later Mook reappeared, and in his massive arms he held a metal-framed bed that had clearly been torn from the wall of the ship. On it were four of the most badly injured survivors. Mook glanced east.

"Mook," he said, then turned and ran into the forest. Evangelyne came next, leading the others out. Most of the survivors were in no condition to run, and the strongest had the weakest leaning on them for support.

"Head to the bolt-hole," yelled Milo, and even though many of the survivors were older than him, they didn't stop to question his order. They shuffled off, moving as fast as they could. Evangelyne leaped from the ramp, changing mid-leap from an eleven-year-old girl into a wolf with silver fur. The off-white linen dress she wore, the leather belt, her shoes, her jewelry, and the small leather pouch that hung from her belt—all vanished. Milo kept meaning to ask her where her clothes went when she transformed, but there never seemed to be the right time for that kind of question.

Evangelyne landed and raced ahead of the survivors, sniffing out the safest route. That left Milo in the clearing with Barnaby, who had lapsed into unconsciousness.

"Oakenayl!" yelled Milo.

There was no answer.

"Oakenayl . . . please!"

When it was clear the tree spirit was not going to come help him, Milo stood, caught Barnaby under the armpits, and began to drag him from the burning camp. Barnaby was heavy, the terrain was not accommodating, and Milo ached from the shock of the blast. But he had to do the job or leave his friend to die.

Milo summoned all his strength and dragged Barnaby into the woods.

As the foliage closed behind them, Milo glanced up to see Oakenayl step out of the smoke and stand there. Watching him. Offering no help. The tree spirit looked pointedly at the twigs and branches covering the injured Cajun. Oakenayl spat a lump of sap onto the ground between them; then he turned away and stalked back into the smoke.

FROM MILO'S DREAM DIARY

Last night I had a strange dream.

Stranger than normal, even for me.

It wasn't like any dream I'd ever had before. There were no aliens, no Stingers, nothing connected to the Swarm or the Huntsman.

In my dream, I was awake and sitting in a big chair in a dark room, reading a book. It wasn't like any book I'd ever seen before. The covers were of heavy wood and had carvings of all kinds of animals and monsters. And when I opened the book, I could feel the carvings move—but only when I wasn't looking at them. When I closed the book and looked at the covers, there were different animals and different monsters. Little kids and strange birds, hunting cats and unicorns, dragons and trolls, and many other things. I didn't know the names for a lot of them, because I was pretty sure they didn't have names.

No matter how long I stared at them, they wouldn't
 change.
That happened only when I opened the book and
 looked inside.
Then the covers would move and change.
I knew that I should be scared by that.
I wasn't, though.
I felt something else, a different feeling.
When those carvings were changing, when the animals
 and monsters were moving around, coming in, going
 away, I felt sad.
So sad.
Maybe it's because the book was sad. Not the story.
 The book itself.

Chapter 11

Milo dragged Barnaby for what seemed like a year. It was probably not more than fifteen minutes, but it felt longer. And he was certain that it was all uphill, which it wasn't. The pod leader moaned piteously, caught in the haze between agonized awareness and dangerous shocked unconsciousness. At least half the sweat that poured down Milo's face was from fear of not getting his friend to safety in time.

Then Milo heard the bushes rustle and he crouched, still holding the groaning Barnaby, and his heart sank. If it was a shocktrooper, he was done. He had no traps ready, no convenient alligators. Nothing.

"Milo," said a voice, and Lizabeth stepped out from between two wild rosebushes. She had moss and leaves in her hair, and her pale eyes were filled with strange lights.

"Lizzie!" gasped Milo. "Barnaby's hurt. Help me. I think there are more 'troopers coming and—"

"Don't worry, Milo," said Lizabeth. "They're gone."

"You can't know that. They're after us and we need to get Barnaby to the bolt-hole. He's hurt bad."

Lizabeth stepped closer. Her jeans and blouse were stained with grass and pollen, and the side of her blouse was slashed open and soaked with blood.

"You're hurt!" Milo gasped. He reached for her but she stepped quickly back and shook her head.

"No," she said. Then she glanced down at the cut in her shirt and lifted the hem to show that the skin beneath was untouched. "See?"

"Geez," said Milo, relieved, "I thought you were . . . you know . . . I mean . . . Whose blood is that?"

"Something died in the woods," was all she said. When Milo pressed her, Lizabeth gave him the strangest look. Then she turned away and slowly knelt beside Barnaby.

"He's hurt bad," said Milo, "and I don't know what to do for him."

"He'll be okay," she said. "I brought something for him."

Lizabeth reached into a pocket, removed some items, and held them out to Milo. There were herbs and plants that he recognized from wilderness first-aid classes—calendula, cloves, garlic, and echinacea—and many he didn't know. She even had a loose ball of spiderwebs and a few useful roots.

"These will help," said Lizabeth. "To prevent infection and reduce pain."

Her voice sounded strange to Milo. A little distant and a little older than the way she normally spoke. *She's in shock,* he thought. It was sad, but it was also understandable. Right now, everyone had to be jolted out of their normal mind. He knew *he* had been.

Milo carefully lowered Barnaby's head and shoulders to the ground and squatted down next to him. He glanced up at Lizabeth. "You're a lifesaver, Lizzie. How'd you even know he was hurt?"

Lizabeth shrugged, but there was a pause before she did so, as if her mind was somewhere else. Without waiting for Milo's permission, Lizabeth knelt beside Barnaby and removed the bloody compress around the spike. Then she pressed the herbs and spiderwebs carefully around the edges of the wound.

"Give me your knife," she said, and Milo drew his hunting knife and passed it to her. As she accepted it, her slender fingers brushed his, and Milo was shocked at how cold they were.

"You're freezing," he said. "We need to—"

"I'm fine," she interrupted. When Milo protested, she ignored him and set about cutting a long strip of cloth from the hem of her blouse. Then she gently applied it as a fresh compress around the wound; it also served to keep the mixture of herbs in place. Lizzie reversed the knife in her hand and offered it handle first to Milo.

Was she more careful this time not to make contact skin to skin? Milo thought so, but couldn't understand why.

Almost immediately the Cajun boy's moans of agony diminished and he lapsed into a more natural and comfortable sleep. Even his color improved, going from a gray green to a faded pink. Not good, but much more encouraging.

"Lizzie," said Milo, "that's . . . that's amazing. Really incredible. Thanks."

She said nothing. Instead she got to her feet and walked a few paces away, looking back toward the camp.

"You should make a travois," she murmured. "If you don't, he'll die before you get him back."

"I don't have time—"

"Yes you do," she said, her voice still distant and strange.

Milo frowned. "Are you okay, Lizzie?"

But Lizabeth didn't answer.

Milo wasted no more time. Making a travois—a kind of stretcher that one person could pull—was one of the thousand things they'd learned in survival class. Milo hated taking these precious minutes to make it, but he knew that Lizabeth was right. Without it, he'd never get Barnaby to the bolt-hole. Not alive. He set to work.

First he found two long, straight branches. He had to use a piece of line wrapped around a heavy rock to snag the branches and pull them down from the trees. That took muscle and about a gallon of sweat, but Milo managed to break them off. They were each about twelve feet in length. Then he found two shorter branches— one four feet long and the other five feet. He used his hunting knife to strip them of leaves and twigs and any jagged knots. Then he lashed the heaviest ends of the long poles together to create the "foot" of the device.

"Oakenayl's not going to be happy with this," Milo said while tying the knots.

Lizzie said nothing. She watched him work, not helping, but instead running her cool fingers over the injured boy's brow.

Milo lashed the crossbars in place and attached his shirt as a sling. He used up all his own ball of heavy-duty twine, and some he found in Barnaby's pocket. Then he quickly wove vines together and wound them about each joint for reinforcement.

He could feel the seconds ticking away on the big warning clock inside his head. "Come on," he muttered to himself. "Come on, come on . . ."

When the travois was finished, the next part was quicker but much, much more difficult. He had to get Barnaby onto it. The Cajun was in and out of consciousness and was in terrible pain, but he was a practical young man and understood what Milo was doing. Just as he understood the need for speed and silence.

"Gimme a stick, you," he mumbled, and when Milo found one, Barnaby placed it between his strong white teeth and then nodded.

"Lizzie," said Milo, "get his other arm."

Lizabeth hesitated, then positioned herself opposite Milo.

"On three," said Milo, and then counted down.

It was horrible work. Fresh blood darkened the bandage

Lizzie had placed, and a strangled scream tore itself from Barnaby's throat. By the time they had Barnaby on the travois and tied in place, both boys were panting and the Cajun had bitten all the way through the stick. Milo was flushed lobster red, and Barnaby was as pale as death. Lizzie was not breathing hard and was still as pale as a ghost. She merely stepped back and stood to one side, watching with her ice-blue eyes.

Milo positioned himself between the two long arms of the travois, squatted, grabbed the bars, and straightened his legs. The physics of the travois didn't make Barnaby's weight feel like a load of feathers, but it made lifting and pulling him possible.

Barnaby moaned softly.

"You take one pole and I'll get the other," Milo said. When Lizabeth didn't answer, he looked up.

She was gone.

He looked wildly about, but the woods were still and quiet except for the buzz of insects. Normal Earth insects.

"Lizzie!" he called in a terse whisper.

There was no answer.

Milo stood and glanced around, but there was no sign of her. He studied the ground to see if he could tell by her footprints which way she had gone, but except for his shoe prints and those of Barnaby, the immediate area was undisturbed.

"What—?" he said aloud, but then Barnaby groaned

as a fresh wave of pain shot through him. There was no more time to waste. "Hold on, buddy." Milo gritted his teeth as he picked up the handles and began to pull. It was still hard work, but it was easier than using sheer muscle. Soon Milo and Barnaby were far away from the battle site, the red ship, and the dead shocktroopers. All the while, Milo keep looking into the woods to see if Lizabeth had followed, but he saw no sign of her.

No sign at all.

Chapter 12

It was Killer who greeted them as they arrived at the bolt-hole. The little dog came out of the tall grass like a four-legged missile. He ran past another of the big chunks of debris tagged with the fierce demand of the Huntsman.

I WANT WHAT YOU STOLE

Killer ran right at Milo, tail wagging at full speed; then he jolted to a stop at the smell of blood. Killer sniffed Barnaby and whimpered softly.

"Get Shark," begged Milo, and the little dog was gone.

Two minutes later, Shark and Evangelyne came hurrying through the woods. They bent over Barnaby to assess the wound.

"Oh, man," groaned Shark, "this is really, really bad."

It was only two "reallys," which was of mild comfort to Milo. Three and he'd have lost hope.

Evangelyne lifted the compress and studied the herbs. A deep frown line appeared between her brows. "Where did you learn this magic?"

"It's not magic," said Milo. "It's herbal medicine."

Shark looked too. "Is that lobelia and *Epipactis*? Why'd you put those on there?"

"I didn't," said Milo. "Lizzie did."

"When?" demanded Shark.

"I don't know . . . twenty minutes ago."

Shark and Evangelyne stared at him.

"Dude," said Shark, "what are you talking about? Lizzie's been at the bolt-hole for half an hour."

"No she hasn't. I just saw her."

"You can't have," said Evangelyne. "She led the wounded there and hasn't left."

"No way," insisted Milo. "Look, that's a strip of her blouse."

Shark touched the edge of the compress. Blood had soaked it so thoroughly that it was impossible to see the flower pattern.

"This is strange," murmured Evangelyne. "That combination of herbs . . . that's very old magic. Lizabeth could not have known this. Maybe some of it is from your own herbalists, but not this."

"And, like I said," said Shark, "she's been here the whole time."

"You guys are nuts," growled Milo. "But forget that for now. C'mon, Shark, help me get Barnaby into the bolt-hole."

It took ten careful minutes to rig another sling and lower Barnaby down. Mook was already inside. He raised his powerful arms to accept the burden and lowered Barnaby to the concrete floor with surprising gentleness. Then he climbed out to make room for the other survivors to begin working on the Cajun. The bolt-hole was cramped with all the wounded refugees, so Mook, Shark, Milo, Evangelyne, and Killer stood outside. A few seconds later Lizabeth climbed out too.

"I'm glad you made it back," she said, touching Milo's arm.

He wheeled on her. "What's going on with you? Why didn't you tell everyone I needed help?"

"What do you mean?" she asked, snatching her hand back in surprise. "We were waiting for you—"

"What do you mean, what do I mean?" snapped Milo. "First you show up out of nowhere with those herbs, then you take off without a word, and now I find you here and you didn't bother to send anyone out to help. And what's with your blouse? It was covered with blood and now it's not. What'd you do? Stop to do laundry? What's with you?"

Lizabeth stared at him like he was speaking a foreign language. "Milo, I—"

"You're allowed to be weird, Lizzie, but that was just mean."

Tears sprang into her eyes and she turned bright red. Shark shifted and put his arm around her.

"Hey, back off, man," he growled. "What are you dumping on her for? I told you, she was here the whole time."

"Oh yeah? Then how come there's a piece of her shirt around Barnaby's wound?"

"A piece . . . ?" began Lizabeth, but Milo snaked a hand out and tugged the hem of her blouse out of the top of her jeans. The fabric, which must have been washed, was completely dry.

"See? Right . . . here . . ."

His voice trailed off because the hem was intact. Clearly nothing had been cut from it. Shark, Evangelyne, and Lizabeth stared at him. Even Killer seemed to give him a skeptical and accusing look. Mook shook his head.

"Mook," he said.

"No," said Milo, "that's impossible. Lizzie, I *saw* you."

"Saw me where? What are you talking about?"

Milo went through the story, and as they listened he could tell that none of them believed him. When Milo was done, Shark climbed down into the bolt-hole and returned later with the bloody bandage and held it out to Milo.

"This is what was on Barnaby."

Before Milo could take it, Evangelyne plucked it from Shark's fingers, knelt, and laid it out flat on the ground. The cloth was thoroughly soaked, but in the downspill of sunlight they could see a faint pattern. It was exactly the same as the pattern on Lizabeth's blouse.

"Okay," said Shark, "that is really, really weird."

"That's not mine," said Lizabeth very quietly.

Milo's mouth went dry. He looked around at the faces of his friends. "I—I don't understand . . . I *saw* you, Lizzie. I spoke with you."

Lizabeth shrank against Shark's side and shook her head.

"Mook," suggested Mook.

Milo turned to Evangelyne. "What did you mean when you said those herbs were old magic?"

The wolf girl looked uneasy. "There are as many kinds of magic as there are leaves in a great forest," she said. "Earth magic and ice magic and fire magic and—"

"Yeah, got it. Lots of kinds of magic," interrupted Milo. "Get to the part that makes sense."

"I'm not a healer, but I know some of the properties of herbs and roots. I could have made a compress that might have helped, but . . ." She shook her head and, Milo thought, looked deeply uneasy. "That combination is strange. I've only seen something like it once before."

"Where?" asked Milo and Shark at the same time.

"It was tied into a bundle and placed as an offering at a shrine honoring the Daughter of Splinters and Salt."

"The who?" asked Milo.

"The what?" asked Shark.

"Mook?" asked Mook.

Lizabeth whimpered and pressed more tightly against Shark.

"The Daughter of Splinters and Salt was a very powerful witch who belonged to the Chitimacha people, who lived in southern Louisiana many years before the Europeans came to these lands. It's said that she's seen sometimes wandering in these woods."

"Then maybe it was her you saw," said Shark.

"Why would she pretend to be Lizzie?" asked Milo, but Evangelyne shook her head.

"We don't even know if that's what you saw," she said. "This is a mystery."

Lizabeth looked deeply frightened by this conversation, and Milo certainly couldn't blame her. But not knowing the answer was driving him nuts.

"Has to be something like that," insisted Shark. "'Cause Lizzie was here with us, right?"

She nodded mutely.

"Besides," added Shark, "lately there's been a whole lot of weirdos running around in these woods."

Instead of taking offense at Shark's comment, Evangelyne shook her head again, very slowly. "No, that's not possible. . . ."

"Why not?" asked Lizabeth in a tiny voice.

"Because," said Evangelyne, "the Daughter of Splinters and Salt died a thousand years ago."

The others stared at her. Even Mook seemed unnerved. Then one by one they looked at Lizabeth, and finally at each other.

The little blond girl stood there, looking not at any of them but down at her own fingers as she slowly traced the faded outlines of flowers on her blouse.

"Okay," said Shark, holding up his hands, "I got nothing. Anyone else have even a clue as to what's going on here?"

"Mook," agreed Mook. His head made a grinding sound as he shook it.

"How does *any* of this make sense?" asked Milo. "Are you saying a ghost of some dead witch showed up pretending to be Lizzie and did first aid on Barnaby? 'Cause, seriously, Evangelyne, even though things have been weird lately. that's really weird."

"That's really, really, *really* weird," Shark said emphatically.

Evangelyne turned away and stared into the forest the way Milo had come. "There are many mysteries in the world," she said. And that was all she would say on the subject.

What's she hiding? he wondered. His next thought was far more disturbing. *What's she afraid of?*

Lizabeth went back to the bolt-hole without saying another word, though she paused at the top of the ladder. Milo saw the expression on her face and it chilled him to the bone. Her eyes were so cold and so strange that for an instant, she did not look like Lizabeth at all.

She gave him the smallest of smiles and then vanished into the bolt-hole.

Chapter 13

Mysteries, even ones that raised goose bumps all over Milo's body, had to wait.

"We got to make sure no one's tracking us," said Shark, and the others nodded. They split up and went into the woods, each taking a different direction. After ten minutes they met again outside the bolt-hole. The good news was that the woods seemed to be empty of Dissosterin 'troopers or any of the Swarm's mechanical hunter-killers. They knew that this didn't mean they were safe, just safe for now.

The bad news was that Barnaby was still hovering on the edge of death. None of the survivors had the skill to remove the spike and do the surgery to save the Cajun's life.

"What do we do?" asked Milo.

"Death comes for everyone in the end, boy," suggested Evangelyne, but Milo barked at her.

"Whoa, don't you dare say that. We're *not* going to let him die. Not him or anyone."

The wolf girl cocked an eyebrow. "And how do you propose saving them, boy? None of us are healers of *that* kind."

Milo chewed his lip, then cut a look at Shark. "Dude, that circuit board you were working on . . ."

"Yeah?"

"Is that really all we need to get the ship to fly?"

Shark snorted. "Sure, it'll get off the ground, but that's about it. No way it would make it to orbit. Pretty sure the coolant circuits are close to being fried, so starting the engine might blow them out."

"What would happen then?" asked Evangelyne.

Shark put his fists together, then mimed something blowing up.

"You're sure, boy?" asked the wolf girl.

"Sure? Are you nuts? Gimme a break. I'm *eleven*. Of course I'm not sure. I've never rebuilt a spaceship before."

Evangelyne colored and looked briefly flustered. Mook chuckled, and when she glared at him he suddenly seemed to find something interesting to look at up in the trees. Although it was nearly impossible to read the stone boy's facial expression, Milo was certain Mook was grinning.

"Shark," he said, "do you think the ship would last long enough to get us across Lake Pontchartrain?"

"I think so. Maybe. I don't know. Why?"

"The other day, before the patrol left, Mom said that there was a rally point in the basement of an old church in Mandeville. Maybe we can find some EA soldiers. They'll probably have a portable field hospital, and if not, they can get Barnaby and the others to one."

NIGHTSIDERS

Shark sucked a tooth while he thought about it. "Well . . . ," he began slowly, "first we'd have to find the circuit board. I dropped it and ran when those Bugs attacked us. Then I'd need maybe half an hour to install it. Maybe less, depending on how well the Bug system accepts my repairs. I had to fudge some stuff. Then we'd have to bring it over here to pick everyone up. . . ."

Evangelyne said, "That's already taking too much time. The Bugs will track us."

"Hey," said Milo, "I'm open to other suggestions."

The wolf girl said nothing.

"And then," said Shark, picking up where he'd left off, "depending on how good the engine's working, figure at least half an hour to Mandeville. Longer if we do it smart and fly low and keep to the trees, fly along the coast. We'd be nuts to fly right across the lake in plain sight. I mean, the hive ship is right there over New Orleans, and there are always scout ships and barrel-fighters around. It's not going to be easy."

A groan of pain floated up from the bolt-hole. Lizabeth climbed out, went to the muddy bank of the bayou, picked up a handful of mud, and then climbed back down into the bunker. They watched her go.

"She's a strange one," said Evangelyne.

Shark snorted. "Coming from you, that's saying something."

"Shark," said Milo, "I'm telling you, I saw her in the woods earlier and the whole side of her shirt was bloody.

She used my knife to cut a bandage off the hem."

"And then what, dude?" asked Shark. "She found an identical shirt, came back here, and slipped back into the bolt-hole without anyone knowing? Without Vangie knowing?"

"Don't call me that," said the wolf girl automatically, but she also nodded. "The boy's right. She was here the whole time."

Milo had no way of proving what he'd seen and there was no time for an argument.

"We have to get the wounded out of here," said Milo. "We have to try."

"Yeah, I guess we do," said Shark. "But we got, like, one chance in—"

"I don't care," interrupted Milo. "We have to take whatever chance we have."

"Yes, sir, Captain Fearless."

"Oh . . . bite me," said Milo. They grinned at each other, then they all decided to leave Lizabeth with the wounded. Mook agreed to stay with her to guard the survivors in the bolt-hole, and he took up station like a stone colossus.

Milo, Shark, Evangelyne, and Killer went running into the woods, taking the fastest safe route back to where the big red ship waited. As they ran, Milo wondered if they were about to effect an escape plan or simply run directly into a Dissosterin trap. Surely the drop-ship would have been reported missing by now. If it was a random patrol, how long would it be before the Bugs came looking for it?

And . . . did the Huntsman know that his ship had been found? Was he waiting too? Was the monstrous alien-human hybrid already there with his pack of deadly Stingers?

These were very bad questions to have banging around in one's head. Milo wished he could flush his brain clear, but that's not how the world worked.

With terror setting fires in his soul, he ran.

Chapter 14

They approached the camp from the north, coming in along a game trail that snaked and twisted down through a dense stand of trees. Milo still had his satchel, but he had zero interest in ever using an alien grenade again. One had failed to explode, and another had nearly killed Barnaby. Not a good track record for tech he didn't really understand. He tapped the pulse pistol shoved into Shark's belt.

"You good with that thing?"

Shark drew the gun and turned it over in his hands, careful to keep the focusing jewel pointed away. "You have any idea how this thing works?"

"Nope."

"That's useful."

"It's Bug tech," said Milo. "Shouldn't be too hard to figure out. I just haven't had time."

Shark made a sour face and shoved the pistol back into his waistband. "Hope I don't blow my butt off."

When they passed through a clearing, they could see the pall of smoke that hung over the forest. It was pale, though, and not very dense.

"The fire burned itself out," said Shark, but Evangelyne shook her head.

"That's not what happened."

She did not explain her remark, though, and the boys exchanged a brief, confused look and a shrug. They ran on.

They stopped a hundred yards from the camp. Evangelyne touched Milo's arm and leaned close to whisper, "Let me check it out first. You boys stay here."

Before Milo could say anything, there was no longer a girl next to him. In the blink of an eye, her features had blurred and melted into the shape of a gray wolf, which leaped forward and ran without a sound through the woods.

Shark said, *"Yeep."* Very small, very high-pitched.

"I know," agreed Milo.

"I am never, *ever* going to get used to that."

"I know."

"I mean, she's cute and all that—but seriously, dude, that's just freaky."

"It's a long way past freaky, if you ask me," said Milo.

They hunkered down to wait. Killer did not seem interested in following the wolf and instead huddled close to Shark.

"Werewolves and sprites and monsters," said Shark under his breath. "Oh my."

Milo sighed. "I know."

Shark tapped his arm. "Hey, whatever happened to that little one? Halfwit, was it?"

"Halflight," Milo corrected, "and don't make fun of her. I like her. She's really cool."

"Cool? Dude," said Shark, "she's two inches tall and rides around on a hummingbird."

"So what? You got a problem with sprites on hummingbirds?"

Shark snorted. "Actually, I have no idea on earth how to answer a question like that."

Milo grinned. "Yeah."

"So . . . where is she?" asked Shark. "Halflight, I mean."

"I have no idea."

During the invasion of the hive ship and the battle with the Huntsman, the tiny faerie had used up a dangerous amount of her magical life energy. She'd fallen into a deep sleep—or maybe it was a coma, Milo didn't know—and Evangelyne had taken her off into the woods that first night. Milo hadn't seen Halflight again, and every time he asked Evangelyne about it, the wolf girl dodged the question.

"You think maybe she died or something?" asked Shark. "Like . . . burned out, or whatever little fire faerie thingies do."

"I don't know," said Milo, then added, "I hope not. She was really nice and she *cared*, you know?"

Milo could feel Shark staring at him, but he focused on the woods and didn't say anything else. After a long, tense five minutes, they saw Evangelyne—in human form—step out from behind a huckleberry bush and wave at them.

"It's clear," she said when they joined her. "The dead Bugs are still lying where they fell. The Swarm haven't come back yet to collect them."

They followed her cautiously into the trees and emerged inside the clearing they'd used as a camp. The red ship was only partly hidden under its canopy of leaves, but one side was exposed because of the burned oak tree. A few of the surrounding trees were burned too, though only the oak appeared to be destroyed. Bug carcasses lay here and there, and the ruins of the drop-ship and their sky-boards littered the site.

"I'm really surprised the fire went out," said Shark. "I thought for sure we'd have a forest fire."

"Not here," said Evangelyne.

"Why not? Is there something special about this place?"

"Yes."

When it was clear she wasn't going to say more, Shark said, very distinctly and slowly, "What. Is. Special. About. This. Place?"

But Evangelyne only shook her head.

It was Milo who answered. "Oakenayl." He glanced at Evangelyne. "Am I right? He stayed behind to fight the fire?"

"Yes," she said quietly, obviously reluctant to discuss it. Milo wasn't sure how she could possibly know, but he thought she was aware that the oak boy had refused to help him save Barnaby.

"Is he still around?" asked Shark, who wasn't aware of the incident. "Maybe he can help us look for—"

"No," said Milo. "I don't think he's going to help."

"Why not?" asked Shark. "I thought he was on our side."

Milo looked at Evangelyne, who met his gaze with a mixture of regret and defiance.

"No," said Milo, "I think Oakenayl's playing for his own team."

"What? Why?" asked Shark. "How's that work?"

"It's complicated," was Evangelyne's reply. "You wouldn't understand."

"Try me," insisted Shark. "I'm not as dumb as Milo looks."

"Hey," said Milo.

The wolf girl stood firm. "Oakenayl's life is his own. His actions are his own. I will not stand in judgment."

"Not asking for judgment," said Shark belligerently. "But a little cooperation would be pretty nice right now, since we're *all* fighting the Bugs. Oakenayl may be a weirdo tree kid, but he lives here too." He emphasized his point by stamping his foot on the earth they all stood on.

But Evangelyne simply shook her head.

Shark turned to Milo. "Any of this make sense to you?"

"I stopped trying to understand this right around the time we found out that pretty much everything that goes bump in the night is real."

"Except dragons," Shark reminded him, holding up a finger like a wise teacher making a point in class. "Let's keep some perspective. Dragons are just silly."

"Right," agreed Milo. "Who would believe in anything as weird as that?"

Evangelyne made a small, very lupine noise of pure disgust.

"Boy," she said tersely, jabbing Shark in the chest, "stop being stupid and find that circuit."

"First," said Shark, "stop calling me 'boy.' We're the same age . . . *girl*."

Milo turned aside to hide a grin. When they'd met, Evangelyne had constantly—and annoyingly—referred to him as "boy." Now she was mostly using that label on Shark. The wolf girl had been raised only around adults and tended to try to act like one instead of letting herself be a kid. For Milo's part, he knew he needed to be smarter about things, but he never wanted to grow up. Not really.

"Second," continued Shark when it was clear Evangelyne wasn't going to reply, "I'm not being stupid, I'm being freaked out. I thought everyone understood that by now. And third, I *am* looking for the circuit. You could stop acting like the queen of planet-freaking-Earth and help."

Evangelyne sniffed haughtily, but she joined in the hunt. So did Milo.

The circuit board was not where they thought it should be, but with all the explosions and commotion, that didn't mean anything. As they searched, all of them kept looking up into the sky, seeing only a blue dome and puffy white clouds but dreading what might appear at any time.

"Here!" cried Evangelyne from the far side of the camp. She turned and held up a piece of printed circuitry. "Is this it?"

Milo and Shark raced over to her, and Shark snatched it out of her hand and cuddled it to his chest as if it were his precious child. "Come to Papa!" he said.

"Is it okay?" asked Milo breathlessly. "Is it damaged . . . ?"

They stood in a tight cluster as Shark examined the circuit board. "No. I think it's . . . yeah . . . it's good," he said, turning it over and peering at every inch of it. "There's one little crack, but it's just on the plastic. The wires and leads are all intact."

He blew out his cheeks in obvious relief, then glanced nervously at the ship, then up at the empty sky.

"You still have your tool kit?" asked Milo.

Shark shook his head. "Lost it when I ran. Let me see if I can find—"

"No time," said Milo, unclipping his own from his belt and pressing it into Shark's hands. Then Milo slapped him on the shoulder. Hard. "Go!"

FROM MILO'S DREAM DIARY

Before all this happened, before I met Evangelyne and
the other Nightsiders, I never believed in prophecy.
I mean, sure, I knew the word, and words like it.
Prophecy, divination, fortune-telling, all that stuff.
I've read enough books and stories to know about
people who said they could tell the future. Prophets
and seers and like that.
Even after I started dreaming about the Witch of the
World, it was all just faerie-tale stuff. Lord of the
Rings and Harry Potter stuff.
I never thought it would be real.
Now I know different.
Which makes me wonder about the new dream. About
the book.
Is that just me being my usual weird self? Or is
someone trying to send me a warning?
'Cause that's pretty much how these things have been
working out for me.

Chapter 15

Shark hurried inside the ship, refusing any offer of help, saying he worked faster alone. That was fine with Milo, who stayed outside to scavenge anything of value from the Bugs. He found seven pulse pistols that looked to be undamaged, as well as knives, alien tool kits, and more of their unnameable gadgets. There were more of the grenades, too, and these he gathered very gingerly and put in his satchel. He knew he didn't have time to disassemble the wrecked drop-ship, but he managed to salvage three sky-boards, and these he dragged onto the red ship. If they were really able to find an Earth Alliance team, then this tech could be a game changer, especially if the scientists could reproduce the stuff. The thought of EA soldiers on sky-boards and armed with pulse weapons made his heart race. That might actually level the playing field.

If only things worked out right.

Evangelyne drifted along with him, watching him but saying very little. Every now and then she would touch the small leather pouch that hung from her belt. Although he had not seen her put the black jewel in there, Milo was certain that's where the Heart of Darkness was. She carried it with her just as he carried the crystal egg with him. Two jewels. Perhaps the two most important items in the world, and they were being carried around in a bag and a pocket by a couple of kids.

As far as Milo Silk was concerned, the world as he knew it was totally nuts.

He knelt by one of the fallen shocktroopers and studied it. Even in death the alien soldier was frightening. So big, so heavily armored, so strange. Milo touched the creature's natural chitinous shell. It was as cool and rough as lizard skin, but as hard as lacquered wood. He ran his fingers over the lifelight, even though the jewel was now dark, showing no signs of the fierce life that had driven the 'trooper.

"So strange . . . ," he murmured.

"What is?" asked Evangelyne.

"These 'troopers . . . don't you ever wonder about them? About what they think?"

"No. Why would I?"

He glanced up at her haughty, harsh face. She was pretty, but her scowl made her look like a carving of some stern ancient queen. Regal, but completely removed from the people around her. Evangelyne was like that even around her own kind. Milo knew it was a defense mechanism—against her fear, against the grief of having lost contact with her family, against the dread of what the Huntsman and the Swarm were trying to do. And maybe against having to feel anything at all. It was easier to fight, and to go on fighting, if you felt nothing. Milo had heard some of the adults in the camp, even his own mother, talk about that. Emotions were fatal, they all said. They made you act rashly, they sparked stupid risks, they created dangerous hesitation.

But Milo wasn't so sure about that. He wanted to be stronger than he was, and he knew that circumstances had forced him into the role of (reluctant) hero. It was a role that fit like someone else's clothes. He was a kid and he was okay with just being one. If growing up and getting tough meant he had to stop feeling, then he wanted no part of it.

He touched the darkened lifelight again as he said, "From what I saw when I was inside the Huntsman's head, it seems pretty clear that these shocktroopers are all . . . I don't know . . . kind of like slaves. Or drones, I guess. Their brains are programmed to obey before they even hatch."

"So what?" she asked coldly. "The whole Swarm is evil."

"That's just it," he said. "I'm not so sure about that. Isn't evil a choice?"

Evangelyne came around and knelt facing him, the dead 'trooper between them. Her expression of scorn and out-of-hand dismissal seemed to falter.

"Tell me something, Milo," she said in a softer voice. "If you had head lice, wouldn't you wash your hair with herbs or a medicine that would kill them?"

He nodded. "Sure, but—"

"And if you had an infection and one of your Earth Alliance doctors wanted to give you a shot, wouldn't you take it, even though all those bacteria would be destroyed?"

"Yes, but—"

She placed her hand flat on the creature's chest, inches away from his. "This insect is part of a swarm that wants to destroy our world."

"I know."

"Are you actually telling me you feel *sorry* for it?"

Milo withdrew his hand and sat back on his heels. "Hey, don't get me wrong, I'm not saying we should start Hug-a-Shocktrooper Day. It's not like that, and I'm not really sure what it is. I guess maybe it's the fact that the 'troopers *don't* have a choice that's bothering me."

"I don't understand."

"Well, think about the whole Dissosterin race. I mean, sure, they're not like us, and they don't think like people and maybe they don't even have much in the way of feelings . . . but they're not just dumb bugs. They're not. They built those hive ships and all this tech. They evolved somewhere and somehow. They must have a pretty advanced civilization, don't you think?"

"They're a plague."

"No," he corrected, "they're a swarm. Guys like this one follow orders. It's the queens who tell them what to do. And, now, the Huntsman, too."

She shivered at the mention of his name.

"What does it matter who makes them kill?" she asked in a hushed voice. "All that matters is that they want to kill us, and that means we have to fight back."

"I know," said Milo. "I get that, I really do. And I'm scared of the shocktroopers and the Stingers and the whole Swarm. I hate the Swarm and everything they've done. It's just that I don't know if I actually *hate* guys like this one."

"It's not a 'guy,' boy," she said. "It's a killer."

"So are we, Evangelyne."

"It's not the same thing and you know it."

He nodded. "Sure, it's not the same thing."

"But—what?" she asked, her brow furrowed. "Why are you bothering with these kinds of thoughts?"

It was a very tough question, and while he thought about it he stood up and walked over to look at the red ship. Evangelyne soon joined him. In the gloom beneath the camouflage cover, the red of the ship was as dark as dried blood. It squatted there, serving as both a hope of escape and a reminder of the enormity of what they faced.

"I don't really know what I'm trying to say," Milo murmured. "I really don't. It's just that . . ."

Evangelyne half turned and touched his arm. It was the gentlest thing she'd ever done, and it humanized her more than anything had since they met. "It's what, Milo?"

"You're going to think I'm nuts."

"Too late," she said, and it took him a little to realize that she'd made a joke. It was the first one he could remember her making.

He grinned at her. "We killed a lot of Bugs up on the hive ship, and if we get the ship and this tech back to the EA, we're going to try to kill a lot more. All of them, right? That's the plan? To wipe them out completely?"

She said nothing, but gave him a single grave nod.

"When we do that—if we even *can* do that—I hope it doesn't make us like them."

"What do you mean?"

"It shouldn't be like stepping on cockroaches."

"We have to stop them."

"I know we do."

"So . . . ?"

He shook his head. "I don't want to kill because it's what we're supposed to do, any more than I want to do it because we have to. No . . . that's wrong." He closed his eyes and wrestled the thought into words that would make sense to her and to himself. "I don't want to believe that killing them all is the only choice we'll ever have."

"They haven't given us another choice, Milo."

"I know," he said. And sighed. "I know. But . . . I don't want to accept that. There has to be another way."

When he glanced at her face, all he saw was doubt and disagreement. She turned away. As if what he'd said and what he felt made *him* the strangest of the two of them.

Maybe, he thought, it did.

Milo changed the subject. "Can I tell you something?"

"What?" Her voice was guarded.

"It's about a funny thing that happened today. Or, at least I think it happened."

"What do you mean?"

"It could have been a dream."

"Another dream of the Witch of the World?" asked Evangelyne, suddenly excited. "What did she say?"

"Huh? Oh . . . no, it's not that. I saw something in the woods but I was kind of out of it for a couple of minutes and now I'm wondering if I daydreamed it. It's hard to explain."

She studied him, then nodded slowly. "Maybe you should tell me."

So Milo told her about the ring of mushrooms, the shimmering air, the dancing little pointy-eared soldiers who seemed to want him to come and play with them. He told her about the smoky shape that seemed to be turning into the Huntsman, and about the regal little female creature who threatened to burn everything Milo cared about. Evangelyne went pale and touched his chest with the flat of her hand.

"Are you telling me the truth?" she demanded. "Did this really happen? When? Where? I mean, exactly where? What color were their clothes?"

She rattled off a dozen questions and he tripped over himself trying to answer. Even though the details were fuzzy in his mind, he was able to pull out some of it, including a few words from the song.

"I don't know what it means," he admitted, "but they said something like, 'Come to the *Sidhe*, Milo. Come play with us.' Stuff like that."

Evangelyne recoiled as if he'd tossed a hunter-killer into her lap. *"Aes Sidhe!"*

"Yeah, what is that?" he asked. "You mentioned that word when we first met. *Sidhe*. They said it too. What does it mean?"

"Did they touch you at all?" she barked.

"No, I—"

"Did you enter their ring? Tell me the truth, Milo Silk, did you enter the faerie ring or eat the mushrooms?"

"No. I didn't—" he protested.

"Did they come out of it?"

"No."

"Are you sure? Did any of them step outside the ring?"

"No, I'm positive. Why? What is it? What's all this mean? Are these more of the Nightsiders? And what's with them saying that the Huntsman was their champion?"

Evangelyne turned from him and stared at the trees. Her hands were balled into knots by her sides, and her body was stiff with tension. "Milo," she said without turning, "how did you get away from them?"

As she asked that question, her voice was not the voice of a young girl. It was the deeper, more feral, and far more threatening growl of someone who was a heartbeat away from revealing herself as the monster she truly was. Milo felt instantly terrified.

"Tell me, Milo," she said in a tone filled with unspoken threats. Her face was hidden by her hair, and in that moment Milo was positive her face wasn't human. No, not at all. "It's important that you tell me the truth. Tell me *now*."

"It was K-Killer," he stammered. "He came running out of the woods and seemed to pull me back. I heard him barking in the forest and—I don't know how to describe it—I kind of woke up."

After a minute, the great tension in Evangelyne's back eased. She still took an extra moment before turning toward him again, and he was greatly relieved to see that her face was entirely human. At least, it was now.

"You are a very lucky boy," she said softly.

"Why? What *was* that? Who were they? I mean, they were Nightsiders, right?"

"Yes . . . and no. They are what you would call 'supernatural,' but they are not like us. Not like my friends, or my family."

"Then what are they?"

"They are the *Aes Sídhe*. They are faerie folk who live deep beneath the world. Or perhaps it would make more sense to you if I said they live *beyond* our world. Apart from it."

"That doesn't actually help," said Milo. "Isn't Halflight a faerie?"

"Halflight is a sprite. Mook and Oakenayl are spirits of the earth, or elementals. Before today you never met a true faerie, and it was almost your doom to have encountered them."

"Why? I thought faeries were cool. Tinkerbell and like that."

"Don't be stupid, Milo. I'm talking the *real* world."

"Um. Sure. Okay."

"There are many kinds of faerie folk, Milo," said Evangelyne. "Most live so completely apart from the rest of the world that you could see them and never know. Others, some of the higher Courts of Faerie, are part of my world, and many of them went into the realms of shadow when the Swarm invaded the Earth. But there are others still, Milo, who are not friends to your people or even to mine. They are the *Aes Sídhe*—the people of the mounds—whole courts of faerie warriors and sorcerers who were driven from their lands into the earth thousands of years ago. Their lands were taken by invaders from Europe, by your ancestors. Humans who came like a plague to the lands of magic. They did to the *Aes Sídhe* what the Swarm have done to this world—invaded, destroyed, exterminated, and ruined. The *Aes Sídhe* went into darkness—both in where they lived and in *how* they lived—and there, in that darkness, they have grown very strong and very wicked."

The whole day seemed to become still as she spoke, and Milo felt a chill in his heart that had nothing to do with the temperature of the air.

"Yeah, okay, well, that's . . . um . . . scary," he said weakly, swallowing hard, "but we're all fighting the same fight now. I mean, you and the Nightsiders, us—it's all us against the Swarm, isn't it?"

Evangelyne gave him a pitying look. "You know so little of how this world works, Milo," she said. "You think that everyone has a good heart, don't you? That all people need to do is open their eyes and they'll suddenly 'get it.'"

"No . . . ," he said hesitantly. "I'm just being practical. It really is *us* against them. We all live here." He bent down and tapped the ground with his knuckles. "If we don't stand by each other, then that only makes it easier for the Swarm."

She shook her head. "There are some who don't see it that way. Even Oakenayl thinks that we should step away from you and fight this war on our own."

"Why? We need each other. Or are all bets off, now that you have the Heart of Darkness back?"

"No. Not as far as I'm concerned," she said, smiling faintly. "Mook feels the same, and Iskiel. The bats are with us, and there are others who will fight with the Orphan Army. However, there are some who will always want to stand apart. Many more than want to stand together, sad to say. And some are not merely bitter, like Oakenayl. Some, like the *Aes Sídhe,* hate all humans. Their ruler, Queen Mab, has never made a secret of her hatred, and that spite is very old. It runs as deep as the bones of the earth."

"Queen Mab . . . Hey, do you think that's the red-haired lady I saw? The nasty one?"

"Did she wear a golden torc around her neck?"

"Not sure what a torc is, but she had a thick gold ring around her neck."

"That's a torc. And yes, that was probably Queen Mab. You're lucky, Milo. Very few people have ever escaped her enchantments. She is immensely dangerous."

"I kind of got that impression. But look, how's she connected with the Huntsman? He was beginning to appear inside that circle. How's that make any sense?"

Evangelyne looked frightened. "I . . . don't know. Magic circles like that are used to conjure demons, to bring them forth from their dimension with the promise of an offering, usually of blood or flesh, and then to enslave them."

"Demons? Geez. What would a bunch of faeries want with a demon?"

"To help them escape, of course."

"Why? I thought they escaped *from* here to wherever they are."

"They did. But they did it the wrong way." She paused. "Goddess of Shadows, there is so much you don't know about my world. Let me try to explain it."

She paused to think. Milo figured it was as hard for her to explain the world of the Nightsiders as it would be for him to explain tech to her. Same planet but very different worlds.

Finally Evangelyne nodded to herself. "When Queen Mab led her people out of this world, she opened a door to a shadow dimension that was well suited to her needs.

The *Aes Sídhe* conquered that place and made it their own. There were other creatures there, and her dark faeries either killed or enslaved them."

"Sounds like the Swarm," said Milo.

"It sounds like every nation everywhere," corrected Evangelyne. "History is filled with conquest. There were oceans of blood spilled here before the Swarm invaded."

Milo nodded, glumly accepting her stern correction.

"However," continued Evangelyne, "the magicks Queen Mab used to protect her people and to safeguard her new world from invasion by the Daylighters backfired. She sealed the door behind her. The *Aes Sídhe* locked themselves on the other side of that doorway of shadow and now no one can pass through in either direction. Only in very rare cases and for very brief periods of time can she or one of her warriors slip between her world and this one. Demons can do it more easily, and some of them know how to create new doorways from world to world."

"What worlds are you talking about? That faerie ring was right here in the forest."

"There are many worlds, Milo, and there are worlds between worlds. And even worlds between those. I suppose you would call them dimensions. They overlap with ours and are mostly invisible to any but the most powerful. Each of these worlds connects to others. Sometimes the doors are sealed shut with the strength of iron, and sometimes they are as insubstantial as smoke. That is how demons move between the worlds, but they are usually pulled back to their own dimensions by cosmic forces that even my people don't fully understand. However, with the right spells, a demon can be summoned who will open such a door."

Milo nodded, accepting this. It made him wonder if magic was really just some aspect of science that had never yet been measured or understood.

"Doors are meant to be opened, though," continued Evangelyne, "and there are many kinds of keys and many kinds of locks. Spells are one kind of key, and the casting of a faerie ring is a powerful kind of spell. If the right spells are cast, then those circles allow for passage between worlds. Not all worlds, just certain worlds. And the circles themselves act like cells. They contain whatever passes through. Do you understand?"

"Sure. It's like the spells are entry codes and the circles are air locks."

She gave him a blank stare. "I have no idea what that means."

"Doesn't matter. I'm following what you're saying. Go on."

"Well, what you encountered in the woods was Queen Mab using a faerie ring to try to summon a being of power. A demon."

"But the Huntsman's not a demon."

"I know, which is why this is hard to understand. Unless . . ."

"Unless what?"

"Unless the Huntsman somehow convinced Queen Mab that he *was* a demon."

"Why on earth would the Huntsman want to do that?" asked Milo.

She considered the question, then shook her head. "I don't know. Maybe I'm wrong. There are several possibilities, but I'd only be guessing."

"So . . . guess."

She thought again. "The Huntsman wants the crystal egg you stole and he wants the Heart of Darkness. The queen has wanted to be free of her prison for many years and she is a powerful sorceress. It's possible—even likely—that she sensed the presence of a being of great, dark power and reached out to him to strike a dark bargain so that they both could get what they want."

"How?"

"The easiest way for a sorceress of her skill would be through dreams. Much as the Witch of the World speaks to you in your dreams. Queen Mab might have offered to help him recover the crystal egg so he could give it back to the Swarm. And they would *both* want the Heart of Darkness. Besides, we know that the Huntsman craves magical knowledge. Who better to teach him than a queen of faeries? It is something she might consider a fair bargain if he helped free her."

"Maybe," said Milo, "but I'm not sure that theory's right. They called him their 'champion.'"

"Of course. If he promised to free her, then that's what he would be. He is already so powerful, and that would be very appealing to her. An alliance between the two would make them each incredibly strong. Ten times more so than they would be alone."

"How would it work, though? He's scary, but all he has is science."

"Maybe," she said dubiously. "There are things even a Daylighter can do on this side of a doorway to help someone on the other side escape."

"Like what?"

"Like a human sacrifice."

"Oh . . . man . . ." It made him sick and dizzy to think that not only could he have died in that circle, but that his death might have doomed the world.

"To do that, though," said the wolf girl, "the Huntsman would have to cross a line that few are willing to cross. He would need to sacrifice his own soul."

"Not sure he even has one anymore. He's a psycho killer, remember."

"That doesn't mean he's soulless, Milo. Even evil people have souls, hard as that is to believe."

"He's half Bug."

"So? What makes you think the Swarm don't have souls? They're alive, and maybe some of them are mindless, the worker drones, I mean, but the soldiers have minds. There's every possibility they have souls, too."

"Even the drones?"

She shrugged. "I don't know."

Milo thought about it; then something occurred to him. "Remember a few days ago when I first met the Huntsman? He tried to kill me and the Witch of the World did some wonky magic and for a minute I was inside the Huntsman's head."

She nodded. "You said it was horrifying."

"It was. We had that whole mind-melding thing and I'm really glad I don't remember all of it. But there are some things I remember. One of them is that long before the Swarm ever got here, back when the Huntsman was just a human psychopath, he was trying to learn everything he could about magic. He's always wanted to *become* magical. He thinks that's part of how he'll become a god. I saw memories of him reading thousands of old books and talking to psychics and doing everything he could to learn about it. He was obsessed with it."

"Oh," she said, looking sick. "That's not good news."

"No it's not." Milo cocked his head to one side. "There's a word kind of stuck in my head since that happened. I've read it in books, too, and I'm pretty sure it's some kind of magic. Like the bad kind."

"What word?"

"Necromancy."

Evangelyne drew back in horror. "Goddess of Shadows! That is the very worst kind of sorcery. Even among the magical peoples there is no one more reviled and feared than a necromancer."

"Why?"

"When a person dies, there is a great release of energy. Not only does their soul fly free, but other forms of energy are released and it is raw and powerful. In sacred rituals around the world, people gather to honor someone as they die and to share in that release. They allow the soul to move on, but sometimes they can gain great insight and knowledge from that raw energy. Much of what we Nightsiders have learned of healing has been learned as one of ours passed through the veil and into the eternal darkness, and we honor them for sharing with us."

She paused and swallowed hard. "But a necromancer is different. He does not wait for natural death. Instead he uses torture and murder to force the release of these energies, and then he steals those secrets for himself. A necromancer is like a vampire except that instead of feeding on blood, he devours life energy and then uses it to read the future, uncover secrets, enslave others, and even raise the dead and turn them into slaves." She shuddered. "There is not much we Nightsiders fear, but we fear a necromancer. Please, Milo, please tell me that you're wrong about what you read in the Huntsman's mind."

Milo said nothing, and he wished he hadn't said a word. Especially *that* word.

Evangelyne shook her head, and he saw her mouth that word.

Necromancer.

"Wait," he said, "so you're saying that they wanted the Huntsman to kill me to free Queen Mab?"

"Maybe. It may be more complicated than that. A single sacrifice wouldn't break open the door. Not with someone new to using magic. Wanting to become a necromancer and actually *being* one are hardly the same things. No, I think they will have to take other lives to set the *Aes Sídhe* free." She pondered this. "It may be that the Huntsman has already killed someone else to gain the power necessary to communicate with the queen. It's a process with many steps. I think what they tried to do to you was something different."

"I probably don't want to know," he said, "but what do you think they had in mind?"

"Binding you."

"What, like tying me up?"

"No. Binding your soul and your life force to those of a necromancer. It would turn you into a kind of slave. You've heard of animals that some witches keep as pets and servants? They're called familiars."

Milo nodded. Scary books were filled with that sort of stuff.

"If the Huntsman were able to complete the spells necessary to bind your life force to his, then you would have no choice but to serve him. That means he could make you as obedient to him as the Bugs are to the hive queens. And you would have to tell him anything he wanted to know."

Milo touched the crystal egg in his pocket and cut a look at the leather pouch at Evangelyne's belt. She followed his gaze and nodded.

"You would have no secrets from him because he would be your master forever."

"Oh, man . . ."

She smiled a twisted smile. "And to think you were saved by an annoying little dog."

"Killer is not annoying," said Milo quickly. "Actually, I think I'm going to be especially nice to that mutt for the rest of my life."

"You should."

Milo felt dizzy. "Why can't the world be simple? It used to be. I can remember when the hardest thing I had to do was put my toys away and brush my teeth before bed. Now . . . every day things get bigger and more complicated. Why can't I just go back to being a kid?"

"I'm sorry, Milo," said the wolf girl. "Life used to be easier for me, too. I used to read my books and run through the woods hunting rabbits and sing to the moon with my aunts. Some of the Nightsiders had learned how to find peace even with you humans around."

Milo sighed.

"Then," said Evangelyne, "the Bugs came. And then the Huntsman, and now the *Aes Sídhe* are trying to make mischief."

"I think it's a little worse than 'mischief.'"

She shook her head. "That word means something

different to the Nightsiders, Milo. Mischief isn't harm-less pranks. Not to us. It comes from an old French word, *meschever*, meaning something done to bring grief."

The word "grief" hung in the air, and it was a word that Milo—and everyone else still alive on Earth—knew all too well. Knew, and feared.

Milo had to clear his throat before he could speak. "Can we . . . *talk* to these faeries? Maybe make them understand who the Huntsman really is and what he wants?"

"I don't know. I doubt it. They don't have a reputation for being reasonable. Trying to reason with them could get us hurt."

"Even if we're careful?"

"I really don't think it's possible. Others have tried to make peace with them, and there was always blood, death, and ruin. All I do know, Milo, is that Queen Mab and her kind—the dark faeries of the *Aes Sídhe* and their allies among the goblins and imps—will never be our friends and they will never be our allies. Not even in this fight. Never."

Despite that, Milo pasted a smile on his face. "My dad had a saying: 'Never say never.'"

Evangelyne's eyes were cold. "Your father is lost, Milo. I'm not sure we can trust his wisdom."

"Don't say that!" snapped Milo. "My dad's missing, not lost. I'll find him. The witch said—"

Before he could finish his statement, Shark stuck his head out the hatchway and yelled, "I did it! Come on!"

His face was covered with grease and sweat, but he was grinning from ear to ear. Killer barked and jumped around him. A few seconds later Milo heard the rumble as the alien engines came to life.

Chapter 16

Milo raced up the ramp, with Evangelyne right behind him. And as if from nowhere, Iskiel came slithering through the scorched grass and managed to get aboard ahead of both of them.

On the bridge of the Huntsman's command ship, Killer barked and ran around in circles, then stopped and jumped straight up in the air a dozen times as if on springs. He couldn't know what was happening, but he had caught the fire of everyone's excitement.

"Will it work, boy?" said Evangelyne, turning a fierce eye on Shark.

Shark ignored her.

"Wait," said Milo, grabbing his friend's sleeve, "can you even fly this thing?"

"Me?" Shark grinned and shook his head. "I could probably figure it out, but you already flew it, so you're elected." He shoved Milo toward the pilot's chair.

"But—" began Evangelyne.

Shark cut her off. "Strap in, *girl.*"

"Not funny," she grumbled.

Because there were so many different kinds of Bugs

in the Swarm, the chairs were made of a gel-like substance that conformed to the shape of whoever sat down.
Evangelyne slid into a seat and shuddered as the gel shifted
and molded itself to her. She made a face of distaste as
she fumbled with the seat belt. The wolf girl couldn't figure it out—technology had played so small a part in her
upbringing—so Shark connected the straps and cinched
them tight.

"Ow!" she complained.

"S'matter? Too tight, Your Furry Highness?"

"Watch your mouth, fat boy—"

"Hey, guys!" yelled Milo. "How about you two shutting
up? I mean, seriously? Is now really the time?"

Shark laughed as he snugged himself into a chair, and
he whistled for Killer, who sprang into his lap. Evangelyne
glowered at them both. Iskiel crawled onto one of the
control panels against the far wall, jumped up to catch
the edge of an open air vent, and vanished inside. They
could hear the skitter of his claws as he disappeared down
the duct.

Shaking his head, Milo belted himself in.

The bridge, like all Dissosterin tech, was simple,
unadorned, and smelly. The air stank of rotting eggs,
old garbage, and other items Milo chose not to name.
Everything was slimy and felt wrong. Everything. Even the
air around them seemed to throb with a sense of threat.

It doesn't want us here, he thought, then scolded himself
for the stupid idea. He couldn't shake it, though, and as

he studied the controls to re-familiarize himself with them, the uneasy feeling persisted.

Bug ships did not have actual physical piloting controls and instead used holographic steering. As soon as Milo had sat down in the command chair, a 3-D hologram of the craft had appeared in the air in front of him. Milo knew that all he had to do was stick his hand inside the projection and then move it in whichever direction he wanted the ship to go. The tech was designed so that even the dimmest of the Bugs could operate it, and configured so that any kind of hand—or insectoid claw—would work. All that was required was a living body sitting in the pilot's chair. It was shockingly uncomplicated, but it required absolute focus. Insects weren't easily distracted and they were conditioned to follow procedures, so they could steer the ship. It was a lot more of a challenge to Milo. He couldn't, say, wipe his nose or scratch an itch, because the ship would follow his hand movements and very likely crash.

He slipped his hand into the glowing hologram, then immediately snatched it back as if stung. It wasn't because anything had actually hurt him. That might have been easier to deal with. Instead it was a weird kind of emotional reaction.

It doesn't like the way my hand feels.

As if the ship was repulsed by his touch.

As if it was disgusted.

Greasy sweat popped out on Milo's face.

"What are you waiting for?" demanded Evangelyne.

"Yeah," growled Shark, pounding the arm of his chair with a fist. "We gotta go, go, go!"

Milo steeled himself and slowly and carefully eased his hand back into the hologram. The ship around them trembled. Everyone looked around, and Milo could see the nervous expressions on their faces. Were they feeling it too? He was sure they were. Even Killer looked nervous: his little tail drooped and he began to whine.

"Hold on," said Milo, as much to himself as to them, and he slowly raised his hand. Immediately the ship responded by spinning up the main engines and firing the antigravity drives. It was so easy.

Except that on a deep level he could feel the ship resisting him.

Hating him.

Had it done that when they'd stolen it that day? Had the ship felt this level of hatred? Had he been so caught up in the urgency of their escape from the hive ship that he simply hadn't noticed?

He could feel it now, though.

This ship belongs to the Huntsman, he told himself. *And it knows it.*

Way down below the surface of his conscious mind, he heard another voice echo that feeling.

Be warned, child of the sun, whispered the Witch of the World. *This ship is sick. It has become polluted by the darkness that dwells within the Huntsman.*

Milo almost yelled. It had been days since the witch had spoken to him. At first he'd feared her presence, thinking that maybe it was proof he was bonkers. Then he'd come to trust her. She wanted this world saved from the Swarm. She wanted him to rise, to become a hero who saved the world. Crazy as that thought was.

Then she'd given him a final, cryptic warning and vanished from his mind, from his waking thoughts, from his daydreams, and from his nightmares. The last words she'd spoken were burned into him. Two statements, and Milo didn't know if they were connected or not.

There are horrors more dreadful than the Huntsman, Milo Silk.

That was something too horrible to contemplate. Nothing seemed more terrifying than the Huntsman.

But then, as Milo had begun coming out of his dream, he thought he heard her say something else.

Your father lives.

If they were separate thoughts, then one was frightening and one was the best news he'd ever had.

If they were part of the same thought, then Milo knew his world was doomed.

Now she was back. And as always she spoke in riddles.

The ship is sick. Polluted.

"You're not helping," he growled through gritted teeth.

"What—?" asked Shark.

"Nothing." Then he repeated his warning. "Hold on."

As he continued to raise his hand, the whole front wall

of the bridge blossomed with a dozen holographic high-def screens that showed the exterior from every possible angle. He saw the camouflage cover slide off and fall away as the red ship began to rise. Milo was careful to do everything as slowly as possible, because a twitch of his hand could send the craft crashing into one of the live oaks or ponderous elms.

"Cool," said Shark. "I was afraid this wouldn't work as well with a human hand."

"Did before," Milo reminded him. "Guess any kind of hand would work."

The ship shuddered and the engines whined.

"Come on," he said under his breath. "Come on . . ."

Then the ship moved. Reluctance notwithstanding, hatred aside, it moved to his commands, rising from the muddy ground, first equal to the tops of the trees and then higher, higher. He moved his hand to the right and the craft responded by swinging out away from the ruin of their camp, away from the burned trees. One of the screens displayed a topographical map of the landscape, and Milo angled his hand and began steering the craft that way.

"Nice job!" called Shark.

"Go faster," urged Evangelyne. "You're going too slow, boy."

"Hey," snapped Milo, "do *you* know how to drive a spaceship?"

She said nothing and her eyes flashed cold fire at him.

Yeah, yeah, yeah, he thought sourly.

The ship began swinging toward the bayou, but almost immediately he realized that it was moving too fast. It overshot the water by a thousand yards, and when he tried to compensate, it swept half a mile the other way. Inside the ship it felt like they were on a big pendulum, and with each swing Milo's stomach lurched. He tried to force the craft back and overshot again. And again.

"Okay," said a green-faced Shark, "I'm going to hurl."

Evangelyne said nothing, but her face was turning the color of milk that had been left in the sun too long.

"Sorry," Milo said as he fought to steady the ship. The engines whined in protest as he forced it to change direction over and over.

By the time he managed to stop the pendulum sway, everyone looked like pieces of moldy cheese. Evangelyne sat clutching the leather pouch and muttering something—possibly prayers—in an ancient language Milo couldn't identify. For his part, Shark seemed way beyond the capacity for speech. He sat clutching Killer with sweaty hands, and there was a strangely plastic smile on Shark's round face.

"Sorry . . . sorry . . . ," Milo kept saying, even after the reluctant craft settled into a mostly steady flight path. He bent forward—careful not to move his hand while he did so—and studied the map. There was a glowing red dot imposed on it to show the location of their ship. It was a tiny but precise replica of the Huntsman's ship. "Okay, here we go."

With infinite care, Milo eased the craft forward, keeping to just above the level of the trees, following the winding brackish waters of the bayou. Flocks of birds exploded from the trees and scattered to the winds. Milo wondered if that was just a reaction to the presence of a flying machine, or if it was something else. Was that the reaction of Earth animals to the presence of a Dissosterin machine? Could fear and hatred of the invaders pulse inside the hearts of ordinary birds and beasts?

He didn't know for sure, but his own heart told him that this was a horrible truth. And if that was the case, then the whole world—from rocks and trees to animals and people—had learned to fear the Swarm.

There was something very sad about that.

At the same time, it made Milo feel he was a part of something great. Something beyond his understanding but not beyond his imagination. He would have to think about it when there was time.

If there ever was time.

"How far is it?" asked Evangelyne.

"Not far. Another couple of miles," said Milo. "We'll be there soon."

"Yeah," said Shark, "but don't push it. I don't like the sound of those engines."

Evangelyne cocked an eyebrow. "And how would *you* know what they're supposed to sound like, boy? You were only on this ship twice and—"

"Same number of times you were, Vangie."

"Do not call me that."

Shark ignored her. "When they took us after the raid and when we escaped the hive ship, I listened to the engines. And before you ask, yes, I paid attention even then. Milo and me are scavengers, but I want to be an engineer. Machines talk to me."

"That's nonsense. Machines have no life force."

Milo opened his mouth to argue, to explain what he'd felt when he sat down in the chair and touched the controls, but Shark was already in gear.

"Not saying that, Vangie. What I'm saying is that if you know what you're doing, you can listen to any machine and tell if it's running smoothly or if there's something wrong."

"He's right," said Milo. "Shark's pretty good at machine diagnostics. Always has been. He gets the best grades in mechanics classes."

"Whatever," she said, clearly out of her depth. "If you can hear this ship, what is it saying?"

"I wish it could just come right out and *say* what was wrong. But from what I can hear, those are not happy engines. Something's busted or maybe loose, but in any case, Milo, *be careful.*"

"Not sure how much more careful I can be," muttered Milo as he slowed the ship even more, letting it drift along below the treetops, only a few yards above the rippling water. On the screens he saw the cold eyes of the patient, merciless gators watching, watching, watching.

"If we have to ditch," added Shark, "try not to put us down in the water. I don't want to be the main ingredient in Cajun Shark soup."

"Yum," said Evangelyne, and both boys shot her a look. Shark actually recoiled from her.

Then a slow, sly smile curled the corners of her mouth. "You should see your faces," she said with a giggle.

Shark's face turned a furious red. His mouth made a dozen different shapes but he couldn't force a single coherent word out. Milo laughed.

"Oh, dude—she *sooooo* got you."

"Just drive the ship, loser," said Shark nastily, which made Milo and Evangelyne laugh even harder.

Then the ship bucked as if it had been struck. Were it not for the seat belts, they'd have been flung from their chairs. Killer began barking furiously.

"What was that?" yelled Evangelyne.

"Are we hit?" yelled Shark.

Milo's eyes clicked from screen to screen to screen as he sought to understand what had happened. But there was nothing. No drop-ships, no hunter-killers, not even a Bug on a sky-board.

"I . . . I don't know," said Milo. He managed to steady the ship, and it flew on with no evidence of damage. "Turbulence—?"

"Not this close to the water," said Shark.

"Not the right kind of clouds for lightning," observed Evangelyne.

The ship flew on and there was no repeat of the disturbance.

After ten more minutes of careful flying, Shark pointed to one of the screens. "There's the bolt-hole. I can see rock-guy, too."

"His name is Mook," said Evangelyne.

"Yeah, sure. Okay. Mook. There he is. Lizzie, too. Looks like everyone's ready to roll."

It was true. All the wounded lay on makeshift stretchers, and the others were clustered protectively around them. Every face was pointed upward with what Milo thought was an even mixture of hope and dread. They'd all been captured and dragged aboard this same ship, so it had to be hard to watch it approach and not feel some serious doubt.

As gently as he could, Milo set the ship down. The landing struts deployed automatically as soon as the undercarriage radar detected a clear landing spot. Another bit of smart, simple Bug tech. The ship settled onto its steel legs, wobbling slightly on the ones Milo had damaged with a grenade during a fight with the Huntsman and his 'troopers. Then Milo withdrew his hand from the hologram and exhaled so long and hard he felt like he was a deflating balloon. He closed his eyes and mumbled a long, detailed, and earnest prayer of thanks.

Then he unbuckled himself and ran for the exit.

Chapter 17

It's hard to be fast and careful at the same time. Most of the wounded could be carried aboard without risking further injury, but there were a few who were very bad off. Barnaby, of course, was the worst. When Milo came to help move him, his heart sank. The young Cajun had lapsed into unconsciousness, and his face was so pale that he already looked dead. Milo had to hold his fingers to Barnaby's throat for a long time before he could feel the flutter of a pulse.

It was so faint, and if it followed any normal rhythm, Milo couldn't tell. He turned in panic to Shark and Evangelyne, but the expressions on their faces only confirmed his fears.

Shark shook his head slowly and offered no comment, but Evangelyne said, "I know he's your friend, Milo. You have to prepare yourself for letting him go. Not everyone can be saved."

"No," he fired back, "Barnaby's *not* going to die. No way. We're going to get him onto the ship and find an EA team and . . ."

His words trailed off as a shadow fell across them, and he glanced up to see Lizabeth and Mook standing there.

They were as unalike as two creatures could be. She was frail and tiny, and Mook was at least eight feet tall and made of dense rock. The little girl had one hand resting on the stone boy's arm, and she held a bunch of herbs in her other hand.

"I found these," she said. "Mook helped me look."

"Mook," he said, but Milo thought he heard some doubt in that gravelly voice.

"He helped," repeated Lizabeth, as if in reply to Mook's denial. She knelt beside the Cajun. "It would be better if he ate them, but I don't think he can. No, of course he can't. Maybe this will be enough." She crumbled the herbs between her palms, rubbing them slowly back and forth until the plants were reduced to small particles. Evangelyne watched her with a mixture of fascination and apprehension.

"How . . . how do you know about those herbs?" she asked. "How do you know about that mixture?"

"Yeah," said Milo suspiciously. "This is like the stuff you gave me in the woods. Or . . . maybe it's like the stuff the Daughter of Splinters and Salt gave me. I don't know. This is making my head spin."

"Shark already told you that I was here at the bolt-hole," said Lizabeth. "How could I have been in the woods with you at the same time?"

"I don't know. My question is how you suddenly know all this herb stuff."

"Yes," said Evangelyne, "that troubles me, too."

Lizabeth didn't look at them, but once more there was a strange smile on the girl's face. A very private smile. It was clear she was keeping some secret to herself. Milo exchanged a glance with Shark, who only shook his head. It was a mystery to them, too. Ever since the raid on the camp, Lizabeth—who was always strange—had become stranger still. So strange that even the Nightsiders thought she was odd, and that creeped Milo out all the way down to his bones.

"Barnaby is dying," she said. "Does anything else really matter?"

"Maybe it does."

But Lizabeth shook her head. "Here," she said to Milo, "hold out your hand."

He hesitated for a moment, but Evangelyne finally nodded. Milo held out his hand and Lizabeth brushed the mixture onto his upraised palm.

"Put it in Barnaby's mouth," Lizabeth said, "between his gum and his cheek. Rub it on his lips, too."

"My hands are dirty," Milo protested.

Lizabeth looked at him with eyes so pale a blue they were almost as silver as Evangelyne's. "Do you think that will matter now?"

Milo had read once that eyes were windows to the soul, but if that was true, then he wasn't sure he recognized who was at home in Lizabeth's frail little body. The expression in her eyes was a strange blend of childlike innocence and something else—something far older and stranger. It made him afraid for her. He and Shark used to joke privately that Lizzie was crazy. Now he wondered if she had actually gone insane, if her connection to reality had been fractured by the things they'd all experienced.

Or was something even stranger happening here? Either way it scared the heck out of him and made the whole day fit the wrong way in his head. He looked at the crushed herbs in his palm, shot a quick look at Evangelyne, who chewed her lip in doubt for a bit, then nodded.

"Do it," she whispered.

Milo gently parted Barnaby's slack lips and pushed the herbs between cheek and gum as Lizabeth had directed. He saved a few pieces and rubbed them over the Cajun's lips. Then he wiped his fingers vigorously on his shirt and used the tip of his index finger to push some of the herbs into place along the gum line. It was a strange thing to do, and under any other circumstances Shark would have been making some kind of crude joke. No one spoke. Milo was pretty sure no one was even breathing.

"Use all of it," Lizabeth told him.

He brushed the last crumbs into Barnaby's mouth and spread them around. Then he sat back and they all watched.

At first there was nothing to see. The Cajun still looked more dead than alive. His face and body were limp, his breathing so shallow that he looked like a corpse.

Then . . .

"Goddess of Shadows," whispered Evangelyne. "What sorcery is this?"

Milo felt his mouth go dry as he gaped at Barnaby. Right before his eyes, the teen's color changed from the gray of near death to a pale flush. He took a long, ragged, audible breath and his eyelids fluttered.

"Oh my God . . . ," breathed Shark.

"This is impossible," insisted Evangelyne. "He was slipping past all hope of healing." She turned sharply to Lizabeth. "Explain this, girl. This is ancient magic. I asked you once before; now I demand that you tell me."

The look in Lizabeth's face was almost indescribable. Cold, remote, detached, and inhuman. She met the wolf girl's harsh stare, and her mouth still wore that strange half-smile.

"I guess I read it in a book," she said in a voice that was only barely like Lizabeth's.

"No, I insist that you tell me."

Lizabeth looked down at Barnaby. "He's stable, but it won't last, you know. We can stand around talking or we can get him aboard the ship and try to save him and the others. Which matters more to you, Evangelyne Winter?"

"C'mon, Vangie," said Shark, "she's right. We got to boogie."

"Don't call me that," snapped Evangelyne, turning away and stalking off toward the ship. Milo saw her waving and shouting orders to the uninjured, who began bringing the wounded aboard.

"Mook?" said Milo, and the rock boy nodded, bent stiffly, and lifted Barnaby with surprising gentleness and care. He headed toward the ship and soon vanished inside.

That left Milo, Shark, and Lizabeth standing together. Shark seemed unable or unwilling to address what had just happened, but Milo couldn't leave it like this.

"Lizzie," he said quietly, "what's going on? What's wrong with you?"

The little girl turned and looked up at him. Lizabeth was as tiny and slender as a flower stem. Her pale hair danced in the damp breeze coming off the bayou. The strangeness in her eyes was less evident and she looked like her old self.

"Wrong?" she echoed. Two tears, bright as diamonds, formed along the lower edge of her eyes, then ran slowly down her cheeks. "The world is screaming, Milo. Can't you hear it?"

"I—"

"There are answers in books," she said. "All you need to do is read the right one."

"Huh? Books . . . ?" Milo asked, suddenly even more confused. "What are you talking about?"

Lizabeth studied him for a minute, and if possible her eyes turned stranger still. So remote. So unlike the girl who'd trained and studied and laughed and played with him, Shark, and the others. Milo was absolutely certain that he did not know the girl he was talking to.

As if reading his thoughts, Lizabeth said, "You don't even know what you know, Milo Silk." She shook her head. "You don't pay enough attention."

Whatever she meant seemed to make her sad. She brushed at the silver tears.

Milo reached out to touch her, feeling a sudden need to pull her to him and comfort her. To keep her safe from something more than the Bugs. She recoiled from him, avoiding his hands.

"No," she said quickly.

"Hey, I didn't mean—"

But before he could finish, Lizabeth turned and walked toward the ship. She paused at the base of the loading ramp and glanced briefly back at him, just as she had done before. There was no smile this time, though. Milo saw her shoulders lift and fall with a sigh; then she climbed the ramp and vanished inside.

Milo turned helplessly to Shark, but his friend just stood there shaking his head.

"What's *wrong* with her?" pleaded Milo.

"Oh, man, I really, really don't know," said Shark.

"What did she mean by all that?"

Shark kept shaking his head. "That stuff about books? How did that make sense? We read every book we can get our hands on, and you read them twice, dude. Is she talking about other books?"

"You got me."

"Is she talking about some special book your *friends* have?" He leaned on the word "friends" and Milo took his meaning.

"If the Nightsiders have any special books, nobody's

told me. Actually, I don't think Evangelyne or any of them have said anything about any books."

"Then I'm out," said Shark, flapping his arms. He tapped his temple with a finger. "I think Lizabeth's gone bye-bye."

Milo grunted.

Shark said, "Come on, we need to get out of here."

But Milo lingered a bit longer, searching inside his mind, hoping to find the process that allowed him to communicate with the Witch of the World. If anyone knew what Lizabeth meant, she would. And if there was no meaning, maybe the witch would know what was going wrong inside Lizabeth's head. He almost told Shark about a dream he'd had recently of a book about a lost little boy, but it was just a dream. Not one of his prophecies, he was pretty sure. And the boy was a boy, not a little blond girl.

So he gave it up for now. The last of the wounded were aboard, and Evangelyne stood at the top of the ramp. Milo looked around as if answers might be hung conveniently on signs nailed to the silent trees. There was, of course, nothing but secrets and mysteries. And urgency.

So he ran for the ship.

A short minute later the red craft lifted off and began its long flight toward the town of Mandeville, where help might—*might*—be waiting.

Or perhaps what he would encounter would be more heartbreak and mysteries.

Chapter 18

The shortest route would have been straight across Lake Pontchartrain, but that was also the worst choice. They'd be as obvious as a black fly on a clean white sheet of paper. Or a bright red fly. The Huntsman hadn't bothered to camouflage his command ship.

There was a pale cloud cover now, and it faded the blue of the lake to an almost uniform light gray. The cloud cover was low enough to hide Dissosterin patrol craft, and Milo coasted around the edge of the lake, flying level with the trees to hide against their shadowy bulk.

Lake Pontchartrain wasn't really a lake, Milo knew, and he pulled from his memory all the details he'd learned. Scavengers were taught a lot of tricks for memorizing data and then recalling important information. Survival, he'd been told a million times, was the most perfect example of the phrase "knowledge is power." For the kids and adults in the Earth Alliance, it was their strongest weapon against the Swarm, and their only chance of ever winning.

So he went through what he knew about Lake Pontchartrain. It was a brackish estuary situated in southeastern Louisiana and connected to the Gulf of Mexico.

It was a big oval that covered an area of over six hundred square miles. According to the charts, it had an average depth of twelve to fourteen feet, which wasn't too bad unless the ship were to sink in it and they couldn't swim out. Even a good swimmer can drown in shallow water if things go sour. Lately things had been going sour a lot more than they'd been going right. Salt water from the Gulf mixed with fresh water from the Tangipahoa, Tchefuncte, Tickfaw, Amite, and Bogue Falaya Rivers and from Bayou Lacombe and Bayou Chinchuba. The lake was surrounded by marshes, hardwood forests, swamps, and wetlands.

For months now, Milo's mom and her team of Earth Alliance resistance fighters had lived in a series of camouflaged camps along the two bayous. Milo knew the geography pretty well, though he'd never had to fly over it before, except for during the escape from the hive ship, but that was more like plummeting than actual flying.

The red ship responded to his commands, but he could still sense its resistance. Its hatred.

Bite me, he thought.

Out of the corner of his eye, Milo saw a glow coming from the open air vent and the quick flicker of the salamander's tongue. The creature peered down at him with his unreadable amphibian eyes.

"Shark," Milo called, and when his friend looked up, Milo pointed to the map. "Where should I put us down?"

Shark swiveled his chair to face the holographic map.

Beside him, Evangelyne leaned forward and studied it too. The fact that the alien map did not have any marker to indicate the presence of an EA camp was encouraging. However, it didn't help them locate it. All they had to go on was the general location and the hope that the camp was still there. When the hive ship had attacked their own camp, the radio equipment had been destroyed. Milo knew that the other camp might just as easily have been attacked, or they might have chosen to move of their own accord, or they might never have been there. All three possibilities held equal weight.

"If we can't find it," said Evangelyne, "set us down anywhere and I'll see what I can do."

Milo and Shark exchanged a look. They knew what she meant by that. Once they were down, she could transform into a wolf to use her far more powerful animal senses. Even though it was a weird thing for a human kid to hear, Milo found comfort in her statement. Evangelyne was strange, and he wasn't entirely sure she liked him anymore than Oakenayl did, but for now they were allies.

Maybe they were on their way to becoming actual friends. It was hard to tell with her. She rarely spoke, and when she did she tried very hard not to relate on a real one-to-one level. Being friends with her was going to take a lot of effort and a lot of time. He hoped they had that time.

"I appreciate the help," he told her, and the wolf girl gave him a grave nod.

"What's the expression you Daylighters use? One person washes the other?"

"Hand," corrected Shark quickly. "One hand washes the other. Totally different meaning."

She thought about it, then nodded. "Oh, I get it. Hand. That makes more sense."

Shark turned away to hide a grin.

"Say, Evangelyne," said Milo tentatively.

"What?"

"Ever since we stole this ship, you haven't said much. Not to me, anyway. Have I done something to, you know, make you mad?"

She looked at him with genuine surprise. "Make me mad? You? No. Why would you ever think that?"

"Well, like I said, you've been kind of avoiding me and all. . . ."

Evangelyne shook her head. "No, it's not like that. We're not—I mean the Nightsiders—we're not like you. We don't . . ." She fished for the right word. "Chat. We don't do much small talk."

"You hardly do *any* kind of talking."

A smile came and went on her pretty face. "It's not about you, Milo. It's us. You don't really understand."

"I'd like to. Why not try me?"

She thought about it, then shrugged and nodded. "It's the Heart of Darkness. It doesn't mean the same to you as it does to us. To you Daylighters it's just a trinket, a beautiful stone. But for us it's the most precious object we have.

It's sacred. And it's important. So, so important. Without it the doorway to the shadow worlds can never be opened."

"I know, but—"

"No, you don't. You think you do, but you can't."

"Then explain it so I can," said Milo.

The wolf girl considered. "You know your mother is out there somewhere. Her patrol and Shark's aunt and the other soldiers, you *know* they're out there, right? I mean, you believe that they're still alive out there, just out of touch for now."

"Sure, I guess."

"And your father, you think that maybe there's a chance he's alive somewhere. Even if he's in a cell aboard a hive ship, you think there's a chance he's alive. You told me that."

Milo nodded.

"And the Earth Alliance resistance groups—millions of people in groups all over the world—you know for sure that they're out there, hiding, staying under cover, working on ways to fight back. You have no doubts they're there, right?"

"Sure, but they *are* there."

"Exactly. Now, imagine that they were all taken away to some distant world and there was only one spaceship left that could get you to them or bring them home to you."

"Oh. And that's what the Heart of Darkness is?"

"Yes. It's the only link that we know of, the only key to the last remaining doorway to the shadow worlds. If it's destroyed or lost, then everyone we few orphans know, and all the millions of Nightsiders of the many supernatural races, will be lost forever." She paused and shook her head. "Forever. With no chance of ever being found again. None. It would be as if they never existed. All we would have is memories and regrets."

Milo understood now, and it horrified him. She was right; he had only thought he understood, but now he truly *got* it.

Evangelyne watched his eyes, looking for that understanding, and nodded when she saw it. She touched the small leather pouch hanging from her belt. "We don't even know how to keep it safe. Halflight might be able to figure it out, or maybe one or two others in this part of the world, but between Oakenayl, Mook, and me, we simply don't know."

"Yeah, about that . . . Where *is* Halflight anyway? I mean, she's still alive, isn't she?"

Evangelyne looked away. "She lives," she said, but there was no enthusiasm in her voice. "Faeries are so powerful but also so delicate. She spent much of her life force to cast glamours when we went aboard the hive ship. She is sleeping, and we can only pray that she wakes up."

"Whoa, wait . . . I mean, she *will*, right?"

Evangelyne would not answer the question.

"What about other Nightsiders?" Milo asked after an awkward pause. "Aren't there supposed to be more out there somewhere?"

She seemed surprised. "Oh, of course. A few. Some are like us—abandoned or accidentally left behind. Some are

renegades who would never help us. And as I told you earlier, there are the wicked ones."

"Queen Mab and the *Aes Sidhe*."

"Yes. Though she is still trapped in her faerie realm.
However, there are others, and some of them are as evil
as evil gets." Evangelyne shivered. "Some are every bit as
dangerous as the Huntsman."

"Okay, so let's not go to *them*, but shouldn't we at least
try to talk to Queen Mab? Maybe if we give her a heads
up about the Huntsman, she'll be grateful. Maybe she'll
be open to working out a deal. Remember, I've been inside
the Huntsman's head, and that put me inside the Swarm's
head too. He wants to conquer everything, and that probably means the faerie world as well."

Evangelyne started to argue, then lapsed into a brief,
considering silence, but ultimately she shook her head.
"Mad Queen Mab's hate and treachery are legendary. We
can't risk any direct contact with her."

"We have to do something."

"Milo," she said, her voice gentle and tentative,
"that's why I've been so silent these past few days. I
haven't been pulling away from you; it's just that I've
been trying to decide what to do and the answers simply
won't come. And I'm getting desperate, Milo. I'm so
scared that I can't keep the Heart safe. I'm so scared
that the Huntsman will find us and take it away and
then all will be lost. Now I have Queen Mab to fear as
well. And if either of our enemies gets the Heart, it will

be my fault, because I wasn't able to protect it."

She looked like she was about to cry, but then she made an angry face and took a deep, steadying breath.

"You know you're not alone, right?" said Milo. "Shark and me . . . and Lizzie . . . we have your back."

"But you're human children. What can you do?"

Milo arched an eyebrow. "First . . . *children?* Really? How old are you?"

She grunted something that might have been an apology, or she could have been clearing her throat.

"Second," continued Milo, "I seem to remember that it was my plan that got us aboard the hive ship. I'm not just some dumb *boy.*"

Evangelyne colored. "I never said that."

Milo laughed. "I'm just messing with you. I guess what I mean is that none of us are alone if we stick together. That's how it works. It takes five fingers."

"It what?"

"Oh, that's something my mom sometimes says when she's talking to the soldiers about working together. It takes five fingers to make a fist."

"Hunh," grunted Evangelyne. "That's a wise statement."

"That's my mom. That's why she was in charge."

"I hope I get to meet her," said the wolf girl.

"Yeah, me too." Then Milo brightened.

"She—" began Evangelyne. Then she suddenly stiffened and sniffed the air. "Wait—what's that smell?"

"What smell?" But as soon as Milo spoke, he smelled it too. "Oh no . . . something's burning."

But Shark was already out of his seat, dropping Killer to the floor, and was running across the bridge. Thin tendrils of blue smoke had begun worming their way through a vent on the far wall. Shark dropped to his knees and began pulling away sections of the panel. Immediately thicker, darker smoke boiled out, driving him back in a coughing fit. Tiny fingers of yellow fire wriggled inside the smoke.

"What is it?" demanded Milo.

"It's the engine coolant," croaked Shark. "I told you it was banged up."

"Put it out, boy," ordered Evangelyne. "Or we'll all burn!"

"I know, I know. See if you can find a fire extinguisher."

"A what?"

"You know, for putting out fires."

She looked confused. "There's no water. . . ."

"First," said Shark quickly, "you don't put water on an electrical fire. Not unless you want to die. Second, we need a fire extinguisher. Probably a red cylinder with a spray nozzle."

But Evangelyne could only shake her head. Either because she was unfamiliar with such a device or—more likely, Milo realized—because there was nothing like that anywhere here on the bridge of the alien ship.

Then Iskiel dropped unexpectedly from the air vent,

scuttled over to the smoking panel, and crawled inside the housing. Shark peered in and gaped.

"He's . . . eating the fire . . . ," he said in an awed whisper.

"He does that," said Evangelyne simply.

The ship suddenly bucked as if it had struck something, but there was nothing on the scanner.

"The engines are going wonky," Milo yelled. Even with Iskiel absorbing some of the flames, the problem was getting worse. Circuits connected to the coolant system began to pop out sparks. The salamander tried to gulp them down too, but it was spreading faster than he could eat.

"Shark . . . ," called Milo. "I'm losing control of the drive systems."

"I know . . . ," growled Shark, who was fanning away the smoke and trying to blow out the flames. That only made them flare brighter. The ship instantly bucked again. And again.

Milo could feel the controls becoming sluggish, and the hologram flickered like a flashlight with a damaged battery. "Do something!"

"I'm *trying*."

"Iskiel can't control that much fire," warned Evangelyne. It was true. The salamander was beginning to glow an angry red, as if his insides were a furnace that had been fed too much fuel. The creature squatted inside the blaze, but it continued to spread.

"Do something," begged Milo.

Shark wore a canvas vest over his T-shirt. He pulled

it off. Then, after a slight hesitation and a nervous glance at Evangelyne, he pulled off his shirt as well. He was very plump, and suddenly there was a lot of brown skin in view. He began vigorously swatting at the flames with the shirt to try to create a vacuum that would rob the hungry fire of the oxygen it needed.

"It's working!" said Evangelyne, clapping her hands together. "Shark, you're a genius."

Milo cut a look at Shark and saw his friend's brown skin turn the color of a ripe plum as he flushed with equal parts embarrassment and pride.

But then the ship bucked again, even harder than before.

"Is the fire out?" Milo cried.

"Yes . . . and the cooling circuits are still intact." Powerful vents kicked in automatically and sucked the smoke out of the bridge. "I think we're good—"

Another buck, this one the hardest of all. The red ship went sideways like a soccer ball that had been kicked by a giant.

And that's when Milo realized what was happening. He pivoted in his chair to look at the holographic screens that showed the air behind the ship. Where once there had been a single glowing red dot to indicate the ship they were on, now there were four dots. One red, and three that throbbed a bright blue. They were being hunted by three alien pursuit ships, and *the Bugs were firing on them*.

"Oh no!"

Like the red avatar, the blue ones were configured as scaled-down images of the pursuit craft, but Milo was sitting too far away to see exactly what kind of ships they were. Because of scavenging, he was mostly familiar with the drop-ships and some of the larger combat vessels. However, he'd seen photos of at least a dozen other types of ships. Everyone in his class—everyone in the EA—had to become familiar with the silhouettes of each enemy ship. He couldn't see these ships well enough to identify them, and it made him wonder how much better Bug eyesight was. All the screens were positioned farther away than was comfortable for ordinary human eyes. The Huntsman had been given alien eyes too, and that seemed to suggest that their eyesight was sharper. It was frustrating, though, because knowing what kinds of ships were attacking them might give him some idea about what the heck he could do.

The ships kept firing. Firing. Firing. And at that distance they could not miss.

"Oh no," he said, this time in a tiny voice. It felt like a huge, icy fist had closed around his heart and was squeezing.

The blasts hammered at the red ship.

In his mind he could almost hear the ship scream in pain.

FROM MILO'S DREAM DIARY

This is what was written on the first page of that book
    I keep dreaming about . . .

Had there been two boys living in Gadfellyn Hall,
    everything would have been different.
So different.
With two minds churning, there would have been games
    and tricks and adventures. With two mouths to
    smile, they would have grinned back the shadows
    and laughed the darkness into its rightful place
    beneath beds and under rocks and into cellars.
    With two brave hearts beating, there would have
    been challenges met and conquered. With two
    sets of bright eyes, there would have always been
    one pair to look forward while the other watched
    behind. With two sets of hands, one pair could have
    held a candle while the other sorted out the right
    skeleton keys.
But there was only one lonely boy living in Gadfellyn

Hall all through that spring and summer and into that terrible winter.

Only one living boy.

Only one human boy.

And so this is a different world than it might have been.

And therefore this is an entirely different kind of story.

. . . and I don't know what in the world that means. Or if it's important. But I kind of think it is.

Chapter 19

Another blast hit the ship, hard enough to jolt Milo's teeth. Killer yelped and went sliding across the floor as the ship canted to one side. The little dog's nails made a desperate skittering sound.

Another blast. Sparks burst from the coolant panels again.

"Get us out of here!" roared Shark as he began once more furiously swatting with his shirt.

But Milo was already wrestling with the controls. Even though it was a hologram, it felt real around his hand and it had started to take on weight. That made no sense to him, though, and he wondered if he was imagining it.

Another blast shook such thoughts from his mind, and from then on he focused only on trying not to kill them all.

He spent one burning second studying the map. The red dot formed the center of a triangle, with the three pursuit ships making up the points. They had closed around the red craft and were taking turns firing. He wondered why they didn't simply open up and vaporize it.

His mind provided the answer, and he knew at once that it was absolutely correct.

They can't risk blowing up the ship, he thought. He could feel the weight and shape of the crystal egg in his left front pants pocket. *If they destroy the ship, they destroy the egg.*

A moment later a pair of blasts told him for certain that the Bugs weren't above damaging the ship pretty badly, though.

They want to make us crash.

It terrified Milo because if the Bugs forced them down, then any survivors would be dragged before the Huntsman. Milo and his friends had defeated and humiliated the monster. The thought of what kind of revenge the Huntsman might exact was almost too much for Milo to bear. He wanted to crawl into a closet and cry.

Bang!

A control panel on the other side of the bridge exploded outward in a fresh shower of smoke and flame, and suddenly the vents and air-conditioning failed.

"We just lost life support," bellowed Shark.

The smoke, no longer vented by the fans, began swirling inside the cabin.

"Do something!" yelled Evangelyne. "I don't want to die up here."

"Neither do I," growled Milo under his breath as he tried to anticipate the next blast so he could bank away from it. Then he had a dangerous little thought. "Shark, look at the scanner. See if you can figure out what model of ships they are."

"Why?" demanded his friend, who was still fighting a fire. "What does it matter?"

"Just do it."

The floor of the bridge seemed to buck under them, forcing Shark to crawl on all fours from the burning coolant panel to a spot close to the screen showing the other ships. He fanned smoke out of the way and peered at the blue avatars.

"Barrel-fighters, I think."

"Are you sure?"

"I—"

"Shark, we need to be sure."

Shark licked his lips, coughed, then nodded. "Yeah. Barrel-fighters. I'm positive."

"Barrel-fighter" was the nickname the EA soldiers had given to a particular type of attack ship. Small, barrel-shaped, with stubby stabilizer wings and a crew of three. Less than half the size of a drop-ship, and built for speed and maneuverability. Milo ran through everything he'd been taught about the barrel-fighter, and everything he'd learned from the two times his pod had scavenged wreckage of this kind of ship. The armor was thinner than a drop-ship's, because the barrel-fighter relied on speed rather than durability. Top speed of Mach 2.3. Designed for planetary combat. Not built for escape velocity, not built for outer space. A cockpit to hold a pilot and two gunners, and everything else was engine. He remembered his mom saying that it was on a par with an F-22 Raptor.

He understood that. He knew the science because that was one of the survival skills he'd had drilled into him.

Barrel-fighters, like their Earth counterparts, were in a design class called supermaneuverable aircraft. They could turn on a dime even at high speeds. Unlike the red ship, however, they were designed to fly only in air, not in the thin upper atmosphere or in airless space. These barrel-fighters were deadly in an aerial dogfight. The red ship was more sophisticated but less maneuverable. So where was the middle ground? What was the balance between trying to outrun the pursuit ships with a craft whose engine was burning itself out, and engaging in a dogfight when no one aboard knew how to fire the cannons?

Another panel blew out, and half the lights on the bridge went dark.

"Are you going to just sit there?" shouted Evangelyne, her voice thick with anxiety. "Or are you going to do something?"

"Shut up," he told her. His voice sounded very calm to his own ears, which he figured was probably not a good sign because inside he could feel panic exploding.

"I have the Heart of Darkness," she reminded him. "If they destroy us, then . . ."

"Please," he begged, "shut up."

She did, but he could feel the heat of her glare on him.

"Shark," Milo snapped, "get back and buckle up."

"No, I have to put the fire out and—"

Two more blasts hit the craft, and the rest of the lights went out. Now the only light came from several small fires and the blue glow of the holograms.

"Do it!"

Smoke was getting so thick that it was hard to breathe. Milo saw Shark stagger across the jolting deck and crawl into his chair. Killer, barking furiously, leaped into his lap. Milo tried not to think about what was happening to the wounded in the hold. What all the jolting and jouncing was doing to the spike in Barnaby's chest.

If Barnaby was even still alive.

"Hold on," ordered Milo. "I'm going to try something."

"What are you going to do?" begged Shark.

Milo closed his fist and began pushing it forward. The engine noise changed from a troubled cough to a roar and then to a scream as the red ship shot forward.

"Milo—the engines can't handle this," cried Shark, but he ignored him.

He raised his hand. Slowly, slowly bringing the ship up, aiming it away from the trees, driving it toward the sky at increasing speeds.

On the screen the blue ships fell immediately behind, and then, one by one, they flared brighter as they kicked their own engines up to full. The red ship was probably faster when it was first built—maybe twice as fast—but in its present condition the barrel-fighters were closing the distance with terrifying rapidity.

Smoke poured from the coolant system and Milo had

to use his free hand to pull his shirt up over his nose and mouth. The smoke burned his eyes and blurred his vision. He heard Shark and Evangelyne screaming his name, begging him to stop, to slow down.

But Milo clenched his teeth in fear and fury as the ship soared toward the edge of space.

The blue ships shot upward, trying to catch the red ship inside the atmosphere while there was still oxygen for their engines to burn.

And then, with a roar of rage, Milo jerked his hand backward, his fist still clenched inside the holographic drive.

There was a scream of protesting metal as momentum and gravity tried to turn the red ship inside out. Milo prayed that the Huntsman's ship was built to withstand those forces. It was the beast's command ship, capable of flight in atmosphere and space. Fast, powerful.

The barrel-ships were directly behind the red ship, all of them traveling at more than twice the speed of sound.

There was absolutely no way for the pursuit fighters to veer away. No chance, no time.

One by one they slammed into the Huntsman's craft and exploded.

And then the red ship was falling.

Falling.

Falling back to the hard, unforgiving surface of the planet below.

Chapter 20

Everybody screamed.

The Huntsman's red ship dropped like a rock from the sky and fell with an escort of flaming wreckage from the three barrel-fighters.

It fell, fell, fell.

The steering hologram winked out as circuit after circuit exploded, melted, or burned. Milo clung to the armrests of the pilot's seat, choking on the thick, oily smoke that now filled the cabin completely. Tears streamed from his irritated eyes, and his lungs felt hot and singed.

Most of the viewscreen holograms had also winked out. Only one was left—and it showed the waters of Lake Pontchartrain rushing up toward them.

"Hold on!" he bellowed. "This is going to be baaaaaad!"

The ship hit the water.

It was bad.

FROM MILO'S DREAM DIARY

I remember a conversation I had with the Witch of the
    World. Not sure if it was in a dream or when I was
    awake. Maybe it doesn't matter.
Anyway, I said, "Everything's getting so complicated. I
    can't keep it all straight."
And she said, "The world has always been complicated,
    Milo. What's changed is that now you're able to
    riotice."

Chapter 21

There are worse ways to wake up than in a burning spaceship that is filling with cold, brackish water.

However, Milo could not think of any.

He didn't know how long he was unconscious. Maybe an hour, maybe only a handful of seconds. His mind was numb and every single molecule of his body hurt. He was sure he was dead and that instead of going to heaven he'd been taken to a world where pain was the only experience. He was certain of it.

He could hear terrible screams.

Screams in voices he recognized.

And overlaying that sound was the gurgling of water. Milo knew he should move, should get up, get out, save himself, save everyone . . . but his body would not respond. His legs felt like they were made of ice, and his hands seemed to hang limp at the ends of dead arms.

"H-help . . ."

He heard the voice through the gurgling. Faint, weak, fading.

Female.

Milo stirred in his seat and tried to make his brain

function so he could attach a name to the voice. He turned with infinite slowness, aware that he was hurt, aware of wet warmth on his face. Blood or oil? He wasn't sure. Probably both.

"*Help . . .*"

The voice seemed so far away. Not just somewhere on the other side of all that water and smoke, but in another place.

"M-Milo . . . please . . ."

He saw something move. No, some*one*.

A pale figure with long, flowing pale hair and eyes the color of winter ice. It confused him, because those eyes and that hair belonged to the voice, and that voice was off to his right, behind the swirling smoke.

"Milo," said the figure, and even with that one word, he knew it wasn't the same voice that had cried for help. This was a younger, thinner, higher voice. Much more familiar, and yet . . . it was as strange as the sound of wind blowing through the charred rafters of a burned-out building.

He tried to find her name. Found something, worked to fit it into his mouth.

"L-Lizzie?"

She came closer, emerging from the smoke. Her hair was wild and her eyes were so strange. Lizabeth's eyes, but also *not* hers.

"Milo," she said urgently, "you need to wake up."

"I—I am awake," he protested. He could see her

clearly now. The same young face and huge eyes, the blouse with the flower pattern and the cut mark.

There was something not right about it all, though, but he couldn't think what it was.

"Milo, you have to wake up."

Lizabeth took him by the shoulders and shook him. Her hands were surprisingly strong, but so cold. Ice cold.

"Lizzie . . . stop . . . I'm awake!"

At least that's what he thought he said.

To his own ears, though, it all sounded jumbled. Gurgled. Wet. As if he was . . .

. . . speaking . . .

. . . . under . . .

. . . . water. . . .

And suddenly Milo snapped awake.

Actually awake.

There was no smoke.

There was only darkness.

Darkness and water.

Because the entire ship had sunk to the bottom of the lake and filled with water.

And he was drowning.

Chapter 22

Milo thrashed in his chair, but he was still belted in. He punched the release, kicked free of the chair, and felt himself rising through the utter blackness. From his angle, all he could tell was that the ship had landed with the bridge tilted forward and to the right. That meant he was moving up and left toward the damaged coolant panels. There was no hatch on that side of the bridge, though. The two exits were the ones that led to the hold—that is, directly behind where he'd been sitting—and the main exit, which was next to where Evangelyne and Shark were seated.

He heard sounds all around him, muffled and distorted by the water. Screams. There were definitely screams, which meant that some parts of the ship might not be fully flooded. And there was a massive pounding sound as if someone were hammering on the walls with a sledgehammer.

And something else.

A sharp sound above him. Small and strange, filled with panic.

Was it . . . barking?

Yes.

Above him somewhere, Killer was barking.

Barking was impossible underwater. Milo kicked upward, fighting the drag of his soaked clothes, his pouch of slingshot stones, and the scavenging pack he always wore. His lungs burned and his head pounded. He wondered if seeing Lizabeth had been a dream of his dying, drowning mind.

The barking continued, and it bounced with distorted frenzy through the cold water as Milo kicked and kicked to try to find it.

Then something struck him hard across the mouth.

Milo recoiled in pain and confusion. It had been something that moved. His face felt mashed, and he pawed the water to try to find the object and fend it off before it hit him again.

It hit him again.

And again.

Finally, Milo managed to get his hands in front of his face and catch the thing. He felt something solid. A shape that instantly made sense.

A shin. An ankle. A shoe.

No, a sneaker with the same familiar tread as his own.

Milo began climbing up the leg to the thigh, the hip. He felt bare skin and a broad stomach. Then a hand reached down into the water, slapped at his head, took a fistful of his hair, and pulled him upward until Milo broke the surface of the water into an air pocket. Killer's bark changed from blind panic to something else, something that was still frenzied but now included a note of happy excitement.

"Milo?" gasped Shark.

"Yeah! Ow, let go."

Shark didn't immediately let go. Instead he pulled Milo until he hit the wall. "Grab onto something."

Milo had to flap around, slapping the walls until he found a section of the panel. Most of the machinery was smooth, but he found the section Shark had opened and he hooked his fingers around that. Then he simply held on as he gulped in lungfuls of air. It was still smoky, but it was air.

"Where's . . . Evangelyne?" he gasped.

He heard Shark make a noise that was fear and anger. "Down there. Hold on, I'm going to try again."

"Again—?" Milo began, but Shark was gone, leaving behind the sound of a splash and the hysterical Jack Russell. He could also hear the pounding sound. It was so powerful that it shook the whole ship, and suddenly Milo understood what it was.

Mook.

The stone boy was in the hold with the wounded and was trying to smash his way out. But he was made of stone and the ship was built of metals and alloys that had been designed to withstand the artillery of Earth Alliance weapons, midair collisions, and the stresses of interplanetary travel. Milo did not believe that Mook was going to be able to smash his way out, not even with all the crushing force of a rock spirit.

Milo bent low to the surface of the water to try to find some clean air beneath the roiling cloud of smoke. He took a small breath, didn't choke, took a longer breath, held it, let it go, took a bigger one, and then dove beneath the surface.

He saw Iskiel there, swimming sluggishly as if dazed, his fiery glow diminished by the dark water. At least he could survive underwater, though not forever if they remained trapped.

Milo kicked toward the back of the bridge, drawn by the sound of Mook's furious hammering. In the dark there was no way to know how close he was to the wall, and he found it by crashing into it. Then he crawled up to the surface, found that the pocket of air was even smaller there, took another breath, and sank down, searching for handholds on the wall, finding only a few, but enough to keep him moving in the right direction. The ship's power was out, but all vessels have a manual release for escapes following accidents, and the alien ships were no different.

It seemed to take a million years to find the lever, which was built into an inset slot beside the hatch door. He gripped it with both hands, braced his feet against the wall, and pulled.

The lever did not want to move. Or maybe it was designed for beings more powerful than a skinny eleven-year-old boy.

Even so, he put everything he had into it, pushing with the big muscles in his thighs, using his core strength.

Using everything he had, until the darkness seemed to be filled with exploding red fireworks.

Just when he thought his lungs would burst and his bones break, the lever moved. First grudgingly, and then all at once. Milo was hurled upward by the sudden release of tension and he shot into the air pocket, hit the ceiling, and dropped again. Then he kicked up, took a couple of quick breaths, and swam back down.

And was amazed that he could see.

Down there in the swirling water was a light. It poured out from the open hatch and he saw bodies moving. Refugees from the camp, some of them swimming with energy, some floating limply as they were pulled by others. He saw the slim form of Lizabeth, moving with the grace of a mermaid. She had an arm hooked around Barnaby and, despite her tiny size, was pulling him quickly through the hatch. Two of the survivors had waterproof flashlights, and it was by their light that they all crowded out of the hold. There was no way for Milo to know how many of them had survived. It was too confusing.

Mook turned and looked up at him and said, "Mook!" But it came out as a watery gurgle.

Then the stone boy turned toward the main hatch. Milo swam down to him and guided Mook's rocky fingers toward the manual release that would allow them to escape the drowned ship. Mook grabbed the lever and pulled. The design may have been nearly beyond Milo's strength, but it was no match for the rock spirit. The lever jerked upward and then snapped off, but the door opened with a *whoosh*.

The water swirled and bubbled, and then something moved *into* the alien ship instead of out of it. A brute of scales and claws and teeth.

Everyone screamed the last of the air out of their lungs.

Chapter 23

Milo shoved people away as the alligator rushed forward, and its whipping tail struck Mook on the side of the head. But the stone boy spun in the water and swung a mighty punch at the beast, catching it with a glancing blow.

The gator instantly jerked around toward the source of the blow, and the very tip of its tail caught Milo in the chest with the force of a boxer's punch. Milo felt himself flying upward once more, and he used the momentum to get up to the air pocket for one last gulp. Killer's barks were filled with wild panic now, and as soon as Milo reached him he knew why. The air pocket was only a narrow slit above the thrashing surface, and the dog was barely able to keep his mouth above the water.

"I'll be back," promised Milo, and then he jackknifed and dove down once more. The flashlight beams were shining all over the place as the survivors tried to fight their way past the gator. Sunlight from outside slanted down through the churning lake water, showing them their route.

But the gator was still there.

It was locked in deadly combat with Mook, who had

wrapped his arms around the thickest part of the alligator's tail. Although the rock boy was powerful and had nothing to fear from the gator, the reptile was much faster and its thrashing body kept bashing Mook against the bulkhead.

Milo dove down below the battling pair and began shoving the drowning survivors out. Then out of the corner of his eye he saw Shark rising from below him, dragging with him a limp form. Evangelyne. Her arms and one leg looked wrong. Crooked.

Broken.

Her eyes were open, but Milo was positive she couldn't see him. Or anything.

There was total panic on Shark's face. Milo's friend was clearly almost out of air. He was dying while trying to save the girl.

How long had all this taken?

Two minutes?

It seemed longer but was probably half that time. Seconds feel like hours when you're struggling to breathe.

Milo kicked hard to reach Shark, grabbed Evangelyne's belt, and together they fought their way through the hatch and out into the lake. Behind them Milo heard a strangled roar of rage and pain. And then there was a bellow of furious triumph.

"Mooooooooooooook!"

There was no time to look. Milo and Shark swam upward. The red ship had settled in about twelve feet of water, and Milo was sure half the lake was inside his lungs. They broke the surface and tried to bite big chunks of air. It was cool and sweet and wonderful. Around them the heads of the survivors were bobbing. People were coughing and crying and yelling. But that only meant they were alive.

"Can you swim?" cried Milo. "Can you get her to shore?"

Shark sputtered and spat. "I—I think so. But—"

Milo didn't stay to hear what else his friend had to say. He took a big breath and dove back down. He followed the rays of sunlight and reached the flooded hatch just as a broken and twisted form floated out.

The gator.

Mook had not been kind to it. Milo half regretted that the gator had to die, but the alternative was too horrible to imagine. Mook appeared in the doorway and tried to ward him off, but Milo ducked past him and swam as hard as he could in and then up. There was no sound of barking to guide him, and Milo's heart began to sink as he fought to locate the pocket of air.

Above him he saw a tiny figure floating there. Not barking, not swimming. Drifting. And as he approached it, Killer's body began sinking down toward him.

Milo grabbed the dog, twisted around, and swam harder than he ever had in his life. Killer was a limp bundle in his hands.

Mook must have seen him. As Milo swam toward the

hatch, a big rocky hand reached out, caught the strap of his satchel, pulled him out of the wrecked ship, and hurled him upward toward the surface. Milo broke into the air, gasping and sputtering, and turned to hold Killer above him as he began furiously kicking toward the shallows. As soon as he could, Milo stood. He slogged through the water to the muddy bank, then dropped to his knees and began working on the terrier, gently massaging his chest to try to find a spark of life.

"Let me," said a voice, and he looked up to see Lizabeth standing there. Even though she had just come wading from the water, her hair seemed strangely dry. She took Killer from his hands and laid him on the grass, then knelt and breathed into the dog's slack mouth.

Once.

Twice.

A third time.

And suddenly the dog's little legs kicked out, and he rolled over and vomited a pint of lake water onto the grass. Then he lay there, panting, tongue lolling, with his tail flapping up and down in a pathetic attempt to wag.

Milo knee-walked over to him. "Lizzie—what did you do?"

She didn't answer but simply backed away and headed toward a section of bank where other survivors were crawling out of the water.

Milo bent and kissed Killer's head, then turned to say something else to Lizabeth, but he couldn't see her.

Instead he saw Mook come striding out of the water holding Evangelyne in his arms. A weak, trembling Shark staggered along in his wake and did a graceless belly flop in the reeds.

"God," said Milo as he got shakily to his feet. He hurried over to where Mook was easing Evangelyne down onto thick grass. "Is she alive?"

"Mook," said the rock boy doubtfully. Milo reached past him and pressed fingers against the girl's throat.

There it was. A pulse. Surprisingly strong despite the obvious injuries. Milo assessed the damage. Evangelyne's left forearm was badly broken, with the ends of bones nearly ripping through the flesh. Both legs seemed to be more crushed than snapped, which meant that there could be multiple fractures. Her clothes were torn and Milo could see long rips in her skin. She'd been on the side of the bridge closest to where the hull had hit the lake bottom, and the collapsing wall must have crushed her. Milo was no doctor, but from what he could see he didn't think there was even the slightest chance of her ever walking again. Not without a lot of special surgery.

He looked wildly around and saw other survivors kneeling over the badly wounded, each of them fighting their own fear, hurt, and exhaustion to give what first aid they could. Iskiel lay on his back at the edge of the water and Milo couldn't tell if he was even breathing. It was a disaster, and Milo was not at all certain that he and his friends would survive it.

Part
Two

MILO AND THE REFUGEES

"From caring comes courage."
—LAO-TZU

FROM MILO'S DREAM DIARY

I keep dreaming about the lonely little kid living in some
   strange place called Gadfellyn Hall. I don't know his
   name or anything about him.
Not until the dream tells me.
All I know is that the dream gets more real every night.
   And in my dreams I'm reading his story. But it's not
   like I'm sitting there with a book on my lap. I can
   hear the story in my head, but it's like I'm telling it
   to myself.
Does that even make sense?

Chapter 24

The day was filled with horrors.

And even though none of those horrors involved more Bugs or Stingers or spaceship battles, the horrors were almost more than Milo could bear.

Friends of his were hurt. Bleeding. Broken.

Dying.

Barnaby and Evangelyne were the worst. They lay side by side on beds of soft grass and leaves. Milo didn't care one bit if Oakenayl would have disapproved of him cutting leafy branches down to provide comfort for them. The tree spirit wasn't here, and when he'd had a chance to offer help, all he'd done was walk away. At that moment Milo would have been happy to turn Oakenayl into a nice rocking chair. Or a campfire. The creep.

Iskiel woke from his daze and slithered through the makeshift camp, using his stored fire to ignite the gathered wood. Apparently he didn't care much what Oakenayl might think either.

Mook, likewise, did everything he could. True to his rocky nature he was tireless and steadfast. He carried the wounded into the woods and helped construct the shelters. And when hungry alligators came sniffing around, Mook picked them up and hurled them into the center of the lake. None of them came back.

The mosquitoes did, though. They swarmed in and brought squadrons of blowflies with them. And as the day wore on, the heat seemed to flow directly out of an oven. The trickiest and most unnerving part of the day for Milo was helping Shark set Evangelyne's broken bones. It was horrific work that made her scream. The pain woke her up, and then the shock slammed her back down into her personal darkness.

When they were finished, Shark sagged back, his face gray and sweaty, his eyes glassy and filled with fear. "That . . . was . . ."

He couldn't finish, and didn't need to. Milo wanted to throw up.

Mook stood over her, standing watch and clearly feeling as helpless as they did.

"Mook?" he inquired softly.

"I don't know," said Milo. "She got hurt before, when we were fighting the Huntsman, but when she transformed she got better."

"Then that's what she has to do," said Shark. "Go all wolfy."

"Right, but she's unconscious and I'm not really sure if she's strong enough to do her transformation."

They looked up at Mook.

"Is she?" asked Shark.

The rock boy spread his hands and shrugged his stony shoulders uncertainly. "Mook?"

As he got to his feet, Milo said, "Mook, could Halflight help her? Could she? Do you know where she is? Can we, I don't know, *call* her?"

The rock boy looked away as if not willing to meet Milo's eyes. "Mook," he said unhelpfully.

"We need help," insisted Milo.

"Mook," said the rock boy again, very softly. He turned and walked over to the bank and stood looking out across the water.

Shark, who had overheard, also got to his feet, and wiped his bloody palms on his jeans. He still had no shirt, and his brown skin was crisscrossed with pink scratches and shallow cuts. Nothing that needed stitches, though. Normally Shark would be terribly embarrassed to be seen without a shirt, but the circumstances had canceled that out. "What was that all about?"

"I don't know," said Milo. "None of them will tell me what's wrong with Halflight. Or where she is."

"You think she's dead and they're just not saying?"

"I don't know. I mean . . . why would they?"

"Don't ask me."

They looked around at the big forest. Some of the trees were young, having grown wild since the invasion. Others were very old, suggesting that for the most part these woods had always been here. That might mean it was state forestland, a park, or the forested edge of some-one's property.

"Where do you think we are?" asked Milo, but Shark was one step ahead of him. He removed his compass from a pouch on his belt and studied it. He turned in a slow half circle and then pointed.

"Okay, our old camp is behind us, so Mandeville has to be north and a bit west of where we're standing."

"How far?"

"No idea. C'mon, let's see if we can find a landmark."

They walked back to the water's edge and peered through the gloom. The clouds were getting thicker as twilight had begun working its way toward them, and the air smelled like rain. A thick mist was drifting across the lake, but Milo could make out something big and angular farther along the bank. He tapped Shark and pointed.

"Is that the causeway?"

Shark made a sour face. "What's left of it."

The Lake Pontchartrain Causeway, according to their geography teacher, used to be one of the longest bridges in the world. Nearly twenty-four miles. It once connected Metairie, near New Orleans in the south, to Mandeville in the north. That was before the Dissosterin hive ships arrived. Now all that remained were the steel and concrete supports and stubby, jabbing shards of the roadway. The rest had been blasted down to pre-vent human resistance fighters from moving troops and equipment. The bridge was crammed with an entire army division when the pulse weapons opened up on it. All those brave soldiers and all those tanks and fighting vehicles had plunged into the water. New Orleans fell the following day, and now a hive ship hovered over it, though currently the monstrous craft was hidden by the clouds.

It was the same hive ship in which Milo and the Orphan Army had fought the Huntsman.

"I'm spitballing it," said Shark, "but I think we're somewhere in St. Tammany Wildlife Refuge. Nothing else makes sense if we're this close to the causeway."

"The EA team was supposed to be hiding out in the basement of an old church," said Milo. "Our Lady of the Lake at the intersection of Lafitte and Jefferson, about a mile east of the causeway. I remember that much, but not much else because my map got soaked."

"Can't be more than seven or eight miles from here. If we can get there, we can find it," said Shark confidently. They looked at the thick clouds. "Question is, do we go now before it's dark, before the rain and all, or do we go at first light?"

As if contributing a suggestion to their conversation, Barnaby uttered a pitiable moan. The boys looked at him and then each other.

"Now," they said at the same time.

But Shark hesitated. "Both of us, though? I think you should stay here."

"No," Milo said at once. "No way I'm going to wait here. I'd go nuts if I had to just sit and wait."

"But one of us should—"

"I agree," said Milo, "which is why I'm going and you're staying."

"Whoa! I didn't mean that."

"I know, dude. But let's face it, you don't have any equipment except what's on your belt, you got no shirt, and I can move faster."

"Why, because I'm fat?" demanded Shark, offended.

Milo grinned. "No, because nothing can catch me when I'm scared, and I've never been this scared before."

Shark angrily kicked a stone into the water. He had his fists balled and his chin stuck out as he fought for some argument that would trump what Milo had said. He kicked another, larger stone way out into the water.

"This really, really, *really* sucks."

"Yeah," agreed Milo, "it really, really, really does."

They spent a few precious minutes going through the meager equipment and supplies belonging to the survivors. The bulk of their supplies had gone down with the ship, including most of the pulse pistols Milo had scavenged from the attack on their camp. He also had the Dissosterin grenades and knives. No food, though, except for some waterlogged power bars and whatever they could find in the nearby woods.

As Milo prepared for his journey, the other survivors offered what they could, and a few of the adults volunteered to go, but none of them were fit. Milo, Shark, and Lizabeth were the only completely uninjured humans in the camp. Mook was strong but slow, and besides, he was standing guard over Evangelyne—and over the whole camp. That was the sole bit of relief for Milo, because there wasn't much that could get past the stone boy. Even the gators had stopped creeping up the banks. Milo had a compass, his knife, some wire and tools, signal flares, a camouflaged rain poncho, and a canteen. He pulled on the poncho and knelt by the water's edge to fill his pouch with sturdy stones for his slingshot. There wasn't even a spare first-aid kit to take, because all those supplies had already been used.

Milo exchanged a nod with Mook and received a vigorous face-licking from Killer, a hiss from Iskiel, and a fist bump from Shark. Then he took his bearings, set his mind, screwed up his courage, and ran into the forest.

As he left the camp, he saw a pale figure standing beneath the arms of a weeping willow. He smiled and waved to Lizabeth, but she merely turned and watched him go. She never said a word.

For reasons he could not explain, just seeing Lizabeth struck him deep in the chest, and for half a mile he tried to understand what exactly it was that he felt. Sadness? Sure, there was some of that, especially if Lizabeth's mind had been damaged by everything that had happened. Anger? A lot of that, too, because the harm she had endured was a perfect example of the kind of damage the heartless Bugs inflicted.

But there was another emotion there too.

Fear.

Not for her.

No.

Milo realized that he was afraid *of* her.

Thinking those—and even darker—thoughts, he ran into the twilight forest as the first rumbles of a coming storm reached his ears.

FROM MILO'S DREAM DIARY

I dreamed about the kid in Gadfellyn Hall again, and just
like always my dream was about me reading a book.
I wrote down everything I could remember. . . .

There were many, many rooms in the big old house.
Rooms filled with dusty furniture in which
cockroaches crawled and over which moths did their
slow, hungry aerial dances. There were rooms filled
with suits of rusty armor, some still occupied by the
ghosts of the ancient knights who had died in them.
There were kitchens and sculleries, butlers' pantries
and closets. There was a great dining hall with a
vast table on which were set a service for thirteen
people and silver trays heaped with enough food for
an army, but only worms and flies had dined upon
it. There were bedrooms by the dozen, but none of
the beds had been slept in. Except one, and it was
too big a bed for a boy as small as him.
There were rooms with chairs for sitting and having

conversations, but the shadows in the room had nothing to say to each other. There was a room with dozens upon dozens of animal heads mounted on wooden plaques on the walls. Some of the animals snarled, some looked surprised, others stared with indifference through their glass eyes. None of them made a sound to stir the air of Gadfellyn Hall.

The boy wandered from room to room to room. He knew them all. Every corner and niche. Every closet and secret stair. Every couch and chair, every lamp and lantern. His wandering footprints were recorded in layer upon layer of dust. They told a story of someone who was looking and looking but had not found the room that waited for him. The room that wanted him.

A single line of his footprints, however, led through a doorway at the end of a forgotten wing of the vast old house. The prints went up to the door, seemed to mill outside for a while, and then the dots of someone walking on tiptoe went inside.

There was no sign at all of the maker of those footprints ever coming back out again.

Never ever ever.

Chapter 25

Like all the kids in his pod, Milo had learned how to judge both time and distance. If the run to Mandeville had been a straight line with no forest landscape to contend with and no aliens to be wary of, he might have made it in well under a couple of hours even at a leisurely jog. Probably in about half that time if he'd wanted to push it.

However, this wasn't that kind of world.

He found an old bike path that snaked its way through the woods, but it didn't run in a straight line at all. After taking it for a while, he realized that it was circling back into a series of switchbacks that would have been nice if he'd been out cruising around on a bike. It wasn't plotted out for speed, so he left the overgrown concrete path and picked a more careful route through dense undergrowth. This part of Louisiana was a swamp, and when the vegetation was left to run wild, it did so with enthusiasm. At times he had to fight his way through dense stands of bamboo and sugarcane; at other times he had to slog through knee-deep streams. Ultimately the way became so cumbersome that he went south and found the bank of the lake again and followed that. It was less safe, though, which meant that even though the route was more assured, safety was not.

Three times he had to run inland to avoid little marshy inlets where alligators lurked with only their eyes and nostrils visible above the brown water. And once he bumped into what he thought was a low-hanging vine, only to have it suddenly try to drop on him. Milo shrieked and backpedaled away from a huge green anaconda.

The big snakes were not native to America, but here, and in Florida and other warm wetlands, anacondas that had been let loose from private collections or had escaped from zoos had become a real threat. He'd heard that in Florida, they were a major predator even before the hive ships arrived, and they were big enough to bring down a wild pig, an unlucky deer, or a skinny preteen dumb enough to walk into one.

Milo ran inland more than two hundred yards to get away from the snake.

By the time he circled back to the banks, twilight had covered the lake with a thick blanket of black storm clouds. Rain began slowly, pattering on the leaves and popping on the lake. Then a bolt of lightning forked across the sky. A heartbeat later a blast of thunder shook the forest. It was so loud that Milo actually reeled and clamped his hands to his ears.

That's when the real rain began.

Not just a downpour but a deluge, as if an ocean were falling from the sky to try to drown the world. Milo cried out as a second blast of lightning burst above him and the rain came down even harder.

Within seconds Milo felt like he was back inside the sunken red ship, drowning. He staggered through a world of rain and mud, his clothes feeling like lead weights. It was impossible to see more than a foot in front of him, and within seconds he lost all sense of direction. He could use the compass if he could find a place to stand where it wouldn't be slapped out of his hand by water.

Standing under trees in a lightning storm was stupid and dangerous, he knew, but he was in a forest and there was nothing *but* trees. The only other option was the lake, and with this kind of rain, he knew he'd never spot a hungry gator. So, what to do when every choice was a bad one?

Milo forced himself to keep going, to find somewhere to hide, somewhere he could wait out the heaviest of the rain. The thunder and lightning were continuous, evidence that the storm was directly overhead.

"Please!" he heard himself say, but he didn't know who he was asking for help. "Please . . ."

And then he heard something. A voice.

Faint and strange, nearly hidden by the roar of falling water and the artillery barrage of thunder.

"Here . . ."

Milo whipped around, and even in his desperation and panic his hands followed countless hours of training and he whipped out his slingshot and a stone, fitted the rock into the pad, and drew.

The woods were a gray smear of shadows and rain.

"Who's out there?" he demanded.

Lightning flashed, casting everything into stark lines of white and black.

"Here," whispered the voice.

And it was a whisper. How he heard it through the rain was a mystery to Milo, though he was half sure that he was imagining it. Or that he was crazy.

"Here . . ."

The voice seemed to be coming from straight ahead of him, from the shadows inside a narrow circle formed by three ancient elm trees. When the lightning flashed again, Milo thought he saw something deep inside that opening. Something that seemed to want to hide in the darkness.

Something.

Or someone.

The rain was too heavy to let Milo see anything clearly.

"Who's there?" he called again, trying to make his voice sound older and stronger. "I'm armed."

"Milo . . . ," came the voice. "Over here."

That's when he recognized the voice, and that realization was like a punch in the gut. It was impossible, but Milo *knew* it.

Absolutely impossible.

"Milo, it's okay," said the voice. "Everything's okay now."

When the lightning flashed again, he saw the figure that matched the voice. The blood in Milo's veins turned to icy slush. His knees buckled and he sagged down to the ground as the figure was revealed by a flash of lightning. Milo could feel his heart beating so fiercely that pain shot through him, darting down all the way to the pit of his stomach and up to his head.

The figure did not venture out of the shadows but instead raised familiar hands and smiled with a familiar mouth.

"It's okay, Milo, I'm here now."

Milo burst into tears.

The figure beckoned him gently, all the while smiling, nodding, reaching.

"Come with me, son. I'll protect you."

Milo stared past his own tears as pain turned knives in his heart. He raised his hands, reaching out, needing to touch those hands. Needing everything that the figure could offer.

"D-Dad . . . ?" he whispered.

Chapter 26

Milo felt like his mind was breaking. The world tilted and spun around him in a sickening whirl.

This was simply *not possible.*

His father had gone missing more than three years ago. He'd been a gentle man, not a fighter, even though he'd carried a gun and gone out on patrols like every healthy adult had. Before the war his dad had taught music, and the Silk home had always been filled with music. Rock, jazz, classical, indie, reggae . . . everything. Music and happiness. Then the Bugs came and ruined all of that. Even so, Dad continued to play his music in the quiet hours in the refugee and resistance camps. He wore a gun at his hip but always had his guitar slung across his back. That was his real power, and his tunes and songs kept the shadows from ever getting too dark.

Then one day his patrol had vanished. The Bugs took them. No bodies were ever found. Just a smashed and bloodstained guitar.

Milo's nightmares were often filled with horrific images of what the Bugs had done to his father—or were still doing to him. Sometimes Milo dreamed of his father pinned to a giant display board along with other interesting humans in a perverse alien collection, the way some humans used to collect butterflies.

Aboard the hive ship the Huntsman had taunted him by saying that the Swarm didn't *collect* anything. The Swarm *use*, he'd said. Then he'd offered to help Milo find him, to save him, if Milo would join his campaign of evil.

Milo had been tempted. So tempted.

But in the end he had fought the Huntsman.

And afterward, when the Orphan Army was back on Earth, Milo had a dream of the Witch of the World and in that dream she said those two terrible things.

There are horrors more dreadful than the Huntsman, Milo Silk.

That was bad enough. Then she said one more thing.

Your father lives.

Those two statements kept beating at him, every hour, every day.

Which is why he stared at those beckoning arms and into that smiling face and did not move.

Could not move.

Dared not move.

Because of the witch's words and because of what he was seeing.

His father was dressed in the same clothes he'd worn the day he disappeared. Jeans, scuffed Timberland boots, an LSU T-shirt. Three years later and after who knew what horrors, and Dad was still wearing the same clothes?

That seemed wrong. Not possible.

"Milo," said his father in a light, happy, encouraging voice, "it's fine, kiddo. Come on in here, under the trees. It's dry in here. It's safe."

"Dad . . . I . . ."

"It's okay, kiddo, it's safe and warm. C'mon, get out of this rain before you catch your death."

Milo did not look into his father's eyes. Instead he stared at the strap of hand-tooled leather that crossed his body from left shoulder to right hip. The leather was dark, and all along it was a rippling music staff on which notes danced. Milo remembered the Christmas morning when Dad had unwrapped the gift. It had been a joint present from Mom and Milo, and the joy in Dad's face was so great they all laughed and cried, and there was music in the house all day.

The strap was connected to the body of the Gibson guitar that hung, neck down, across Dad's back.

Milo stared at it and tried to make sense of it.

That guitar.

The same guitar. The same strap.

Somewhere, back in camp, in the ashes of his mother's burned-out tent, was that same strap. It was the only thing Mom had left of her husband, of Milo's father. She'd touched her fingers to her lips and brushed them along those dancing notes every single morning and every single night since Dad had gone missing.

How could it be here?

How could Dad be wearing it on *that* very guitar?

And how could his father have found him out here in the forest, in the rain, so far from where anyone would know to look?

"Milo," said his father, the smile flickering for the first time, taking on a hint of impatience, "I told you to come here."

Milo pawed rainwater out of his eyes. "Who . . . who are you . . . ?"

It wasn't the question Milo wanted to ask. He wanted to accept this at face value, to run to his father, to hug him so tightly that he could never go away again. To make all this real because he felt so small and so lost and Mom was gone and the world was broken. He needed to believe in this.

And he almost did.

Almost.

Maybe he even would have, if it hadn't been for the guitar strap.

There are horrors more dreadful than the Huntsman.

Yes. There were.

Hope was a terrible thing.

Lies were worse because they made a fool out of you for believing.

"You're not real," said Milo, and it cost him to force those three words out of his throat.

The smile on that familiar face flickered again and then went out, leaving behind a frown of disapproval.

"You're being naughty, young man," said his father. "You come here right now or there'll be consequences."

Milo heard those same words echo inside his mind from long ago. From one night when he was little, when he ran away in a shopping mall. Dad had chased him, but before he could catch up, Milo climbed into a big stone fountain and began scooping up handfuls of the coins people had tossed in to make wishes. Dad had been very angry with him because he was scared for Milo and probably embarrassed, and Milo was soaked and there were people watching. When Milo finally obeyed, Dad gave him a stern lecture about right and wrong, about not taking things that didn't belong to him, and about never running off like that. It was one of the few times Dad had been angry with him, and the only time he'd ever yelled. It was an old memory that Milo hadn't thought about in years, because it belonged to another part of the world.

Now this strange and impossible figure was saying some of those words in exactly the same way. As if he was playing an audio loop straight from Milo's memories.

It was crazy.

And it was wrong.

"No," said Milo hoarsely, his voice almost lost beneath the roar of the rain.

"Right now, young man."

"I . . . can't . . ."

"I don't want to hear 'can't' from you, Milo." Dad

turned one beckoning hand palm up and reached forward with it. "I need you to come here and give me what you took."

"What? I . . . didn't take anything. That was when I was little."

The figure snapped its fingers with impatience. "Don't make me come over there. Don't make me take it back."

Those were *almost* the same words. Almost, but not quite.

And it occurred to Milo that the figure had not moved at all. It stood in the shadows between the trees, beneath the canopy of leaves. It was no more than fifteen feet away and could have reached him in a few quick steps.

But it did not.

Which is when Milo realized that he was thinking of the figure as an "it," not a "him." Not as Dad. Not anymore.

The figure seemed to sense this, and the frown changed into a sneer that was so cold it chilled the air and nearly froze Milo's heart.

"Come here," said the figure.

"No!"

"Come here now!"

This time the words came out as a roar. The voice changed, the things that had made it his dad's voice crumbled and flew away into the storm winds. Now the voice was huge, strident.

Alien.

And familiar in a very, very bad way.

So bad.

"Come here, boy!" bellowed the voice.

And suddenly it was no longer his father's voice. Now it was something else entirely. Something wrong. Something horrible. Something familiar.

"I want what you stole!"

Milo screamed.

Chapter 27

"**I** want what you stole, boy. Give me the egg or I will lay waste to everything you love."

The figure of his father stood there roaring with the voice of the greatest monster who had ever walked this or any world.

The Huntsman.

"No," cried Milo, falling backward into the mud. "You can't have it."

"Give it to me or I'll take it."

Milo retreated through the mud. The stone had fallen from his slingshot, but he dug another one out and fitted it into place, raising the weapon, aiming.

The face in the shadows creased into an ugly smile that Milo knew never had a counterpart of his real dad's mouth. This smile was a leer of malicious hate.

"Give it to me *now*."

Milo pulled back on the strong elastic bands of the slingshot. "If you want it—come and take it."

Milo forced himself to say those words. Forced his voice to sound far, far braver than he felt. He readied his stone to strike as the Huntsman charged.

The *thing* stood there in the shadows, glaring and seething.

But *stood*.

It did not move.

It did not come after him.

It did not step out of the shadows and into the rain.

"This is your last chance, boy," growled the Huntsman.

"Why don't you go back to where you came from?" snarled Milo, and then he let the stone fly.

It was a streak that punched through the rain and struck his father's body right between the eyes.

And all at once his father vanished in a shower of red sparks.

One second it was there, looking like his dad, guitar and all, and then it was gone, changed, torn away to reveal something else entirely. Another figure stood in the shadows.

No, not "stood."

Hung.

It was another man. A human, dressed in the camouflage green and gray of the Earth Alliance. His clothes were torn and streaked with blood. His skin was unnaturally pale. His eyes were completely empty and his mouth hung slack. The front of his shirt had been torn open, and into the pale skin over his heart a Dissosterin lifelight had been driven. Implanted. Wires ran from it up the throat and vanished beneath the flesh under his chin. Other wires disappeared beneath the shirt and sleeves, only to reemerge from the cuffs. They wrapped around each hand and each finger, forming a pattern like the crooked lines of blood poisoning, but Milo could see that they were indeed wires. On the man's face was a cracked device from which smoke now rose.

Those hands still reached for him, but the creature seemed unable to move.

Only when the lightning flashed again could Milo see why. One of the man's legs had been shattered, apparently by heavy-caliber bullets. The other thigh was also punctured. The only reason the man could stand at all was because he was leaning back against the trunk of a tree. The pain from those wounds had to be unbearable, and yet there wasn't even a flicker of it on the man's face.

Milo whipped another stone out of his bag and readied it to fire.

"Who are you?"

The man's mouth worked, but the voice that came out was neither his father's nor the Huntsman's. It was a meaningless, wordless mumble of empty noise.

A cold wind whipped up and down Milo's spine at the sound of it.

Milo backed away from the man . . . or *thing* . . . or whatever it was.

With the device shattered by his stone, the illusion vanished. And so, it seemed, did the connection with the Huntsman. What was this? he wondered. Had the

Huntsman somehow rigged this poor guy with some kind of speaker? Or maybe some other device? A hologram of some kind?

That seemed to be the only possible answer. But it left Milo with so many questions. Like, how could this even *be* here? It couldn't have been set as a trap, because even Milo hadn't known he was coming this way. And why was it here?

Milo rose to his feet, the stone still aimed at the wounded man.

"Who are you?" he asked again, anger and fear seething within him. "Why did you look like my dad? *Why?*"

The man kept making the meaningless mumbling noises. There was no expression on his face, no spark in his eyes, and no sense to the sounds he made. They weren't even jumbled words. Just sounds.

Milo took a hesitant step forward to see if the man would react.

He didn't.

Nothing changed at all. Not one thing.

Milo looked at the wounds. They were awful and the pain had to be unbearable. So why wasn't the man screaming? How could he keep his face so slack?

So . . . *dead.*

It made no sense at all, and terror rose up like a mushroom cloud inside Milo's heart.

"No!" he said as he backed away, at first slowly with

clumsy steps, then more rapidly as the strangeness of this began to overwhelm him. Finally, with a small cry of wordless utter horror, he whirled and bolted.

He got exactly two steps before he ran into a very big man with a very big gun.

Chapter 28

Milo rebounded as if he'd struck a wall. The man was massive, and he didn't even grunt as Milo slammed into him. Instead he raised his very big gun and pointed it at Milo's face.

"Say something," he said. His index finger was stretched along the outside curve of the trigger guard. It would take only a fraction of a second to slip it inside and pull that trigger.

Milo, sprawled on his back in the weeds, stared up at him.

The man was dressed as a soldier, in the camouflage pattern of the Earth Alliance. But he was a stranger and his face was half melted as if he'd been in a terrible fire. There were bloodstains on his clothes, and his shirt hung in shreds. Through the holes Milo could see torn Kevlar and also torn skin. The wounds still bled, the red mingling with rain. The bloody water sluiced down his body.

"I said," the man repeated, "*say* something. Make it good and make it fast."

Milo's mind pretty much froze and he tried to speak, but couldn't.

The soldier slipped his finger inside the trigger guard. "Last chance, little man. Say something."

"I . . . ," began Milo. "I mean . . . wh-what do you want me to say?"

The soldier squinted down the barrel at him, one eye cold and brown, the other a milky white and blind, a leftover from whatever had burned him.

"What's your name and unit?" demanded the soldier.

"I—I . . ." Milo stopped, swallowed, and then said it the way he'd been taught. "Milo Silk, scavenger, Third Louisiana Volunteers."

The brown eye widened for a moment, then narrowed again to a suspicious slit. "The Third Louisiana, huh? That's under the command of Major John Burke, right?"

"What? No. My mom's the commanding officer, Colonel Amanda Silk."

The soldier studied him a moment longer, then slowly lowered his gun. "You're Mandy Silk's kid?"

"Yes . . . ?" Milo said uncertainly.

The soldier suddenly grinned and offered his hand. "Then you're darn glad you met me, kid."

"Um? I . . . ? What?"

Milo accepted the hand, and the big soldier plucked him off the ground and set him on his feet. Milo staggered, but the man steadied him.

"Who are you?" asked Milo. "And what was all that about John Burke? Major Burke's dead. He was killed last October and—"

"Yeah, well, can't be too careful, can we? Bugs have gotten smart. They understand English now, and probably other languages too. And they're using the holo-men to—"

"They're using the who?"

The soldier pointed through the steady downpour to the thing that still stood in the shadows between the trees. "Holo-men," he said. "Or maybe 'zombie' is a better word."

"What—?" Milo gasped. "Who *are* you and what on earth are you talking about?"

The soldier grunted. "I'm Staff Sergeant Jose Ramirez, Fourteenth Regulars out of Biloxi. We came over here to support the Hundred and Third out of Baton Rouge, but we . . . well, we were too late." He walked over to the trees, raised his gun, and flicked on the top mounted flashlight. The wounded man hung here, pinned to the bark by long metal spikes Milo hadn't seen before. The man's eyes were empty, mouth slack. "You see that? It looks like one of our people and it sounds like one of ours, but it's not. Not anymore."

"What do you mean?"

Sergeant Ramirez reached in, grabbed a handful of wires, and with a savage grunt tore them away. There was a shower of sparks, and suddenly the wounded man slumped down and hung like a limp scarecrow. Ramirez hooked a finger under the chin to raise the man's head. There was no expression at all on the face.

"They killed him," said the sergeant. "The Bugs. As

213

far as we can tell, they wiped out the entire One-Oh-Three. Every last man and woman. Maybe all their camp followers too, though we haven't confirmed that yet. And instead of just letting the dead stay dead, those bloody Bugs wired them up with some new kind of tech. Our geek squad thinks it reactivates the central nervous system enough for the dead to walk around."

"Oh my God . . . you mean that man was . . . I mean *is* . . . ?"

Ramirez nodded. "Dead. Two, maybe three days, by the smell. Poor bugger."

Milo turned away, disgusted and close to throwing up. "That's so . . ." He stopped and simply shook his head, unable to come up with a word that described what he felt.

The soldier glanced at him. "Oh, it gets worse. You saw something, didn't you? You saw a friend maybe, or—"

"I saw my dad," said Milo. "He looked like my dad."

"Even sounded like him too, I bet."

"Yes! How did you know?"

Ramirez looked angry and he pounded the side of his fist on the tree. "It's this new tech, and I got to admit that we're struggling to understand it. From what we know, it doesn't just animate the dead—it does something to anyone within range of about forty, fifty feet. It gets inside your head somehow and pulls out a memory, and then uses holograms to make it look like someone you care about. A friend, a fellow soldier, or . . . your dad, I guess."

"That's sick."

"Yeah, it is, and don't ask me how it works because I have no idea. No one does. Almost seems like magic."

Milo said nothing to that.

"We call them holo-men," continued Ramirez. "The Bugs have started using them all throughout the South over the last couple weeks or so. Most of the time you can't even tell they're fake. Not if the light's bad, 'cause that makes the holograms look totally real. Rainy nights like tonight? Heck, they could walk right up to you and you wouldn't know you were in trouble until you were dead."

"He couldn't walk at all."

"Yeah, well, that's where you got lucky. Looks like this one lost a fight to someone. Maybe one of my squads, or more likely a refugee, 'cause my guys would have put it down for good. The Bugs must have propped him up to ambush anyone coming this way. His gun is gone. No knife, either. Not sure what happened there. Maybe a slippery darn scavenger managed to steal them, or maybe the Bug who propped him up didn't have a spare."

"So . . . he wasn't dangerous?" asked Milo.

"Don't think that for a second. If you had gotten close enough, he'd have choked the life out of you. Maybe even bit you. These things are programmed by the Bugs. They'll kill you any way they can." He glanced up at the gloomy sky. "The Bugs have upped their attacks on camps over the last couple of days. They've gotten even more vicious. Nastier, if that's even possible. Not sure why."

Milo was pretty sure he *did* know why, but he didn't tell Ramirez about the crystal egg or the Heart of Darkness. He wanted to, but something made him hold his tongue. He wondered if the Witch of the World was somehow whispering in his ear so quietly that all he could do was react but not actually hear her. What was the phrase he'd read that described that? Subliminal influence? Or maybe subconscious influence. Something like that.

There was a flash of lightning, but now the thunder lagged behind it by almost ten seconds, which told Milo that the storm was moving away. The rain was slowing too.

Ramirez said, "A couple of the holo-men were even fitted out with explosive vests like suicide bombers used to wear back when humans were fighting humans. Insane stuff. We lost a lot of people before we figured it all out, and there are still a lot of others out there who don't know. Unfortunately, even though we've been able to trash a bunch of these holo-men, we haven't recovered much of their tech. The wiring and holographic stuff are pretty basic, but we haven't begun to crack how they read minds and pull out such convincing images. The Bugs have really gotten smarter lately, and now they're using our own memories against us." He shook his head. "And you thought you were seeing your dad? I'm sorry, kid, but that must have been pretty rough. I lost my folks during the invasion and I was already twenty-two. I can't even imagine what you must be feeling."

Milo said nothing. What he really wanted to do was

find a nice quiet spot to sit down and cry. The soldier came over and knelt in front of him.

"Where are your people, Milo?" asked the sergeant. "Where's Colonel Silk? We heard that there was an attack, and we saw the hive ship over the bayou."

Milo wiped at his eyes with the back of his hand. "They attacked us."

He told Ramirez what had happened. Not all of it, but enough. He did not mention the Nightsiders. But he did tell him about the Huntsman. The big sergeant looked frightened at the mention of the alien-human hybrid.

"The Huntsman, huh? Is that what he calls himself? Geez, that's creepy," Ramirez said hollowly. "We've been hearing reports about some weird new Bug critter that's supposed to be half-human, but to tell you the truth I didn't believe them. Or maybe I didn't want to. Geez. Most times when rumors start flying around about that thing being in the area, we lose all contact with our people almost immediately, and if we find survivors, they're half out of their minds. Guess now I have to believe it's all true. You're Colonel Silk's son and you don't seem like you're all that crazy."

"Um . . . thanks?"

"One of the survivors we met—this poor guy who lost his whole camp—said that there was this big monster-looking guy running around with a pack of Stingers like a hunter with his dogs."

"It's true," said Milo. "I saw that up close."

"If you're being straight with me, then that is some seriously scary stuff, though this Huntsman sounds like he stepped right out of a nightmare."

"He's real, all right," Milo assured him. "He destroyed our whole camp and killed most of . . . most of . . ."

The tears suddenly started coming, and it made Milo so angry. He didn't want to cry, but he couldn't stop himself. The big sergeant looked at him up and down, his face stern, and Milo thought the man was going to yell at him, tell him to suck it up. Instead the soldier hooked an arm around Milo's shoulders and pulled him close, hugged him, held him.

The way a father might.

The way a friend might.

The way anyone should.

Milo finally got control of himself. It was hard, though, because until now he'd needed to be strong, to be the strongest one around. Now, with the soldier here and other soldiers close, he was able to be himself. To be a kid in a big, bad, broken world full of monsters.

Ramirez didn't tell him that everything was going to be all right. He wasn't unkind enough to lie like that. Instead he held Milo and whispered in his ear.

"You're alive, kid. You survived. You're tough."

When Milo could manage, he coughed his throat clear and then pointed the way he'd come. "We need medics. Right now. And transport."

Ramirez stood quickly. "Tell me."

Milo did so, and the sergeant took a small, scrambled walkie-talkie from his pocket, keyed it, and made the call to his people.

Hearing him make that call and knowing that help—real help—was on its way hit Milo harder than anything that had happened so far. The tears, newly stopped, came again, and this time he didn't know if they were ever going to end.

Chapter 29

But of course tears end.

Everything ends, and Milo knew that. Storms pass and night turns into day and wounds heal.

Even so, to Milo it seemed as if there was never going to be anything but pain, fear, running, hiding, fighting, and hurting. Nothing else, and no hope of peace or escape.

He tried not to look at the holo-man, but he couldn't help it. With the tech destroyed, the man in no way resembled Milo's dad—but so what? He had. He'd spoken with his dad's voice, worn his face. Had *been* him, even if only for a brief time. The lie was devastating. To Milo this new tech seemed even worse than pulse pistols or the barbs of Stingers. This didn't just hurt flesh or break bones. It broke his heart. It cut him all the way to his soul. It made the pain of the loss of his dad a thousand times worse because it dangled hope in front of him and then snatched it away. It was a kind of wrong Milo had no words for. It made him ache for his father. To have him here, alive and whole, or to *know* that he was dead. Seeing the holo-man only made the doubt burn like a supernova inside his chest. He could feel it like a physical pain. He loved his dad so much, and he missed him so very much.

Right then Milo wanted his mom so badly he could have screamed.

He almost did.

But didn't.

Instead he looked up into the gray sky and imagined the Huntsman's monstrous face. "I'm going to stop you," he whispered slowly, forcing the words out past the tension in his throat and through clenched teeth. "No matter what it takes, no matter what I have to do, I'm going to find you and kill you."

Far away, on the other side of the lake, hidden in the heavy clouds above New Orleans, there was a final rumble of thunder. To Milo it sounded like the deep, unnatural laughter of his most hated enemy. A laughter filled with confidence and cruelty. Laughter that mocked Milo's promise, and threatened worse in return.

As if he were engaged in a real confrontation, Milo stood there, fists balled, glaring his hatred into the windy skies, feeling the seeds of darkness take hold in the soil of his soul. He silently repeated his promise. His vow.

I'm going to find you and kill you.

The rain slowed and slowed and finally stopped, but the swamp dripped and the humidity was oppressive.

Ramirez let Milo have his time, and spent a few minutes talking into his walkie-talkie, receiving intel and giving orders. Soon other soldiers came out of the woods. Like Ramirez they were dressed in camouflage that hid their presence until suddenly they were there. These were well-trained soldiers, highly skilled at moving with almost no sound even through dense foliage. Somehow that level of skill was also a comfort. It proved to Milo that the Swarm had not already won. It made a forceful argument that people—human beings—were sometimes at their best when they were pushed to the edge.

None of these hard-faced men and women mocked him for crying. They nodded to him, acknowledging him, accepting him as one of their own, and that told Milo something about them. They were all survivors, which meant they had all lost something. There was not one person among them who had not shed his or her own tears. Maybe a river of them. Maybe an ocean.

Tears did not make you weak.

Sometimes the courage to cry, to be *seen* to cry, was a mark of toughness. It was a sign that you cared enough about life, about the world, to continue to *feel* even when everything seemed to be falling down.

Milo's tears slowed and stopped. He took a few long, steadying breaths as he thought things through. He worried about what might happen when these soldiers reached the lakeside where Shark and the others waited. The Nightsiders were too smart and way too practiced at not being seen by humans. Mook could just fall apart and look like a pile of rocks, and Iskiel would vanish into the trees. Evangelyne was the problem. As long as she stayed in human form, everything would be okay. What happened if she transformed, though? On one hand, it might help her heal from those terrible injuries. On the other, how would armed soldiers react to a girl suddenly turning into a wolf? No, he thought, call it what it was. How would the EA soldiers react if they were confronted by a werewolf?

What could he do, though? Trying to explain this to Ramirez would never work. No one would believe him, and Milo couldn't blame them. He was already more than four full days into his association with the Nightsiders and he still found it hard to accept.

He fidgeted as he tried to decide what to do.

"Okay, kid, that's done," said Ramirez as he lowered his walkie-talkie. "We have a patrol two miles from that point on the beach. They'll get there first and evac the wounded. We have a skimmer inbound, and that'll get the most seriously injured upriver to an exfiltration point."

A skimmer was a kind of airboat that whipped along on inflated pontoons. Unlike swamp boats, skimmers had nearly silent engines. The EA mostly used them at night for quick runs, but they were rare because they were hard to make. However, it was much safer to use a skimmer than one of the far more dangerous helicopters.

"Where will they take them?" asked Milo. "To the church in Mandeville?"

"Not a chance. One of our people led a holo-man back to the church last night. Thought it was his cousin. Forty minutes later we were hit. A drop-ship, two Stingers, and more hunter-killers than I've ever seen." Ramirez shook his head sadly. "We lost a lot of friends last night, kid. We lost some good people. And that's why we have to get our butts in gear. That holo-man saw you, which means the Bugs saw you. They probably think you're a refugee from the church. We need to put a lot of gone between us and here. You ready to rock?"

"Sure. Let me grab a few stones for my slingshot, though. I'm almost out."

The sergeant grinned. "Don't bother. I got something better." He fished in his pack, brought out a small but heavy pouch, and tossed it to Milo.

The bag made a faint metallic *clink* as Milo snatched it out of the air. He loosened the drawstring and poured some of the contents into his palm. They were gleaming metal balls about the size of marbles but heavier. Milo held one up to examine it, and when he recognized what it was, he flinched. "This is shrapnel from a boomer."

"Yup. One of my guys fried one in a short-yield EMP trap. That deactivated the bomb, so we were able to pick it apart for tech. These ball bearings were packed in with the explosives."

The sight of them sickened Milo. He'd seen what happened when a boomer exploded. Several of them had detonated during the hive ship's attack on his camp. Those ball bearings, hurled with the force of high explosives, were like a spray of bullets.

"Yeah, kid," said Ramirez, "I know how you feel, but tech is tech, and though this is pretty low-tech, these ball bearings are going to hit a lot harder than any stone you use. These will give your slingshot a whole lot more pop. Might even flip the switch on a Bug lifelight, you never know."

Milo didn't want to take them, but as he weighed them in his hand, he thought about the vile deception of the holo-men and how much he'd love to have the Huntsman in his line of fire. It was a dark thought, but it belonged to him now. He nodded his thanks and attached the pouch to his belt.

"Hey," he said, unslinging his satchel, "let's make this a swap. I scavenged some tech too."

"Don't need Bug night-vision goggles, kid. We have a ton of that junk and—"

"Pretty sure you don't have this stuff," Milo said as he opened his bag and removed the two Dissosterin grenades and the gleaming pulse pistol.

The soldier's jaw nearly hit the ground. He took the pistol gingerly, as if it were as fragile as eggshell, and held it up. A couple of the other soldiers stopped and gaped at it. "Holy mother of pearl! How . . . how . . . I mean, seriously . . . *how* . . . ?"

It was all Ramirez could manage to say.

Milo cleared his throat. "I, um, took it off a shock-trooper I kind of ambushed this morning."

And so there was another piece of the story to explain

to the soldiers. He did so very quickly, mindful of their need to flee. When he got to the part about the Huntsman's ship, a dozen of the soldiers stood in a circle around him, eyes and mouths wide, staring at him as if *he* was from another planet.

"It's been a weird week," Milo concluded.

FROM MILO'S DREAM DIARY

Writing down the story that I dreamed . . .

Once the boy had found the library in the huge, dark,
    shadowy, dusty old manse, it was clear that he had
    found a place that had been waiting just for him.
It was the library of Gadfellyn Hall.
A forgotten room in a forgotten wing of a forgotten
    house. Filled with forgotten books that wanted so
    desperately to be remembered.
When he stepped inside, he stood for a long, long time
    just staring at all the books. There were so many of
    them.
So many.
And so many kinds. Tall volumes bound in carved wood,
    leather-bound books in groups, stacks of scrolls
    tied in red ribbon, heaps of tablets made of clay
    and lead, blocks of stone with writing that looked
    like pictures, even paperback books that looked too
    new to belong in such an old library.

So many books on shelves and tables or stacked by
themselves in crooked towers. Books on stands or
laid open on tables or facedown on the arms of
chairs. Books that looked like they were being read
by someone who had briefly stepped away and then
become distracted and forgotten to return. Books
with markers in them—strips of cloth, odd pieces
of paper, folded receipts, anything that would
remember a place. There were books placed side
by side on the table so that the text of one could
be easily compared with the other. There were
small stacks of books beside chairs or on chair–
side tables, patiently waiting their turn. There were
books pulled slightly out of place on the shelves as
if frozen at the instant of being selected.

Books and books and books.

But no people. No sounds at all other than the excited
breathing of the boy who stood and gaped in
wonder.

For the first time in a very long while, the sad and
lonely boy smiled.

For the first time in a very long while, the sad and
lonely boy felt as if he'd found his way home. He
loved books. In books anything was possible—even
the impossible.

Outside, in the hall, there is a single set of footprints pressed into the dust. The footprints lead to the library door and then through it. Each print is filled with dust now.

No footprints lead away, though many years have passed.

Chapter 30

With his eyes still glazed from everything Milo had told him, Sergeant Ramirez led his team away from the clearing and into the woods. The holo-man had been taken down and quickly buried, with nothing more than a fist-sized rock placed over his grave. The idea of a "proper burial" was something Milo knew about only from books. Most of the millions who had been killed during the invasion were never buried at all, and their bones littered the otherwise empty cities of the world.

They went inland, following a path that seemed awkward until Milo realized why. Instead of following any natural path such as an overgrown track, game trail, or deserted road, they went through the densest parts of the forest. The Bugs were highly logical, and if they didn't have an obvious trail, they'd follow the most likely one. It was how the EA teams managed to stay ahead of the Bugs. Two soldiers ranged ahead to pick their trail and watch for trouble; two others worked their back trail, erasing all signs of the platoon's passage. It was done quietly and with great efficiency. Milo knew good wood-craft when he saw it, and these men and women were every bit as good as the soldiers his mother trained.

When they were a mile from the sad grave, Ramirez said, "This hologram tech is new, and it's scaring me silly. Something's made the Bugs take a jump forward. I mean, the actual tech isn't new, but their applications are smarter, more devious. We're losing too many people lately."

Milo said, "It's got to be the Huntsman. He was a soldier and part of him is human. Maybe that helps him set better traps."

"Maybe," said Ramirez, in a tone that suggested he agreed, although reluctantly. "If that's the case, then we could be in real trouble. I mean, in worse trouble. The Bugs have muscle and numbers, but we were always smarter, trickier. And we've started figuring out how a lot of their tech works. I heard that up in Wyoming our guys are test-flying our own version of barrel-fighters and drop-ships. And there's a Special Ops squad working the outskirts of Philly that had some prototype sky-boards." He tapped the pulse pistol that was now tucked into his belt. "This thing is an insane find. We've never had a working Bug gun before. Not in all these years. If we can duplicate the tech and figure out how to make those focusing crystals, then we might even be able to turn this whole thing around."

Except, thought Milo darkly, *the Huntsman is out there.*

Milo knew that the mutant was the most dangerous X factor in the whole war. His imagination, his knowledge of human battle tactics, and his ferocious insanity were unbelievably dangerous. And if he ever got hold of the Heart of Darkness—or any of the secrets of magic—then no amount of tech was going to stop the Swarm. This and every other world would fall. Including the realms of shadow into which most of the adult Nightsiders had escaped.

"That holo-man saw me and read my mind," said Milo cautiously. "Does that mean the rest of the Swarm know I'm here? I mean, right here in this part of the woods?"

Ramirez nodded grimly. "I don't know for sure, but we think that's how it works."

"So the Bugs are coming?"

"The Bugs are always coming, kid. But I know what you're asking, and—yes. Which is why we are not going to be anywhere around here when they arrive. I have scouts watching high and low."

They ran in silence for a while, and then Milo summoned the courage to ask, "Don't suppose you heard anything about my mom?"

"No, kid, sorry. When some shocktroopers were killed, the request was passed down to your camp for her to check it out 'cause your camp was closest. Since then, nothing."

Milo walked for a while with his fists balled in frustration. The big soldier cut him a look.

"Doesn't mean she's dead, you know. From everything I heard about Colonel Silk, she is both tough and sneaky. She has a rep for getting her people out of some really sticky situations."

Almost always, thought Milo. Dad had been on a patrol with Mom when he went missing. But no one can win all the time. Not even Mom, though it hurt him to think it.

"I wish she hadn't gone out," said Milo. "I mean, because of the attack and all."

Ramirez walked a few paces before he responded. "There's a lot of different ways to look at that one, kid. If she'd been at your camp, she might have been killed."

"She could have won the fight. . . ."

"Really? Against a hive ship and that Huntsman dude? I don't think so. No, kid, at most she'd have maybe—*maybe*—gotten some more survivors out, but she'd have tried to make a fight of it, and there are some fights no one can win."

"I don't believe that," said Milo.

The soldier said nothing, but Milo didn't want to let it go.

"I'm serious," said Milo. "My dad and mom both told me that there's always hope. There's always a way. Never say never."

Ramirez merely grunted and they walked on. Ten minutes later the soldier said, "We'll keep trying to get your mom on the radio. The Bugs have been dropping EMP poppers. You know what they are?"

"Sure. Electromagnetic pulse bombs. They fry anything with a computer."

"Right. They've started using them before some of

their raids. They drop some and then once communications are down, they send in their shocktroopers. Your mom's radio could have been fried, but don't worry—the downside to the Bugs' using those poppers is that even though it cuts out the radios, it pretty much advertises that they're coming. Your mom, being smart, would have gone to ground. She could be waiting it out in a bolt-hole, letting her trail go cold, letting the Bugs get gone, you dig?"

"I know."

It was an encouraging thought.

Ramirez had his team stop for a three-minute rest, and he called the rescue team. He spoke very little and listened for a long time, occasionally making noncommittal grunts. Milo tried to eavesdrop, but he could only hear one side of the hushed conversation.

"Good," said Ramirez. "We're four miles out and will come at you from the east, one hundred yards in from the water. Out."

Milo was almost afraid to ask. "Was . . . was everything . . . I mean, how are my friends?"

Ramirez frowned and Milo's heart sank, but then the big sergeant said, "Everyone's still sucking air, so we're good. Couple of your people are in bad shape, but our field medics are top notch. That one kid, the Cajun boy with the spike in him, what's his name?"

"Barnaby Guidry. He's our pod leader."

"He's in the worst shape, but the doc says they can

patch him up. He won't be scavenging anything for a while. They said whoever gave him that herbal field dressing saved his life. What was that stuff, anyway?"

Milo shook his head. "I don't know. My friend Lizzie put it together from things she found in the woods."

"She a medic or herbalist?"

"No, she's a kid. Youngest member of our pod."

Ramirez looked skeptical. "Then someone told her what to gather. The medic said it was a very sophisticated mixture. Exactly the right herbs and roots in exactly the right amounts."

Milo said nothing. Even Evangelyne had been surprised by what Lizabeth had used. She called it "old magic," whatever that meant. Lizabeth hadn't studied any kind of magic, and as far as Milo knew, she'd never taken any herbal medicine classes beyond what was generally taught in their camp school.

"What about the others?" Milo asked tentatively. "One of my friends, a girl, broke her legs and—"

"Really? That wasn't in the report. Must not have been too bad."

Or, thought Milo, *Evangelyne wasn't there at all.*

He hoped she had awakened enough to transform so that she could use the healing powers—however they worked—that were part of being a werewolf.

The other alternative was a lot scarier. Maybe she'd been so bad that Mook had simply taken her away. He had no idea what the death customs were for the

Nightsiders. If she died, would Evangelyne's grave be a small mound in the forest marked by a simple rock? Or something equally sad?

It was a wretched thought.

Suddenly, as something rustled in the woods off to their left, everyone froze and a gun seemed to magically appear in the hands of each soldier. Milo was surprised to see that the big sergeant held the alien pulse pistol in a two-hand shooter's grip.

The woods grew still around them, the darkness of late twilight fading everything into a purple gloom that blurred all outlines into meaningless blobs.

Careful to make no sound, Milo drew his slingshot and fitted a ball bearing into the pad. The metal ball felt heavy and dangerous, and he raised the weapon, ready to hit back at the Bugs with a piece of their own murderous tech.

The sound had come from directly in front of where he stood, maybe twenty feet into the woods. They all crouched, ready to fire, ready to flee.

Then, gradually, Sergeant Ramirez relaxed and straightened. He lowered his pistol and the others slowly did the same.

"Must have been a squirrel or a coon," said one of the soldiers.

"Maybe a possum," said someone else.

They all kept careful eyes on the woods for a while, before deciding that it truly was nothing. If it had been a hunter-killer or a Stinger, there would be no doubt by now. Even a shocktrooper scout would have fired on them, confident in its greater power and weapons.

However, Milo thought he caught the slightest hint of a tree moving the wrong way, and had a momentary image of a face made not of flesh but of wood, leaves, and acorns.

Oakenayl?

Could it be the wood boy? If so, how could he have gotten all the way over here? Milo knew that the wood spirit could shed his body and make a new one from any living tree, but did that also mean that between inhabiting construct bodies he could fly like the wind?

Somehow Milo didn't think so, because surely one of the Nightsiders would have mentioned that.

So whose leafy face had he glimpsed in the deep, dark woods?

Or had he seen anything at all?

"These woods are getting weird," muttered Ramirez.

"You have no idea," said Milo, but he didn't say it loud enough to be heard.

Chapter 31

They reached the lakeshore just as a gibbous moon was breaking through the ceiling of clouds. The nearly full moon painted everything with a cold blue light, and Ramirez's team made sure to stick to the shadows. When they were still fifty feet from the lake, Milo cupped his hands around his mouth and made a sound like a barred owl, one of the night birds common to bayou country.

A few seconds later another owl called in reply.

"That's Shark," said Milo, and he went out to meet his friend.

Shark and Killer were the only members of Milo's camp left on the beach, and they had been hiding beneath a tree with a female soldier. The soldier took Ramirez aside to give her report and Shark did the same with Milo.

"I can't believe you found help this fast," said Shark, greatly relieved.

"Everyone got out okay?"

"The skimmer just left with the last of the wounded," he said. "I said I'd wait here with the corporal."

Milo lowered his voice. "What about our *friends*?" He leaned on the word.

"Been some really, really, really freaky stuff happening here," said Shark. He launched into a quick, quiet explanation of what had taken place. First Lizabeth had found more herbs and roots and applied them to Evangelyne's broken bones. That seemed to ease the wolf girl's pain, and soon she woke up.

"What happened to her?" asked Milo.

Shark looked like he'd been kicked very solidly in the head. "That's just it. . . . She woke up, then she told Mook to take her into the woods. He did, and half an hour later I saw a wolf limping through the marsh weeds."

"You sure that was her?"

"No, it was probably a completely different limping wolf."

"Right, sorry."

"But listen, man . . . I think something bad happened."

"What do you mean? Everything that's happened today's been bad."

"Not that kind of bad," said Shark. "Look . . . after I saw the, um, *wolf* . . ."

"She's a werewolf, man, just call her that."

"Not actually sure I can," said Shark. "That word absolutely does not fit inside my head. But listen, after Mook took her and she changed, after I saw her limping in the marsh, I heard something."

"What? A Stinger or a—?"

"No, no, it was her. It was Vangie. I heard her scream."

"Well, she was pretty messed up, Shark."

"You're not listening to me," insisted Shark, who was clearly having a hard time explaining. "This was after she was mostly healed. I heard her screaming in the woods. Not like a wolf, but in her own voice. Screaming and yelling. And not like she was in pain, and I don't think it was anything to do with the Bugs."

"Then what?"

"I couldn't hear everything she said, but I'm pretty sure I heard her say something bad. About something that really scared her, because that's the kind of scream it was. Like someone who's really, really, really, *really* scared out of their mind."

"What did she say?" whispered Milo, grabbing Shark's arm.

He could see his friend's face by the moonlight and Shark looked really scared too.

"I'm pretty sure I heard her say that it was broken."

"Broken? What was broken?"

"That black stone," said Shark quietly. "She said, 'The Heart is broken.' And then after that, all she did was scream."

FROM MILO'S DREAM DIARY

Writing down the story that I dreamed . . .

The boy built a fire in the cold hearth, and its glow was
    warm and kind. He found a blanket folded neatly
    over the back of a sofa, and he shook the moths
    and spider eggs from it and took it to the chair
    closest to the fire.

The boy spent quite a lot ot time wandering up and
    down the aisles of the library selecting books he
    wanted to read, and he brought them back to his
    seat near the warm fireplace. There were books of
    adventure in which someone very like him went to a
    strange school where he learned how to use magic.
    There were books in which children like him walked
    through closets and found themselves in magical
    lands. There were books about a girl who rode a
    whirlwind to a land of witches and flying monkeys,
    and books about falling down a rabbit hole or
    stepping through a mirror. There were books about

being lost on islands where pirates buried their treasure, and about being lost in the woods with only a hatchet. There were books about spaceships and alien worlds. Books about vampires and ghosts and humans built from parts of dead people. There were books about kids who solved crimes and kids who lived in boxcars. And so, so many others.

There were other books, though. Books that he knew had not been written for eyes as young as his. Books about medicine and books about healing—which he discovered were not always the same thing. Books about law and crime, which were sometimes the same. Books about right and wrong, about good and evil, and sometimes one page contradicted another. There were books about heroes and villains, and sometimes it was hard for the boy to tell one from the other.

He read and read and read.

He read everything he could.

Hours passed while the boy sat and read.

Or maybe it was days.

Or maybe it was years.

Part
Three

"All that we see or seem
Is but a dream within a dream."
—EDGAR ALLAN POE

Chapter 32

As soon as Shark told him what he had heard Evangelyne saying, Milo instantly knew it was true. Horribly, frighteningly, terribly true.

The Heart of Darkness was broken.

He could feel his own heart beating the wrong way, and for a minute he closed his eyes to listen, to feel.

The beat was still there, but it was changing. Skipping every now and then. And slowing.

No.

That was wrong.

It wasn't slowing . . . it was emptying.

It was then that he heard a familiar whisper in the very back of his mind. The whisper of an ancient woman who seemed to speak in a voice of dust.

Milo Silk, whispered the Witch of the World, *my heart is broken. The world is broken.*

"No," breathed Milo aloud.

"Hey," said Shark, "I'm pretty sure that's what she said."

Milo ignored him. He tried to search among the swirling shadows inside his head for the witch.

"Where have you *been*?" he demanded, angry and desperate.

"What—?" asked Shark, but Milo shushed him and stepped aside, touching his head with his fingertips.

"You stopped talking for so long," said Milo. "Why'd you leave me? I *needed* you."

Milo, child of the sun, said the witch in a faint voice as if she were very, very far away, *there is not much time and you must listen.*

"I'm listening, I'm *always* listening. Tell me what to do."

Milo was aware that Shark was staring at him like he'd gone crazy. Even though Milo had told Shark about the Witch of the World, his friend had never been with him when the witch spoke. Shark had to feel like Milo did when he'd tried to eavesdrop on Sergeant Ramirez's call—only much stranger.

When the witch spoke once more in Milo's head, her voice was so faint he could hardly hear her. And with a chill, he realized that she was *not* far away . . . but that her voice was weak.

Very weak.

Fading, or perhaps . . .

Milo did not have the courage to finish that thought. Instead he closed his eyes to concentrate on the fragile voice.

You must find Evangelyne Winter, said the whispery voice of the witch. *You must tell her that the only hope lies with the Heir of Gadfellyn Hall.*

Milo gasped. "What? I dream about that place. Have you . . . have you been giving me those dreams?"

The witch did not answer directly, saying, *Not all secrets have been lost. You and your friends must find the Impossible Library.*

"Wait . . . the what—?"

Milo, listen to me. The answers are there if the Heir will help you. You and he share a love of books. That will matter, Milo. Believe me, that will matter.

"But who *is* he?"

He isn't anyone anymore.

"I don't understand."

Shark was looking at him with increasing alarm.

It was a while before the witch spoke again.

Beware the Huntsman, she said weakly. *He is tireless. His hatred and hunger never sleep. He is changing, Milo. He is getting stronger and I am getting weaker. Keep hidden what you stole. Keep safe what he wants.*

"Should I give the crystal egg to the soldiers and—"

No, Milo. If you give it to anyone else, then all is lost. You have taken it and you are responsible for it. Keep it safe.

"And do what with it?"

When the time comes, you will know.

"Oh, come on . . . can't you be a *little* more helpful than that?"

The future is in motion, Milo. Little is clear except what I have said . . . though I am losing my sight, child of the sun.

"What? Why?"

I am wounded, said the witch. *I am dying.*

Milo was stunned. "No . . . no . . . you *can't* die!"

Shark gaped at him, but held his tongue.

Every living thing can die, Milo, said the witch in a voice that was barely there. *Some live out the fullness of their years, while others are taken before their time. The Huntsman and the Swarm have cut me to the very bone.*

"No! I won't let them. I'll stop them. Just tell me what to do."

Find your friends, Milo. Look for the Heir. He is in the Impossible Library. He will offer you your heart's desire. But be careful what you wish for. Oh, be very careful indeed.

"What's that supposed to mean?"

Time is burning like a fuse, Milo Silk. You must hurry . . . hurry . . . hurry. . . .

That last word echoed and then faded into nothing, leaving his head filled only with his own confused and frightened thoughts.

Chapter 33

"**W**hat," said Shark, "was *that* all about?"

Milo held up a hand, needing a minute to try to remember exactly what the witch had told him. He was sure that every detail, even the ones that made no sense, was important. Understanding things takes time. Knowledge often needs to be planted in the mind and given time to sprout roots and grow. Milo knew that for sure.

So Milo told Shark about his conversation with the witch. That also meant explaining about the Heir of Gadfellyn Hall.

"We need to find Evangelyne *right now*."

"Dude, we're about to be evacuated to a safe zone. The soldiers—"

"Don't understand what's really going on."

"Then we need to tell them."

Milo shook his head. "No, I don't think so. Think about it, man, you're having a hard time dealing with this and you saw it firsthand. You want to tell me that a bunch of soldiers are going to just suddenly believe in werewolves and sprites because a couple of kids say they're real?"

"Well, when you put it like that . . . ," said Shark slowly.

"Besides, the witch told me to keep this all secret. She said that I shouldn't give the crystal egg to anyone."

"Did she say why?"

"Not really. She just kind of hinted that it would be bad."

Shark made a face. "You know, I've read a lot of stories about magic and wizards and quests—Percy Jackson and Frodo and Harry Potter and all that—and it seems to me that if spooky characters would just come right out and *say* what's going on, life would be a lot easier for everyone. There ought to be a rule that no one's allowed to be vague."

"I don't think she was being vague on purpose," said Milo. "She's hurt."

"Hurt?"

"Yeah. Maybe dying. And she was scared, Shark. Really scared."

Shark took a deep breath and exhaled slowly. "So . . . what do we do to help her?"

Milo chewed his lip in indecision. "I need you to cover for me. I've got to find Evangelyne and the other Nightsiders. If she's feeling better, then we need to go find this 'heir' and see how he can help."

"Help how? Did she say anything about fixing the Heart thingie?"

"Not straight out, but I'm pretty sure that's what she meant."

"So," said Shark, eyeing him suspiciously, "what do you mean about me 'covering' for you?"

"When Sergeant Ramirez asks where I went, point in the other direction and—"

Shark punched him on the arm. Hard.

"Ow! Hey, what was that for?" cried Milo.

Shark bent forward and jabbed Milo on the chest with a stiff index finger. "For trying to ditch me, bonehead. You think I'm going to let you go running off into the woods without me? If so, you're nuts."

"This isn't about you, Shark. This is something I have to do and—"

Shark punched him again.

"Ow! Stop hitting me."

"I'll knock some sense into you if you don't stop with that junk. *We* have to find Evangelyne and *we* have to find that Hairy Gadfluey kid and *we* have to help save the world because *we* both live here."

Milo rubbed the sore spot on his arm. "It's the 'Heir of Gadfellyn Hall,'" he mumbled.

"I don't care if it's a Hair on Killer's Butt. We do it together or I'll rat you out to Sergeant Ramirez."

As if in agreement—or perhaps because his name had been mentioned—Killer began enthusiastically wagging his tail. Milo wanted to argue, but Shark could be very stubborn when he thought he was right.

"Okay, okay," Milo said reluctantly. "But if you get eaten by a Stinger, it's not my fault."

Shark, despite the harsh realities of what they were about to do and all the countless dangers built into it, grinned like they were about to split a big slice of chocolate cake.

"Hey," said Milo, suddenly looking around, "where's Lizzie? Did she go with Barnaby?"

"I . . . think so?" It came out as a question. "They took everyone else away. I told them I wanted to stay here until you came back, but . . . I guess Lizzie left."

Milo nodded, but Shark's uncertainty about Lizabeth made him feel vaguely uneasy. Lizabeth had become so strange—far stranger than normal—since this morning. Milo was really worried about her.

They glanced about. The soldiers were busily removing all traces of the impromptu camp Shark and the others had made. They moved with silent efficiency, their eyes watchful, guns ready. Sergeant Ramirez came striding past, glanced at them, walked on, stopped, and came back. "Listen, kids, here's the plan. The skimmer's coming back and will take you two to join your friends. If you have any gear around, grab it and be ready to move out. There's a big cypress over there, see it? Leaning out over the water. Go wait there out of sight. The skimmer will pull in there. You guys will get on it. Understood?"

"Sure," said Milo.

"Absolutely," said Shark.

"Good. It's been a rough week for you boys. Now you get to go somewhere safe. We even have a generator and

DVDs. Got a whole bunch of old superhero movies, if you know what they are. Superman, Avengers, like that."

Milo and Shark grinned at him.

The sergeant nodded and went off at a brisk walk, snapping orders to his people. The grins on Milo's and Shark's faces vanished as if switched off. They looked at each other, then at the cypress leaning out over the water. It was right at the edge of the marshy place where Shark said he last saw Evangelyne. Shark picked up Killer and they walked over to the tree, glanced around, ducked under it, gave a final look to see if anyone was watching, then turned and ran as fast as they could into the marsh. They were a mile away before they heard the soft hum of the skimmer, but they didn't even bother to look for it.

They had more important things to do.

Chapter 34

As they moved through the woods, Shark had Milo go through the mental conversation he'd had with the Witch of the World. When Milo was finished, Shark grunted. "Man, you are a freakjob, you know that?"

"Yeah, I know."

Shark paused, then said, "It's kind of cool, though."

"Huh?"

"I mean, dude, you're like a hero on an actual quest."

"I may be a lot of things, but I am not a hero," Milo said flatly. A few days ago the Witch of the World had tried to convince Milo that he was a hero, or at least needed to become one. Even though he'd come up with the plan to recover the Heart of Darkness from the Huntsman, and revised the plan when they wound up aboard the hive ship, Milo did not feel like any kind of hero. Lucky, maybe. Determined, no doubt. And probably more than a little nuts. He was okay with that. Hero? Not so much.

It would be nice, though, to suddenly become one. But he was small, scrawny, young, lonely, heartbroken, and scared. Hardly the qualities of a hero.

"Definitely not," he said, shaking his head.

Shark ignored that and said, "So if you're the hero, I guess that makes me the plucky sidekick." He thought about it. "Not sure 'plucky' is the right word. Not even sure what it means. How about 'intrepid'? Or 'stalwart'?"

"'Stalwart'? What's that mean?" asked Milo. "I keep seeing it in stories."

"Not sure. I think it means 'tough.' Or maybe 'determined.'"

"I'd go for 'annoying sidekick.'"

"Cute."

"'Fart-tastic sidekick,'" suggested Milo.

"I'm going to hurt you."

"'Smelly sidekick' . . ."

"Or," suggested a voice from the shadows, "how about 'Idiot Boy and his *loudmouth* sidekick'?"

They whipped around and saw her standing there. Pale eyes, pale hair, pale skin, looking ghostly in the moonlight.

Evangelyne.

"I thought you boys were supposed to be skilled in woodcraft," she said coldly.

"We were whispering," Shark said defensively.

"A deaf rock troll could hear you half a mile away," she fired back. "You're only lucky that there are no shock-troopers around."

Milo was glad it was dark, because he was dead certain his face was as red as a boiled lobster. Then all thoughts of his own embarrassment vanished as he saw the tear tracks on her cheeks and the wild look in her eyes. Her sarcasm had probably been an attempt to keep herself from going crazy with fear. Milo could certainly understand.

He took a half step forward. "How are you?"

She shrugged, and that simple action made her wince in pain. She stood awkwardly and looked worn out. "Healing," she said, dismissing it. "It's not important. We have matters far more grave than a few scratches."

Her bones had been shattered, and even now, healing through the powers of her lycanthropic nature, she must be in severe pain, but Milo didn't pursue it. Evangelyne was very proud and seemed to need to appear unaffected by things that bothered ordinary mortals. It was all put on, but if it helped her deal, then Milo was okay with it.

"Look," he said, "I know about the Heart of Darkness. I know it's damaged."

"What? How? Who told you?"

Shark very unkindly said, "You screamed it loud enough for even a deaf rock troll to hear."

Evangelyne turned a lethal stare at him, but Shark managed not to wither and die.

"What happened?" asked Milo. "Was it damaged when we crashed?"

"When *you* crashed?" she said in a voice that was nearly a snarl. Making it a clear accusation. "The wall crumpled inward on my legs and . . . well, the Heart was damaged."

"How bad is it?"

Evangelyne considered his question, then with great reluctance reached a trembling hand into the pouch slung from her belt and carefully withdrew an object. She held her hand out and then uncurled her fingers. There on her palm was a jewel, like a multifaceted diamond except that it was as black as midnight sky. Milo had seen the Heart of Darkness before, had held it, had fought alongside Evangelyne and the Orphan Army to recover it from the Huntsman, but now it looked different and wrong to him. Instead of a jewel that felt alive, and that seemed like a window through which he could see an infinity of glittering stars, it was ordinary and small and totally without luster. The moonlight accentuated its damage by highlighting a jagged crack that ran from one side to the other.

"Oh no . . . ," he breathed.

When he glanced up at Evangelyne, he saw that the wild look in her eyes was worse than he'd thought, and he realized that she was on the very edge of total panic. Maybe even despair.

"It's all lost," she whispered. "All lost."

"No," said Milo, "it's—"

She wasn't listening. Evangelyne clutched her hand tightly around the stone and pressed her fist to her chest, directly over her own heart. She kept talking, but Milo was pretty sure her words weren't directed at either him or Shark.

"The Heart is broken. All doors are sealed to us, all pathways blocked. We're lost and the worlds of shadows are closed to us. We called ourselves orphans before, but now we truly are. This is the end of all songs. This is the last page of the ancient story of the Nightsiders. We have survived so much, suffered and sacrificed so much, and it ends here because a stupid little boy did not know how to fly a spaceship. That doesn't even sound like a real story. It can't be real. The Heart of Darkness cannot be lost because of some human boy. It can't have come to me, it can't have been mine to protect, if it all ends so easily and so . . . so . . . so . . ."

As she spoke, her voice rose and rose, going from nervous to shrill to something bordering on hysterical. Milo tried to stop her, calling her name over and over again, but Evangelyne seemed like she was going away from them.

"Dude," breathed Shark. "Do something. She's getting loud. . . ."

Killer began to whine.

". . . and we are all going to die. The Huntsman will destroy the forests and the mountains, and the Swarm will suck away the oceans and turn this world into an empty shell. He'll take all the magic with him and he—*he* will build a new dark heart and *he* will find a new doorway into the shadow worlds and then all will be—"

Milo grabbed her by the shoulders and pulled her close until they were nose to nose. Risking it all, he shouted at her. Loud. Loud enough to break through her hysterical shrieks.

"We can fix it!" he yelled.

Everything stopped.

Her shrill rant, the sounds of insects in the woods, even the sound of Killer's whines. It all stopped.

Until Evangelyne—who still stared with wild eyes—said, "Wh-what?"

Milo took a breath. "We need to find the Heir of Gadfellyn Hall. We need to find some kid who lives in a big old house that has this crazy-huge library. The Witch of the World said that if there's any chance of fixing the Heart of Darkness, he's the only one who'll be able to help us."

Evangelyne kept staring, her fist still pressed tightly to her chest.

"Listen to me," begged Milo. "Can you understand what I'm saying?"

Her lips moved, forming four words that meant nothing to Milo. Not yet. In a ghost of a voice, Evangelyne said, "The Vault of Shadows."

Milo flicked a glance at Shark, who spread his hands in an "I got nothing" gesture.

To Evangelyne, Milo said, "What's the Vault of Shadows?"

"It's a secret room in Gadfellyn Hall that only the Heir of that mansion can enter. It contains an ancient library where the most powerful and dangerous of magical texts are stored. But . . . but . . ."

She stopped and shook her head.

"What?" demanded Milo. "If it's somewhere far away, who cares? We'll manage. Just tell me where this Gadfellyn Hall place is and how we get there."

She blinked the wildness from her eyes and then looked at him as if he were the one who had gone a little crazy. "Gadfellyn Hall," she murmured, "is not even a real place. It hasn't been for a long, long time. The Heir is long dead. Turned to dust and shadows."

"What?" yelled Milo and Shark together.

"It was destroyed more than a century ago. It exists now only as a dream."

"Oh, man," breathed Shark, closing his eyes and banging his head lightly on the closest tree. "This is just great."

Milo released Evangelyne and staggered backward. "No . . . ," he breathed. "No, that can't be. The witch told me to find the Heir of Gadfellyn Hall. She *told* me."

A strange, slow smile blossomed on Evangelyne's face, chasing more of the madness from her eyes. "Then we'll find him."

"But . . . but you just said he was dead."

She looked at him, surprised. "And why should that matter?"

Chapter 35

Milo and Shark stared at her.

They both said, "Um . . . what now?"

Killer whined in confusion.

Evangelyne opened her hand and looked once more at the stone. There was still some wildness in her stare, but far less. She used the fingers of her other hand to brush errant strands of pale hair from her face and to smooth the tear tracks into her skin until there was no trace of them. If she was embarrassed, she didn't show it. Instead she cleared her throat and spoke as if this were any normal conversation on any other day than this one.

"Do you know the story of Gadfellyn Hall?" she asked without taking her eyes from the jewel.

"Only some of it," Milo confessed. "Just what I remember from dreams."

"Tell me."

Milo did. He told about the lonely little boy in the empty house, about how he was lost for a long time—cold and hungry and abandoned—and then found comfort among the endless rows of books in the Impossible Library.

"That's just a story, though," he said. "I think."

"Everything is a story," said Evangelyne. "Even the truth is a story."

"Nope," said Shark, "didn't get that one at all."

She ignored him and kept her eyes on the crystal. "Haven't you ever heard that there is a little bit of truth in every tall tale?"

"Well . . . sure," said Milo.

"Except when there's not," Shark pointed out. "People do sometimes just make stuff up."

"Not this time," Evangelyne said. "There is much more than a 'bit' of truth in this story. This may be our best hope, and I'm a fool for not having thought of it." She blinked once more and then seemed to totally snap out of her distraught state. She looked around, as if surprised to discover that they were standing in the woods under a spill of moonlight.

"You okay?" asked Milo.

"It's just that dealing with a ghost is frightening. They are so devious and strange. And besides, they never do anything for the living without payment."

"What kind of payment?"

"There's no way to know until we confront him. All I know for certain is that ghosts always want something from the living. Always. And no matter what the Heir demands of us to repair the Heart of Darkness, we will have to pay it."

They stood there as the enormity of what they were

about to undertake rose above them like a tidal wave. It made Milo feel very small and very tired. The others looked like they were on the ragged edge too.

"Maybe we should rest up a bit," he suggested.

"No! We're wasting time," she said decisively, sounding very much like herself. "If you truly heard the voice of the witch, Milo, then we have work to do. We have a long journey ahead of us, and it will take us on strange paths."

"No kidding," Shark muttered.

"You don't have to come, boy," snapped Evangelyne.

"Hey, this is weird, so I'm allowed to complain. Doesn't mean that I'm not all in on this." Then he added, *"Girl."*

Evangelyne studied him for a moment, then nodded. "Fair enough. We need Mook. Let me call him."

"How?" asked Shark. "We don't have a radio or—"

She smiled at that, raised her head, and uttered a single piercing, rising cry. The sound of it sent a chill down Milo's back, and the cry was echoed—in a tiny, screechy chorus—by Killer.

It was the plaintive howl of a wolf.

Somehow, hearing that sound and seeing it come from the lips of a normal-looking girl reinforced the strangeness of it. Milo would not have reacted with such unease had she howled like that while in wolf form.

Shark actually *yeeped* again and jumped backward.

Evangelyne ended her call, took a breath, and sighed, her shoulders sagging. But she was nodding to herself.

"What if the Bugs heard that?" whispered Shark, clearly alarmed.

"Then they would think it was a wolf," Evangelyne said simply. "And they would waste a lot of time looking for one. Besides . . . you may know the science of circuits and alien tech, but I know acoustics. Unless I howled more than once, no Bugs would ever be able to find me. Not if I sent it up to the winds in just the right way."

"Okay," said Shark, "that is both really, really cool and really, really creepy."

Evangelyne smiled faintly, but Milo thought she was pleased, perhaps by both parts of Shark's observation.

"Will Mook be able to find us, though?" he asked.

"Of course. Mook is Mook."

"Couldn't be clearer than that," said Shark to himself.

"Others, too," said Evangelyne. "If we're lucky." She did not elaborate.

"I think Oakenayl's around here somewhere," said Milo. "I'm pretty sure I saw him in the clearing where I saw my dad . . . I mean, where I met that holo-man." Milo saw her look of confusion and he quickly filled her in on the new and utterly horrifying tech being used by the Dissosterin.

"That is quite dreadful," she said. "They made you see your dead father?"

"Hey, my dad's not dead," insisted Milo, immediately angry. "The holo-guy was dead. This was some kind of weird mind-projecting. Don't you go saying my dad's dead."

"I'm sorry," she replied quickly. "I only meant that it was a cowardly and appalling thing for them to do."

"Because up till now," said Shark dryly, "they've been so nice and fuzzy with everyone."

"Hey, guys, let's stay on the subject here," snapped Milo. "I saw Oakenayl. Or at least I'm pretty sure I did."

Evangelyne frowned. "I . . . don't think so. He promised me he would protect the Hummingbird Grove."

"The what?"

The wolf girl flushed. "No. Forget I said that."

"Too late," said Shark. "Hummingbird Grove? Let me guess, that's where Halfpint is hiding out until she recovers."

"Halflight," said Evangelyne and Milo at once.

"Right. Whatever. That's where she's at, right? And it's some big secret Nightsider place that we Daytimers aren't allowed to see. Tell me I'm wrong."

"Daylighters," corrected Evangelyne, "and yes. But no, I won't talk about it. Some places are sacred to us— different places for each of the Nightsider clans. The Hummingbird Grove is one of the most sacred places of the fire sprites, and believe me, Oakenayl will defend it to his last leaf, his last drop of sap."

Shark opened his mouth, clearly intending to make a joke, but Milo cut him off. "Okay," he said, pointing the way he'd come, "then who did I see in the woods? It was definitely a tree face. Are you saying there's others like Oakenayl around somewhere?"

"Yeah," agreed Shark, "I thought they all left and that's why there's only a couple of you still here."

Evangelyne shook her head. "No. Most of the Nightsiders departed for the worlds of shadow. My family left. So did Mook's and Oakenayl's. Most of them, anyway. There are always some relatives—cousins, distant uncles and aunts—who linger, but we can't assume they are our friends, just like we can't assume the *Aes Sídhe* are."

"The who?" asked Shark.

"Tell you later," Milo said quickly.

An owl hooted in the night and all three of them— and Killer—paused to listen.

"Burrowing owl," said Shark, and Milo nodded. "A real one, I think."

It was common for Earth Alliance soldiers to use bird calls for communication. So far, at least, the Bugs did not seem able to tell the difference between real bird calls and faked ones. The owl hooted again.

"It's real," agreed Evangelyne, relaxing a fraction. "Nothing to worry about. We're safe."

Milo remembered how real the holo-man had looked and sounded. "Not sure we're ever going to be safe again."

Shark and Evangelyne nodded, accepting that hard truth.

The moon seemed to have chased all the clouds from the sky.

"The night is burning," said Evangelyne as she carefully returned the Heart of Darkness to its pouch. "I don't know how long the jewel can be broken before it's dead."

"Dead?" echoed Milo, and he remembered the feeling he'd had when he first heard about the damage to the stone. It was like listening to the heartbeat of someone fading toward permanent blackness. "What do you mean, dead? Is it actually *alive*?"

She looked at him as if he had just asked something intensely stupid. "Of course it is."

"Ah," said Shark, "just when I thought things couldn't actually get freakier."

"Where exactly are we going?" asked Shark. "I mean, if this Gadfellyn Hall kid is dead, are we supposed to go to a cemetery and dig up his bones? And if so, then what?"

"Don't be absurd."

"I'm not," he said defensively. "I'm just trying to understand the rules here."

Evangelyne thought about that, then nodded. "Fair enough. The boy known as the Heir lived in a mansion—"

"Gadfellyn Hall, got that," said Shark. "Is this an *actual* place? One we can touch?"

"It hides behind a real place. Or maybe it *haunts* a real place. I'm not sure how to explain it. We can find where it was. I saw it once. There is an old antiques store there now, and that is very real. Bricks and stone and glass, if the Bugs haven't destroyed it."

Shark blew out his cheeks. "That's something."

"Where is it?" asked Milo, excited.

She gestured toward the water. "Over there. In New Orleans."

Shark winced. "In New Orleans?"

"Yes."

"The, um, same New Orleans where the Bugs have a hive ship?"

"Yes."

"The hive ship that *we* nearly wrecked? The one we stole the crystal egg from?"

She raised her chin. "Yes."

"In a city crawling with about a million shocktroopers?"

"Yes," she said once more. "Why so many stupid questions? Are you afraid?"

"Oh, I'm way past afraid. I'm all the way over into epic terror," said Shark. "Want to know why? Because I'm not stupid. Oh, and because I'm not actually out of my mind."

"Like I said, you don't have to come."

Shark actually laughed. "Ha! Nice try, but I wouldn't miss this for the world."

Milo didn't look at him, worried he'd see the wild look in his friend's eyes. He wondered if it was in his own. He closed his eyes and rubbed them, then yawned so wide his jaws creaked.

"God, is this still the same day?"

Shark nodded. "And it ain't over yet."

"I'm so tired I could sleep forever." He yawned again. His whole body felt heavy and there was a weird little fluttering feeling inside his chest. Too much adrenaline, too much exertion and fear, not enough rest. Milo knew that he was in absolutely no condition to set out on any kind of journey. Not a hunt, not a rescue mission, not some kind of bizarre heroic quest to find a magic mansion in a city dominated by creatures who wanted to kill him. He could feel Shark and Killer watching him.

He said, "Let's get moving."

FROM MILO'S DREAM DIARY

Writing down the story that I dreamed . . .

The boy read every book in the library. Every single
    one.
And then he read them all again.
When he was done, he went looking for more books.
    A white rabbit hopped out of the shadows, and the
    boy followed it through a doorway behind a doorway
    that was behind another doorway. And there,
    beyond that, were more books.
So many more.
Too many to count.
But not too many to read.
No, not too many for him to read. After all, he had all
    the time in the world.

Chapter 36

Getting from St. Tammany Wildlife Refuge to New Orleans meant going halfway around Lake Pontchartrain. Without a skimmer or the red ship, and with the causeway, Route 11, and Interstate 10 bridges long since destroyed, they were looking at a hike of fifty-five miles. If they pushed on without a break, it would be a minimum of eighteen hours.

That was best-case scenario, and Milo knew better than to plan around things going smoothly. The reality, given what was happening in their lives, was something else entirely. Moving with caution, avoiding Bugs and their hunter-killers, steering clear of well-known Dissosterin patrol zones, and keeping to the cover of the woods and overgrown places would stretch the journey. Milo did the math in his head and predicted that it would take them at least two full days, allowing for a few three-hour breaks for catnaps and food. And the circuitous route would be closer to eighty miles.

He shared this with Shark and Evangelyne, who nodded fatalistically, accepting the hard truth as their only truth.

Two miles into their walk they encountered Mook. The rock boy simply stepped out of the shadows and fell into step with them as if this were all normal. Shark and Milo exchanged a look, shrugged, and kept walking.

They'd covered only four miles before Shark said, "Look, guys, I'm all for plowing ahead and getting as far as we can, but I got to tell you—I'm beat. This has been an insane day. I think we should find a dry spot, eat something, get some sleep, and then start out bright and early."

Evangelyne clearly wanted to argue, but she'd been limping heavily and lagging behind, so she made a sour face and nodded. "Very well. But once we start out tomorrow, we push on as far and fast as we can."

"Absolutely," said Shark, in a way that Milo interpreted as "We'll see how that works."

They found a safe spot, shared dried meat and water. Mook moved off into the darkest shadows to stand guard while Milo brought Shark up to speed on everything that had happened that morning: Queen Mab and her dark faeries, the toadstool ring, and the Huntsman's experimenting with magic. Shark listened in open-mouthed horror and frequently cut looks at Evangelyne, who nodded to indicate Milo was telling the truth.

Finally Shark cut him off. "No, wait, wait . . . you said this was a circle of mushrooms? On that path you took this morning? Oh, man . . . oh, man . . ." Shark's face had gone milk white.

"What is it?" demanded Evangelyne.

"What's wrong?" asked Milo, suddenly very alarmed.

"Lizzie!" said Shark.

"What about her?"

"That's where I found her."

"What are you talking about?"

Shark was blinking rapidly as if he'd been punched. "This morning, I told you she went off into the woods and I found her."

"Sure," agreed Milo, "you said she walked into a tree."

"That's what she said, but that's not what I mean. It's *where* I found her. She was in a clearing, totally unconscious, lying *inside a circle of mushrooms.*"

Evangelyne grabbed his arm with both hands. Her eyes were wild. "What? What did you say?"

"It's the truth. That's where I found her."

"Where? How? Tell me everything."

Shark looked scared. "There's not a lot to tell. I was checking the woods and I saw Lizzie lying beside some of that junk the Bugs dropped and—"

"Which junk?" interrupted Milo.

"The food cart. You must have passed it when you went down to the bayou."

The image of the cart with its demand written in bloodred letters was vivid in Milo's mind.

"Lizzie was there?" he asked weakly.

"Near there, sure. I saw her and at first I thought she was crawling around to try to scavenge something, but then I realized she wasn't moving. I ran over and checked her. She woke up, but she was really out of it and said she must have walked into a tree. She had some bruises on her face and her clothes were all messed up, but she didn't look really hurt. Not hurt hurt, you know? Just dazed."

"What about the toadstools?" urged Evangelyne.

"I didn't notice them at first," explained Shark. "I was focused on Lizzie, you know? It was only after I helped her up that I saw there were a bunch of them growing in a circle. A pretty regular circle, which is kind of weird."

"Tell me about how you felt," snapped Evangelyne. "What did you feel?"

"Was the air really cold?" asked Milo. "Like it was around the pyramid we found? The one the Heart of Darkness was in?"

"No . . . I don't think so," said Shark slowly. "Or at least I didn't notice."

"Was she entirely inside the circle?" asked Evangelyne.

Shark had to think about that. "Not really. Only her legs. The rest of her was outside on the grass. A couple of the mushrooms were smashed like maybe she'd kicked them. Now, come on, Vangie, what's all this mean? Did something happen? Is that why Lizzie's been acting so freaky?"

Evangelyne looked very worried. "Where was this? Exactly, I mean?"

Shark dug a laminated map from a belt pouch and spread it out on the ground. Then he shifted out of the way to allow the bright moonlight to fall on it. Shark and Milo both pointed to the same spot.

"Right there," said Milo.

"Yup," said Shark.

"Goddess of Shadows," breathed Evangelyne. "That is the grove of the shrine."

"What grove of which shrine?" demanded Shark.

"I already told you," she said hollowly. "A thousand years ago there was a medicine woman of great power and knowledge. These swamps and forests were hers, and it is said that she wielded incredible powers. Her magicks ran very deep and strange."

Shark snapped his fingers. "You mentioned her earlier, didn't you? The sweet and salty girl? Something like that?"

"The Daughter of Splinters and Salt," corrected Evangelyne sternly. "And be careful, boy. Mock her at your peril."

"Why? I thought she was dead."

"She is."

"But maybe roaming around the woods and helping us out? Doesn't sound too evil to me."

"Evil?" Evangelyne shook her head, then shrugged. "Actually, I'm not sure. I really don't know much about her other than some old stories from the Chitimacha native peoples who my aunts were friends with. People around here feared her, I can tell you that, but they also honored her with offerings. They built a shrine to her."

"The mushrooms?" asked Shark, confused.

"No. The clearing itself is her shrine."

"It doesn't look like a shrine," said Milo. "It's just a clearing."

"To some people," said Evangelyne, "anything can be sacred. A hill, a tree, a mountain. You don't need to build a temple out of stone to honor the great mysteries. All that is required for a place to be holy is that people believe it to be."

"So this clearing is a shrine," said Shark. "Got it. Weird, but whatever. What does that have to do with a ring of mushrooms? Five minutes ago you guys were telling me about some bizarro faerie queen and Milo seeing the Huntsman. Now we have Native American witches. Should I be taking notes or something? Is there going to be a test?"

Evangelyne gave Shark a tolerant and almost apologetic smile. "Let me explain something to you boys."

"Stop calling us boys," said Milo tiredly.

She continued without commenting on that. "Before we met . . . no, actually before you two found the pyramid, the world of shadows was beyond you. It was always around you, and it was *all* around you. As it always is and always was, but it was hidden. Not exactly invisible, but your eyes could not see it because you were not looking for it. Your world and mine are not really the same. We Nightsiders are able to see more of the shadow world than you, just as you can probably see more of the Daylighter world than we can. Think about the ant and the hawk."

"Huh?" grunted both boys.

"An ant and a hawk may live in the same forest, but are they really part of the same world? They never interact. The ant lives on the ground and does what it does, living out its span without knowing or caring if the hawk exists. It may never even be aware that such a thing as a hawk exists at all, because the hawk's existence isn't any part of the ant's life. The same can be said of the hawk. It has its life, others of its kind, its enemies, its prey, its places of rest, its hunting grounds, and even though it has keen sight, it is never looking at the ant. The ant is not part of its experience."

"Oh," said Shark.

"Yeah," agreed Milo. "So magical stuff's always been around but not in any way that we'd run into? Or see? Is that pretty much it?"

"Well . . . yes, I suppose," agreed Evangelyne. "It wasn't always like this, though. The Nightsiders and Daylighters shared the world at times, even peacefully in places. But mostly both species fought and hunted each other. And killed each other. Then . . . as your kind built cities and moved away from the natural world, the Nightsiders started looking the other way. Niether side needed to see each other, and eventually both sides hardly needed to believe in each other. The Daughter of Splinters and Salt lived in these forests five hundred years before Europeans came here to conquer what they called the New World. Perhaps the native peoples who once lived here had memories of her, but they're gone now. Gone, and with them any human memory of the shrine and of the one it was made to honor."

"Again I ask," said Shark, "what's this have to do with cranky faeries and the Huntsman?"

"I don't know," confessed Evangelyne. "It can't just be a coincidence that Queen Mab grew her toadstool ring at that spot."

"My mom says not to believe too much in coincidences," said Milo.

"Your mother is wise," said Evangelyne. She thought about it in silence for a while. The boys exchanged nervous looks, and the darkened forest seemed to loom huge and black and threatening around them.

Milo broke the silence. "This Daughter of Splinters and Salt was some kind of witch, right?"

"Yes."

"Was she a good witch or a bad one?"

"I told you I don't *know.* Besides, good and evil, right and wrong, what does it matter?" mused the wolf girl. "Those concepts don't apply to everything, Milo. Why even ask?"

"Kind of for the obvious reason," said Shark, jumping in. "If she was a bad witch, then maybe this Queen Mab weirdo is tapping into her negative mojo. If that makes any sense . . ."

"Ah," Evangelyne said, then shook her head. "I don't know the whole story of the Daughter, but I can't believe she would willingly help someone who wanted to destroy the world."

"Does she even have a choice?" asked Milo. "Couldn't the *Aes Sídhe* just kind of hijack the energy of her shrine? Does it work like that?"

From the expression on Evangelyne's face, he knew that his question had hit the bull's-eye. "That's not as stupid a question as you might think," she said.

"Thanks," mumbled Milo. "I think."

"Any place as important as the shrine of the Daughter of Splinters and Salt would have been drenched with magical energy. This energy would have soaked into the ground and infused everything within a certain range. Even now, even with the Heart of Darkness removed from it, the area around the pyramid has power."

"We felt it," said Milo, and Shark grunted agreement.

"Queen Mab may have chosen the Daughter's shrine for exactly the purpose of amplifying her own magic."

"That makes sense, I guess," said Milo. "If she was trying to control the Huntsman, she'd pretty much have to go nuclear with her magic."

"More or less," said Evangelyne, nodding.

"Okay," Shark said, "I'm starting to see how this works. But it doesn't explain anything about what happened to Lizzie. Queen Mab tried to sacrifice Milo, too, right?"

"Possibly," said the wolf girl. "The more I think about it, the more I believe that she was giving him to the Huntsman as a gift of trust."

"A what?"

"In magical bargains there is an exchange of gifts. Things of great value, but not like gold or jewels. Power items. Things that help the other person but also show that you trust them. Look at it like this: If two soldiers from different countries wanted to join up to fight an enemy they both hated, they might shares supplies or even weapons. That would show each of them that they were in it together. Do you get it?"

"I do now," said Shark, "but it's creeping me out. Milo was a gift bag for the Huntsman?"

She gave him a blank look, clearly not understanding the reference.

"Ignore him," Milo said to her. "But tell me this: If the Huntsman materialized inside the faerie circle, wouldn't he be trapped too?"

"No, it wasn't that kind of thing. I believe it was only his aspect you saw, not his actual physical body. It was like one of those holo-things. . . ."

"Hologram," supplied Shark.

"Yes. They were conjuring his aspect so that the queen could share energy with him, and so that he could receive her gift. His real body is wherever he was, probably in a conjuring circle of his own. It would be in a place where he would be heavily protected. But enough of his essence would exist within the queen's circle so that he could take possession of the gift. And, before you ask, it would be actually physical possession. If you had stepped inside the *Aes Sídhe* circle, then the magic would have sent you to the Huntsman. You would have been his."

"Like a teleport," said Shark.

Again, Evangelyne didn't get the reference. Milo explained and she nodded.

"Wait a sec," said Milo. "When we first met, you made some crack about real names and how you Nightsiders could conjure with them."

"So?" she asked. "What of it?"

"Does someone *need* a real name to do that whole conjuring thing?"

"Of course but . . . oh, I see your point."

"I don't," said Shark.

"If Queen Mab was trying to conjure the Huntsman, in flesh or in aspect, she would have to know his real name."

"So?" asked Shark and Milo both.

"Well, if she had discovered it through some magical means and was conjuring him to be her slave, that would be one thing. Bad, but not the worst that could happen. The Huntsman as a slave would be less fearsome."

"Still not following. Less fearsome than what?"

"The Huntsman as an ally," she said. "The other alternative is that he *told* her his name, so that she could not only summon him but cast spells that would give him powers without her turning him into a slave. It means that they would have to trust each other, and that they would be truly working together."

"Oh," said Shark, his face turning a sickly greenish brown. "That's not good."

"She could give him enough power to find us and destroy us. That spell in the faerie ring might have been the queen and the Huntsman trying to recover the crystal egg. No . . . more than that. If Milo had been forced all the way into the ring, Queen Mab could have cast a spell of enslavement on him and then he would have had no choice but to tell her where the Heart of Darkness could be found."

That was a truly terrifying thought, but it was so big, so overwhelmingly enormous, that Milo did not know how to properly think about it. He stared into the middle distance, barely seeing anything but the nightmare images conjured by his imagination.

"But what about Lizzie? Why go after her?" asked Shark, his voice weak and afraid. "I mean, she knows you have the Heart, but we haven't told her or any of the others about that egg. Far as I know it's Milo, you Nightsider guys, and me, right?"

"Right," said Milo. "So the Huntsman couldn't have gotten that information from her. There must have been another reason to try to get her into the faerie ring."

"Yes," agreed Evangelyne.

"What happened to her, though? Why's she so weird?"

Evangelyne shook her head. "I—don't know. I really don't. There are only two possibilities I can think of. One is that Lizabeth never fully entered the circle, not at any point, which means the *Aes Sídhe* weren't able to sacrifice her to the Huntsman. And since you saw her lying across the edge of the toadstool ring, that seems likely. Or the ceremony was interrupted somehow and when the enchantment collapsed, so did she. Magic is very powerful, so she could be feeling some kind of aftereffect. She might shake it off after a few days."

The boys considered this. Shark began nodding, but Milo wasn't so sure. "That doesn't explain how I saw her in the woods when she was already at the bolt-hole. And it doesn't explain that thing with her blouse. I *saw* her cut off a strip to use as a bandage, and that bandage was on Barnaby's wound. You both saw it. How'd she do that and then we all saw her with her blouse all normal? No cut, nothing."

"Don't look at *me*, dude," said Shark. "I gave up trying to understand this a long time ago."

Evangelyne shook her head slowly. "There are many mysteries in this world, Milo. Maybe now it's that you can see things you couldn't before."

"Oh, so I'm the ant who suddenly sees the hawk?"

She shrugged. Then she gave Shark a strange look. "Where is Lizabeth now?"

"She went with the others on the skimmer," said Shark.

"You're sure."

"I—I *think* so," said Shark dubiously. "Everyone else left."

"Did you actually see her get on that boat?"

"No. Not exactly. But where else would she go?"

The wolf girl suddenly tensed and looked into the forest with such intensity that Milo and Shark stared too. But all they saw were shadowy trees and hairy vines.

"Evangelyne," whispered Milo, "what is it? What's wrong?"

Before Evangelyne could answer, there was a sudden crashing sound in the woods, and they wheeled around just in time to see Mook's head come flying like a cannonball toward them.

Chapter 37

They dove for cover as the ball of rock whipped by, trailed by a long bellow.

"*MOOOOOOOOOOOOOOOOOK!*"

The stone boy's head struck a live oak and both tree and rock exploded, showering everyone with debris. One piece struck Shark square in the center of the chest and knocked him flat. Evangelyne tried to dodge the spray, but another piece caught her on the temple. She uttered a sharp, shrill cry of pain and spun away in a clumsy pirouette, then fell hard. Milo jumped for cover and landed badly, the air whooshing from his lungs.

Immediately the brush parted and something massive and monstrous burst out at them. Milo saw what it was and screamed. Because screaming was a very appropriate response on being confronted by the thing that now stood in the clearing.

It was a *Stinger*.

These monsters were nightmare creatures, feared by even the toughest soldiers. The Dissosterin scientists had taken ordinary mastiffs and wolfhounds and then rebuilt their DNA, combining it with that of *Leiurus quinquestriatus*, the aptly named deathstalker scorpion from North Africa and the Middle East. The Stinger's body had all the mass and bulk of the fighting dogs, but it was completely covered in hard, dark arachnid armor, and above its back curled the segmented tail with its deadly barb. Even a few drops of venom could knock out a fully grown man, and a full dose would kill anyone. This twisted science had created a monster more fearsome than any creature that had lived anywhere on earth since the age of dinosaurs. With its speed, armor, and venom, it was more than a match even for a grizzly bear or Siberian tiger.

Milo, Shark, and Evangelyne had fought Stingers only a few days ago, but it had been mostly a matter of more good fortune than skill that had allowed the kids to escape death. Now the three of them sprawled on the ground, shocked into helplessness as more than two hundred pounds of savage fury and alien evil stalked forward.

Shark was on his back, frozen in terror, with the Stinger nearly atop him. Killer stood nearby, tail curled tightly under his body, his teeth bared, ready to defend his master. Pieces of Mook were scattered all around them, and for an instant the Stinger stood there with dark triumph blazing in its eyes. Then the tail rose, the barb quivering and poised to strike.

"No!" screamed Milo as he rolled onto one knee, whipped out his slingshot, and loaded a steel ball bearing into the pouch. "Yo! Bug-Face, over here!"

The Stinger twisted its head sideways and hissed at

him. Mandibles like those of a locust stuck out on either side of the canine snout, and they twitched and snapped as a long line of hot drool dripped onto Shark's chest. The creature began to tense for a leap at Milo, but then suddenly twitched as if stung, turned away from him, and leered hungrily down at Shark.

"No, no, *no!*" Milo yelled, and fired the slingshot. He had no plan other than to distract the creature so that Shark might get up and run for it. Milo had fired his slingshot at other Stingers and accomplished nothing more than irritating the already furious and murderous creatures.

This time, though . . .

The little metal ball whipped through the air faster than any eye could follow, and it struck the Stinger on its armored cheek.

The Stinger instantly recoiled, yelping aloud in pain. Blood burst from a deep crack in the armor. It flowed in lines of red and green—Earth blood and alien blood that shared the same veins but never mingled together.

Milo gaped.

So did Shark.

So did the Stinger.

Terror held as they all reassessed this new factor in the way the world worked. Little boys with slingshots did not cause injuries to alien mutant monster dogs. It didn't work that way.

Except . . .

As if annoyed that his mind was frozen in shock, Milo's hands suddenly jerked into motion and loaded a new ball bearing into the sling. Milo drew and fired even as the Stinger shook off its shock and lunged at him.

This time the metal sphere hit it between the eyes.

It was a dead-solid perfect hit.

Armor burst apart and drops of dark red and vile green seeded the air. The creature staggered backward, more in uncertainty than in actual fear. It roared in real pain, though, and eyed Milo with caution and naked hatred.

Milo reloaded his slingshot and drew it back, but before he could fire, a hissing shape dropped from the closest tree and landed heavily across the shoulders of the Stinger.

"Iskiel!" cried Milo as the salamander whipped its powerful tail around the Stinger's bull neck and buried his long, needle-like fangs into the face wound Milo had inflicted.

The Stinger went insane with pain as Iskiel injected acid venom into the beast. The barb shot forward and stabbed the salamander through the body, but that was the wrong thing to do.

Iskiel exploded.

The Stinger's head and shoulders, and most of its tail, vanished into a fireball that was so hot, the force of it picked Milo up and flung him into the wet bushes. The headless body stood there for a minute, legs quivering, red and green lines running from the horrific wounds. Then its knees buckled and it collapsed.

Shark shrieked and managed to roll aside just in time, though he was bathed in alien blood.

Milo stared, shocked by what had just happened, his slingshot still raised.

Then he heard a branch snap behind him. Shark glanced up, and his eyes filled with new horror just as Milo felt something hot and wrong on the back of his neck.

The fetid breath of another Stinger.

There was no time to run. There was no chance left at all. Milo closed his eyes and winced, bracing against the inevitable jab of the barbed tail.

The moment stretched and stretched, becoming unbearable. He could feel the animal hatred, the intense desire to kill, and yet the monster did not act. Instead he heard it . . . *sniff?*

The creature pressed its snout against his satchel, then pushed on each of the pockets of his vest, sniffing, sniffing.

Which is when Milo understood. It wasn't here to kill him. His friends, almost certainly, but not him. Not yet. It had been dispatched like a hunting dog to find and retrieve the thing that pulsed with unnatural energy deep in Milo's pocket.

The egg.

These Stingers weren't just attack dogs—they were hunters. Retrievers. And now they'd found what their master had sent them to find. Milo heard the inquisitive sniff abruptly pause as the monster bent to the level of his jeans pocket. Then Milo heard a low, mean, terrifying growl of triumph.

The shadow of the Stinger's tail fell over Milo, bathing him in darkness. This was his death. Right now.

"Milo—*move!*" yelled a voice that was harsh and feral. Not Shark's and not Mook's. A girl's voice that was filled with its own canine growl.

Milo instantly flung himself forward as Evangelyne came up off the ground, changing in shape from a dazed girl into something wilder and more primitive. The wolf jumped in and slashed at the Stinger with her fangs.

The Stinger howled in pain, but it shook the wolf off and whipped its tail down again and again. The wolf yelped and dodged, evading the killing blows by mere inches. Then the wolf faked left and darted in right, moving at incredible speed. Her powerful jaws snapped shut, and without even breaking stride the wolf tore the lower leg from the Stinger.

The Stinger had five more, though, so the attack caused pain but little else.

Milo rose to his knees and fired the slingshot, but nothing happened. During his dive to safety he'd lost the ball. He dug frantically in the pouch, found another, loaded it, pulled back, and fired—and very nearly hit Evangelyne as she lunged in under the Stinger's tail to strike again. Her teeth tore at a pincer on the side of the Stinger, snapping it, and at the same second Milo's ball hit the creature in the mouth, snapping off one of the mandibles.

The Stinger howled in greater pain, and now there was a small note of fear in its cry.

We can do this, thought Milo, and somehow just thinking that—as uncertain as his belief truly was—gave him new strength. He fired another ball. And another, each one hitting hard, doing damage, *hurting* this monster.

Shark lumbered heavily to his feet and shoved Milo. "Out of the way!"

As Milo staggered, he saw his friend raise something that gleamed with silver fire and flashed with blue lightning. There was a hot, burning *zap!*

And then the Stinger was falling backward, its head gone as surely and completely as its companion's. Evangelyne staggered sideways, wolf eyes bugged wide in shock.

The Stinger collapsed. Its big scorpion tail rose sharply, trembled, and then flopped down too. The creature lay still.

Everyone—Milo, the wolf, and the little dog—turned toward Shark, who stood with the Dissosterin pulse pistol gripped in two brown hands. He looked every bit as shocked as they did. Then he slowly lowered the gun and stared down at it as if surprised by what he had just done.

No one said a word.

Milo turned at the sound of clacking stones and watched as splinters of stone and small rocks rolled together and began slowly—almost painfully—forming themselves into the lumpy shape of Mook. Those movements were the only movements in the clearing. When Mook was reassembled, he turned and looked at the figures around him. And at the destroyed Stingers. He slowly raised his eyes and stared at Shark.

"Mook?" he asked tentatively.

"Yeah," said Shark a little breathlessly, "I agree. Mook."

"Mook," said Milo, then coughed out a jagged little laugh.

Evangelyne transformed from wolf to girl. She wiped alien blood from her face.

"Mook," she agreed.

Killer looked at everyone else and just barked. His version of "Mook," Milo figured.

Chapter 38

"Is everyone okay?" asked Milo.

"Well," said Shark as he ran a trembling hand over his cornrowed hair, "I'm pretty sure I need to change my underwear."

Evangelyne looked aghast. "Eww. Really?"

"No," he said, giving her a nervous grin. "Close, though."

Mook went over to the first of the dead Stingers, bent stiffly, and picked up a four-inch piece of leathery tail. "Mook."

"Um," began Shark, "Milo, you say that Iskiel kind of *does* this, right? Blows up and comes back? Like a phoenix?"

"No," said Evangelyne, "a phoenix explodes into flame and rises from its own ashes. Iskiel regrows his body from remnants."

"Oh, right, that's totally different. What could I have been thinking?"

Evangelyne gave him a narrow-eyed look, uncertain whether he was messing with her. Milo figured she'd catch on eventually. If Shark couldn't be snarky, *he'd* probably blow up.

"Well," continued Shark, "do we wait for him to re-lizard himself?"

"He's a salamander—an amphibian," Milo corrected, but Shark ignored him.

Mook held up the piece of tail. "Mook," he explained.

"Which means what, now?" asked Shark.

"I think it means we take him with us," said Milo.

The rock boy nodded. "Mook."

"Sure," agreed Shark. "Portable lizard parts."

"Amphibian."

"Shut up, Milo."

"We can't stay here," said Evangelyne. "These Stingers found us too easily. We need a safer place to hide while we rest."

Milo looked around. "I don't suppose you have any magic caves or grottos or anything like that around?"

She shook her head. "These are not my woods. We could be at the doorway to a palace of shadows and I couldn't tell. If we were closer to home, maybe."

"I don't get that," said Milo. "Earlier you seemed to be saying that because I've seen magical things, I can see more of them. The ant and hawk thing. That's why I could see the faerie ring. So why can't you see magical stuff around you?"

She shrugged. "It's complicated." When it was clear that wasn't going to be enough of an answer, Evangelyne explained, "Like all Nightsiders I can see some things that only our eyes can see. I can see the smile of the goddess of the hunt in the face of the moon. I can tell which fire-flies are fireflies and which are fire sprites. I can hear the song of certain trees."

"Um. Oh," said Milo. "That's maybe the coolest thing I ever heard."

"Yeah," said Shark, his mouth and eyes wide. "Definitely the coolest thing."

But the wolf girl looked annoyed. "No, you don't understand. That's like you looking at an oak tree and recognizing it because of its leaves. It's ordinary stuff. These aren't things that can help us right now. We have to get moving. I don't care how tired we are, we have to get away from here. Someone sent these Stingers—either shocktroopers or the Huntsman—and in my experience, hunting dogs seldom run that far from the hunter."

No one could argue with that, so with bodies jittery with adrenaline and limbs heavy with exhaustion, they packed their meager supplies and left the scene of slaughter behind.

Evangelyne became the wolf again and ranged far ahead, picking out a trail. It was soon apparent that there were other hunters in these woods, and the safe passage she picked was neither straight nor fast.

The moon abandoned them, and as it set, the forest was plunged into an almost impenetrable darkness, lit only by starlight. This slowed them even more and turned a difficult hike into one of constant paranoia and danger. Milo and Shark had flashlights, but they dared not use them except to navigate ravines, and even then they had to smother virtually all the light because even a little glow could be seen easily at night. A flashlight could only mean the presence of humans, and nothing hunting in these woods was friendly to their kind.

Several times Milo recoiled from monstrous shapes that seemed to rear up in his path, and each time the shape turned out to be something harmless: a stunted tree draped in Spanish moss, or the rusted hulk of an old piece of farm equipment. Though once he whipped out his slingshot because he was absolutely certain there was a figure pacing them in the woods not thirty feet from the trail.

"What is it?" asked Evangelyne, hurrying to his side.

"I—don't know," he admitted. "I thought I saw someone. A face. Or eyes at least. Watching us."

Without a word Evangelyne became the wolf and ran into the woods, but after five fruitless minutes she returned as a girl, shaking her long pale hair. "No, there's no one there. No Bugs. All I can smell are the trees and flowers."

"I saw a face," said Milo firmly.

"What kind of face?"

He hesitated. "I think it was the same tree face I saw earlier. Like Oakenayl but different. Or at least I think I saw it."

They looked at the woods around them, but there was no sign of anyone or anything.

"Can't you smell whoever's out there?" asked Milo.

Evangelyne looked annoyed. "If it was a person or animal, sure, but if this is a tree spirit of some kind, then no. Remember, they *make* bodies from the woods around them, which means that they smell like the rest of the forest. I can smell the forest and each plant, but there's no way for me to pick out a scent like that."

"Swell," muttered Shark. "Any chance you can find us a place where we can crash for a bit? I'm dead on my feet."

Without another word the girl leaped forward, became the wolf, and vanished into the woods. The boys stood there, exhausted and uncertain.

"Wait," said Shark, "did she go looking or did I make her mad?"

"Don't ask *me*, man," said Milo. "I gave up trying to understand her."

"Mook," agreed Mook.

They waited for ten minutes; then Evangelyne appeared out of the gloom and transformed into girl-shape, looking weary but less stressed. "I think I found a safe place."

"Finally!" cried Shark, who had been having the hardest time. He was strong and quick, but he carried more weight than Milo, and that had worn him ragged.

"You won't like it," said Evangelyne, sounding almost happy.

"I bet I will," said Shark, panting and mopping sweat from his face.

As it turned out, they didn't like it.

The place Evangelyne had found was an old rusted boxcar that was the only car left standing from a freight train that had been derailed by a pulse blast. Hundreds of other cars were twisted and heaped along the tracks, or crammed into the gully that ran beside the rails. More still had gone flying like grenades, lifted by the force of the blasts and thrown into a row of houses that lined the east side of the tracks.

As they approached, a wall of smell hit them like a tidal wave, and the boys reeled back, coughing and covering their eyes. It took Milo a few seconds to understand what it was. More than half the cars had been tankers, and their contents had spilled. Most of the stuff must have been cleaning products, because there was a heavy stench of bleach and other poisonous chemicals. Even now, years after the invasion and with season upon season of rain and evaporation, the stench was nearly unbearable.

"Stingers can't smell us through this," Evangelyne assured everyone, then seemed to be momentarily embarrassed by her choice of a hideout. "It's better inside."

As they climbed inside, Shark unclipped his flashlight and pulled the pulse pistol. He swept with the light and the weapon together, exactly the way the EA soldiers did. The interior was stacked with wooden crates that had long since been broken open, their contents scavenged. Even so, the smell inside the boxcar was far less toxic. Still not pleasant, but Milo was sure the air was breathable. Mook remained outside, once more taking up his guard duty. Milo suspected that the rock boy was embarrassed and probably angry about not having stopped the Stingers, but as Milo's mom once said, "Anyone can be caught off guard. Absolutely anyone."

Milo was certain that Mook would be paying even greater attention than before, and he would likely make someone else—Stinger, hunter-killer, or shocktrooper—pay for what had happened. Because Mook did not need to sleep, eat, or go to the bathroom, his standing guard left the kids free to rest. Shark curled up in one corner, hugged Killer to his chest, and dropped off at once. His deep, regular breaths were calming to Milo's jangled nerves.

Milo dragged one of the empty crates across the floor to create a kind of compartment behind it, and he offered this to Evangelyne.

"It's not much, but it's private," he said.

She glanced at him strangely, as if uncertain how to react to simple courtesy. "Thanks," she mumbled awkwardly, and vanished into the shadows at the back of the boxcar.

Milo trudged over to the corner opposite Shark, made a nest out of old half-rotted packing materials, and tried to sleep. He wanted to and needed to, but sleep didn't come easily. Instead he lay there and thought about Evangelyne. They had known each other for five days now and even though they'd been through so much together, Milo knew they were still mostly strangers. Friendship—even when it's born in battle—takes time and effort to grow. Evangelyne was unlike anyone he'd ever known. Even discounting for the moment that she was a werewolf—which, he had to admit to himself, was hard to forget. But the girl herself was odd. She'd grown up around adults and tried to act like one. She was bossy, cold, abrupt, sarcastic, occasionally mean, weird, vicious, intense, and, on very rare occasions, funny. She was entirely who *she* was, and entirely unlike Milo. He had a few eccentric friends—Barnaby and Lizabeth—but he'd never known anyone quite like Evangelyne.

He wondered if he and she would still be friends when this was over. If it was ever over.

If it even could be over.

He wondered what would happen if the Swarm were somehow defeated and driven away from Earth. Would the Nightsiders fade back into the darkness again, shunning Milo's world? Would the old hostilities and hatreds come back once there was no shared enemy? Or could humans and monsters learn to live together and maybe learn to value the world they'd nearly lost?

Milo didn't know, and he was too mind-weary and bone-weary to figure it out.

Sleep took him when he wasn't looking. He drifted down into shadows.

Down to where his dreams were waiting.

FROM MILO'S DREAM DIARY

I dreamed about my mom and dad.

Mom looked like she did when I last saw her, dressed
    in camos, carrying a gun, seeming hard and angry.
    And a little sad. The way she always is.

Dad looked like he did when I was little, from before
    the war. He wore scruffy jeans and a really ugly
    Christmas sweater with dancing reindeer on it. He
    had on his wire-framed glasses and that goofy grin
    that always made Mom laugh despite herself. He
    had his guitar and the three of us were sitting in
    the living room, by the fireplace, singing Christmas
    songs. Dad sometimes made up his own lyrics.

"Grapenuts roasting by an open fire."

"Jack the Ripper tweaks your nose."

We were laughing so hard we couldn't sing. Dad made
    me snort hot chocolate out my nose.

Funny thing was, Killer was there, and he wasn't our
    dog.

Then the doorbell rang and Dad got up to get it.

It was late and we weren't expecting anyone. I'd
    stopped believing in Santa Claus already, so I
    figured it would be one of the neighbors dressed up
    to play the part. Mom picked up a comforter and
    wrapped it around her 'cause there was a cold wind
    outside and some of it always managed to sneak
    inside. We had an old house and I guess old houses
    are like that.

I heard Dad humming to himself as he opened the door.

"Oh," I heard him say, "I'm glad you're here. Milo's
    been waiting for you."

Mom and I grinned at each other, knowing what was
    coming.

"Don't peek," she told me, and I hid behind my hands.

"Who is it?" I asked, really excited. Happy. Back when
    I could remember what happy felt like. I already
    knew who it was, but asking was part of it. "Who is
    it?"

"Ooohhh, it's someone who really wants to see you,
    Milo," said Dad. "Have you been a good boy, Milo?"

"Yes!" I yelled. "Yes, I've been really good."

"Are you suuuure?" asked Dad, drawing it out. Having
    fun with it.

"I promise, I've been really good."

"Okay, but don't peek now. It'll spoil everything."

"I won't, I promise."

"Good boys don't peek."

I pressed my hands to my face and scrunched up my
    eyes behind them, but I was laughing. So was Mom,
    so was Dad. And so was . . .

That's when I heard him. Not Dad. Him. He said, "Are
    you a good boy, Milo Silk?"

"Yes!" I said.

"I don't know . . . I heard you've been bad this year."

I tried to move my hands, to look, but Mom put her
    hands over mine. "No peeking," she whispered.

"I've been good," I said. "I promise."

"Have you?" asked the voice. "Have you been good?"

"Yes."

He was right behind me by this time, and now it didn't
    feel like I was hiding my eyes so I wouldn't peek. It
    felt more like I was hiding behind my hands. Like I
    didn't want to look.

"Good boys don't steal things that don't belong to
    them," he said. "Do they?"

I heard Killer begin to growl. And another sound. It was
    Mom, and she was crying.

"Daddy," I said, "tell him to go away. Tell him I've
    been good. I didn't steal anything."

"Milo." This time it was Dad's voice. "Milo, look at me."

I wanted to but I didn't want to.

But I did.

I mean . . . of <u>course</u> I did. It was Dad. I had to look.

Even though <u>he</u> was there too.

I didn't take my hands away but kind of lowered my
head and ducked under them, then looked up,
expecting this to be bad.

It wasn't bad.

It was worse.

<u>He</u> stood there, right next to my dad. All of that
muscle, the insect armor, the multifaceted eyes,
the extra arms. The hate.

The Huntsman. In my house. Right there.

Mom was to his left, kneeling on the floor, her hands over
her face like mine had been. I could see blood leaking
out from between her fingers. It ran along her hands
and wrists and dripped onto the white carpet.

And Dad . . .

God.

Dad was on the other side of the Huntsman.

Dad.

Dad.

What was supposed to be Dad.

Same jeans and stupid shirt. Same hair and bedroom
slippers. But there were wires running everywhere,

poked through ragged holes in his sweater, sticking right into his skin, coiled around his wrists, jabbed through his cheeks, threaded between his teeth.

That wasn't the worst of it, though.

His glasses were gone.

So were his eyes.

Instead he had blue jewels, like the lenses of the pulse pistols.

He wasn't a holo-man. He was something else, something worse. Something I didn't know the word for and didn't want to know. Couldn't know. Never ever wanted to know.

The Huntsman stood next to him and his mouth mandibles clicked and clacked.

"I want what you stole," he said.

And I screamed myself awake.

Chapter 39

A hand clamped over his mouth and a voice whispered in his ear.

"Dude—shut up!"

Milo stopped screaming. Right there, no arguments. As terrifying as the dream had been, this was the real world and it was much, much scarier.

Shark knelt beside Milo, his bulky frame outlined by the pale light of early dawn. His face was puffy from sleep but his eyes were sharp, alert, and annoyed. Another figure stood behind him looking equally disheveled and angry. Evangelyne.

Milo pushed Shark's hand away and gasped, "It's okay, I'm all right."

Shark sat back on his heels, then heaved out a sigh. "Another one of your weirdo dreams?"

"Yeah."

"Looked like you weren't having any fun."

"Not much." Milo sat up and rubbed his eyes.

"You shouldn't scream when we're being chased," scolded Evangelyne.

"No kidding," Milo muttered. "What time is it?"

"Late. The sun's been up for five whole minutes," she snapped. "We need to go."

Before Milo could reply, Evangelyne yanked open the boxcar door. She glanced over her shoulder at them. "I'll scout the area. Be ready when I get back."

"Hey, Vangie," called Shark.

"What?" she demanded.

"While you're out there . . . see if you can find some manners and maybe a sense of humor."

Milo tensed, expecting a brand-new war to explode right there. But Evangelyne surprised him by grinning. "Maybe tomorrow morning I'll let the wolf wake you up."

Then she transformed and leaped into the slanting morning light.

Shark swallowed hard and looked at Milo. "She was joking, right?"

Milo couldn't answer. He was too busy laughing.

"You're as weird as her," groused Shark. He offered a hand and pulled him to his feet. "The Mookster found us some nuts and berries and stuff. Not exactly pancakes and scrambled eggs, but it beats starving. C'mon, we need to hustle. You pack up your stuff, I'm going outside for a pee."

When he was alone, Milo took a minute to try to remember the dream, horrible as it was, and write it into his diary. Mostly he wanted to forget it because it made him sick to think what the Bugs could have done to his dad in all this time. Killed him and used his body for raw materials to make more Bugs. That was enough to drive Milo completely crazy. Or maybe his dad was working in one of the mines the Bugs had dug around the world, laboring with millions of other humans to tear key minerals out of the earth so the Bugs could build new ships and repair their old ones. Or had they really turned him into some kind of cyborg slave? There had been rumors of that sort of thing for years, though no one in the EA had confirmed it. The Huntsman was a cyborg, of course, but not a slave. He was a cyborg general, and he was part Dissosterin now as well.

Too many of Milo's dreams had held bits of prophecy, so he knew he couldn't simply dismiss this one, much as he wanted to. If there was a chance that even one secret hid among those nightmare images, he had to find the courage to hunt for it.

He heard a sound behind him as the boxcar door slid open, and then Shark said, "Say, Milo? There's, um, a *tree* here to see you."

Chapter 40

Milo turned, expecting it to be Oakenayl, and he had some pretty hard things to say to the oak boy. Most of which were phrases he'd have gotten in deep, deep trouble for saying around his mom.

It wasn't Oakenayl . . .

. . . but it was a face Milo recognized.

A tree face. A woodland spirit face. One that Milo had twice glimpsed briefly in the forest on this side of Lake Pontchartrain. Now, in the clear glow of morning light, Milo could see that it definitely wasn't the oak boy. The face wasn't covered in oak bark but was instead the more graceful bark of a weeping willow, and it was framed by long tendrils of soft green leaves. And it wasn't a boy. Even though it was impossible to tell gender by the strong body of living wood, the face had a decidedly feminine cast. Cleaner lines, more delicate shoulders, larger and more expressive eyes, and a general air of grace that Oakenayl never displayed. The eyes were filled with sadness, and there were worry lines etched around the corners of her mouth.

"I ran into her while I was out doing my business,"

VAULT OF SHADOWS

said Shark. "And yes, I'm traumatized, thanks for asking."

"I was not spying on you," said the tree girl quickly. "I am here seeking the keeper of the sacred jewel."

"Wh-who *are* you?" stammered Milo.

She narrowed her eyes as she studied him. "You are a Daylighter."

"Pretty much, yeah."

"Where is the werewolf?"

"Actually," said Shark casually, "she's right behind you."

The tree girl spun and Milo hurried out of the boxcar. Evangelyne was crouched down, eyes blazing and teeth bared. Beside her was Mook, who had his rocky fists balled. Shark, with a snarling Killer beside him, stepped a few paces back and raised his pulse pistol.

"No!" cried the stranger, raising her hands. "I am a friend and I come only in peace. I will tell you my name if you swear not to conjure with it."

"Conjure?" echoed Shark. "Geez."

"We're not much for conjuring," Milo assured her.

"Mook," said Mook.

The wolf growled and then shape-shifted to human form. "By the Goddess of Shadows we swear not to conjure with your name," she said tersely. "But play false with us and we will roast our breakfast on a fire made from your bones."

"Harsh," murmured Shark, though there was admiration in his eyes.

309

The tree girl straightened and with great dignity said, "I am Fenwillow Longleaf of the House of Salix. This forest is my home."

"Milo," said Evangelyne, "is this the spirit you told me about? The one you saw?"

"I think so," said Milo. "Yes. Yes, I'm pretty sure."

The wolf girl took a threatening step toward Fenwillow. "Why are you spying on us? Speak truth. Lie, and I will know."

Fenwillow's movements were quick and nervous, and she flinched back from Evangelyne until she bumped up against the boxcar. The leaves that formed her long hair were clearly from a weeping willow, but her skin was much smoother, and Milo thought that maybe she was very young. A sapling, if that word applied to tree spirits, and her eyes were almond-shaped and slanted, giving her a vaguely Asian look.

"I will tell you true," she said. "I also swear by the Goddess of Shadows."

Evangelyne relaxed by one sliver of a degree. Speaking with even more than her usual formality, she said, "Then speak. Be quick, girl, for we are in a hurry and time is not ours to waste. Why have you been following us and why do you ask about the dark heart?"

"There have been whispers through the leaves and vines," said Fenwillow. "Evil roams the land."

Shark made a sour face. "Really? No kidding."

"We know that," snapped Evangelyne, pointing

sharply in the direction of New Orleans. "The world is being torn apart by an alien swarm."

"No, that's not what I meant," said Fenwillow quickly. "I speak of an evil that is of *this* world. Or . . . mostly of this world."

Evangelyne shot a brief look at Milo. He gave her a tiny nod in return, knowing what was coming.

"The *Aes Sídhe* have wearied of their own world and wish to return to ours. Not as allies in this war but as conquerors," said Fenwillow. "Queen Mab has summoned her greatest sorcerers and seeks to bargain with a demon the like of which I have never seen. He is half man and half monster, but he is not a Nightsider. Nor a Daylighter, either. He is a necromancer and he is the most savage and horrible thing I have ever seen."

"He is called the Huntsman," said Evangelyne. "We already know of him. And we think that Queen Mab is either deceiving him or working out a deal of some kind."

Fenwillow said, "Oh, a deal, to be certain, and a black one. They have been speaking to each other through faerie rings. They have been trying to devise a spell powerful enough to tear open the way from the realm of the *Aes Sídhe* to our world."

"You're sure they're working together?" asked Milo.

"I'm positive," she said, then added, "though I don't know if it started out that way. An owl who is a friend of mine said that at first they fought with one another, each struggling to dominate, but then this Huntsman offered the queen a deal. He promised to free her and give this world to her in exchange for her using her faerie charms to lure a perfect sacrifice into the toadstool ring."

"They tried and failed," said Evangelyne, nodding to Milo. "This Daylighter boy was saved before the spell could be completed. And there was another attempt that failed too. A girl, another Daylighter, was nearly lost to the queen and this Huntsman, but somehow survived."

"I'm glad to hear that your friends survived," said Fenwillow. "Not everyone has been so lucky. This necromancer has already spilled blood in failed attempts to gain power and break open the door to Queen Mab's realm. And I fear he will spill more unless he destroys himself in the process."

"That'd be great," said Shark. "What are the odds on that?"

It was Evangelyne who answered. "A magic circle can be used as a channel to allow ancient and very dark energies to flow into one's own body. To fail even once is to die and be utterly destroyed. But to try and survive? Every time the Huntsman survives a conjuration, he becomes more powerful because he allows more dark energy into his soul."

"I really, really, really, *really* don't like the sound of that," complained Shark, and Milo agreed.

"This Huntsman must be mad, for only a madman would ever attempt that process," said Fenwillow.

Evangelyne nodded. "We are not talking about the life

energies of this world, or the natural forces that run like breath and blood through the planet. No, such a spell can tap into the force of pure, destructive chaos."

"Wouldn't that destroy the Huntsman?" asked Milo hopefully.

Evangelyne chewed her lip. "Only if he makes a mistake. He is no magician, no sorcerer. His weapons are science. He *wants* to use magic, but without the Heart of Darkness he cannot possess that power. Performing spells of this kind *should* tear him apart. They are not meant for mortals, and the Huntsman is no Nightsider."

Fenwillow interrupted her. "He could survive the rituals if he makes the right kind of sacrifice."

"Whoa," said Shark, "what does that mean?"

"It means that if the Huntsman makes an acceptable offering, the darkest of ancient powers will protect and reward him."

"Yeah, but what kind of sacrifice are we talking about?"

"An innocent soul," said Fenwillow. "A pure soul. They are rare and precious, and the act of destroying one releases vast and terrible powers."

"What would they have done to Milo if he hadn't gotten out of there?" asked Shark.

Fenwillow glanced at Evangelyne. "For a human sacrifice? Would he have used a firedirk?"

Evangelyne shivered. "Almost certainly. Making one is not easy, but Queen Mab could have taught the Huntsman how to do it."

"Firedirk?" asked Shark. "Ugh . . . that sounds nasty. What is it?"

"A firedirk is the weapon of a necromancer. It allows him to drink the life energy from his victims. When used as a sacrificial blade, it kindles the fire of true magic inside a human heart. Especially in a dark, dark heart. With such a weapon, a necromancer can speak to the dead and force them to betray any secret they possess, and it can give the user a measure of control over the slain."

"Geeeeez," breathed Milo, his pulse quickening. "Do you think that's how he controls the holo-men?"

"I don't know much about science," she admitted, "but if he is using the dead as his minions, then yes. Nothing else makes sense. The firedirk would give him the power to force the dead to obey him, to share their secrets, and to betray their friends."

"The one I met wasn't anyone I knew," said Milo. "But he looked like my dad."

"I know, so this is something new. Something the Huntsman and Queen Mab must be creating together. A new form of magic that blends sorcery with science. The firedirk must be more than a sacrificial knife; perhaps it allows them to share their energies. It is a terrible weapon of evil."

"What's it look like?" asked Shark.

"A firedirk is a long-bladed thrusting dagger," explained the wolf girl. "In certain kinds of magic spells, the steel of the blade is transformed into a special kind of fire that burns as cold as ice. Although the blade looks like it is composed only of fire, it cuts like ordinary steel. However, the magical fire is there to sever the connection between the victim's body and their soul. The firedirk transfers that energy into the person who wields it, increasing their magical powers. It is one of the easiest ways for someone to gain such power, but it is the very darkest of magic. Among my people, anyone committing such a sinful act would be destroyed."

They all stared at each other, shocked and horrified by all of this. Milo tried to wrap his mind around the idea of such a blade stabbing into him and draining his life away.

Suddenly Evangelyne cried out. "By the Goddess! Now I understand. Now it all makes sense."

"What does?" asked Shark.

"What blind fools we've been. The faerie rings should have told me, but I was too upset about the Heart to listen. Goddess of the Shadows, I'm an idiot."

"Stop ranting and tell me what's going on," ordered Milo.

"The faerie rings," repeated Evangelyne. "When you told me about what happened to you, Milo, I thought it was an attempt by Queen Mab to enslave the Huntsman in the way a wizard might enslave a demon, but that's not it at all. We're looking at this the wrong way around. I think this is all about the Huntsman. I think *he* was the one who reached out and offered a deal, to Queen Mab. But he's so sly, so cunning, and he's so careful. We

know this about him. If he has become a necromancer, then he would never risk releasing the *Aes Sídhe* unless he could control them, and he couldn't control them unless he already possessed magical powers."

"Right," said Milo, "but he tried that twice and failed twice."

She looked at him with deep sadness in her eyes. "Did he, Milo?"

"Of course. Killer saved me, and Lizzie never went all the way into the circle."

"Milo, don't you see it? Queen Mab tried to lure you inside the circle, probably as an offering to the necromancer who promised to help free her. I don't think they ever planned to kill you. Did you see a flaming knife in the Huntsman's hand as he materialized?"

"No."

"Then I'm right, and a dark night is falling for all of us."

"What are you taking about? He *didn't* stab me. The spell was broken. They failed."

She shook her pale hair, and beside her Fenwillow looked terrified.

Evangelyne touched Milo's arm. "When you saw Lizabeth in the woods, you said there was a cut on her blouse. Show me where."

Fear was beginning to claw at the inside of Milo's chest. He touched his chest, just off center of his sternum. "Right here."

"And she was covered in blood?"

"Well, I thought so, but there was no mark. Not even a scratch. She showed me."

"There wouldn't be, would there?" whispered Evangelyne. She closed her eyes and bowed her head, and two tears broke and fell down her cheeks. Beside her, Fenwillow also hung her head and wept tears of sap.

"Oh, Milo," said the wolf girl, "I am sorry. I am so sorry for not having seen it. For not having known. For being so wrapped up in my own problems that I did not see."

"See *what*?" yelled Milo, though he realized that he already knew.

Shark got it too, and he put his face in his hands. "No, no, no, no . . ." His big body began to shudder with heavy, silent, wretched tears.

"That is where a necromancer would stab with a firedirk. Right there at an angle so as to pierce the heart."

"No!" growled Milo. "No way. I saw her. I talked to her."

"So did Shark at the bolt-hole, and no one can be in two places at the same time, Milo," whispered Evangelyne. "Only spirits can do that." She paused as a sob broke in her chest. "Only *ghosts* have that power."

Milo suddenly felt as if the ground were falling away beneath his feet. He staggered sideways and reached out for the edge of the train car doorway. Missed it. Grabbed nothing.

Fell.

Fell hard.

Fell into a heap.

He tried to yell the word "no." To shout it loud enough to make the world change back, to fix the hole that was now burned in Milo's life. A hole shaped like a little girl with wild hair. A girl only two years younger than himself. A girl who was a bit mad and a little strange and entirely innocent.

He tried to say "No!"

Instead he said her name. Or rather, he screamed it.

"Lizabeth!"

Chapter 41

They sat on broken crates inside the boxcar. They all knew that time was flying past them, but for now they could not move. Fenwillow, who could not bend enough to sit, stood against the wall near the door. For a long while no one said anything; then Shark begged them to explain it all. He kept crying and Killer leaned against him, whining piteously.

"I *saw* her," Milo kept saying over and over as he shook his head.

"You saw her ghost," said Evangelyne. "And it's very likely you saw the ghost of the Daughter of Splinters and Salt. If Lizabeth died on her shrine, then their spirits would have become mixed. Entangled. I've read about such things. The Daughter has been dead so long, she has no body left and probably no memory of it. That . . . or maybe she took Lizabeth's form so that she could fool you."

"Why?" asked Shark. "Why would she do that?"

"I can only guess. Queen Mab and the Huntsman have done something very wicked, something truly evil. Sacrificing an innocent on a sacred spot. That is a terrible sin and it would offend the ghost of the witch. She would want revenge, but she would also need to know what was happening. Appearing as Lizabeth was probably her way of trying to understand us."

"So . . . you're saying that wasn't Lizzie at all?" asked Shark. He pawed at the tears in his eyes.

Evangelyne chewed her lip. "I really don't know. The power of that shrine might have brought Lizabeth's spirit back too. We may have seen both of them at different times. And it's even possible they are sharing the same spirit body. They may have become fused together." She shuddered. "This is ghost magic and it is beyond my understanding. All I know is that this foul murder has given power to the queen and the Huntsman. There is so much old power there. It must have been like . . . like . . . What do you Daylighters call it when you use one car to energize another one?"

"A jump start," said Milo in an empty voice. "Is that all Lizzie was? A bit of juice for that . . . that . . ."

He stopped because he didn't know any word bad enough to describe the Huntsman. He wanted to throw up, but he kept it down, and kept his fury inside. It burned him, though. He could feel it leaving scars on the walls of his soul.

"Milo," said Evangelyne, "I know it hurts to hear this, but . . . yes. I think that's exactly why they picked her. Her innocence was a great source of power, but the ritual must have awakened the Daughter of Splinters and Salt."

Milo dragged his arm across his eyes. "If they got

power from . . . from . . ." He couldn't say the word. He shook his head angrily. "If they got so much power, then does that mean the queen is free?"

Evangelyne shook her head. "We'd know it if she was. No, I think something must have happened during the sacrifice. My guess—and it is only a guess—is that the Daughter somehow interfered with the transfer of magical power. It is, after all, her shrine. I think the queen and the Huntsman will need to try it again, as they tried when they almost lured you, Milo, into the ring. They'll keep trying until they murder another innocent, but next time they won't risk doing it on a sacred shrine. That was a risk that might have made them invincible, but it backfired."

"Backfired?" cried Milo. "Lizabeth is *dead*!"

"I know, Milo . . . and I'm so sorry."

"Where is she?" asked Shark. "Her body, I mean?"

Fenwillow spread her leafy hands. "I'm sorry, but I don't know."

"I don't know either," said Evangelyne. "Buried, maybe. Or taken by the Huntsman. All any of us ever saw yesterday was her ghost."

"It doesn't make sense. She wasn't all the way inside the faerie ring. I saw her, I should know."

Evangelyne shook her head. "You said that her legs were inside and the rest of her was outside. If she was inside the ring when she died, she would have fallen down across the arc of the ring. Her legs would be closest to where she stood."

Shark put his head between his hands, and his sobs filled the train car. Grief was like a whip that kept hitting them and hitting them. Mook laid a heavy hand on Shark's shoulder.

"Mook," he said softly.

"Maybe Lizzie's not dead," said Shark, his voice thick and his face streaked with tears. "I touched her. She was *real*. She wasn't a ghost."

"Have you ever touched a ghost before?" asked Evangelyne.

"Well . . . no . . ."

"Then how would you know what one feels like?"

"But you're talking *ghosts*. You can't touch them. It'd be like trying to grab smoke."

The wolf girl shook her head. "It doesn't work like that, Shark. There are as many kinds of ghosts and spirits as there are sprites. Thousands of them. Even we Nightsiders don't know all of them."

"You don't?" asked Milo, surprised. "But I figured they were part of your world."

"Why would they be?" asked Fenwillow. "We are alive. Ours is the world of living things, even if we are strange to you Daylighters. Ghosts are not part of our world any more than they are part of yours."

To Evangelyne Milo said, "But you said the Heir of Gadfellyn Hall was a ghost."

"And so he is," she replied, "but I never said he was a Nightsider. He is what he is, and no one I know can claim to understand what that means. He's a dream, but one that lingers in the world. And he has dreamed so long and with such power that even his home, Gadfellyn Hall, lingers on as a kind of ghost. When we go there, we will all be stepping into the unknown. Mook and I will be as much strangers there as you and Shark."

Fenwillow stared at her. "Gadfellyn Hall? You're going there? By the Goddess, *why*?"

Milo saw that Evangelyne was uncertain whether to decide whether to trust this young tree spirit, but in the end she nodded. The wolf girl carefully removed the Heart of Darkness from its pouch and extended her palm to show it to Fenwillow. The willow girl's eyes flew wide and she covered her mouth with two leafy hands.

"Goddess of Shadows! The rumors are true. You *do* have it." She began to reach out to touch it, then instantly thought better and snatched her hand back. "I have heard the bats whisper about it. They tell of a great battle with this Huntsman and how many of them died to help you recover it. But you know bats gossip and brag. . . . I hardly believed it until now."

"It's real," said Evangelyne, "but it is also damaged. See? There is a crack through its heart, and we are all now in grave danger."

Milo thought Fenwillow would faint, and once more there were sappy tears glistening on her cheeks. "Roots of Heaven!" she cried. "Tell me we are not all lost."

"Shhh," soothed Evangelyne, closing her hand around

the stone. "Shhhh, now. We have yet a chance of repairing it."

Fenwillow straightened, and snapped her twiggy fingers. "That's why you're going to see the Heir. You believe the old stories are true."

"I *hope* they're true."

"What stories?" asked Milo. His heart was so heavy that he wanted to leave and get lost in the woods, to give it all up. To walk and walk until he could forget, but he knew that there was no place on any map where memories and the truth could not find you. It was hateful. The world was so cruel, so cold. Lizabeth was the gentlest and most innocent person he'd ever known, and the idea that it was those qualities that had urged the Huntsman to sacrifice her was beyond imagining. It was beyond sick. So despite his despair, he made himself remain a part of this conversation, this hunt. "What are you talking about?"

Fenwillow turned to him. "The Heir lives in a house with—"

"—a great big library," finished Milo irritably. "The Impossible Library. Yeah, yeah, I know. What about it?"

When the willow girl looked surprised, Evangelyne quickly said, "Milo has prophetic dreams sometimes."

"Oh. That makes sense, then."

Does it? wondered Milo. *Feel free to explain that to me.* But he didn't say this aloud, and instead gestured for Fenwillow to continue.

"They say that the Impossible Library is where all books go when they die. Books that have been burned by people afraid of new thoughts or old wisdom. Books from cultures that have passed away into history, even into legend. Books that have been forgotten. The scrolls from the Library of Alexandria, which was burned by the Romans. The books from the Abbasid Library of Baghdad, which was destroyed by the Mongols. The lost writings of Archimedes, Plato, Agatharchides, Ctesias, Lucan, Protagoras, Hua Tuo, Tertullian; the *Necronomicon*; the *Badianus* manuscript, an ancient Aztec medical codex; *Cardenio*, a lost play by William Shakespeare; Homer's *Margites*; the missing volumes of Charles Dickens and Dr. Seuss; and thousands of others. And stories . . . so many stories written in journals and diaries and never shared."

She paused, and her bark darkened as she became flushed with excitement. When she realized that everyone was staring at her, she turned an even darker shade. "Oh, I'm sorry. I rattle on, don't I? I—I love books. When I read them, I can hear the voices of the trees that were turned into book paper. When a tree becomes a book, it doesn't die. Stories are immortal. They exist—like ghosts, I suppose—in the care of him who lives in that library."

"Okay," said Milo grudgingly, "that's kind of cool. But how's that help us?"

"Reading all those books and learning all those secrets," continued Fenwillow, "has filled the Heir with the knowledge of the ages. Of all the ages. And because he is ageless and because all the great sorcerers and witches left our world to escape the Swarm, the Heir is thought by many to be the last true doctor of magic."

"Ah," said Milo.

Even Shark looked interested now, and he pawed his face clear of tears. "I get it now."

"Getting to Gadfellyn Hall will be so difficult," warned Fenwillow. "New Orleans belongs to the Swarm. The hive ship and all those 'troopers are there. And the Huntsman is either in league with Queen Mab or he's stolen her secrets to discover the magic himself. Either way, he will be more powerful than he was when you fought him before. How can you even hope to succeed? And what assurance do you have that the Heir will even help you? How would you *pay* him? Ghosts always demand payment, but discovering what it is they value is so difficult." Her voice was rising to a hysterical note.

"Hey, hey, it's okay," said Milo. Mook reached out and patted the tree spirit's gnarled shoulder, offering rough comfort. Fenwillow looked deeply distressed.

"This is crazy," said Shark. "Sounds like it's impossible, but man oh man, I can't stand the thought of the Huntsman beating us. Not after everything that's happened."

Milo stood up, walked over to the door, and looked out at the morning sun, wondering how it could have so little regard as to shine while someone like Lizabeth lay dead somewhere. It wasn't right. The skies should turn cloudy and the world should weep for her. Even then there wouldn't be enough tears.

"When we started this," he said without turning, "it was all about saving the world and stopping the Huntsman. Just yesterday morning it was all about that. Us and him. I could understand that. It was simple, like playing chess."

No one spoke.

"Now everything's different. The more I find out about the way the world really is, the bigger, uglier, and meaner it gets. Most of my friends are dead or hurt. My dad's missing; my mom's somewhere, maybe dead. And now Lizzie."

Outside the birds sang in the trees, and life—despite everything—moved forward. Still no one spoke.

"How are we going to do this? Get to New Orleans, slip past the Bugs, find this Heir kid, figure out how to pay him, get him to fix the Heart? I have no idea. Maybe we won't. Maybe we'll all die trying."

Now he turned, very slowly, and every eye was on him.

"But I can tell you guys something, and you can believe it or not," he said. "I'm going to kill the Huntsman. I'm going to make him pay for what he did. You hear me? I'm going to make him pay."

Without saying a word, Evangelyne stood and walked over to him. She stopped and stared deep into his eyes. Then she wrapped her arms around him and hugged him. A half second later Shark gathered them both in a bear hug, and then two huge rocky arms engulfed them all. Milo felt a thin, leafy hand on his shoulder, and a small furry body squeezed in between his ankles.

No one said a word.

No one had to.

Chapter 42

They gathered their belongings and stepped down from the boxcar. Fenwillow stood to one side, looking awkward and nervous.

"I will come with you, if you ask," she said to Evangelyne. "I would give every leaf and every splinter of my heartwood to help you restore what has been damaged."

"No," said the wolf girl, "but there is something you *can* do for us."

"Anything! I will jump into fire if you need that of me."

Evangelyne smiled thinly. "I will not ask that, but what I need won't be easy. Tell me, do you know Oakenayl, son of Ghillie Due?"

Fenwillow went pale and took a half step back. Then she cleared her throat. "Of course. I mean, I don't *know* him, but I know *of* him."

Milo caught something in her tone of voice. She was being defensive and trying to hide it. "Let me guess," he said. "You don't like him either, right? What a surprise."

"He has a certain reputation," she said, blushing

329

again. "Oakenayl believes in the old ways and he has a well-known, um . . . *dislike* . . . of Daylighters. Actually, he seems to have a dislike of most things, even other kinds of trees. He is a difficult person to admire."

Milo almost smiled. So Oakenayl was a jerk even to the world of supernatural creatures. It figured.

"Oakenayl can be intense," admitted Evangelyne carefully, "but he is no friend to the Huntsman. The shocktroopers have burned whole forests, and many of Oakenayl's family were killed."

"How may I help?" asked the willow girl.

"Find him," said Evangelyne. "He's in the Hummingbird Grove. Do you know where that is? Good. Go and tell him what's happened. Tell him everything. He may be difficult, but he can be trusted."

"Trusted to do what?" asked Milo.

"To do what has to be done," said Evangelyne, and beyond that she would not explain.

The willow girl fluttered her branches in what Milo figured was some kind of bow or salute. Then she turned and hurried into the forest with surprising speed and grace. Despite the heavy ache in his heart, Milo decided that he liked the little tree spirit. In some way she almost reminded him of Lizabeth.

And in thinking that, both anger and urgency rose up in his chest.

"We're wasting time," he said. "Let's get going."

No one argued.

Within ten minutes they were leaving the train tracks and all that stink behind. Milo had stuffed his pockets with pecans, bull grapes, hackberries, and red mulberries, and he shared these as they walked. Between quick meals they all kept a small piece of tough, chewy root in their mouths so saliva would keep their throats lubricated. That made it easier to breathe. Miles fell away, and soon they got into a rhythm of walking, jogging, walking, resting. The scout pace of alternating between light running and walking kept their muscles loose and devoured the distance. Twice they passed small towns that had been thoroughly destroyed by the Bugs. Dead cars littered the broken streets and weeds choked everything. Some areas were flooded from the heavy rains, and they had to skirt these for fear of gators and other water creatures.

They made sure to stick to the shadows as much as possible. Because nature here in Louisiana had gone wild once people stopped tending to it, there was plenty of useful foliage. Birds sang in the trees, which Milo took as a good sign; birds generally stopped singing when Bugs were around, and they even hushed when the mechanical hunter-killers came prowling. Not that the travelers took the birdsong as an invitation to slack off on caution. They absolutely did not.

Most of the time Evangelyne stayed in wolfshape, and each time she changed back, Milo noticed that more of her injuries were healed. When he asked her why she didn't just remain a wolf until she was entirely healed, she said, "It's not as simple as that. The longer I'm a wolf, the more I risk forgetting I'm a girl."

"Really?"

"Oh yes . . . there are wolves in the world who are really werewolves who lingered too long on four legs and forgot who they were."

"But I thought you had your human mind when you changed."

"Why on earth would you think that?"

"Well, 'cause you don't kill me and eat me when you change."

She laughed. "Maybe I just haven't been hungry enough."

Still chuckling to herself, she walked on ahead and then transformed into a wolf and ran into the brush. Milo called after her.

"Hey, you're just joking, right? Right? Hey—right?"

Shark burst out laughing too. "You should see your face."

"Don't mess, chubster," snapped Milo, jabbing Shark in the stomach. "You'd make an even better meal for a hungry wolf than I would."

Shark didn't take offense and instead patted his thick middle. "Dark meat tastes better. Everyone knows that. Does it bother you that you're so scrawny a werewolf won't even bite you? Wow, can't be good for your self-esteem."

Milo tried to come up with a crushing reply, tripped

over it, and shut up. It had felt good to laugh, and he was surprised that any of them could. Somehow he found that encouraging rather than a betrayal of Lizabeth's memory. If laughter could still happen, then surely hope could still exist. To Milo they went hand in hand.

The miles burned away but the hours of the day seemed to drag.

They slept again, this time in the vault of an old bank. The Bugs had no interest in money, and the Earth Alliance traded only in food and supplies. As far as the world was concerned, the stacks of bundled fives, tens, twenties, fifties, and hundreds on which Milo and his friends would make their bed were relics as disconnected from their world as dinosaur bones.

Milo went hunting at dusk and came back with three rabbits. Shark, who was the best cook among them, skinned and roasted them on a million-dollar fire.

They sat on sacks of cash and nibbled their first hot meal in days. The fire turned Shark's brown skin the color of honey, and turned Evangelyne's white hair gold. Milo noticed that Evangelyne ate her food with great delicacy and good manners. It made him wonder if she did that to remind herself she was not a wolf. Maybe that was why she was so formal all the time. Was it a struggle to keep the two sides of herself separate?

Evangelyne caught him watching her. "What's wrong? Do I have something between my teeth?"

"Huh? No," he said quickly, "I, um, was just thinking

that we'll be outside New Orleans by noon tomorrow."

"Yes," she said, clearly unconvinced that Milo had been thinking about logistics. But she ran with it. "We'll have to scout the area and then find the best route into the city. Gadfellyn Hall is in the French Quarter, a few blocks from Jackson Square. The Bugs will be everywhere."

"Yeah, they will," agreed Shark, "and I'm kind of worried about that. I mean, not just the fact that they'll be there, but after what happened yesterday with the Stinger. He was sniffing Milo. I think he could smell the crystal egg. I think that's why he didn't just kill him."

"You're right," said Milo. "He was sniffing my pocket when Evangelyne attacked him. Another second and he'd have torn it open."

"My point exactly," said Shark, nodding. "So how smart is it, us waltzing into New Orleans with the crystal egg? Won't they smell it? Maybe it'll set off some kind of alarm. I mean, heck, the hive ship is right there."

"It's a little late to be worrying about that, boy," said Evangelyne.

Milo turned away, frustrated. He kept hoping the Witch of the World would pop up and say something useful. Or anything at all, for that matter. The only thoughts inside his skull, though, were his own and they were a jumble.

They set off on the last leg of their journey. Their bellies were filled with food, and there had been a rain shower overnight, so finding clean water to drink was easy. They'd allowed themselves an extra hour of sleep so they'd be ready for whatever the day had to offer.

As they walked, Milo saw that Mook held a small creature in his hands, and when he asked the stone boy what it was, Mook showed him. Curled asleep in the big rocky palm was a miniature salamander with familiar red stripes.

"Is that . . . *Iskiel*?"

"Mook."

"He's so tiny."

"He'll get bigger," said Evangelyne, glancing over. "It takes him a couple of days to come all the way back."

Shark bent close and gently poked at the amphibian. Tiny puffs of steam escaped from Iskiel's nostrils, but the creature did not wake.

"He's kind of cute."

"Mook," agreed Mook.

During the trip Milo noticed a change in the relationship between Killer and Evangelyne. Until now the little Jack Russell had been shy of the girl in either of her aspects, and particularly the wolf form. Now whenever Evangelyne transformed and went running ahead as the wolf, Killer wagged his tail and ran after her. Soon they were scouting together and even play-fighting during breaks. Shark and Milo exchanged a look.

"I have no idea what to even say about that," confessed Shark. "After the last couple days, my weird-o-meter is all burned out. I actually don't think anything can freak me out at this point."

They came through a dense grove of old hardwood trees that was clogged by younger saplings. Milo reckoned that they were getting close to the city. It wasn't until they emerged from the grove that he realized just how close they were.

It was right there.

The ruined, blackened, overgrown sprawl of New Orleans.

And hovering above it like the fist of a titan from old myths hung the vast egg-shaped monstrosity that was the Dissosterin hive ship.

They stood in the shadows and stared up at it, mouths open in awe and horror. Killer's sense of fun melted away and he shrank against Evangelyne's side, whimpering softly.

The hive ship cast its shadow across the city, and inside that shadow thousands of shapes moved.

Bugs.

Hunter-killers.

Stingers.

And more.

Thousands and thousands of them. Maybe millions.

And all of it between them and Gadfellyn Hall.

Chapter 43

They climbed a towering oak and stared in horror at New Orleans.

Milo had seen this city only once since the invasion. It had been on a clear morning when the kids in his pod had gone on a long march with his mother and her soldiers. They'd crouched in the weeds in Manchac Wildlife Management Area on the west side of Lake Pontchartrain. His mom had been scouting for a new location for their camp and had thought to settle on the far side of the wildlife park, closer to the much smaller Lake Maurepas. She ultimately chose to move deeper into bayou country.

It wasn't really a city anymore. It was mostly destroyed, burned black, the buildings' brick skin torn away to reveal the naked bones of wood and iron. And hanging over the ruined town like a storm cloud was the hive ship.

Seven of those massive ships had come to Earth after an interstellar journey of thousands of years. Impossibly huge, ugly, made up of patchwork metal from thousands of unknown sources. Milo thought that this one looked less like a well designed ship and more like some half-digested garbage spat out into space.

Milo could hardly believe he'd been aboard the thing. If it hadn't been for little Halflight and her glamours—spells that disguised Milo and the Orphan Army as shock-troopers—they'd never have managed it. He wished he had the little fire sprite with them now, because getting into New Orleans looked like it was going to be even harder than getting aboard the hive ship.

The town was crawling with Dissosterin. Literally crawling. Shocktroopers were everywhere, their many hands gripping pulse pistols. Others, bigger insects that looked like gigantic rhinoceros beetles, towered over scuttling hordes of cockroach-like drones, snapping at them with steel-barbed whips. Stingers on chain leashes walked beside them, growling and snapping at the worker bugs. In the main streets, segmented millipedes the size of school buses lumbered along, their backs hung with net bags of cargo. There were tens of thousands of green lifelights. Every shocktrooper, every drone, and every single one of the unnameable alien insects had a life-light. Milo touched the pouch of metal ball bearings at his belt. He had plenty of shot left, but even if he had had a truckload he wouldn't have had enough to make a dent in that seething mass.

Swarms of flies bigger than vultures flew in and out through the openings of the hive ship, each of them carrying what looked like I beams and sheets of metal. Dense black smoke billowing from the openings carried the smell of welding torches and hot metal. And below the ship was a growing heap of twisted deck plating, shattered machinery, and other nameless junk, including the bodies of hundreds of Dissosterin.

When Milo and the rest had stolen the red ship to escape from the monstrous craft, Milo had flung some grenades into the main birthing chamber. He knew that he'd done damage, but from the intensity and scope of the repair work, it was clear he'd accomplished more than he'd hoped.

Nice.

In its way.

The greater the damage, the greater the desire for revenge on the part of the Swarm.

Oh well, he thought, *they can't want to kill us any more than they already do.*

Beside him Shark quietly said, "Wow."

"Yeah," said Milo.

"Mook," said Mook.

"At least," said Shark, "I don't see any hunter-killers."

Evangelyne pointed to a side street that was nearly choked with debris from a row of collapsed buildings. Weeds were thick and a few young trees poked crookedly from between the piles of shattered brick, evidence that the street was disused.

"That's our way in," she said. "Come on."

They climbed down and began moving toward New

Orleans. The Bugs had done so much damage during the invasion that there was plenty of wreckage to hide behind. Evangelyne asked to see Milo's map and he spread it out on the ground. She tapped a group of streets that made up a neighborhood that used to be called the French Quarter—back when human beings lived there. Then, using a stick, Evangelyne drew a larger map in the dirt of a few of those streets to indicate where Gadfellyn Hall was located.

"We'll need to be sharp, because it won't look like what it is," she said.

"Which means what?" asked Shark.

"The house is a ghost too. Another building has been built where it used to stand, but the old hall is still there. It's inside, hidden in the shadows."

"Okay, that's really, really creepy. How are we supposed to find it?"

"I can get us to the front door," Evangelyne assured him, "but once we're inside, we'll have to search for it. There has to be a clue. Maybe a hidden passage or a door that's been sealed up. Something."

"Wait," said Milo, holding up a hand. They all looked at him, but he kept his hand up and closed his eyes, trying to remember something. Then he snapped his eyes open, unslung his satchel, and pulled out the battered little notebook he used as his dream diary. Milo riffled through the pages until he found an entry from a few nights ago. "Here. This is something I wrote down after

one of my dreams. It's about the Heir and the library.
Maybe this will help."

He held it out for them all to read.

When he was done, he went looking for more books.
A white rabbit hopped out of the shadows and the
boy followed it through a doorway behind a doorway
that was behind another doorway. And there,
beyond that, were more books.

"Okay," said Shark, closing his eyes and rubbing them
wearily, "so what you're saying is that we have to go to
Wonderland?"

"How would I know? It was a dream."

"Wonderland?" asked Evangelyne sharply. "What is
that?"

"It's a story," said Shark. "About a little girl who follows a white rabbit down a hole and winds up in some
wacky magical kingdom."

"There's nothing about a hole here," insisted Evangelyne.
"It says he went through doorways."

"Might be one of those . . ." He snapped his fingers as
he fished for the word. "What do they call it when something means something else?"

"A metaphor?" suggested Milo.

"Right. Maybe the doorways are metaphorical rabbit
holes. Or something. I might have that backward."

"No," said the wolf girl, "I get you. You're saying we have to look for something that is *like* a rabbit hole. A magical doorway of some kind, right?"

"Something like that."

She looked at him and smiled. "You may actually be smarter than you look."

"Gee," said Shark. "Thanks. Loads."

Milo put his book away. "C'mon, let's go."

Evangelyne went first, dropping into wolfshape and running on four silent paws. Her silver-gray fur allowed her to blend in with the gray and dusty rubble. The boys and Mook watched from behind the burned shell of an Abrams tank until Evangelyne made it across a crammed lot that had once been a hotel. She became a girl again and pressed backward against the wall, looking up and down the street. Then she waved them on. Shark went next, moving low and being careful to make maximum use of ground cover. Killer, silent and tiny, darted ahead of him.

Milo turned to tell Mook to go, but there was only a pile of loose stone behind him. The rock boy had shed his body, and Milo knew—weird and creepy as it was— that Mook's spirit was somehow traveling through the pieces of stone and brick and shattered granite to where Evangelyne waited.

"Freaky," Milo breathed, and then he was running.

As soon as he left the cover of the dead tank, he saw a 'trooper walking across the avenue on four powerful

342

legs, a pulse rifle held in two hands, its head swiveling left and right. Milo froze and tried to will himself into the landscape, to become as unobtrusive as any piece of debris. The shocktrooper was too far for Milo's slingshot to be of any value, and Shark's pulse pistol was too loud. Evangelyne could not defeat a shocktrooper alone.

Milo tried to be a statue.

He tried to be invisible.

The 'trooper scuttled slowly across the avenue, and for a moment it looked like the 'trooper would not see Milo at all.

Just for a moment.

But that moment passed.

The 'trooper stiffened in surprise and immediately swung its rifle around toward Milo. The green lifelight on its chest seemed to flare with indignation, and the sound of angry clicking filled the air as the creature's mandibles twitched.

"Run!" shouted Shark.

Evangelyne morphed into wolfshape and began sprinting toward the alien warrior.

And then the shocktrooper seemed to fly apart in a sudden mass of green goo and chunks of shattered armor. Something huge and gray rose up behind it, arms sweeping wide to scatter the pieces of the alien across the rubble-strewn street.

Milo gaped, caught in the split second between

acceptance that his death was inevitable and disbelief that the end wasn't here at all.

The gray mass resolved itself into a shape. A very recognizable shape.

"Mook," said the shape—as if any statement of personal identification was necessary.

Milo nearly collapsed with relief.

All at once Mook collapsed, falling to pieces as he had only a minute ago. Milo turned to follow a rippling line of disturbance in the rocky debris on the ground. A few seconds later, Mook re-formed against the wall near Evangelyne. For a creature incapable of facial expression, he nevertheless managed to look immensely smug.

"Mook," he said.

"Well," gasped Milo, "I suppose so."

He ran to catch up.

Chapter 44

They made their way through the occupied town, taking time, being careful, often hiding in destroyed houses or the trunks of burned cars. If this had been the city of New Orleans before the war, it probably would have taken them maybe an hour to reach the edge of Jackson Square. As it was, dodging and hiding and moving as slowly as caution demanded, it took seven long hours. The sun was already beginning its descent toward the distant trees. Not that sunlight was much of a factor, as most of New Orleans was blanketed by the perpetual shadow of the great hive ship. The dense gloom was useful. It saved their lives a dozen times that day, and Milo thought it ironic that the greatest symbol of the Swarm's power, the hive ship, was also one of its weaknesses.

Now they were hiding inside the moldering corpse of a giant alien worm that had died and been left to rot in the hot sun. Milo had to fight the urge to throw up. Shark lost the fight and hurled up everything he'd eaten that morning. As soon as the smell of it was in the air, Evangelyne turned and vomited against the wall.

And so did Milo.

Once the danger was past and they were preparing to leave the huge corpse, Evangelyne muttered, "We are never going to talk about this."

The boys could only manage weak nods.

Milo crouched in the mouth of the monstrous worm and used Shark's compact binoculars to study the way ahead. Evangelyne knelt beside him.

"We're only a block away," she said quietly, then nodded toward the row of houses on the left side of the street. "See that alleyway? We can go down there and stay off the main street."

"Good," said Milo, "but just in case we have to make a run for it, everyone goes a different way and we meet right back here in the worm. I don't think even a Stinger could sniff us out in here."

"Ugh," said Shark behind him.

"Okay," said Milo, "let's go."

But as Milo went to rise, Mook clamped a stony hand on his shoulder and forced him down. "Mook!" he said fiercely, pointing to something in the air above the houses.

Milo flinched away from what he saw and had to shove half his fist in his mouth to keep from crying out.

Not eighty feet above them, standing like a dark colossus on a sky-board painted the color of fresh blood, *was the Huntsman.* Killer whined and retreated all the way into the stomach of the dead worm. The half-grown Iskiel dropped from Mook's shoulder and scuttled after him.

The Huntsman's sky-board was different from the ones used by the six shocktroopers who flew in two angled lines behind him. Theirs were simple disks controlled by foot pressure, but the Huntsman rested his hands on a control column that rose up from the front of his machine. Milo studied him through the binoculars. The great hybrid monster had changed a lot in the last few days. The last time they'd seen him was aboard the hive ship, and they'd left him unconscious and injured in the ruins of the egg chamber. Evangelyne, in werewolf form, had bitten off the killer's left hand, and Mook had shattered his jaw with a mighty punch. Milo had stabbed him, though that had been only a scratch. If Milo had had any hopes that the Huntsman would be suffering from those wounds, he was thoroughly disappointed.

The Huntsman's jaw now gleamed with a new armor of bright steel, and Milo suspected it was a cybernetic repair job—something that enhanced rather than merely fixed the shattered bones. And in place of his missing left hand was a new one that was made of the same gleaming metal, with six long, segmented fingers and a row of wicked spikes sprouting from the back. He wore metal gauntlets on both wrists and forearms, and matching greaves on his legs. The werewolf would be taking no more trophies from him. And there was a wire cage around his green lifelight that Milo suspected would withstand any number of ball-bearing slingshot rounds. There were pistols on each hip and knives strapped to his thighs, and rising above his right shoulder was the handle of some great sword of alien design. The Huntsman also wore a skullcap of the same metal, and on his forehead was an empty socket that looked just big enough to hold a small faceted stone.

It didn't require much thought to guess what stone the Huntsman planned to use to fill that socket. Milo handed the binoculars to Shark, who took a look and passed them to Evangelyne and Mook.

The Huntsman flew slowly across the sky, his sky-board forming the point of a V, the six shocktroopers making up the arms. The way he stood there made Milo think of some ancient warrior in his battle chariot.

"Oh, man," said Shark, and the way he said it reminded Milo of just how small and young they all were, and how big and dangerous everything else was.

It also reminded Milo of something the Witch of the World had said to him in his dreams. Milo had said, "Everything's getting so complicated. I can't keep it all straight." And she'd replied, *The world has always been complicated, Milo. What's changed is that now you're able to notice.*

Sometimes there were things that seemed to hammer that home to Milo with greater force. This was one of them. He'd lived in camps for years, hiding from the Swarm, protected by his mother and her soldiers, feeling safe and distanced from the ugly realities of the world. Now his mind and all of his five senses seemed to want to shout the truth at him.

He lived in a conquered world. His world was a battle-field. And there was not much hope that there was going to be a happy ending to his story.

No, not much hope at all.

It should have made him want to cry, to crawl away and hide, to fall down. To give up. That truth should have done all those things and more to Milo Silk.

Should have.

Instead Milo rose from his place of hiding and stepped out into the street to watch the Huntsman fly away. Then he turned toward the alley that led to their destination.

"Come on," he said.

Together the Orphan Army, such as it was, went to war.

Chapter 45

They cut across the street and then slipped into the narrow alley. There was enough rubble and weeds to allow them to move quickly without being seen. Not that anyone was looking. This part of the French Quarter was relatively deserted except for dozens of destroyed military vehicles and uncountable skeletons. There had been a terrible battle here, but it had happened years ago and even the stubborn stink of gunpowder had long since faded. Now only the weeds and scampering vermin held dominion.

It was quiet enough for Evangelyne to share a few words with Milo.

"I'm so sorry about your friend," she said. "Lizabeth seemed like a nice girl."

"She was," said Milo, flinching at the pain her words—however kindly meant—inflicted.

"Please," said Evangelyne, "don't let anger or a need for revenge pollute you."

"Pollute me? What do you mean by that?"

"Revenge can summon the bad kind of darkness into a person's soul. I see it growing like root rot in Oakenayl.

He has lost so many of the trees he loves, and so much of his family, that now all he knows is hate. He's even pulling away from the other Nightsiders. Soon the darkness will own him."

Milo nodded. "Is that what happened to Queen Mab?"

"Yes. Once, many thousands of years ago, she was a queen of light and beauty, and her faerie lands were filled with joy. But now her mind feeds on her hatred of you Daylighters—and of the rest of the Nightsiders—because she thinks all of the supernaturals should have stood with the *Aes Sidhe* in a war to exterminate all of humankind." Evangelyne shook her head. "I . . . I can understand it too. You and Shark think I'm cold and that I'm always trying to be the grown-up, and maybe that's true. But it's only part of it. Mostly I'm fighting to keep control."

"Control of what? Your hate?"

"Yes. It's always there, right beneath the surface. Like the wolf, or maybe it's part of the wolf. The hate wants to own me, and sometimes, when I'm tired or weak or scared, I think maybe I should let it. Perhaps that's the only way I'm ever going to fight back and win."

Milo walked a few steps before he answered. "Yeah," he said, "I get that. I really do."

She touched his hand. "Please," she begged, "don't let it take you. You're a good person, Milo. You don't have much darkness in you. Maybe that's why the Witch of the World speaks to you and not to me or Oakenayl.

Maybe she chose you because there is more light in your soul than shadows."

"It doesn't feel that way."

"Please," she said again. "My aunt once told me that it takes a lot more courage to do what's right than to do what's easy. And hate is easy." She gestured to the ruined world around them. "Hate is way too easy."

Shark, who was walking point for their party, suddenly stopped, one fist raised in the classic signal for everyone to freeze. Then, after some nervous hesitation, he waved them on, and Milo, Evangelyne, and Mook caught up and saw what had jolted Shark.

It jolted them, too.

They were standing at the mouth of the alley and could see the street before them. Directly across from the alley was a building. It was the only structure left intact on the whole block. The grimy, scorched sign outside said that it was an antiques store, but Milo knew that this had to be the real-world face of the mysterious Gadfellyn Hall. There were no shocktroopers, Stingers, or hunter-killers. However, on the ground in front of the building, all the concrete paving stones were shattered, and rising up from the dirt were the domes of sixty pale, diseased-looking mushrooms. They formed a large circle in front of the door.

A faerie ring.

The toadstools were broken and pieces of them lay scattered.

However, there was something inside the ring. A

humped shape that lay curled in a blackened ball of charred bones.

"No!" growled Milo, and he broke from cover and ran across the street before anyone could stop him. A sleek gray shape raced past and halted between Milo and the ring. The wolf became the girl, and she turned and held her palms out.

"Wait!" she ordered.

The others came up behind Milo, and they spread out to study the grisly remains.

That the figure had once been human was evident, but that was all they could tell. It was small, so it could have been a woman or a teenager of either gender. There wasn't enough left to say.

"Tell me that's not Lizzie," said Shark, his face gray.

Evangelyne became the wolf and bent to smell the corpse. The wolf walked around it and studied it from several angles, then abruptly backed up a step, and became a girl again.

"Goddess of Shadows," she breathed.

"What is it?" asked Milo.

"I think this was a faerie."

"A faerie? I thought they were tiny." Milo said, frowning at the twisted form.

"No. They're the same size as us. When you saw them, it was through the distortion of the faerie ring."

"Wait, wait, I don't get this at all," Shark said. "You're saying this is one of those *Aes Sídhe* characters? Why would they have sacrificed one of their own kind?"

"I don't know."

"Mook," said Mook, and Evangelyne pursed her lips in thought.

"That's possible," she said, then explained to the boys. "There are some scattered faerie folk around this city. *Sidhe*, but not of the *Aes Sidhe*. There are many courts of faerie. It's possible that Queen Mab or the Huntsman captured one and used its death to break the enchantment that keeps the *Aes Sidhe* on the other side of their doorway."

"That doesn't sound good," said Shark. "Does that mean she broke out?"

Evangelyne picked up one of the toadstool pieces, studied it, then tossed it away. "I don't know. If Queen Mab has come through to our world, then things have gone from bad to worse."

"Worse? Really? There's still a worse?"

She looked at him with no trace of humor. "Things can always get worse, boy. Always."

"Swell." Shark looked around. "I'm hoping this is a good sign, but I don't see a whole army of faerie warriors anywhere around. Are you sure they came through?"

"I'm not sure of anything, Shark," she said. "Spells like this require tremendous amounts of energy. It's possible that only the queen herself managed to come through."

"That would be a lucky break," said Shark.

"No," replied the wolf girl, "it wouldn't. If only she came through, then the queen would be desperate to sacrifice as many innocent lives as possible in order to smash the doorway and free her people."

"Just once can you find something positive to say? Seriously? Just once."

"Will you guys cut it out," barked Milo. "We don't know how much time we have left. Let's get moving."

They stepped carefully around the faerie ring and approached the front of the antiques store. The window glass was still intact, though a jagged crack ran from upper right to lower left. The lock and door handle were burned, and the wood around them was charred. Milo touched them—and snatched his hand away.

"It's hot." He pushed against the door with the toe of his shoe and it swung inward, the lock destroyed.

Shark looked deeply uneasy. "You think Queen Mab's in there?"

Evangelyne didn't answer, but her silence seemed more like an evasion than a lack of opinion. Shark sighed.

"Swell," he said. "Does that mean we're walking into a trap?"

Again she didn't answer.

"You got to tell us something," persisted Shark. "What kind of magic stuff can she throw at us? Are we talking death spells or is she going to turn me into a frog or what?"

"I don't know," said Evangelyne. "I'm sorry, but I really don't. You boys keep asking me as if I know *everything* about the magical world. I don't. No one does. You don't know everything about your world, do you?"

"Well, no," conceded Shark, "but we don't know what you don't know and we don't know what you *do* know." He paused and smiled. "You know?"

That put a faint smile on her face. "Look, I'm sorry, I don't mean to be difficult."

"Too late."

She punched him on the arm. Pretty hard, too.

"If Queen Mab's been trapped for all this time," said Milo, "won't she be pretty rusty when it comes to fighting?"

"I wouldn't count on it," said Evangelyne.

"What about tech? Shark has a pulse pistol. No way she's ever had to deal with that kind of thing before. Won't that give us an advantage?"

The wolf girl brightened. "That's a good thought. I'm not sure if the gun would kill her, but it might weaken her enough for one of us to finish her off. If we can remove her golden torc, then she'll lose much of her power. Without the torc she would be as vulnerable as anyone."

"Moooook," said the rock boy, drawing the word out to suggest that he would be happy to take a swing at the evil faerie queen. Shark patted his shoulder, clearly getting Mook's meaning.

"I'm with Stony McRockshoes here," he said. "That's the first good news I've had since . . . let me think . . . *ever*?"

"Don't be overconfident," warned Evangelyne. "Even if she is unfamiliar with your gun, Queen Mab is still incredibly dangerous. Underestimate her at your peril."

"Sure," said Shark, "'cause why should we be optimistic for more than a nanosecond?"

"Look," said Evangelyne, "I'm not trying to depress everyone. You asked."

"It's cool," said Milo. "Shark's just messing with you."

"It's what I do," admitted Shark.

Evangelyne gave a grudging nod. "If I were a sorceress, I wouldn't turn you into a frog."

"That's nice—"

"I'd turn you into a rabbit. Wolves eat rabbits."

"You," said Shark, pointing at her, "made a joke. A very, very scary joke."

The wolf girl turned aside to hide another smile. Then she straightened. "I just thought of one thing," she said. "There are a lot of stories and legends about Gadfellyn Hall. It's supposed to be very strange inside. Bigger than you'd think, and filled with many halls and corridors, cellars and attics, and countless rooms."

"So—?" asked Milo.

"So no one knows exactly where the library is. It can only be found by luck or instinct."

"Again, so?"

"So even if the *Aes Sídhe* are inside, it doesn't mean they'll know how to find the library. Some of the legends say that most of the people who enter Gadfellyn Hall get lost. Forever lost."

"How's that help us? Are you saying we're going to

spend the rest of our lives playing hide-and-seek with faerie warriors?"

"No, that's not what I'm saying at all. Queen Mab doesn't know how to find the Impossible Library. Neither will the Huntsman if he gets here. But Milo, you *dreamed* of it. You watched the Heir find his way there. You can follow memories of those dreams, can't you?"

"I can try," he said doubtfully.

It seemed like a thin thread of hope, but it was something, and Milo felt the ground to be more firmly under his feet. He glanced at the others and they shared a nod.

Shark drew his pulse pistol and Milo fitted a ball bearing into his slingshot. Evangelyne morphed into wolfshape, and Iskiel—now grown nearly to full size—scuttled onto Mook's shoulders and uttered a low hiss of challenge. His eyes blazed with heat. Even Mook's placid face seemed to change into a brutal war mask.

Milo went first, his slingshot raised.

Shark held his flashlight in one fist and rested the pulse pistol atop it. As he came in, he shifted right to cover Milo but also keep him out of the line of fire. Evangelyne crept along on silent paws. The only sound was the dull thud of Mook's heavy feet.

From outside, the antiques store looked like what it advertised. Through the grime on the windows they'd seen old Victorian chairs, crystal chandeliers, ornate wardrobes, and tall, delicately painted vases.

Once they stepped inside they saw none of this.

Stepping through that doorway was like stepping into another world. It was colder, older, and stranger, and nothing they'd seen from outside was in here. They entered the large vestibule of what was clearly a huge old house. The vestibule was wider than the entire facade of the store.

"Okay," murmured Shark, "this is freaky."

They walked to the end of the vestibule. There were dried leaves and the white skeletons of small animals on the tiled floor. An urn made of hammered brass stood against the wall, and from it sprouted a dozen walking sticks and umbrellas that were draped with dusty cobwebs. The desiccated husk of a long-dead spider hung inside one web.

There were three doorways at the far end of the vestibule. The left one led to a small sitting room furnished with ugly and uncomfortable-looking chairs. A dusty piano stood in one corner. The doorway on the right opened into a larger room with leather chairs, a massive globe hung inside a wooden frame, and a huge old oak desk. On every available piece of wall were the mounted heads of animals Milo had only ever seen in books. Wild rams, lions and tigers, bison, moose, zebras, and even a rhinoceros. They were ancient and covered with dust, their fur or hide worn away, their glass eyes dull and empty. Milo hated that room. Like everyone in his pod he was a hunter, but everything he killed went into a stew pot. The thought of hunting just to gloat over the stuffed heads seemed weird to him.

They moved back into the vestibule and approached

the last doorway. This one brought them into a long hall-way with framed pictures of disappointed-looking people in old-fashioned clothes. None of them looked any happier than the animal heads they'd seen on the wall.

At the end of the hallway was a long stairway that swept upward into shadows.

"What is all this?" asked Shark. "How can all of this be in here?"

"We're in the ghost of a house," said Milo, remembering what Evangelyne had told him. "This is Gadfellyn Hall."

They stood at the foot of the stairs and listened for any sound. The old building creaked and moaned as cold winds blew through its bones. Milo had expected the place to feel dead, like a spent battery or a crashed drop-ship, but it wasn't. It *looked* dead, but it felt . . .

He tried to put it into words in his head. When he'd piloted the red ship, there had been a sense of resistance and resentment, but that's not what this was.

It knows we're here, he thought.

A small gust conjured a tiny dust devil on the landing above them. It dissipated and the dust floated down toward them.

It knows we're here and it doesn't like it.

He almost said that to the others, but when he glanced at them, he saw they were all looking nervous enough already. They were feeling uneasy, too.

Evangelyne changed back into girlshape and stood chewing her lip, one foot on the bottom step.

"I don't see any footprints," said Shark, trying to sound hopeful. "Maybe no one's come in yet."

"Faeries don't leave footprints," she said.

Shark sighed.

"The Huntsman would, though," said Milo. "We saw him flying the other way. I don't think he's been here yet. That's something."

Evangelyne said nothing, which Milo assumed was not a good sign.

"Look," said Shark, "tell me this much at least. These dark faeries . . . can we fight them if they're here? I mean, we're not exactly a pack of bunnies. I got my gun, Milo's an ace with that wrist-rocket, and you three are all sorts of creepy-weird-dangerous. Tell me we at least have a chance."

Mook clacked his fists together and gave a single stern nod. "Mook."

As before, the rock boy's meaning was clear enough.

"Glad to hear it," said Shark.

Milo didn't feel too reassured. If Queen Mab was here, they were about to face a dark sorceress of legendary power. He wasn't all that confident in a bunch of kids— however tough they were—fighting someone like her.

He didn't say it, though. No one needed to hear that right now.

Without another word they all began to mount the stairs.

Chapter 46

When they were halfway up the stairs, Shark asked, "Maybe I don't want to know the answer to this, but how did Queen Mab even know we were coming here?"

Evangelyne climbed several steps in silence, clearly unwilling to answer.

"Yo, Vangie," said Shark, "if you know something, maybe you'd better share."

She paused and her hand strayed to the leather pouch. "It's the Heart of Darkness."

"What about it?"

"It's hurt."

"Yeah, we kind of *know* that. It's pretty much why we're here. What does that have to do with Queen Mab?"

Evangelyne sighed. "The stone isn't just a piece of rock, it's not a simple piece of quartz. It's *alive*. It's attuned to the heartbeat of the world."

"So?"

"The heart of this world is the heart of magic," she said. "It is the heartbeat of all shadows. This jewel is the last of its kind left on this Earth. All of the others have been destroyed or have been taken into the shadow worlds.

That's why this stone is so important. Now that heart is wounded to its core, and anyone who is in harmony with the magic of our world can hear it scream."

Shark's mouth hung open.

"Mook," said Mook sadly, nodding.

"Queen Mab can *hear* the Heart of Darkness?" gasped Milo.

"Yes. And she would know that we wanted to heal it, just as she would know that we had to seek out the last doctor of magic. The Heir."

"I'm going to bang my head on a wall for a while," said Shark. "Really, I think it'll help."

"When were you planning on telling us?" demanded Milo.

She gave him a funny look. "Never. I thought we'd get here long before Queen Mab escaped. I never thought it would come to this."

Milo wanted to yell at her. Instead he ground his teeth together and pushed past her as he ran up the steps. The big clock inside his head was starting to ring its alarms.

The others followed at a run.

Evangelyne caught up to him as he reached the landing. "Do you know where you're going?" she asked. "Are you being guided by your dreams?"

He grunted, realizing that he probably was but hadn't been aware of it until she asked. He looked down the shadowy length of the second-floor hall and all at once knew that this was familiar to him. These were the halls the Heir had walked all those years ago. There were doors on either side of the corridor, and he immediately knew which ones would open onto drab rooms filled with sheet-draped furniture and which doors would be locked. None of these doors led to where they needed to go.

He rubbed his eyes and then blinked to clear his vision. His feet had never been here, but somehow he could remember each quiet footfall of the Heir as he prowled this vast and ancient house in search of . . .

Of what?

He hadn't been looking for the library. The Heir had found it by accident.

What had that lonely kid been looking for? Why had he been abandoned here? What had happened to the people, the adults, who should have lived here?

None of those answers were in his dreams, and therefore they were not in Milo's head.

"This way," he said quietly, and moved forward.

"You sure about this?" called Shark in a low, urgent voice.

"No, of course not," said Milo. But what he wanted to say was, *Yes*.

The corridor ended in a T-junction. Each of these halls was even longer than the one down which they'd come, and there were at least twenty closed doors on each wall. Milo took a step toward the left hall, then stopped and shook his head.

"No," he said.

Mook walked a couple of paces past him; then he also stopped and retreated, shaking his head.

"Why?" asked Evangelyne. "What's wrong? What's down there?"

"I—don't know," admitted Milo. "But it doesn't want us to go that way."

"What doesn't?" asked Shark.

"The house."

Shark stared at Milo. "The house," he echoed flatly.

"Yes. Don't ask me to explain it, because I can't. I just know that we're not supposed to go that way."

"Why not?"

Milo just shook his head. He didn't tell them the thoughts that filled his head, because it was hard to put his feelings into words. There were secrets down those halls, maybe important ones, but they weren't today's secrets. Maybe, if he lived through this afternoon, through this day, he'd return to Gadfellyn Hall and go exploring. Like the Heir had gone exploring.

Maybe he would get lost in this house.

He was almost certain he would. The house wanted him to go that way, just not now. Not today. The longer he lingered there, the more a coldness built up inside his chest.

Come back, a voice seemed to whisper. *Come back and stay.*

"No," murmured Milo.

Come back and play with us.

Milo almost took a step forward. Almost.

But the more he thought about his dreams, and the more he listened inside his head to that whispery voice, the more he heard something else.

A sound, deep and low. A thump, like a weak hand striking a drum. Not in a rhythm. It was awkward and painful to hear. It shouldn't have been, he knew that with every fiber of his being. It should have been a strong, steady, beat.

No . . . not just a beat. A pulsing beat.

A heartbeat.

The chill in his chest swept through his entire body as he realized what he was hearing.

It was the dying, struggling throb of the Heart of Darkness.

So weak. So fragile.

Milo made himself turn around and look down the other hall. The sound was louder that way. Or . . . maybe not louder, but clearer. More correct.

He could feel everyone watching him, but they said nothing. They knew that this was his to do, this part of it at least. Finding the way.

"Come on," he said hoarsely.

Milo began walking quickly, then broke into a run, passing door after door, knowing they weren't the right ones even though he didn't know exactly what he was looking for. He could remember his dreams as something hazy and indistinct. They were, after all, only dreams. In dreams, nothing looks the way it does in the real world.

Not that Gadfellyn Hall was within a million miles of the real world.

Absolutely not.

The corridor ended at another T-junction and again Milo took the hallway on the right, increasing his pace, racing now, with the others following as fast as they could. Mook lagged behind, his rocky feet pounding on the old floorboards. Evangelyne could have turned into a wolf and outrun them all, but she didn't know the way. So instead she ran at Milo's left side and Shark huffed along on Milo's right, with Killer at his heels.

"How big is this place?" grunted Shark as they ran down a hall that seemed to grow and stretch out before them, adding more and more doors that were shut and locked against them.

"A lot bigger than this," said Milo, though even he didn't know what he meant by that; he only knew it was true.

At the end of the next hall they slowed to a stop at what appeared to be a dead end. Instead of a door, there was a huge picture mirror that stretched from wall to wall and from ceiling to floor. The glass was shattered, though, and pieces lay everywhere on the floor. Some jagged splinters were still stuck in the edges of the frame.

Milo stepped forward and stood amid the glittering pieces of mirror. At first he only glanced down to see his reflection, but then he did a double take because the reflection in those pieces was all wrong.

So wrong.

In one he saw himself as he was. Eleven, on the skinny side of slim, short, with a scuffle of brown hair and dirt on his face. Haunted eyes that were filled with sadness and fear. That's how he knew he looked. The real him.

But there were other versions of Milo Silk. Some were memory images, others were not.

He saw himself as a little boy in the days before the Swarm came. Wearing footie pajamas with the Ninja Turtles on the chest. Rosy cheeks and bright eyes that were filled with laughter. But right next to that image was one whose nature horrified Milo. It was a broken, distorted version of himself. No longer entirely human. His body had been torn apart and rebuilt with gleaming metal and patches of ugly green-brown Dissosterin armor. Clicking mandibles forced their way out between teeth and cheeks, stretching his mouth into a permanent grin of alien hunger. Instead of his own eyes, he had the multifaceted eyes of a monstrous fly. It sickened him, because in that image he was a miniature and tortured version of the Huntsman. A pet or, worse, an apprentice.

Milo tore his gaze away but then saw himself in another terrifying aspect. Standing mute and gray-skinned, with a network of wires running in and out of his flesh and a visage that flickered back and forth between his own grim dead face and one that pretended to laugh normally as if inviting his friends to come and play. It was a lie, though. The laughter was a trap, because in that reflected image

Milo was a holo-man. A corpse used as a living land mine to trap and murder his friends. Like the holo-man who had appeared as his dad and nearly killed him.

There were other images. In one he knelt over the still and silent body of his mother. Her eyes were open but a thin line of blood leaked from the corner of her mouth. There were pulse-blast burns stitched across her chest. In that image Milo screamed and screamed and screamed, even though the piece of shattered mirror made no actual sound.

He saw his dad, playing guitar and laughing.

He saw his dad turned into a hybrid.

He saw his dad lying dead.

He saw his dad in silhouette, twisted and strange, transformed into something more monstrous than anything Milo had ever seen.

He saw his dad standing with a gun, his face scarred but alive, his eyes filled with power. And Milo prayed that this image was true, that it was more than his own weak hope that his father was still alive somewhere, fighting the aliens. Fighting to come back to him.

He saw Lizabeth, her shirt burned, her hair tangled with twigs and leaves and dirt, her eyes empty.

He saw Lizabeth rising into the air, her skin aglow as if all the starlight in the universe shone through her flesh, a sword of fire in one hand.

He saw himself staggering through a world where everything and everyone lay dead. Shark was there, his brown skin torn by blade and pulse blast. Evangelyne was caught between wolf and girl, and in that mismatched phase she had died, cut down by the *Aes Sídhe* or the Huntsman.

He saw all these things and many, many more.

Death and life. Defeat and victory. Despair and hope.

Then he turned back to that one sliver of glass that reflected his face as it truly was in this moment. The Milo in that reflection spoke to him, and Milo heard his own voice inside his head. But it wasn't the voice of a kid. It was an older, stronger, deeper voice. Still his own, but not his yet.

These aren't real. They're lies and predictions. They're hopes and dreams. The future is a storm that rolls and changes, Milo. Nothing is set. Nothing is certain. Not victory and not defeat. This is a universe of chaos and every possibility exists. Do you hear me? Every possibility still exists.

Milo tried to reply in thought only, but he couldn't, and so he answered aloud.

"Help me," he whispered.

"Milo?" called Evangelyne, concern in her voice, but he waved her off.

You walk in a dream, Milo. Anything is possible. Be very, very careful. Follow your heart in all things. That's more powerful than sorcery or spaceships or death.

"How do I know what's right, though?"

You aren't alone, Milo. There are allies you can't see. You are not alone in this war. Others are fighting too. Some will rise to fight beside you. Others will make their own stand in their own places to fight the Swarm and to fight the dark magicks that have been unleashed. Don't give in to despair. But know this: In the end you will be called on to lead an army the likes of which this universe has never seen, because only such an alliance can ever hope to prevail against what the Huntsman will become. Darker times are coming, Milo. Be strong.

And that's when Milo realized the voice he was hearing was not some older version of himself.

It was the voice of someone who had been lost. Taken. Maybe destroyed.

Milo reached a trembling hand toward the fragment of mirror. "D-Dad—?"

Be strong, son. Be true.

And then the voice was gone.

Milo's knees buckled, and he would have fallen if Evangelyne and Shark hadn't caught him and held him up.

"Geez, what's wrong?" cried Shark.

Milo pushed them away and staggered across the hall to lean both palms against the wall. The mix of emotions swirling and boiling inside him was almost too much to contain, and he threw back his head and screamed.

The sound that erupted from him was not right. Not normal.

It was the roar of a monster, a *thing*. It was an animal roar of primal rage and endless need, and all along the hallway the doorways cracked and shuddered in their frames. Pictures fell from their hooks and shattered on the floor. Cracks whipsawed along the ceiling, and the pieces of broken mirror exploded into clouds of glittering silver powder.

The frame that had held the mirror suddenly swung backward, turning inward on hidden hinges. Milo's scream seemed to be pulled like smoke through a fan, vanishing into the dark recess that was now revealed.

Milo pushed off the wall and stood there gasping, his chest and throat hurting, strange lights bursting like fireworks in his eyes. His fists tightened into balls and he bared his teeth at this new doorway.

His friends had recoiled from him and were standing back, fearful and wary.

Then slowly . . . so slowly . . . the storm that had exploded inside Milo passed. It blew out of him as if pushed by a freshening wind.

No one asked him to explain what had just happened. They were in a ghost of a house and nothing here was real.

Except that Milo was absolutely certain it was all real. In some way, maybe in a thousand different ways, this was all real.

Without saying a word to anyone, Milo bent and picked up the slingshot he hadn't realized he'd dropped. The ball bearing was there on the carpet, and he looked at it and saw yet another distorted reflection of his face.

Then he pushed the hidden door open and stepped through into darkness.

One by one, the others followed.

Chapter 47

They stepped into a narrow space that looked like it had been built as a walk-in closet. There was barely enough room for them all to fit. The door swung shut behind them, plunging them into darkness. But almost immediately the far wall swung away from them to reveal another door, and another, and another.

Milo understood what was happening. The Heir had come this way, going through one doorway to find another and another and another.

Until they found the last one. Shark swept his flashlight beam around and the beam fell on a large crystal doorknob that was faceted like a big diamond. Milo took a breath and glanced at the others, who nodded encouragement. None of them offered to touch it, though. They were letting him run this hunt.

He was only sort of okay with it. He knew he had to, but he really didn't want to. Those strange, cryptic words spoken in his dad's voice echoed inside his head.

Be strong, son. Be true.

Whatever that meant. Be true to what? Or to whom?

Milo was no philosopher. He wasn't sure what he

was. Maybe he wasn't really a kid anymore. Not completely. He felt himself changing. Not into the hero that the Witch of the World wanted him to be. Into something else, but he had no idea what label to hang on it.

Be strong.

They were searching for a ghost in a house, with dark faeries and the Huntsman at their heels.

Be strong?

Geez.

He gripped the handle. It was so cold. Much colder than it should have been. And as he touched it, the air became filled with familiar smells that made no sense. The scent of burnt toast and of orange peels.

"Do you guys smell that?" he asked.

"Smell what?" asked Shark. "I don't smell anything."

"I do," said Evangelyne. "Burned bread and oranges."

"Yes!" said Milo. "What's that about?"

"People sometimes smell those things when they are in the presence of great psychic energy. Those two smells. I read about it in one of my aunt's books, but I'm not sure why it's those things."

"Weird," said Shark. "My list of really, really weird things is getting really, really long, you know that?"

"Welcome to my world," said Evangelyne.

"Yeah, I guess."

"Mook," said the rock boy, tapping Milo on the shoulder.

Milo nodded and turned the handle.

It took effort; it was as if the door was reluctant to yield. Milo put some muscle into it, and the handle shifted and then turned. There was a soft click, then the door opened and a warm light washed over them. Milo went in first. He felt strange and he realized that this place felt *important*. Not just magical. It felt special in a way that was almost like stepping inside a church, an institution Milo hadn't been to since the invasion.

The others followed. No one spoke. They were all in awe.

All these books.

Not just books, but scrolls and clay tablets, too.

Milo walked over to the closest shelf and ran his fingers along the spines. He knew them from his dreams, and he remembered what he'd written. Or rather, he recalled what he had transcribed, because in his dreams he was reading a book about the Heir of Gadfellyn Hall. The words came back to him now as if they were printed in the air.

So many books on shelves and tables or stacked by themselves in crooked towers. Books on stands or laid open on tables or facedown on the arms of chairs. . . . Books and books and books.

A long, long time ago the Heir had come to this place, and upon finding these books he had smiled for the first time in a long while.

The boy had been abandoned and lost, and when he came here he'd found his way home. Milo knew that, though he didn't understand it. Just as he knew it wasn't required of him to understand it. Knowing it was enough.

Milo loved books too. He read every single one he could scavenge, even though many were burned and missing pages. When he read a book like that, Milo wrote his own endings. Or dreamed them.

He knew that if he looked for those damaged books, he would find whole ones here. They had to be here. Maybe every book that had ever been written was here.

It made him wonder if these were only books from his world, from the Daylighter world. Were the books of the Nightsiders here too? Maybe even the books of the Swarm? After all, the library was impossible, which probably made anything inside it possible. He almost smiled at how ridiculous that sounded, but he also knew that it was probably true.

What had he read in the Heir's story and then written down in his dream diary? In books anything was possible— even the impossible.

Shark came up beside him, his eyes fever bright as he looked at the books. "This place is insane!"

"I know," said Milo. Despite everything that was happening, he was excited, even happy, to be in among all these thoughts, all these stories, and all this knowledge.

"Say, dude . . . when this is all over, I mean, if we get through it and stuff, any chance we can come back here and, like, never leave?"

Milo looked at him. "I—"

He never finished his reply because Evangelyne called out to them. "Here! I found something."

When they turned, it took time to locate her because she had wandered down one of the long aisles, but Shark spotted her footprints in the dust. She was almost invisible in the shadows, crouched down and running her fingers along the floor. Mook stood over her, bending his stiff body to look.

"What is it?" asked Milo.

"Shark, give me your flashlight," she said, holding out a hand. He passed it to her and she held it at an angle to show them. "See here, beneath the dust. Do you see it?"

They knelt and peered at some faint marks. Evangelyne bent and brushed at them, revealing the distinct shape of a child's shoe. Smaller than shoes worn by Milo, who had average feet for his age. The sole looked smooth except for a series of round nail-head marks.

"Old-fashioned shoes," observed Shark. "But I don't get it, it looks like it's been painted there."

"There are others, too," said Evangelyne. "I don't think it's paint, though."

Milo ran his fingers over the footprint. "It's not. You know what it looks like to me, Shark? Remember when we went on that two-week hike with your aunt Jenny and we scavenged that museum way over in New Iberia? Remember those pieces of fossilized wood we saw in one of the rooms? It was wood that had turned to stone. Remember how it looked? That's what this looks like to me."

"How's that even possible?" asked Shark; then he grunted. "Okay, I heard it as I said it. Impossible Library. Got it."

"Are these *his* footprints?" asked Evangelyne. "The Heir's, I mean?"

Milo nodded. "I think so. In my dream there was something about his footprints being the only ones in the library. But . . . they were only footprints. Not sure why these have changed like this. I mean, this library isn't *that* old." He glanced at her. "Is it?"

"We're in a dream of a house, Milo. Who knows what's possible or not in here."

The footprints ended at the wall, as if the Heir had simply walked through it, but Milo didn't think this was so. There were so many doorways in the place, and they had already found secret ones. He shifted closer to the wall and began feeling along it, looking for a hidden hinge or release.

"It's behind here, I think," he said. "Help me look."

"What's behind there?" asked Shark. "Are we looking for this Heir kid's corpse or something? I'm not sure how this actually works."

"There's got to be a secret door," Milo said. "There was another library inside this one. Where all the really rare and special stuff was kept."

"The Vault of Shadows," said Evangelyne, nodding. "It's the library of magic."

"Oh," said Shark dubiously, "that's not scary at all."

"Everything here is scary," said Evangelyne, and she shivered. Not with cold but with obvious unease. "I don't like it here. Ghosts frighten me. I want to do what we have to do and get out. We can discuss these mysteries when we are far away from here."

"So what do we do?" asked Shark. "Bust through the wall?"

"No!" said Evangelyne quickly. "This is the house of a ghost and the Vault of Shadows belongs to him. It would be suicide to try to force our way in, even if we managed to find it. The last thing we want to do is anger a ghost."

"Why? I mean, okay—*ghost*, that's scary to begin with, but why should we be extra-special careful with them? We've already got the Huntsman, the queen of the dark faeries, and the entire alien race mad at us. How much deeper trouble could we get in?"

"I don't know and I don't want to find out," she said sharply. "Ghosts have powers I don't understand and they are very, very hard to get along with. We haven't even figured out what we can afford to pay the Heir to repair the Heart of Darkness."

Shark sighed. "Last week the worst thing I had to worry about was Stingers. Now . . . hey, I'd love to only have to worry about Stingers. I mean, Stingers—bring 'em on. I can at least make sense of them."

They retreated from the wall and stood there for a long time, just staring at the books. Milo imagined that they were whispering to him. Calling him in, wanting to tell their stories to him. And these were whole books, not damaged fragments. More books than he could read in a lifetime. Enough books so that he could spend forever reading them and never get to the last page of the last volume on the last shelf.

Never ever.

It was the most wonderful thing he'd ever seen. And in a way, the presence of all these books seemed to make a statement about the people of Earth. They raised a collective voice to shout, "We are here!"

We're real.

We matter.

It made Milo swell with pride.

And then a moment later he shivered in fear at the thought of how fragile this all was. Paper and parchment on wooden shelves, while outside this place the Swarm were ever ready with the blue flames of their pulse guns and their total indifference to humanity.

The fear was followed immediately by a ferocious return of Milo's resolve to smash the Bugs off the planet. To save not just the people of Earth, but everything they had built and everything they had learned.

"Hey, what's that?" asked Shark, interrupting his thoughts. Milo looked where his friend was pointing. Across the library and lit by the warm glow of the fireplace was a low table on which had been set several gleaming silver trays of food. Fresh fruit and bowls of bread, cheeses and cut vegetables, geometrical stacks of pastries, and tall crystal carafes of clear water. They hurried over to take a look, and Milo felt his stomach do a backflip. It was all fresh and real and right there.

There was something else, too. Leaning against the side of a row of empty goblets was a stiff piece of notecard. On the outside was a single word:

WELCOME

"Was this here a minute ago?" asked Shark.

Evangelyne shook her head. "I don't think so."

"Let's see what the card says," Shark suggested, though he made no move toward it. Neither did anyone else; however, Mook placed a hand on Milo's back and gave him a gentle but irresistible shove forward.

"Mook," he suggested.

"Gee, thanks," said Milo. He gingerly reached out to take the envelope. It didn't explode and nothing nasty happened. There was a handwritten note inside, penned in a flowing script. Milo read it aloud.

I know what you want.

I know why you're here.

I will be with you when I can.

Relax. Eat. Read a book.

"Is this for real?" asked Shark as he peered over Milo's shoulder.

"I—don't know," admitted Evangelyne.

"I mean, is this for us or are we looking at someone else's lunch?"

"I don't know."

Milo said, "This was left for us."

"How d'you figure that?" asked Shark.

"It's on the card. He says he knows why we're here."

"He? You think the ghost of a dead kid fixed us all a nice lunch? Am I the only one who thinks that's a little strange?"

"Give me a better explanation, man."

"This is so freaky."

Evangelyne said, "Is it really freaky or really, really freaky?"

Shark laughed. "Really, really, *really* freaky."

Iskiel scuttled down from Mook's shoulder and crawled up onto the coffee table. He sniffed the food suspiciously. Killer leaned in to give everything a thorough sniff too.

"So do we just chow down and wait?" asked Shark, who was eyeing the baked bread with naked hunger. "'Cause I'm okay with that."

Iskiel reached out a clawed foot, grabbed the fattest strawberry in the bowl of fruit, and ran away with it like a thief. He climbed onto the backrest of an overstuffed chair and proceeded to eat it. Very noisily and messily.

Milo and the others looked at him, at each other, and down at the food.

They fell on it like vultures.

For several minutes all they did was eat. Since the invasion, food had often been scarce. Plus everything here was fresh and incredibly delicious. Milo wasn't sure he'd ever eaten anything as good in his whole life. Shark kept saying repeatedly that he had not. Evangelyne didn't waste any breath on conversation and instead made serious headway on the pastries.

After a while, though, Milo took a plate of food with him as he began to explore the endless rows of books. After all, the note had extended an invitation to read.

He found three books about survival in the wilderness and brought them back to the couch and settled in to read. First thing he did, though, was make sure the books were intact. No missing pages. Even though each of the books appeared to have been read—possibly many times—they were in excellent condition and complete. Milo found that deeply satisfying.

One by one the others went and found books and brought them back to the chairs by the fire. Even Mook found a heavy book and opened it on his lap. Milo expected it to be about rocks or geology, but it was an oversized hardbound copy of the fairytales of the Brothers Grimm. The rock boy sat there, chin on his chest, and read.

After a while Milo heard Shark say, "Isn't this kind of weird? Us just sitting here stuffing our faces and reading? Shouldn't we be looking for the Heir? Or hiding from the dark faeries. Or . . . something . . . ?"

But his voice seemed to be coming from far away. Between the warmth of the fire, a full belly, the comfort of the couch, and the seeming safety of the library, Milo found himself drifting. The words on the pages began to lose their anchors and drift across the page.

He fought to stay awake. He knew he should.

He closed his eyes to rest them. Just for a second.

He thought about all that had happened. All that still was happening. He thought about all he'd lost and everything he stood to lose. He thought about being the hero that the Witch of the World wanted him to be, and the ordinary little kid he knew himself to be.

He wished he could be that hero.

He wished his mom and dad were here to help him, to protect him. To *be* with him. To prove they were still alive and they still loved him.

He wished that he was strong enough to just stand up and fight the Huntsman. To kick him off the planet along with the whole stinking Dissosterin Swarm. And while he was at it, to kick the *Aes Sídhe* back through the doorway to their little shadow world. The world had enough problems without dark faeries complicating things.

He wished he had one of those magic weapons he read about in books. An ancient sword or a ring of power. Maybe a high-tech device that could eliminate the Bugs with the flick of a switch. Why not? If all the other things from books could be real—alien invaders, werewolves, cyborgs, faeries—then why couldn't there be a magic weapon? It was only fair.

That's what he thought.

That's what he wished for.

While he drifted into sleep there in the Impossible Library, Milo Silk wished to have that kind of power.

Chapter 48

A voice woke him.

Small, faint. Familiar.

Milo opened his eyes and saw that everyone else was asleep. Mook and Shark leaned against each other, both of them snoring in unison. Evangelyne was curled up with Killer snuggled against her. Iskiel was dozing in the embers of the fire. The library was almost silent except for the faint popping of the burning logs.

Something buzzed near Milo's ear and he brushed at it, thinking it a fly or moth.

"Milo!" said a musical little voice. "Milo, wake up."

He turned and saw that it was not a moth at all. Instead a gorgeous little hummingbird hovered in the air inches from his face, its wings beating so fast they were only a blur. And sitting astride the bird was a tiny girl no bigger than his little finger. She wore a dress of shimmering silver and gold, and instead of hair she had living fire streaming from her head. Colors burst like fireworks around her—wild blues and purples, brilliant yellows and greens, appearing and then fading, only to burst again.

"Halflight!" cried Milo in delight. His heart lifted at the

sight of the little sprite. He had met her at the same time he'd met the other Nightsiders. She was kind and smart and wise, and he thought she was the best person of any species he had ever met. Halflight was able to use strange magicks and could cast glamours—illusions that had allowed Milo and the orphans to sneak aboard the Huntsman's ship disguised as Bugs. However, those magicks drew directly on the sprite's own life force, and she had risked so much that she had nearly died. "Halflight, it's so great to see you. Are you okay? Are you better now?"

The hummingbird swung around in front of him and Milo's heart suddenly froze in his chest as he saw that Halflight did not look recovered at all. The bright colors were more wishful thinking on his part than how she really looked. Her head hung between slumped shoulders and her fiery hair seemed to be burning out.

"Milo . . . ," she gasped in a thin, faded voice filled with pain and fear. "The Huntsman is coming. He's almost here. You must wake up."

"I *am* awake," he told her.

"No," she said. Then she turned suddenly in her saddle and looked toward the library door. "He's right outside. Oh, please wake up . . . wake before it's too late. . . ."

The door burst open and *he* stood there. Massive and powerful and totally alien.

The Huntsman.

"It's already too late," he said in a deep and booming voice that was filled with dark amusement.

Milo shot to his feet and waved the hummingbird away behind him. He had his slingshot out and loaded in half a heartbeat. "No! Get out of here or I'll—"

The monster cut him off. "Make threats when you have a chance to carry them out." The insectoid pincers on either side of his wet teeth clicked and snapped. He had his whip draped over a hook on his belt and his knives and pistols ready, but the Huntsman held nothing in his hands. The threat of him was like a hurricane. It was vast and it filled the room with the dark promise of horrible things. His face, already filled with malicious intent, darkened to a mask of hate. "Now . . . give me what you stole. I can hear it beating, I know it's here. *Give it to me now.*"

Milo fired the slingshot. The ball, crafted from some steel alloy designed by Dissosterin science, flew like a silver missile. It was a blur and it flew straight at that evil face.

And the Huntsman snatched it out of the air as if it were nothing.

Nothing.

He held it up between thumb and forefinger, studying it. "You know," he said thoughtfully, "two days ago you might have actually hurt me with this. This is a tullinium alloy. You won't have heard of it, but the entire Swarm uses it. That's why the Earth Alliance weapons have so little effect. Fifty times harder than steel. A useful bit of metallurgy the Swarm stole from a planet they devoured a million years ago." He bounced it in his palm and smiled at Milo. "Two days ago something like this could have hurt me. Maybe even killed me. But now? Ah well, now everything's different. My lady the Queen has helped me discover how powerful I truly am."

"What are you talking about?" demanded Milo.

The Huntsman's smile broadened, becoming a leer. "You know what I'm talking about. You know what I did the other day. You know how I *fed*." He laughed, and the sound of it was so ugly it hurt Milo's head. "Lizabeth VanOwen. Who would ever guess that such a skinny little child like her would have so much *life* in her? The very young and the very innocent are the most powerful, did you know that? All that purity, all that love and hope and all those unspent years . . . they're like nuclear fuel." His leer became a demon's mask. *"And I drank every drop of her life."*

"Noooooooooo!" Milo screamed as he loaded another metal ball and fired. And another, and another.

The missiles flew like mad, striking the Huntsman in the chest, in the face, clanking off him, ricocheting to smash into the walls. The monster laughed and laughed.

He still held the first one he'd caught and, still laughing, he whipped his hand toward Milo, throwing the ball with ten times the speed and force of the slingshot.

Milo felt a punch.

He coughed.

He looked slowly down at his chest.

At the dark red hole in the center of his sternum.

Milo opened his mouth to say something.

Nothing came out.

His eyes rolled up in his head and he felt himself falling backward and downward into the well of forever.

He felt himself die.

Chapter 49

A voice woke him.

Again.

"Milo. Milo, you have to wake up."

It was a female voice. But not Halflight's. Not Evangelyne's, either.

He opened his eyes and he wasn't in the library anymore. He wasn't in New Orleans.

He stood in the swampy woods. Mosquitoes thrummed in the air like fighter squadrons. Spiderwebs glistened with morning dew. He could hear bullfrogs and nutria down by the bayou. He looked up and saw the sky through the canopy of trees. The moon was out.

No, not the moon.

This was something closer and uglier and it moved slowly across the sky, pushing through the clouds, insulting the very air with its presence.

A hive ship.

"Milo," said the voice again, and he turned. Behind him was the shattered bulk of the food cart from his camp, and the Huntsman's demand was painted on its side.

Give me what you stole.

A slim, small figure stood in the shadows thrown by the cart, but even in that purple darkness her hair glimmered with pale light.

"Lizzie—? Oh my God—*Lizzie!*"

He ran to her, needing to hug her and force her to be real and to be alive again. He would never let her go, never let death or the Huntsman take her. He had no siblings, but Lizabeth was his sister nonetheless. Just as Shark was his brother. But before he touched her she stepped away, evading his touch, shaking her head.

"No!"

That word stopped him in his tracks. "What is it? What's wrong?"

Shadows covered her face and he couldn't read her expression, and when she spoke her voice was different. Wrong. Not the voice he knew. It was too old and she had an accent he'd never heard before.

"Milo," she said, "you must wake up. Worlds turn and turn and you must wake up."

He drew back, suddenly afraid of her.

"Who are you? Where's Lizzie?"

"You know what happened to your friend. She is gone. *He* has stolen her life just as his masters steal the life from our mother world."

"Who are you?" Milo repeated. "Why do you look like Lizzie? Why are you doing this?"

The figure pointed to the ground and Milo saw a fairy ring there, and in the disturbed dirt he could see the impression of a small, slim body. He closed his eyes for a moment, feeling the pain, the loss.

"It's not fair," he said. "Lizzie never hurt anyone."

"There is such power in innocence," said the figure. "Such wonderful power. Had she lived to grow up, Lizabeth VanOwen would have been a healer. She would have served life itself. The Huntsman stole that from her when he stole her from the world."

"I want to kill him," snarled Milo. "He's got to pay for what he did."

She said nothing and instead looked up at the hive ship. Milo glanced around the clearing and then suddenly thought he understood what was happening.

"I'm dreaming," he said.

"Of course you are. Life is a dream."

"No, I mean I'm actually dreaming. I'm back in the library and I'm asleep and this is just a dream."

"Just a dream?" she said, repeating the words slowly. "You live in a world at war with itself. Science and magic are in collision. Doors are breaking open and dreadful things are being set loose. Tell me, Milo Silk, how is that just a dream?"

He studied her face, seeing the alien light in her eyes and understanding what it was. "You're *her*, aren't you? You're the woman who was buried here all those years ago. The Daughter of Splinters and Salt, and this is your shrine."

"I was her," she said. "Now I am shadows and dust."

"Were you here when Lizzie died?"

She pointed to the ground inside the faerie ring. "That is my grave. The Huntsman desecrated it with his foul deed."

"You saw what happened. Did it . . . did she . . . ?" He stopped and started several times, trying to push the words through the ache in his chest. "Did it hurt? For Lizzie, I mean?"

"The Huntsman is a monster and a necromancer. He feeds on pain and fear. He was like that before he became a necromancer, and now he has become a kind of vampire but more frightening. It was dreadful to behold."

"I should have been here. Maybe I could have done something."

"You would have died too. And the world with you."

"You're wrong. I'm not important. I'd have given him the crystal egg if he had let her go."

The Daughter of Splinters and Salt stepped out of the shadows. She still looked like Lizabeth, but Milo could see it wasn't her. The lights in her eyes were so different. As alien, in their way, as the Huntsman's. Her eyes now blazed with intensity.

"You must not say such things. You must not. Listen to me, child of the sun," she said. "You have been charged with a great task. It does not matter that you do not think you are strong enough. Few of this world's greatest champions were born as heroes. You are young, you are small, and you think that makes you weak. But you are so wrong. The Witch of the World told you this. *I* tell you this. The mountains and the forests of the Earth tell you this. And the Heart of Darkness screams it as she dies. You must rise, Milo. You must find a way."

He shook his head. "Where is she? Where's Lizzie?"

The ghost touched a hand to her chest. "She is here," said the Daughter of Splinters and Salt. "She is with me and of me. We are beginning a journey together, she and I, and not even the fates know where it will end."

"I don't understand."

She smiled. "It is not yet to be understood. We are adrift in the waters of eternity and possibility, Milo Silk."

"I don't understand that and I don't care. All I need to do is kill the Huntsman for what he did to Lizzie."

The smile faded. "Seek revenge and you seek your own death. Give in to that kind of hatred and you steal from this world its last hope. Being a hero means thinking of everyone, not of oneself."

"Will you people get off that? I'm *not* a freaking hero. Why can't anyone understand that? I just want to stop the Swarm. That's the only thing I want. Why's that so hard to understand? It's the only thing that matters."

The Daughter of Splinters and Salt began to reply, then stopped and stared upward. Milo followed the line of her gaze. Far above them, the hive ship opened massive gun ports, and from them emerged the focusing crystals of enormous pulse cannons.

The cannons fired and the whole swamp exploded in blue fire.

Milo felt himself *burn.*

Chapter 50

Milo woke up. Again.

He stood on a vast barren field from which columns of smoke rose into a dark and troubled sky. Above him, a hive ship was burning as thousands of small fighter craft swarmed around it. Milo stared in shock. The fighters were all built like the red ship he'd stolen from the Huntsman but they were painted with the round blue-and-green logo of the Earth Alliance.

This was a counteroffensive. It was the kind of battle he'd dreamed of, and as he stood there and watched, Milo knew—somehow knew—that this was because of him. He'd brought the red ship to the EA, and the scientists and techs had scavenged it, reverse-engineered the tech, and used it to build a fleet.

An entire fleet of ships that were as fast and powerful as the Huntsman's craft.

Swarms of barrel-fighters clashed with the EA ships, but one by one they exploded as the resistance fighters of Earth showed them what would happen in a fair fight.

It was wonderful.

It was everything Milo had wished for.

Explosions rippled along the body of the hive ship as its internal engines ruptured.

"Enjoy your moment," said a voice, and Milo spun to see the Huntsman behind him. The hybrid was bleeding and he leaned on a makeshift crutch fashioned from a piece of metal tubing. His pincers were broken, one eye was missing, and his body was crisscrossed with wounds that bled red or green. Even now the creature's human and alien blood refused to mingle despite flowing through the same veins. "Enjoy your victory, general."

It took Milo a few seconds to realize that the Huntsman was indeed addressing him. But . . . *general*?

"We're going to wipe you off the planet," Milo said, and the sound of his own voice startled him. It wasn't a kid's voice. It was an adult voice. Deep, strong, filled with confidence. "And then we're going to hunt your kind across the universe. We won't rest until we wipe you out of existence."

The Huntsman coughed and blood ran from the corners of his mouth. "I remember when you were a boy. Such a little thing, all those years ago. I should have killed you when I had the chance."

"You should have," said Milo. He could feel the power in his body. He was tall, strongly built. A warrior.

A hero.

Standing with the battered and dying Huntsman beneath a sky filled with fire and death.

"It would have been different if I had gotten the Heart," said the monster. "You know that. You know you could never have won."

"Then it's a good thing you didn't get it."

There was a malicious gleam in the Huntsman's remaining eye. "Such a shame that you failed to get it repaired. Ah, such a pity. All that power lost. All those doorways shut forever." He cocked his head. "That is what you wanted, wasn't it? Your greatest wish was to defeat the Swarm, no matter what the cost. And you have. Tell me, General Silk, was it *worth* the price you paid? Can you even remember the names of the friends you buried along the way? The werewolf girl? The fat boy and his dog? Your own parents? Any of them? Was winning this war worth shutting out all those lights?"

In the air above them the entire hive ship exploded.

Eight hundred billion tons of interstellar craft. Seventy gravity drives. Six thousand nuclear reactors. Fifty million pulse-gun power packs. All of them detonating in the same instant.

Milo saw the Huntsman throw back his head and laugh.

And then there was nothing.

Milo woke up an instant later.

He was in the woods miles from his camp. In front of him was a small pyramid made from stones and hidden in the forest. Nearby was the debris from a crashed Bug scout ship.

Milo stood there, his skin still tingling from the heat of the nuclear explosion. He trembled as he tried to understand what was happening.

Before him was the damaged pyramid that had housed the Heart of Darkness. It was gone, and he knew that it had been taken by the Huntsman.

But this was wrong. He couldn't know that yet because this was a memory. This was a week ago, when he had first found the debris field and the pyramid. His scavenger pod was in the woods, and he knew with absolute certainty that if he turned around, he would see the face of a wolf.

He would be meeting Evangelyne for the first time. And then Oakenayl would grab him and they would demand to know what he'd done with the Heart.

"This is nuts," he said aloud. "This is where it all started."

Or, he thought, *this is where it all started going wrong.*

He closed his eyes.

"No," he said. "I don't want to do this all over again."

Except that maybe he did. If he could go back, then he could warn his camp. He could save everyone. Lizzie wouldn't be dead. Barnaby wouldn't be dying. Mom would still be with him.

Could he really go back, or was this all a dream? What was real? Milo was losing his ability to tell.

He heard a voice whisper to him from the shadows beneath the trees. Not Evangelyne's voice. Not a voice he recognized at all.

"Be careful what you wish for."

Milo shook his head. "I just want to do the right thing."

He closed his eyes.

When he opened them, he was in the rainy woods near Lake Pontchartrain and his dad was there. Except Milo knew now it wasn't his dad. It was a holo-man that simply *looked* like his father, using an image stolen from Milo's mind.

"Milo," the holo-man said in the voice of his father, "give me what you stole. It's wrong to take things that don't belong to you. Just give it to me and I'll make sure to return it. Then we're going to have to have a little talk about consequences, young man."

"You're not my dad!" Milo yelled. Lightning forked in the sky and thunder boomed loud enough to drown out his words.

"You're being rude, Milo."

"You're not my dad," Milo repeated, more to himself this time. Weaker. Lost. "I want my dad."

The image of the holo-man flickered as if the tech was shorting in the heavy rain. It flashed, sparked, and then winked out, leaving only the slumped form of the dead man leaning against the tree.

Then the lightning flashed again and Milo saw, to his horror, that beneath the holographic image was the real face of his father. Actually there. Cold and dead.

He screamed himself out of the memory.

He woke up again, this time on the blackened corpse of planet Earth.

Nothing moved.

Nothing lived.

The moon was gone, blasted to a million chunks of debris. Without its gravitational pull, the tides had stopped and the oceans sat, vast and still and stagnant.

Milo walked and walked and walked through the wasteland of the world he'd tried—and *failed*—to save.

Alone.

Filled with despair.

Walking through black ash under a relentless sun.

Looking for some trace of life.

Finding absolutely nothing.

He woke up again and he was with the Earth Alliance. Older but still a kid. Orphaned, desperate. His mother was gone and now he could remember seeing her fall, watching her die, weeping as she was buried.

Her grave was next to Shark's.

Milo fought his way through the months and years, losing a little more hope every day. Fighting the gnawing pain of knowing that he could have made a difference but hadn't tried hard enough.

He fought and fought.

And died.

And woke up.

Again and again and again and again . . .

Chapter 51

When Milo woke up again, he found that he was back in the library once more. He had no idea if he was really awake or still dreaming.

He was alone by the fireplace and he looked around, expecting to see everyone either gone or dead.

They were all there, though. Evangelyne sat on the floor across the room and there were fresh stacks of books around her. For once she looked like a normal kid. Pretty, a little shy, into her own thoughts, happy to be lost in the book that lay open on her lap. Shark was seated on the top step of a wheeled ladder, his shoulders hunched as he bent over what looked like a big book of maps. Mook was reading a *My Little Pony* graphic novel.

"O-kay," Milo said to himself. "This is us saving the world."

He walked through the library, wandering aimlessly up and down the aisles, finding new ones and following them, rediscovering old ones that brought him back out to the main room. He kept expecting something bad to happen, kept expecting to be shot or stabbed. Kept expecting this to be another dream.

Kept expecting it to all go wrong again.

The things he had dreamed about haunted him. His father, the Daughter of Splinters and Salt, dear little Halflight. The Huntsman. His own future selves. .

His failures.

The end of everything.

It was so much to carry that it all seemed to weigh him down.

He wished the Witch of the World would say something to him.

He wished the darn Heir of this place would show up. Or materialize. Or whatever ghosts did when they were done wasting everyone's time.

The Huntsman was out there somewhere. Maybe the queen of the dark faeries was too. The Swarm certainly were.

And here they were, hanging out, eating, goofing off, reading books.

It was unreal.

So he figured it had to be another dream. But if that was the case, where was the action? What was the theme of this dream? What was supposed to happen?

That question was answered when he went down another of the seemingly endless number of aisles, rounded a corner, and found himself in a little alcove that was lit by dozens of candles. There was furniture here, but it had been pushed outward against the wall so that the center of the floor was clear.

Well, not clear. Not really.

The floorboards had been torn roughly apart to reveal black soil. Milo knew that it should have been concrete or some kind of foundation materials, but it was dirt.

And growing up through that dirt were dozens upon dozens of mushrooms with pale yellow caps and scaly stems.

A faerie ring.

Here.

Inside the Impossible Library.

And . . . worse than that.

Far worse.

Standing inside the ring was a woman. Tall and regal, with masses of flaming red hair, gleaming silver armor, and a torc of carved gold around her throat. Her eyes blazed with green fire and her red mouth smiled. The air around her shimmered as if boiling. Little arcs of electricity ran up and down her body, twisting and hissing like yellow snakes.

"Milo Silk . . . ," said Queen Mab. "I see you've come to set me free."

And she reached for him.

Chapter 52

Milo screamed.

And this time he did not wake up.

This vision—this horror—persisted, forcing Milo to accept it as real. As something that was happening right now.

So he screamed again. Louder.

"GUYS! SHE'S HERE!"

The queen of the *Aes Sídhe* laughed at him and lunged forward with ten dagger-sharp, red-lipped fingernails. Milo stumbled backward against a shelf, lost his balance, and fell, dragging a dozen heavy cookbooks down with him. They pounded Milo to the floor and then went skittering through the dust. One struck the outside edge of the faerie ring and instantly burst into flame. Milo scrabbled at his belt for his slingshot, spilled half the ball bearings from his pouch trying to load it, and then jerked his arms up to fire.

The queen stood there, laughing as the air shimmered around her. Milo fired.

The tullinium alloy ball flew straight and true.

And it exploded in midair.

The queen laughed even harder.

"Stupid child," said the queen, "how can one as stupid as you be the favorite of the Witch of the World? How is that possible?"

The fire on the burning cookbook was beginning to spread, so Milo kicked the cover shut. The flames snuffed out and thin tendrils of smoke curled upward. For some strange reason they smelled like spaghetti sauce. At any other time Milo would have been both dazzled and delighted by the concept of a cookbook's smoke containing smells from the recipes inside. It disturbed him now, though. It suggested that these books were far more real than they appeared. That the knowledge in each of them was somehow alive.

That bothered him because living things can die, and that cookbook might have actually died. All around him were hundreds of thousands, perhaps millions, of books. If they were all alive, then they would die—just as Milo and his friends would die.

Queen Mab nodded as if able to read his thoughts. "Oh yes, Milo, that would hurt you, wouldn't it?"

"Shut up," he said. Then he cupped one hand around his mouth and yelled for his friends. There were faint answers but they seemed impossibly far away.

The queen stood inside the faerie ring, and through his shock Milo realized that even though something had changed, the queen was still trapped. The shimmering air was like a giant force field, And it was then that he realized that Queen Mab was not alone in her prison. All around her feet capered the tiny figures of her warriors. Candlelight glinted from their armor and from hundreds of miniature swords.

"Free our queen!" they cried. *"Free our lady so that she may free us."*

In that split second of time, Milo understood the pattern of this thing. The pieces tumbled into place. The Huntsman, craving knowledge of magic, had sought out someone magical with whom he could make a deal. He found the *Aes Sídhe* and struck up an alliance with Queen Mab. She taught him enough about dark magic to set him on the path of becoming a necromancer. The murder of Lizabeth—and whoever else he killed—generated raw power. The Huntsman took some and shared the rest with Queen Mab. The spells holding her in the shadow dimension were weakening, but just for her. She was almost ready to step out into this world. And she would reward her champion with even greater magical knowledge.

Milo knew that if this were something healthy, it would be called a symbiotic relationship. But what was it called when two parasites helped each other? Was there even a name for it?

He heard voices calling his name, but they seemed so far away.

"Guys!" he shouted again. "Back here!"

The queen smiled. "I hear that you've seen your father's face recently. How pleased you must be."

"Shut up," he said. "Besides, that wasn't really my

dad. You don't know my dad. You don't know anything about him."

"Oh, but you're wrong, human child. I know everything about him."

"You're a liar."

"Am I? Would you bet your life I know nothing at all of Michael Harper Silk? Musician and teacher."

That was like a punch.

"You could have gotten that information from your boyfriend," Milo said in a voice that was little more than a low growl. "Nice try."

"I could have," she conceded. "My champion is so generous with everything he has and knows and is. But even he could not have shared this with me."

She swept her hand across the inside of the shimmering wall of the faerie ring and a face appeared. His *father's* smiling face. Plucked from Milo's own memories. Not a static image, but something closer to a video loop. His father was looking away and then burst out laughing as he turned toward Milo. It was silent, but Milo remembered that laugh and the circumstances. It was during the second year of the invasion. They were sitting around a campfire and his dad had been singing funny songs he'd learned from a man named Weird Al, who lived in one of the other EA camps. It was a silly song, and as Dad finished it he burst out laughing. Everyone was laughing. It was one of Milo's happiest memories. But now the queen twisted it and made it a whip with which she lashed at him.

"No . . . ," he breathed in a weak voice. "No."

"Tell me, boy, how could I, queen of darkness, mistress of the faerie realms, know anything about a mere mortal?"

The world seemed to collapse down to the two of them. His friends were still calling his name, but Milo could not process that. All he could do was stare at this woman. Her smile was the cruelest thing he had ever seen. She seemed to be feeding on his pain the way the Huntsman fed on the life energy he stole.

Vampires.

The word burned in Milo's head. Not the correct word, but more than close enough.

He fought for control of his voice. "Yeah? So what? Just because you creeps can use some truths to tell even bigger lies doesn't prove anything. No, I'm wrong, it just shows that you're both a pair of total freaking scumbags."

She held up one slender finger. "Oh, be careful now, my little Daylighter. Mind your manners or there will be consequences."

"What are you going to do? Kill me? Torture me? Pretty sure I already know what you want to do."

"Ah, how naive you are. You think you understand the horrors that await you? A human imagination could never stretch that far. You think torture is only what we will do to your flesh. And you probably think that you'll die before it gets too unbearable. But, child of the sun, you do not know what an immortal faerie queen can do to you as years turn into centuries and centuries become millennia."

Milo's mouth went so dry he couldn't manage even a tiny reply.

"Do you want a taste of real pain? Behold, Milo Silk." She flicked her hand across the laughing image of his father and it was instantly replaced by a new picture.

A figure stood in a badly lit metal hallway that looked like one of the corridors aboard the hive ship. He stood just beyond the downspill of light, and it cast his face in shadows. There was enough light to see most of his body, though. He wore a mix of chitinous insect armor and the steel and leather worn by shocktroopers. However, this was not a 'trooper. Nor was it the Huntsman, as Milo had feared. There were no extra limbs, no pincers, no snapping mandibles or antennae. But the head shape was wrong.

It was only when the figure stepped into the light that Milo could see what was wrong. Instead of human eyes, this man had the multifaceted eyes of a blowfly. Dark red and inhuman. The flesh around them was scarred and melted from recent and brutal surgery. The man raised his hands and began flailing wildly as he fought to orient himself with these eyes. He touched his face and brushed his fingers across those eyes, then screamed as he stumbled backward, trying in vain to escape what had happened to him.

Despite the monster eyes, Milo knew that face. He knew that scream.

So he screamed too.

"DAD!"

The man froze in place, head raised to listen, staring with those mutant eyes. "M-Milo . . . ?"

"Dad! Dad, it's me. Dad, where are you?"

"Milo!" cried his father. "Milo, where are you? I can't see you. What's happening to me?"

"I'm right here, Dad. I'm in New Orleans. Where are you? What's happening to you?"

"Milo? Are you safe?"

"Yes. Yes, I'm with friends. Where are *you?*"

"Where's your mother? Is she okay? Oh God, Milo . . . are you both safe?"

"Dad, I—"

And the queen snapped her fingers to extinguish the connection. His father vanished, and there was a silence so heavy that it crushed Milo. Absolutely crushed him.

He dropped to his knees and caved forward, beating the floorboards with his fists as dry sobs broke like grenades inside his chest. Was this true? Was his father alive? Had he really just spoken to him?

If so, what were the Bugs doing to him? Were they transforming him into another monster like the Huntsman? Or was Dad some kind of lab animal for them to experiment on? And *where* was he? Was his father on the New Orleans hive ship? Or somewhere else? There were six other hive ships on Earth, and hundreds of other craft. Thousands of ground installations too.

"Milo . . . ," said the queen, almost singing his name, the way people do when they want to tease. "I know that you would like to kill me now. I would expect nothing less."

He didn't even look at her. He squeezed his eyes shut and wished he could teleport away to anywhere else.

"You can be my enemy, Milo Silk," she said, "and suffer every hurt and indignity that I can devise—and my imagination runs so deep, Milo. Cruelty is an art, and no one can claim to have a more skilled hand than Mab, Queen of the *Aes Sídhe*. Not even my champion, and he is a master of the art of pain."

"Shut up."

"Shhh, listen now. You can oppose me, or"—her voice became silky—"you can serve me. You can earn my gratitude and my favor, Milo. I reward my friends, and as cruel as I am, I can be even more generous. So much more generous. Would you like to know what I would give to you if you were to do a little favor for me?"

Milo tensed, hating himself for wanting to hear what she offered. But fearing the offer too.

"I can restore your father to you. And not as the misshapen thing you saw. I can *restore* him, healthy and whole, to you. Your mother, too. I can reunite you with your loving family and then offer you protection so that no harm will ever come to you."

Milo slowly raised his head. "You're pathetic and you're a liar. The Huntsman tried the same trick. He said he'd give me whatever I wanted if I gave him the Heart of Darkness. Now you're telling the same lies. I hate you."

Queen Mab seemed to grow in size, and the crack-ling electricity that ran up and down her body intensified, forming arcs with the shimmering wall around her. The tiny faerie warriors cowered back and fled into the earth at her feet. "Do you dare to call me a liar?" she said in a voice like thunder.

"Yeah, I do. You're all liars. You and your *boyfriend* and the whole Swarm."

The queen glared at him for five long seconds; then her anger changed into something else and her scowl of rage was replaced by a mask of cold dignity. "Know this, Milo Silk: I may be many things, and most of them are unpleasant to one such as you, but never in fifty thousand years have I told a lie. The very powerful do not need to hide behind lies. When I say that I will restore your family and keep you safe, it is truth and I will give a blood oath on it. There is no more powerful bond in this or any uni-verse than the blood oath of a faerie queen."

Milo stared at her. His face was as hot as a burning match and his fists hurt from pounding the floor.

"Milo!" came the call of a voice that seemed strangely far away. Evangelyne. Desperate and frightened.

He tried to speak, to answer, but he couldn't. All that he could manage was to kneel there and look at the smil-ing face of the faerie queen while her words echoed in his head.

I will restore your family and keep you safe.

Milo's mind was filled with ten thousand memories of

his parents. From before the war, from the first years after, and in the things he'd seen in those twisted visions. He missed them so badly he wanted to scream. He wanted the world to reset and go back to the way it was and to be the way it should have been.

"Be quick, Milo Silk," purred the queen. "Serve me now and have my gratitude forever."

He raised his eyes to meet hers. They burned with green fire.

"What do you want me to do?" he asked.

Chapter 53

Her smile was as cold as ice and as merciless as death.

"All you need do is gift me two little gifts. One is in your pocket. I can hear it buzzing like a locust. Lay the crystal egg of the hive queen on the edge of my faerie ring. Do that and I will save your father from a life of torment."

"What about my mom?"

"Mothers are so important, aren't they? And yours is so fierce and strong. A warrior and a hero. Many would sacrifice their lives for her." The queen ran her fingers along the shimmering wall and suddenly an image of his mother appeared. She was in uniform, hunkered down behind the stump of a shattered tree, rifle in hand, a smear of fresh blood across one dirty cheek. Behind the tree was a Stinger and it was coming toward her. His mother tensed, fitting the stock of her rifle to her shoulder as she prepared to fight the horrible creature. Then the queen snapped her fingers and the image winked out.

"No!" cried Milo.

"Is that the past and did she die? Or is it the future

and may she yet be saved? Or . . . is this happening right now and only my champion, the Huntsman, can call off his hounds?"

"Do something. Save her!"

"Only you can do that, my child. Only you have that power." She leaned toward the wall. "Go find the little werewolf girl; shoot her with your slingshot. When she falls and becomes human, take the Heart of Darkness from the pouch at her waist. No, don't look so surprised. Do you think such things could be hidden from a queen of faeries? Go and do this now. Lay the Heart of Darkness beside the crystal egg. Do that and everything your heart desires will come to pass. You have my word."

"He won't let you," said Milo. "The Huntsman won't let you help me. He won't let you save them. He'll make you into a liar. He'll kill everyone."

The queen laughed. There was no trace of doubt in her eyes or in that mad laugh.

"You think my champion will oppose me? You have so much to learn about the universe. Now," she said, her laughter over and her smile fading, "do as you are told."

The yells of Evangelyne and the others faded and went away. There was no sound at all from the library.

"Your friends have abandoned you," said the queen. "While mine are bound by oath and love to me." The little faerie warriors had crept from their holes and were standing in glittering ranks around her. "And my champion is coming. He knows what is needed to bring me into this world. You saw part of it when you arrived, did you not? My champion sacrificed a woodland faerie to try to break the spell, but alas it was not pure enough to shatter the last lock. His firedirk will drink the life from your fat friend or perhaps the werewolf. They are young and pure and full of energy. Their lives will finally free me from my exile. And then *I* will repair the Heart of Darkness. I know spells that can bind even a ghost like the Heir, and I will force him to do what needs to be done. Oh yes, little Daylighter, everything is flowing forward as I have foreseen it. Everything is as I will it. Now . . . earn your place in the court of Queen Mab by doing as I have asked. It is a little thing but the rewards are great. *So* great."

Milo stood up very slowly. It felt like there was a ton of weight pressing down on him, but he managed to get to his feet, and he stood swaying. Weak inside and out. He dug one hand slowly into his pants pocket and removed the crystal egg; then he held his hand out toward her, careful not to touch the shimmering wall.

"You'd give me my dad back for this?"

"So I promised."

Milo closed his eyes, and in that brief personal darkness he saw himself with Mom and Dad. Together. Alive. Happy.

Safe.

It would be so easy to give her what she wanted. He had the tullinium alloy ball bearings. One of them would be enough to take down the werewolf. She was, after all, only flesh and blood.

He nodded.

"Okay," he said.

"Yes!" she cried in delight. "You have made the wisest choice. You are—"

"Okay," he repeated, "I'm only going to say this once."

Her flow of words stopped and she half-recoiled from him.

"First," said Milo, "bite me."

The queen went pale with rage.

"Second, Your Majesty, I hope you stay locked in your faerie world for about a million years. I hope you rot in there. You and all your little jerk warriors. I hope you get some horrible disease that makes your face fall off. If I had any way to do it I'd toss a couple of grenades in with you, 'cause you deserve to get blown to pieces. You're no different from the Huntsman. I didn't think I could ever hate anyone as much as I hate him, but congratulations. You're just as much of a parasite as he is."

With that he returned the crystal egg to his pocket and very slowly, very deliberately turned his back on her.

He did not see her face, but her screams of rage filled his ears and the threats she made—or perhaps they were promises—struck his back like a rain of arrows. Milo fled the alcove and went searching for his friends.

His heart was breaking and he had never in his life felt more wretched. The images Queen Mab had showed him of Mom and Dad were like nails driven into his heart. Had he just condemned them to horrible deaths? Had he done that?

"I'm sorry, Dad," he said as he broke into a run. "I'm sorry, Mom."

He ran as hard as he could through the winding aisles of the Impossible Library. All the time, he wondered where the Heir of Gadfellyn Hall was and if he knew what was happening.

And if he cared at all.

Chapter 54

Milo rounded a corner and skidded to a stop, understanding all at once why his friends hadn't managed to find him.

Something else had found them.

The queen of the *Aes Sídhe* had not lied or even exaggerated. She'd said that her champion was coming for her.

And here he was, in all his hideous reality.

The Huntsman.

The door to the library hung open and shattered, dangling from one twisted hinge. The Huntsman stood just inside the room, filling it with an overwhelming presence. The others stared in shock.

"Give me what you stole," said the monster.

Mook roared like a stone lion and swept Shark and Evangelyne out of the way as he stepped forward to put himself between them and death. The Huntsman did not retreat from the stone boy. Instead he smiled.

"Ah," said the Huntsman with a trace of amusement, "how gallant. The Colossus of Louisiana." He ran his fingers over the steel augmentation that had been surgically attached to him to repair the damage from Mook's fist. "I have you to thank for this," he said to Mook. "And make no mistake, I will crush you to sand, and fire you into space." He smiled. "Oh yes, I know what would happen to a rock elemental if you were unable to build a new body from the stones of this Earth. You'd die out there, and your debris would float forever in the vast nothingness of space."

He laughed, and it was the coldest, cruelest sound Milo had ever heard. It rumbled through the air, colliding with the rows of books, making the dust on the floor twitch and dance. It hurt Milo's ears to hear it, and to know that this was a cruel promise and not simply an empty threat. Mook and Oakenayl could make an infinite number of new bodies as long as some part of them was able to touch the Earth. That was why Milo had thought them so brave to accompany him when he'd snuck aboard the Huntsman's red ship.

Mook, for his part, did not waver. He was as steadfast as the rock that made up his body. He slammed his fists together so hard that jagged splinters of stone flew through the air.

"*Mook!*" he bellowed.

"Whatever," said the Huntsman, unimpressed. "Give me what you stole and you may live past this hour. Refuse me and I will drag you into space, you pile of useless rock, and cast you adrift far, far from this Earth."

"Yeah?" growled Shark. "Well, eat this!"

He snapped off three quick shots with his pulse pistol,

filling the aisle with intense azure light. The Huntsman must have guessed this attack was coming, because before Shark had finished raising his gun, the monster had whipped something from a hidden sheath and held it before him. The blasts from the pulse pistol hit what looked like a spike of white-hot fire, and the blue force bolts exploded, showering the books on either side of the Huntsman. The books immediately caught fire.

The Huntsman laughed.

He stood there holding a flaming dagger with a long, narrow blade. It was not a steel blade covered in something flammable, but a blade of living fire. The glow of it gave the Huntsman a strange blue-white radiance.

"Oh, great," muttered Shark, backing up, "he has a freaking *light saber.*"

But it wasn't that. It wasn't anything from old books or movies from before the invasion. No, Milo knew exactly what this was. It was the thing that the Huntsman had used to steal the life force from Lizabeth.

It was a firedirk.

"Necromancer," snarled Evangelyne, and she loaded that one word with bottomless hatred and contempt. "Defiler! Despoiler. Slayer of the innocent."

The Huntsman laughed aloud and even offered her a mocking half-bow.

"All of those things, little girl, and so much more. It is nice to be recognized for one's accomplishments."

"You killed my friend," said Milo in a voice he barely

recognized as his own. "You killed Lizabeth."

"Killed her? Of course I killed her." The Huntsman shrugged. "Who cares? What is she to me but a means to an end? She was a worthless and unimportant nothing, and only in the act of dying did her life have any meaning."

"You *murdered* her."

He nodded. "As I will murder each one of you. Surely you understand that it must happen that way. You stole something from me and you stole something from the Swarm. Those are unforgivable crimes. I can't even consider mercy because you're young and stupid and don't understand what you've done. And do you know why? Because I've been inside your mind, as you were in mine. I know that you are capable of grasping the enormity of your sins."

"Sins?" snapped Evangelyne. "You dare speak of sins to us?"

He straightened and sneered. "And why should I not, you filthy little mongrel? What are you? *Nothing.* What am I?" He took a heavy, threatening step toward them, while on either side of him precious books withered and died inside their wreaths of flame. *"I am a god!"*

The heat from the burning books washed down the aisle toward Milo. The flames were spreading, killing more of the books and sending dense smoke up to the ceiling. In his mind Milo heard voices crying out in fear and pain, as if the characters in all those books were caught in the flame. Burning and dying.

The Huntsman had used the word "sins," and in truth Milo had never much considered what that meant. He believed in God and prayed every night that the Swarm would leave and the world would be saved, but it didn't go much deeper than that for him. Concepts like sin never much mattered except on a general scale. Some of the adults in his camp talked about the sins of the Dissosterin, but it had always seemed like another word for crime or wrong or evil.

Now, in a fragment of a second as the Huntsman's proclamation echoed through the smoke and dust in this impossible place, the word "sin" took on a new meaning for Milo.

He understood what it was, what it meant. It was not exactly a religious understanding for him. It was more a glimpse into the sheer depth of the importance of things. The Swarm had wanted to conquer the world and exploit it for any resources they could steal. They were not evil, just as a disease, however destructive, was not evil. Milo understood that. The Huntsman, he knew, *was* evil. He reveled in destruction and he fed on pain. Before, when they'd fought him on the hive ship, Milo had thought he understood the full scope of that evil.

He was wrong.

There were depths and dimensions to it he hadn't understood before. Or maybe it was that he hadn't been *able* to grasp it before. Not before Lizzie.

Evil went so much deeper and was so much darker

than Milo had ever understood. Evil wasn't just about destroying things. No, it was about *having* them. Owning them. Controlling and using them.

The Huntsman had craved magical power, but the path he'd chosen was the most vile imaginable. Necromancy. Magic and knowledge that were only possible through the pain and death of innocents. Could there be a worse crime? A worse sin?

No.

Milo had no intention of charging at the Huntsman. It was the furthest thing from his mind. It was a stupid and suicidal thing to do.

But it was what he did.

He ran straight at him, his slingshot empty, his eyes half blind with red rage, murder in his heart. He gathered every ounce of strength he possessed and swung a punch at the monster before him.

And the Huntsman swatted him away as if he were nothing.

There was a burst of blinding pain and then Milo felt himself flying. He slammed into the wall of burning books. It felt exactly like what it was. Intense heat, choking clouds of smoke, fiery ash, and the humiliation of being discarded like a piece of trash. Milo dropped to his knees.

Then he realized that his clothes were on fire.

So was his hair.

He screamed in pain and rolled away from the

Huntsman, trying to snuff out the flames on the carpet. Then something landed heavily on him. He felt slick, scaly skin and sharp little claws, and all at once the intensity of the burn was gone.

"Iskiel!" gasped Milo as the fire salamander drank in the flames and even the burning heat from Milo's skin. Then the creature turned and belched it out again, shooting it like a stream of napalm at the Huntsman.

This time the monster did not laugh or deflect the attack with the firedirk. The flames engulfed him and drove him back, and a terrible roar of agony tore itself from the Huntsman's throat. The firedirk fell from his hands as the Huntsman beat at flames that caught on his insect armor and the patches of human hair that still clung to his misshapen head.

"At him!" yelled Evangelyne, and instantly the wolf was racing forward, snarling, white teeth flashing. Shark tried for a shot, but the wolf was in the way. So he and Mook ran after her.

The Huntsman reeled away from them, and between his howls of pain he cried out in the clicking, inhuman language of the Swarm. There was an instant response from across the library, and the doorway blew inward off its hinges. Milo looked up, and watched in horror as a squad of shocktroopers poured in through the smoke.

Chapter 55

"**W**atch out!" screamed Milo, but everyone already saw that things had gone from bad to much, much worse.

Shark flung himself behind a couch, snapping off wild shots with his pulse pistol. There were so many of the 'troopers that it was impossible to miss. Three of them went flying backward, their chests exploding, lifelights instantly going from a bright green to fragments of lightless black.

Their corpses knocked down several of the alien warriors, but other 'troopers returned fire and soon the library was filled with blue lightning. Chairs and paintings exploded in clouds of splinters. Rich tapestries on the walls turned into sheets of flame.

And the books . . .

The ancient paper and parchment of the books caught fire. Each book screamed as it burned, and the cries filled the place with a nightmare din that threatened to break Milo's mind.

The Impossible Library was dying.

They were killing it. The Swarm and the Orphan Army. Each was inflicting cruel damage on the world's last repository of books.

It was hateful and hurtful and Milo saw no way to stop it.

He fumbled for his slingshot as he struggled to his feet, loaded it, and ran into the smoke. Aiming at every lifelight he saw. Firing, reloading, firing. Seeing those awful green lights explode, seeing misshapen bodies fall.

A gray form leaped past him, and Milo pivoted as Evangelyne struck the Huntsman with her front paws just as the killer was reaching with his metal hand for the fallen firedirk. The werewolf's claws raked the Huntsman's armor, leaving deep parallel gouges. With a snarl of fury, the Huntsman shoved her away and snatched up his weapon. Then he bore down on her, raising the weapon to strike.

Milo loosed a ball bearing from ten feet away. Not at the Huntsman's face or lifelight, but at the back of his alien hand. There was a heavy *clang* as metal struck metal, and once again the magical dagger went flying. The very tip of the blade cut a burning line across Evangelyne's cheek, and the wolf yelped in pain.

Across the room, Mook had picked up a heavy oak mission table and was using it as a shield as he rammed into the 'troopers. Their pulse blasts blew chunks off it, but the rock boy was too close and moving with too much momentum for them to stop him in time. The burning oak crushed them back; then Mook released it, cocked a mighty fist, and punched all the way through one and into the unlucky aliens behind it. Green blood splashed high on the walls of books.

Shark was down on the ground, using a smaller table for cover as he fired a steady stream of shots at the legs of the 'troopers. Already a bunch of them had fallen, and Killer—the tiniest and least dangerous of the orphans—darted in and out, biting alien faces, scratching insect eyes with his tiny claws. Doing his part.

Evangelyne lunged once more at the Huntsman and drove him back, and the two fell into the flaming wall of books, vanishing inside a cloud of smoke and sparks. Then she went flying across the room, hurled with savage force by the Huntsman. She vanished into a wall of fiery smoke, but Milo heard her strike something solid. There was no yelp or cry. Only silence and stillness.

Grinning at his victory, the Huntsman looked around, spotted his firedirk, and reached for it. As he snatched it up he turned to Milo, a wicked smile on his face.

"And now, boy, let's see if your life force is pure enough to free my queen from her prison. How would that be? To die so that the queen of all the dark faeries can join me in our conquest of all space and time. Do you think you will rest easy in your grave knowing how thoroughly you have failed those who counted on you?"

Milo scuttled away, tossing a small table down between him and the advancing Huntsman. A stack of books fell too and slid across the floor on their leather covers. The Huntsman kicked them out of his way.

"Where is the Heart of Darkness?" demanded the monster. "You know where it is, don't you, boy? Tell me now and I may even let you live. Would you like that? You can be my pet, like a monkey on a chain."

Milo backed away, searching through the smoke for Evangelyne.

Shark, Mook, and Iskiel were still holding their own, using the dense smoke to manage a hit-and-run battle against the shocktroopers. That couldn't last, though. And besides, more and more of the precious books were catching fire.

Where was the Heir? Where was the secret door to the Vault of Shadows?

Where was even a splinter of hope in all this madness?

From the back of the library Milo heard the queen yell for the Huntsman to free her and to slaughter Milo and his friends. Her voice boomed as if from a loudspeaker.

Laughing, the Huntsman strode forward to commit those murders—for his new partner and to satisfy his own red hungers. He shook out his whip and cracked it at Milo, but Milo flung himself into the smoke. The tip of the lash missed him by an inch and the sonic boom it made half-deafened Milo.

"I'll get you, boy, and I'll tear the flesh from your bones!" roared the monster.

"Bring me his heart!" screamed the queen.

Terrified, Milo ran, but he barely got ten feet before he tripped over a figure that lay slumped on the floor. He fumbled through the gloom and found a slack arm. When he bent close and blinked his eyes clear, he saw who it was.

"Evangelyne!" he cried, dropping to his knees beside her. She was no longer a wolf. Sprawled and bleeding, her eyes open and glazed with pain, her mouth smeared with blood, one fist clutched tightly to her chest, the leather thong of the small pouch hanging from between her fingers.

"M-Milo . . . ?" she called in a faint, fading voice.

"I'm here," he said. Burning books fell from the shelves all around her, and Milo swatted them away. He knelt and pulled her to him, leaning over her, wanting to shelter her even if it was the last thing he could do. "We have to get out."

They could hear the Huntsman and the queen yelling and promising bloody horrors. Evangelyne looked at him and then up at the burning library, her eyes filled with panic and despair. It was all ending. This was no heroic fight. This was a slaughter and a failure and it could only end one way. The Huntsman would win. Then he would free Queen Mab and the whole of the universe would tremble as it began to die.

"Oh, Milo," whispered Evangelyne, "I'm sorry."

Milo wasn't sure what she was apologizing for. Bringing him here, failing to protect the Heart, losing her fight with the Huntsman? Or maybe she was as sorry as he was to see all these books burn, and to know that everything everywhere would also burn.

The smoke darkened as a figure came toward them.

It was over.

Then a voice said, "What have you done to my books?"

Chapter 56

Milo looked up to see a boy standing there. He looked to be no older than eight or nine. Dressed in old-fashioned clothes and shoes, like someone from the nineteenth century. Brown hair combed to one side, big eyes behind small glasses. But all of this was transparent, like an image painted thinly on glass, or like a weak hologram. Milo could see all the way through him. But his gaze was drawn to the boy's eyes. They were filled with such deep hurt that it made Milo's own eyes sting.

Milo recognized him from his dreams.

Here was the Heir of Gadfellyn Hall. A ghost of a lonely boy who had lived and died in a forgotten library a long, long time ago.

"I . . . I . . . ," began Milo, but he couldn't finish the sentence. He had no idea how to properly address a ghost.

The Heir, however, was not looking at him, and Milo turned to see the Huntsman coming through the smoke, pushing it away as if its presence offended him. The firedirk blazed in his powerful fist. Behind him the battle raged and the fire spread out of control.

"No," said the boy. "No."

His voice was soft, but somehow it shook the whole place. Milo could feel it strike him in the chest.

And in the next instant the room changed.

Everything *stopped*.

The fire froze in place as if it were something painted on the air. The smoke, too. The shocktroopers were caught in a tableau, some of them leaping forward. Glowing bolts of deep blue destructive energy hung in the air in front of their guns. Mook was crouched down, turning to shield a screaming Shark as huge splinters of rock were blasted from the stone boy's body. But it was stopped. Halted in the midst of Mook being blasted apart. Killer was frozen in midbark.

And the screams of the queen had stopped too, as if she were equally frozen.

Milo looked down at Evangelyne. She was frozen too. Utterly still.

Even the Huntsman—with all his devastating power— was caught immobile, a foot raised to step within striking distance of Evangelyne. Like everyone else, he had simply stopped. On the floor near where they stood lay the firedirk.

But Milo was not frozen. He looked up at the Heir and saw tears glisten on the boy's transparent cheeks.

"My books," murmured the ghost. "Look what they've done to my books."

"I'm sorry," said Milo.

The Heir looked down at him and studied him for

what seemed like a long time. "You're so full of fear. You're afraid of everything," he said.

Milo said nothing because he didn't know how to respond to a statement like that. The Heir nodded, though, as if Milo had spoken.

"Why did you bring your war to my house?"

"I didn't mean to," said Milo. "We came here because we needed your help."

The Heir pointed to the Huntsman. "You brought *him* here."

Although the face and body were those of a child, the voice was different. Older, sadder, stranger.

"I'm sorry," said Milo.

"Are you?"

"Of *course* I am. I'm sorry he followed us here. I'm sorry he brought Queen Mab. I'm sorry we started a fight. I'm sorry your books got burned. I'm sorry for everything." Milo let go of Evangelyne. She didn't fall but remained where she was, as if she still leaned against him. He got heavily to his feet and faced the ghost. The fact that this actually *was* a ghost terrified him. The fact that the ghost had the kind of power he'd just demonstrated brought Milo beyond fear into something he didn't even have a name for. Milo steeled himself to say the rest of what he had to say. "But I'd do it all over again if I had to."

The ghostly boy wore no expression on his face. "Why?"

"Is that a serious question?"

The Heir nodded. "Why would you bring all this pain and violence and destruction here? Why would you want that?"

Milo's fists clenched into knots. "Want? *Want?* I don't *want* any of this. My friends are dying. A lot of them are already dead, including a little girl who never did anything to anyone. The Huntsman killed her. My dad's missing, and maybe he's dead too or maybe they're turning him into a monster. My mom's missing too, and she could be dead right now. I've lost almost everything and everyone I ever cared about. Why would I do all this over again? 'Cause maybe if I did I'd get it right. Do it better. *Fix it.*"

"How is that my concern?" asked the ghost coldly. "What do I care about the world? What do I care about people? My books are my family, and because of you people, some of *them* are dying."

"Then you have to know how I feel. Do you think I want any of this to happen? I'm not actually nuts." He pointed to the Huntsman. "If you want to be mad at someone, be mad at him."

The ghost studied the Huntsman but made no comment. He took off his glasses, removed a handkerchief from his pocket, cleaned the lenses, and put them back on. Milo could see all the way through him and it was totally freaking him out. His own hands were shaking so badly, he wanted to hide them behind his back.

"Look," said Milo, "you left us that note. You said you

know why we're here. Does that mean you know about the Heart of Darkness?"

The boy shrugged.

"You know it's damaged?" Milo asked.

Another shrug.

"Do you know what will happen if the Huntsman and Queen Mab get hold of it?"

This time the Heir did not shrug, but he seemed to be listening.

"My friends and I came all this way to ask you for help," Milo said.

"Why?"

"Because the Heart of Darkness is broken and you're believed to be the only one who can fix it," said Milo. "Is that true? They call you the last doctor of magic. Is that what you are? If so, then we need your help. The whole world needs your help."

The Heir bent and took the pouch from Evangelyne, opened it, and spilled the cracked jewel into his palm. Milo made no move to stop him, because he was dead certain there was nothing on earth he could do.

"Pretty," said the Heir, then held it to his ear. "Still alive."

"But it's dying," said Milo. "You can hear that, right?"

"Of course."

"Can you fix it?"

The ghost shrugged again.

"Is that a yes or a no?" demanded Milo.

"Fixing this is easy," said the Heir. "Tell me why I

should. What would you do with the Heart of Darkness if I repaired it?"

"Keep it safe," said Milo at once. Then he thought about it and added, "And see if I can help my friends use it."

"To do what?"

"To find out how it works. To re-learn the spells, I guess. To figure out how to open the doors to the shadow worlds."

"Why?"

"Because . . . because . . ." Milo fumbled for an answer that would make sense. "Because if we don't, then we can't stop the Swarm and the Huntsman. They'll destroy everything and ruin everything, and all the Nightsiders will be lost forever in the shadow worlds. And all the Daylighters here will die."

"There are worse things than death," said the ghost.

"Maybe when I'm dead I'll understand that. Right now, though, I'm trying to do the best I can to save my friends and find my parents. I'm trying to stop the Huntsman and Queen Mab and the Swarm from ruining everything." Milo walked over and stood in front of the fire that had paused in the midst of burning a wall of books. "You think that the worst thing that could happen is the Huntsman burning your books? I watched my whole camp burn. I watched *friends* of mine burn. And die. They were real people, real lives. Real stories. Gone. Just like that. I'd give anything to stop that from happening again." He turned and pointed to Evangelyne, to Shark and Mook, to Iskiel and Killer. "The Swarm are taking everything away from me. Everything."

"But why should *I* help you?" insisted the ghost. "I'm already dead. I've been dead for hundreds of years. None of this can touch me."

"They'll burn down the rest of your library." Milo saw the Heir's face twitch and knew that his words had struck home.

"Yes," said the Heir, turning to study the Huntsman and Queen Mab. "There is that." He stood for a minute, lips pursed as he considered. Milo waited him out. The room—the world—remained frozen. "If I were to help you, Milo Silk, what would you be willing to give me?"

"Anything I have."

The ghost turned. "And what do you have to offer? Would you give me the Heart of Darkness?"

"No."

"Why not?"

"It doesn't belong to me. I can't give it to you."

The Heir nodded as if that was the answer he wanted to hear. "Then what would you give me?"

Milo thought about it, and then nodded to himself. All the way here he'd thought about this very moment, when the Heir of Gadfellyn Hall would ask for payment. Everyone had warned him that ghosts were devious and that discovering what kind of payment one would accept was hard. Even Evangelyne had no answers.

Milo, though, thought he knew what the Heir might want.

He took a deep breath and reached into his pocket. Then, as he had done with Queen Mab, he withdrew his hand and held it out to reveal the crystal egg. It looked inert and dead, with no trace of the inner lights that sometimes pulsed within its depths. Maybe it, like everything else, was frozen.

"I'll give you this," he said.

For the first time the ghost seemed surprised. "What is it? That's not of this world. Tell me what it is and tell me why you think I might want it. Be quick and be careful. We spirits have little patience with the living, and mine is burning away."

Milo swallowed. "This is a book," said Milo.

The ghost narrowed his eyes suspiciously. "What?"

"A kind of book, anyway," said Milo quickly. "This egg contains the genetic record of an entire hive ship of the Swarm. It has the DNA of one of their queens, all the DNA of her soldiers, all their science and battle knowledge. Everything. Stored in here. I guess this is *their* library. The Swarm want it back so bad they sent the Huntsman after us, and he's so desperate to get it that he's turned himself into a necromancer to find it."

"Don't be so sure you know why the Huntsman sought to learn the dark arts," said the ghost. "Not entirely. He was already walking a shadowy path long before you even heard of him. He wants the Heart of Darkness."

"Yeah, okay, there's that. But he has to get this back or the Swarm will blame him for it. They probably already do. They have to know that he screwed up and wasn't able to stop me from taking it. In its way, this thing is every bit as valuable as the Heart of Darkness."

The ghost seemed very interested now. He came closer and reached out to take the egg. But then he jerked his hand back.

"No," he said. "No, this does not belong in my library."

"Why not?"

But the ghost merely shook his head.

Milo stood there, stunned and helpless. He'd been sure the egg would be exactly the kind of thing to use as payment. It was unique, and in its way it really was a book. The ghost turned his eyes on Milo and there were strange lights there. Dangerous lights. It was then that Milo realized he was in danger every bit as dire as a minute ago when the Huntsman was stalking him with the firedirk. The ghost, though still looking like a boy, now seemed infinitely stranger and more dangerous. Darker in some way Milo's mind refused to define.

"You have not met my prize," said the Heir in a voice that sounded like wind blowing through a midnight graveyard. It chilled Milo to the bone.

"Look, please," begged Milo. "We tried. I'll give you anything I have. You can kill me if you want to, but please help my friends. Or . . . at least let them go."

The lights in the room began to fade as if the shadows were consuming them.

"Did your Nightsider friends not tell you the consequence of failing to meet a ghost's price? You don't just get to walk away. Not you . . . and not anyone who has invaded my home."

"No! Why would you do that? That's not fair."

The ghost moved toward Evangelyne and Milo tried to block his way, but the specter passed straight through him. It was the oddest and most disturbing sensation, like a wind blowing through his flesh. Milo staggered, then spun around as the Heir crouched over the frozen wolf girl.

"She should have told you what would happen," said the Heir. "Or maybe she was afraid that if you knew, you would not come."

Even though he could not protect her, Milo ran to get between the ghost and Evangelyne. He had one last idea. Slim and shaky and probably useless, but it was the only thing he could try.

"Take me," he said, dropping to his knees.

"And why would that meet my price?"

"Because," said Milo, "I have dreams."

"Everyone dreams."

"Not like me."

The ghost studied him. "What do you mean?"

"My dreams come true. Not always, but a lot of the time. I even dreamed about you." Milo shrugged off his satchel and dug his dream diary out. He held it up to show the ghost. "I dreamed about you and this place. I know what happened to you. I know that you got lost here. I know that you died here. I dreamed it all. Just like

I dreamed about the Swarm and the hive ships and the Huntsman. And I wrote it all down. If you want a book for payment, then okay, take me. I'll stay here in the library and I'll dream and I'll tell you what I dream. I'll be a book, but one that keeps changing. I'll tell you everything I dream. Everything. If you let my friends go, I'll stay and tell you every dream. I'll write them down so you can read them if you want, or I can just tell you. Whatever you want."

The ghost looked at him and then at the diary and back again. "That is filled with prophetic dreams?"

"That . . . and other stuff."

"What other stuff?"

Milo hesitated. "Just stuff. Things I think about. Sometimes conversations I had with people. And the stuff I learned. About scavenging, about surviving. About the Swarm. But other stuff too. About my folks. About things I remember. Christmas mornings and birthday parties. Sleepovers with my friends when I was a kid. The songs my dad used to sing. My dog. Some of the funny stuff Shark says. And about other stuff. The Nightsiders and how cool and scary they are. About Evangelyne and her friends. Mook and Halflight and Oakenayl. Iskiel, too. I write everything down. That's why you should take me. There are so many stories I can tell you. But only if you let my friends go."

"You would stay here with me?"

"Yes," said Milo.

"Forever?"

"Y-yes." This time Milo stumbled over the word. But he meant it. As much as it terrified him, he meant it.

"You'd be a storybook for me?"

"Yes. For as long as I lived."

"And when you died?"

"Then I guess I'd be a ghost like you. Maybe I'd still have those dreams, so I guess I'd still be here."

The ghost was silent for a long time.

A long, long time.

The battle and the fire and the pain around them remained frozen.

"Let me see that book," said the ghost. "Prove to me that it's full of dreams."

With trembling fingers Milo extended his dream diary. The ghost was only a ghost, so he wasn't sure how the Heir could actually touch the book. But as the boy closed his fingers around the diary, Milo felt a tug. He opened his hand and let it go.

The ghost stepped back and leafed through the book, saying nothing.

The frozen moment stretched and stretched.

Then the ghost raised his eyes and peered over the diary at Milo.

"No," he said.

Chapter 57

Milo felt his heart fall. It seemed to plummet into some deep place in his chest that was like a well of despair. He spread his arms as if there was some way he could protect Evangelyne from what was coming.

"Wh-what . . . ?" stammered Milo. "Didn't you hear me? I'm giving you a *living* book. I'm—"

The ghost closed the diary with a sound like a gunshot. It shocked Milo to silence.

"I will take this," said the ghost.

Milo stared at him for what felt like an hour, during which his mind went numb and then blank and then seemed to come back online like a faulty piece of tech.

He said, "What—?"

The ghost pressed the dream diary to his chest with the same intensity with which Evangelyne had held the Heart of Darkness to hers.

"This is a book of dreams, Milo Silk," said the Heir. "Do you have any idea what that means to someone like me? Ghosts can't dream. We can't and it's so . . . horrible. We can learn, we can think, but dreams belong only to the living. Especially prophetic dreams, because they are about the future and a ghost has no future."

Milo had no idea what to say. In an instant his terror of the ghost changed to pity. To compassion. To not be able to dream *did* seem horrible, even for someone like Milo who often had bad dreams. But now he saw them differently. Dreams of any kind were a proof of life.

"I . . . ," he began. "I'm sorry."

The ghost smiled. "I'm in your book," he said. "You dreamed of me."

"Yes."

"I will take this as payment."

"You will?"

"If you are willing to part with it."

"Sure," said Milo. "You can have it."

The ghost stroked the cover and Milo thought he once more saw tears in those ghostly eyes.

"I—I'm sorry about your other books," said Milo.

The ghost nodded. "To destroy a book is to destroy someone's dreams. That may not matter to the living, but it is devastating to someone like me."

"No," said Milo, "I get it. I feel it too. I wish I could have done something to stop it. I'm sorry."

The ghost gave him a long and quizzical look. Then he turned toward the Huntsman.

"What happens now?" asked Milo. "What about the Heart of Darkness? Can you really fix it?"

The ghost smiled. "Fix it? Why would I fix something that is already healed?"

He held the diary in one hand and extended his other. On his palm rested the glittering Heart of Darkness. Milo gasped.

The stone was perfect.

There was no trace of damage. It was as if there never had been any.

"I don't . . . I don't . . . ," he said, repeating it over and over again without being able to finish the statement. Then he shook his head hard enough to unscramble his thoughts. "How?"

"Magic, of course," said the ghost as if that were a stupid question.

"No, I mean, when? You were right here the whole time?"

"Was I? Are you so sure?"

"I was standing right here the whole time."

"Yes," said the Heir. "You've been standing in that exact spot for days."

"What? No. We just came here a little while ago and—"

Which is when Milo realized that there was no smoke in the air. None. And although there were scorch marks of fire on some of the shelves, there was no actual fire. No sign of burned books. He spun around and saw that the Huntsman was gone. Evangelyne still lay on the floor, and over by the door Shark, Mook, Iskiel, and Killer had not budged, but the shocktroopers were gone and the door had been repaired. Milo ran down the rows of books to the alcove and saw that Queen Mab was gone too and the floor had been repaired. His brain spinning, Milo hurried back to where the Heir stood, still holding the diary and the Heart.

"I don't understand. How is this even possible?"

The ghost shrugged. "This is the Impossible Library. Anything is possible here. And I have all the time in the world."

"But you didn't even move!"

"No," said the ghost, "it was you who did not move. Just as your friends have not moved."

Milo's mouth hung open.

"What happened to the Huntsman and the queen? Are they dead?"

"No," said the ghost, and he gave an odd, twitchy little shrug. "They were not mine to kill."

"But you were going to kill me!"

Those strange lights twinkled once more in the Heir's eyes. "You came to ask for my help and nearly failed to meet my price. That meant you were in danger of breaking a spiritual contract. Certain rules apply."

"But the Huntsman—"

"He came here to kill you and to gain the power to free his queen. That had nothing to do with me." He paused and gave Milo a brief, sly smile. "However, they did burn some of my books."

"What did you do to them?"

The ghost shrugged. "They wanted to be together," he said. "And now they are."

"What?"

"Who knows . . . the Huntsman may even enjoy the shadow world of the *Aes Sídhe*."

Milo stared at him for a few seconds, then burst out laughing. "You banished him to the queen's dimension?"

The ghost shrugged again. "It may not last, and probably won't. But it will give you and your friends a chance to get out of this city. I suggest you hurry. You've already been here too long."

"What about you? What about your library?"

The Heir gave him an enigmatic smile. "This house lingered here because it wanted to be found. I guess I did too. But now . . ." He shook his head. "After you leave, if anyone comes looking for Gadfellyn Hall they'll only find a ruined old antiques store."

"What if we need to find you again?"

The Heir gave him another of his unhelpful shrugs. Then he offered the Heart of Darkness to Milo, who took it with great care, as if the stone might fall to pieces in his hand. But as soon as his skin touched it, he knew he had no need to worry. The Heart throbbed with incredible power.

No, that was wrong.

It felt totally and completely *alive*.

"Thank you," he said.

The ghost held up the dream diary. "You struck a fair

deal, Milo Silk, and I think I may have come out ahead." But then his smile faded. "But be warned—there are long, dark roads ahead of you. I do not need the gift of prophecy to know that. You have been marked by destiny. I pity you."

"What's that supposed to—"

Milo never finished the sentence.

The world closed around him like a dark fist and then the Heir, the Impossible Library, the endless rows of books, his dream diary, and everything simply vanished.

Chapter 58

Milo woke up.

Again.

He was not in the library.

It took him a long time to understand where he was. Everything was dark. And the darkness stank.

A lot.

Milo sat up very slowly and looked around.

The walls were metal. So was the floor. And there were heaps of old, decayed packing materials heaped around him.

It was the boxcar where he and his friends had slept. He was sure of it.

Which meant what?

Had everything been a bad dream? Like so many other bad dreams he'd had? Was that what this was—just a dream?

He heard Shark outside, talking and laughing with someone. A girl's voice. Evangelyne. Then the raspy grunt of Mook.

Had that happened before when they were here? Or was this then?

His mind seemed to be limping through a field of broken logic and twisted possibilities.

He got to his feet, swayed, steadied himself by leaning against the wall. When he was sure he wouldn't fall down, he began checking his pockets. All the usual stuff was there. If this was real and everything that had happened in New Orleans was a dream, then how could he prove it?

Or . . . how could he prove that Gadfellyn Hall was real?

Milo cast about him looking for his satchel, saw it right where he'd been lying, bunched up as a pillow. He snatched it up, tore it open, fished inside for his dream diary.

And found it.

His heart sank.

It was only a dream after all.

With a sour grunt of anger and frustration, he pulled out the diary and let the bag drop. Then he stood for maybe thirty seconds staring at the small book.

It was a diary.

But it was not *his* diary.

He opened it and flipped through the pages.

They were empty. Every single one.

Empty.

Waiting for dreams to be written down on them.

The door slid open and he turned to see faces.

Shark, grinning at him, a bandage wrapped around his

head and one arm in a sling. Mook, with fresh chips gone from his rocky hide and a fully grown Iskiel crouched on his shoulder. Evangelyne, smiling brighter than the sun, with a black jewel hung around her neck on a golden chain.

And more.

Behind them were two leafy faces. One smiling and happy, one scowling. Fenwillow and Oakenayl.

And hovering in the air, filling the day with a pure light, was a tiny figure seated astride a hummingbird.

Halflight.

He looked past them, hoping to see one more face. A little girl with flowing blond hair and pale eyes. But there was no one else.

He wondered if he would ever see her again. The ghost of his friend or the ghost of the other one. The Daughter of Splinters and Salt. He had a feeling that he would. Just as he had a feeling that this was all real. That he was not dreaming. That everything in Gadfellyn Hall, as impossible as it seemed, had been real.

His friends all stared up at him.

"He's alive," said Oakenayl, and he managed to sound deeply disappointed.

"You're awake," said Evangelyne, and her smile widened.

"I hope so," he said. Then he corrected himself. "Yeah, I'm awake."

Shark said, "Dude . . . we all woke up here and that's really, really freaky. You got any idea how?"

"And the Heart of Darkness is healed," said Halflight.

"How did you manage it?" asked Evangelyne.

"Mook?" asked Mook.

Milo climbed down from the boxcar. "You guys don't remember?"

"After the shocktroopers broke in," said Shark, "my whole brain kind of went kerflooey."

"I don't know what 'kerflooey' means," said Evangelyne, "but I'm pretty sure that's what happened to me, too."

The hummingbird buzzed directly in front of Milo's face, and Halflight searched his eyes with hers. "Do you know what happened, Milo?"

Milo leaned back against the train and rubbed his face with his hands. "So," he said, "I met this ghost . . ."

He told them all about it. Every word that he could remember, and he could remember a lot.

As he spoke, the sun climbed high into a perfect sky of blue and he felt himself detach, as if the version of him who stood there and related the strange encounter with the Heir of Gadfellyn Hall were temporarily disconnected from his inner mind. From his private self.

He drifted into his own thoughts, matching the beauty of the day, the peace of the moment, and the presence of his friends against the realities of what was out there.

The Swarm with their shocktroopers and Stingers, hunter-killers and holo-men, and all their alien tech. Relentless and numberless. They wanted the crystal egg that lay nestled in Milo's pocket.

The Huntsman and the queen were still out there too. Maybe trapped for now, but Milo wasn't optimistic about how long it would be until the two of them broke free. And when they did . . . well, there were probably no words for that kind of anger or that level of hatred.

His dad was out there somewhere too. A prisoner of the Bugs. And his mom was somewhere fighting for her life.

Milo knew that he and his friends had won a major victory. The Heart was repaired and hope had not become extinct.

The war, though, was far from over.

FROM MILO'S DREAM DIARY

I had a dream last night.

I dreamed that I was standing on the lakeside watching the hive ship burn. My friends were with me. Shark, Evangelyne, and the others. But there were people there I didn't know. Other kids and some soldiers. And other Nightsiders, too. We were all messed up from a big fight. I could hear someone crying.

But we were cheering. Most of us were, because the hive ship was burning.

Then I heard a sound and looked up. We all looked up.

Everyone stopped cheering.

Everyone started screaming.

There was another hive ship.

And another.

And another.

The sky was filled with them.

These weren't the hive ships from around the world.

No.

NIGHTSIDERS

There were too many of them.

Forty. Maybe fifty.

I knew what it was, and I screamed too.

It was a second Swarm.

That's when I woke up.